DRIFTING
(AUGUSTA)

GIL T. ENGELKE

authorHOUSE®

AuthorHouse™
1663 Liberty Drive
Bloomington, IN 47403
www.authorhouse.com
Phone: 1 (800) 839-8640

Published by AuthorHouse   01/09/2015

ISBN: 978-1-4969-6169-3 (sc)
ISBN: 978-1-4969-6168-6 (e)

Library of Congress Control Number: 2015900334

*Any people depicted in stock imagery provided by Thinkstock are models,
and such images are being used for illustrative purposes only.
Certain stock imagery © Thinkstock.*

This book is printed on acid-free paper.

Contents

Contents

Written at the urging and prodding of my friend

Lenny Bjerke

@

SAVANNAH MOOSE FAMILY CENTER 1550

ABOUT THE BOOK – DRIFTING (AUGUSTA)

J AKE GOES THROUGH HIS LIFE living in six to nine year life segments, new name, new position, new state, new city, new everything.

Totally aware of everything that he has encountered in all eight or nine segments and has yet to reach his twenty eighth birthday, due to one camping trip, one damn trip.

Because of the Trip, the government and happenstance, he was changed and he now changes the lives of many, in many ways. Some good and some not so good, this book is the story of his Augusta, Georgia, Segment of Life.

ABOUT THE AUTHOR

GILBERT T. ENGELKE JR. WAS born in New York, New York, and now lives in Savannah, Georgia with his wife, Janet. He has a degree in engineering, and served in Vietnam with the U. S. Army, as a Combat Medical Specialist from 1966 through 1968. He is a life member of the Disabled American Veterans Organization, and a member of the VFW and American Legion. He is also a member of the Loyal Order of Moose reaching their highest level, The Pilgrim Degree of Merit.

He enjoys the outdoor sports of golfing and fishing and the inside activities of darts, reading, writing and spending time with Janet, and their two dogs, Al and their Pug, Kim.

This book is dedicated to:

My Wife, Janet
My Sister, Pat and her family
My Cousins, Jeannie & Sly – The Myrtle
Beach Flash
My Friends, David Smoot & one of
my biggest fans Lisa, Bill Fischer,
Ken Fisher, Ken and Martha Smith,
R. Wayne Allen, Matt Scarpitti, Rod
Winters, Danny Walker, Rocky Johnson,
Renny Johnson, Jimmy Parham, Robert
Cowart

Thank you to Stephen King, John Sanford, and Jack
Saul for your gift of inspiration

Books by G.T. Engelke
<u>Detective William Ryan Series</u>
Classified
Random
Ballot
Flavors
Payback

<u>Others</u>
America (The Death Of!)
Drifting (Augusta)

<u>COMING SOON</u>
Tracks
Click
America (The Change)
Drifting (San Diego)

CHAPTER ONE

J AKE LIFTED THE LAST BOX of his possessions out of the
rear seat of his Blue Chevy S10 extended cab pickup
truck. The truck was clean, but not too clean, nor too
dirty, as to not stand out or be remembered. He bumped
the door closed with his hip and turned towards the
doorway that led to his apartment, on the second floor
of the four car garage, he rented yesterday.

He had gotten into town a week ago, and was staying
at the Jamison Suites off Washington Road. On his
first day in town he had gone to the County Sheriff's
Building and reported in to the HR department. This
was to confirm his starting date and it also included
a Meet and Greet tour of the facility to make him feel
comfortable. He got his parking and access passes,
and made sure he was also taken to the Security and
Forensic Departments. He made sure that he met the
Security Department's Director and his office personal,
also the Forensic Lab Director, Dr. Claude Andrews.
He had learned that the best way to not be noticed was
to be the first one to take the step to meet and greet,
from then on, for the most part, they would just nod
and pass you by.

He had then spent a few days just driving around
the town to get familiar with it and understand the

tone of it. Every town or city's residential areas have a flow to them, some areas going up, some areas going down, and the original areas trying to maintain their presence. He had driven out of the city and turned on Fury's Ferry Road, just because he liked the sound of it, and had driven up and down the cross roads, the last being Millikin Road.

As he drove down Millikin Road he saw the mix of new and old, big and small, as he got to the end of the road there were Dead End signs but the road really ended another 1200 feet in a circular turn around. The homes off of the circle were quite large and sat well off the road.

He had seen the small handmade sign with "Garage Apartment for Rent" tacked to a yardstick and pushed into the front lawn, beside the drive, on the circle on Millikin. It was his sixth day of looking, and third trip around the Fury Ferry and Millikin Road areas. He had spent hours driving around each block moving outward from that location, until he had seen each house, on each street, for four blocks surrounding the house and apartment's location. The adjoining properties held two or three areas with each being built in what looked to be twelve to fifteen year growth patterns. In the first adjoining properties each of the homes in the area looked to be somewhere between forty to fifty years old, and all were reasonably well kept. Now and in its heyday, this had to be the area of town local residents strived to live in.

The day before yesterday he had scoped out the newer area of large modern homes where the current movers and shakers lived. There were lots of new shiny cars, and manicured lawns, alongside the large brick or stucco homes that look like no one lives there.

After numerous drive arounds, he had returned to the apartment for rent sign and pulled into the home's drive, and stopped where the walkway to the front door met the driveway, gotten out and walked up to the Oak front door. The door was larger than most modern doors, it was forty eight inches wide, eighty inches high and he guessed two inches thick. The hinges were large brass scrolls with dead pins in each that prevented removing the hinge bolt. There was a large brass knocker shaped like a fish and the knob was also shaped like a swimming fish. He was fully aware that someone in the house was watching his progress from the truck to the door. Once he reached the door he lifted the brass knocker and taped it twice, and stepped back so the storm door could be opened without hitting him.

It was just seconds before the door opened slowly and standing before him was a woman that looked to be in her sixties, neatly dressed and a smile on her face. She opened the storm door saying, "May I help you?"

Jake smiled and replied, "Yes Ma'am, I hope so, if it is still available I would like to inquire about the apartment for rent."

Then as she replied, the woman opened the storm door wider, "Why yes, it is still available, please come in."

Jake took hold of the storm door so that the woman could step back into the house and then he stepped in allowing the storm door to close.

The woman looked up at Jake and pointed towards her left saying, "Please have a seat." She turned towards the staircase that spiraled up to the home's second floor saying, "Teddy, there is someone here that wants to discuss the apartment." She pushed the door closed and Jake heard it latch.

A voice followed them towards the chairs in what appeared to be the living room, "Be right there."

The woman gestured towards a chair saying, "Young man you look to be around twenty six, and out on your own," and then sat in chair that paralleled the one Jake sat in.

"Yes Ma'am, last month, on the birthday part, and a few years on the on my own part," Jake replied with a grin.

Just as they were seated Teddy walked into the room with his hand extended saying, "Ted Jacobson, Teddy to most," and turning towards the woman in the chair continued with, "and this is my wife, Marian."

Jake stood and shook the man's hand, noticing the older man was almost six three, just an inch shorter than his six four frame, saying "Ken Jackson Smith, Jake to friends"

Teddy said with a smile, "Jake, please take a seat. The apartment has two rooms and a bathroom. The one room is a bedroom with a decent size closet and the main room has a reasonable size sitting area and a kitchen area. One of the garage bays goes with the apartment, and it has a wall separating it from the other three bays. All of the plumbing, wiring and HVAC are only two years old and it is wired for cable."

"Teddy, Slow down, you'll scare the young man off with your abruptness," Marian turned to Jake saying, "Young man would you like a glass of tea?"

Jake looked at her and smiled replying, "Yes, Marian, and please, it's Jake. Looking at Teddy he replied, "It sounds like it will work for me, but I will need to see it. What are you asking per month?"

Marian stood saying, "I'll get the tea while you discuss the money." With a smile she waved her hand saying, "Jake, don't take his first offer."

Teddy made a shooing move with his hands towards Marian as she moved out of the room, and looking at Jake said, "Six Fifty a month, and that includes electric and water, if you want cable that is your responsibility."

Jake replied, "That will work, but before we come to an agreement I would like to see the place."

"Of course, of course," Teddy stood and walking towards the door Marian had left thru continued with, "This way, we'll have the tea when we get back."

Once thru the door Teddy said, "Marian, we'll be out back for a few moments," Jake was surprised to be in a hallway, it had a kitchen door to the left and what he presumed to be a library door to the right, with the rear door at the end. Teddy led the way opening the rear door and proceeding to the door on the left end of the garage. He pointed to the first garage door, as he unlocked the apartment door, and said, "That will be yours."

Jake smiled and thought, "It seemed his decision had been made for him."

Teddy stepped into the doorway saying," The door has a three point lock with a security bar that locks into the top, bottom and lock edge. Don't ask, just something I felt was needed." Teddy continued up the stairs until he reached the second floor landing. He turned to Jake and said, "Look around and come on back to the house and we'll discuss whatever questions you have." He handed Jake the keys and started back down the stairs without another word.

Jake watched him go down the stairs then turned and looked at the apartment; it was furnished with what looked like all new furniture and appliances. There was a 60" flat screen TV hanging on the wall that faced a couch and two recliners in the living area, and an island work area with a counter, stove, oven and microwave with wall cabinets just beyond in the kitchen area. He walked over to the kitchen area and started opening draws and cabinet doors. Cups, plates, bowls, glasses, platters, just about everything one could want or need. At the end of the wall counter there was a taller cabinet that held a small washer/dryer unit. On the wall next to the counter closest to the stairs there was what looked like a fourteen inch TV, he pushed the ON button and was surprised to see a split screen color display with one view of the apartment's entrance door and the other gave a full view of the driveway as it climbed to the street. A button switch under the screen was marked entrance door, he pushed it and heard the door lock engage, he pushed it again and it unlocked. There was nothing that he could think of that the kitchen did not have, "Amazing" he thought.

He walked around the outer walls and checked each window; he was surprised to find each window to have six position locking pins to allow the window to be open but still secure from access at different levels. The window looking out the rear of the apartment overlooked what he believed was the Savannah River. He shook his head and walked into the bedroom and was not surprised to find it perfect and the bathroom the same.

He was sold, the price was right, and everything else was pretty much as he would have built it. He walked back down the stairs and after locking the door walked back to the house. He grinned when he saw the for rent sign leaning against the fence that surrounded the trash cans. He knocked once, and opened the house's door and stepped into the hallway.

"We're in the kitchen Jake" Teddy's voice came down the hall.

Jake walked into the kitchen and walked over to the table where Teddy and Marian sitting. There was a tall glass of tea in front of them and one at the empty seat next to Teddy. He walked to the seat and after he sat down Teddy reached over and placed a business card in front of him.

Jake picked it up and it read:

Theodore and Marian Jacobson

4030 Millikin Road -AAA

Evans, Georgia 31920

706-224-3445

Marian began to speak, "Should you need to contact us, or if you need to list an emergency contact, please feel free to use us, also please use the same mailing address, the AAA after the street name identifies the apartment. I know we have assumed a bit, but in reality you are the only person we have actually talked to about the apartment. You just seem to fit, you know?"

Teddy started before Jake could respond, "We will need your full name, a contact number, and if you want, the contact info for whom you might want contacted should something occur, that of course is your choice. We would like one month's rent for security and the date when you want to move in. We will be here if you need anything, but unless you ask you will not be bothered."

They both sat there sipping their tea and waited for his reply.

Jake lifted the glass and sipped his tea before replying, "Well, it looks like you have a tenant, I will move in tomorrow, and bring the deposit money in the morning, if that is ok?

They both smiled and said, "That will be fine, almost in unison."

Jake finished his tea and standing shook Teddy's hand saying, "I'll see you tomorrow morning around ten."

Teddy held up his hand saying, "Wait a moment," he turned and walked out of the room. Marian stood and walked over to the counter and opened a draw, taking out a 3X5 card out she turned and handed it to Jake saying, "This is a list of emergency numbers and a few local restaurants that have takeout and or delivery and the cable company. If you want basic cable let me know and I'll have it turned on for you, I'm sure that we will cover that, it will be a small extra to our existing coverage. No, I'll just have it turned on. If you want any special channels or coverage you can get that."

"You don't have to do that, I…"

"Nonsense, it's done."

Jake took the card, folding it and pushed it into his back pocket saying "Thank You, Marian."

Teddy came back into the room and handed Jake a third key to the apartment saying, "This is the only other key to your apartment, the lock is a special order and it would be difficult to get the tumbler changed or extra keys made."

Jake gave Teddy the key back and said, "You keep it, I have no problem with that. If you feel you need to use it, so be it. Thank you both very much and I'll see you tomorrow." He shook Teddy's hand and gave Marian a slight hug, it just seemed right. He turned and walked out the backdoor, the way he had just entered, shaking his head and with a smile on his lips.

It had been a great way to start.

★★★

After climbing the stairs Jake placed the box on the kitchen counter, stepped over and opened the refrigerator and took out a soft drink. He walked over to the recliner facing the TV and sat down sighing and thinking, another new town, new name, new position, ya'da, ya'da, ya'da and hopefully he would be good for at least five or six years.

CHAPTER TWO

JAKE SAT THERE LOOKING AT the blank TV screen thinking, this was the ninth, no, the tenth move, and new life to be started, since leaving Wheatland, Wyoming. He had left after his twenty second birthday, one day after the camping trip that changed his life forever. The longest stay anywhere after that had been 7 years, in Nome, Alaska, but it was not possible to stay much longer in any one place without questions, questions, and eventually accusations.

He stood and looked at himself in the full length mirror that hung on the wall in the hall, Marian had picked his age at 26 and he had agreed. In reality he was eighty six, the image looking back was one of a twenty five - six year old male, six four, two hundred twenty pounds with rugged good looks under sandy blond hair. He shook his head and sat back down thinking back to the camping trip, the camping trip, the trip, that damn trip.

His birth name was Thomas Grayrock Jr. and in 1948 he had just returned from the military along with three of his best friends. They had all just returned from serving in the military, Army, Navy, Air Force and Marines. They had all signed up right out of High School and purposely gone in separate branches of the service so they would not be distracted by their friendship should they be in combat. He had been the one in the Army, serving four years, with a few being in combat. They had all served, and served proudly, but now they were home and needed to bond with each other, and the world, they had stepped away from for four years.

★★★

They planned a camping trip to the Laramie Mountains, the mountains are anywhere from 4500 feet to 10,200 feet high. They would drive his pickup to the foothills, getting as high up the trail in the truck as they could and then back pack another few hours until they reached ten mile steppe. They would set up camp and spend a few days fishing, hunting and telling stories. Everything went as planned for the first night and the second day turned out to be much warmer than normal. With the heat of the day upon them they decided to spend the mid part of the day exploring a cave that they had found on their climb to the steppe. None of them remembered it from trips they had made many years before, while in high school.

Once at the cave entrance they realized that the opening was more a cave in than a normal cave opening. After entering and proceeding in about fifty feet the walls of the cave became smooth and after further investigation they were sure that the opening was man made. They continued to proceed deeper into the tunnel, they felt they had gone well over a mile when there was a light about three hundred feet in front of them. They continued going deeper, and it kept getting lighter, until they turned around a long arching corner and found themselves in front of a large smooth door. The door seemed to be made of glass and all they could see beyond it were rows and rows of Lab desks and what looked like ovens.

He now knew that they were an attempt be what we now know as fume hoods and were to prevent contamination.

They had forced the large door open with debris they found and began to look in each of the fume hoods not realizing that as they opened each one they were tempting fate. Once they had searched the room and found nothing, they walked on and entered a smaller room that had larger cabinets and other doors on what looked like vaults. They started opening the cabinets and found all of them to be empty so they turned to the vaults.

They never gave it a thought that they could be in danger, hell they had survived the war.

They picked the largest vault and it took two of them to turn the large handle and pull the door open. They were surprised to find over a hundred glass containers, with a few broken and on the floor, each with what looked like a scorpion in them. What was even weirder the scorpions were still alive, and a few were almost as large as the containers they were housed in. Tom and his friends entered the vault slowly and were bent over looking at the broken containers on the floor when fifteen to eighteen inch scorpions fell from above on to their backs. Before they could react each of them was stung multiple times.

Tom woke up lying on the floor of the vault to see his friends lying dead, their skin looked wrinkled and old like sun dried leather. He stood and stepped out of the vault shaking uncontrollably not believing what he was seeing. His friends had aged seventy or eighty years in what he was sure was only hours.

It had taken him many hours to retrieve gasoline from the truck to burn the Lab, and then to get his friends bodies, and all of their camping equipment back to his truck and then back to his father's ranch.

★★★

His father, Thomas, after hearing the story from his son had called Doc Tim, a friend of his that he knew was in the service of the government, and gave him a brief description of what had happened. His friend had told him to not talk to anyone else until he got there and they talked first. Stating that what was done was done and a few more hours delay in notifying the three men's parents would not affect anything.

Tom's father never knew what his friend Tim did nor why he was called Dr. Tim, but he had moved into the community well over ten years before and had been well received.

Dr. Tim arrived about forty five minutes after the call and after shaking hands, and then looking at the bodies of the three young men, asked Jerry to have his wife and Tom join them in the living room.

Tom and his mother and father sat on the sofa looking at Dr. Tim, as he pulled a chair around and sat facing them.

Dr. Tim looked at each of them and said, "Well, to get to where we are now, I guess I need to go back about twenty years or so. A little over twenty years ago a department of the federal government built the

Lab complex that Tom and his friends found. It was an extremely secret project that had almost unlimited funds and very few people knew about it back then and even fewer know today. On the short, the project was attempting to derive a serum that would prolong life. Well, they were successful with only one species of living things, Scorpions, and that was one out of thousands. Every other species that the serum was administered to died. They aged at a rate so quickly that nothing could be done to cure or stop it."

"But there were hundreds of jars in that vault that we found" Tom blurted out.

"Yes, well over three hundred, three hundred out of 40 to 50 thousand attempts of administering the serum. But every living thing that the serum was administered to, besides Scorpions, died, a 100% failure rate every time. The project was cancelled and it was believed that everything had been destroyed. The people that worked there were dispersed across the county and they were forbid to contact each other in any way, ever. To disobey this command meant losing all earned benefits and to be discredited publicly or even jailed as a spy."

Thomas Grayrock lifted his hand off of his knee saying, "Dr. Tim, If everything was destroyed how did those jars get there and be allowed to remain there to cause the death of Tom's friends, our friends sons, and what is going to happen to Tom? Just what.............."

Dr. Tim Witherspoon held up his hand and stood up, he looked at them saying, "Thomas, I have been living here for twelve years on a permanent basis and spent hours, days, months, no years searching for anything that might allow this to occur. I never was given the location or access to the Lab site. Twelve years ago a Scientist that had worked on the project was found in an apartment room in Dallas Texas dead. All that was found was an open jar and a 16" Scorpion on his chest feeding on his face. I was dispatched here to find out how and when he removed a specimen of a defunct project, from an unknown location without anyone knowing and why."

He sat back down and continued, "There are only eleven people left alive in this country that know anything about this project and four of them are in this room. This project was ordered by the President of the United States back then in an effort to extend his life. When it was ended and everything thought to be destroyed all paperwork concerning it was destroyed.

When the discovery was made in Dallas a few people in power sent me to investigate everything. What I did discover is that the dead Scientist had lived out in the mountains for five or so years. I summarized that somehow he had hidden the samples and then he had gotten access to the closed Lab and continued the work for another five years. It was felt that he was in Dallas to meet with another Scientist that worked in the field of ageing and or the prevention of."

The sound of a large truck penetrated the room, they all started to rise, "please sit back down, that is just some of my people starting the cleanup process."

"What? Your people, clean up, Tim just what is going on? Thomas asked.

Dr. Tim's voice changed and it became much more forceful, he talked for well over six hours about what happened and what was going to happen, now and for an unknown future period. Every aspect and event that would, could or might occur was touched, expanded on and explained. Tom would spend some time with government doctors and the three young men's families would be notified and through a few government projects in the area, they would be provided for. It was also the last day Tom Grayrock Jr. existed.

It was made perfectly clear that it would be this way or it would be very bad for all concerned.

★★★

Jake spent the next few years totally controlled by the government, day after day of testing, testing and more testing, vile after vile of blood, more testing, so on and so on. Jake's ability to comprehend and learn grew exponentially, almost daily. He completed his college education in six months, his masters in two.

It was not until after six or seven months he realized that he could throw his mind at will to anyone and anywhere. He protected and hid this information/ ability from his government handlers and used it to slowly work his way to release from them. He worked diligently to get them to the point of releasing him from their containment and being allowed to rejoin the world at large.

★★★

Jake would lay awake at night allowing his mind to search out each of the Doctors, that he considered his handlers, and search their thoughts and plans that were currently being used to control his life and the goals they need him to reach to consider the research on him complete. He manipulated their thoughts a little at a time getting him closer and closer to release.

After a period of time Jake realized that he could enter a person's mind and have them perform what he wanted, but they would only remember doing or saying what they wanted. He had tested this on his Doctors and other workers that he was allowed to interface with.

He had wandered through one of the workers minds, the man creeped Jake out, to find that he was a very bad person. Jake had him send a letter to the local police explaining that he was a pedophile and that he could not help himself from harming children. The worker gave dates and times of where different occurrences had occurred, all the while the worker believed he was writing a letter to his mother. Not to Jake's surprise the worker was not seen again.

Jake accidently found out about another ability that he had, one that made him very nervous and put him in deep self thought and self evaluation. The only female worker that he interfaced with had been a young woman in her twenties. At one point her demeanor in actions and personality had changed greatly. Jake had questioned her about it and she had become tearful and sobbed that she had been diagnosed with breast cancer and told she would have to have chemo and radiation treatments the following week but the outlook did not look good. She had moved into his arms sobbing, Jake had held her telling her that anything could happen and she could end up fine. The woman had left in tears and Jake did not see her again for a few weeks.

A little more than two weeks later she had burst into his room, and hugging him, saying "I've been cured, they took more tests and it's all gone, it's gone. You said I would be okay, thank you, thank you." He never got to respond to her in any way, in a flash she turned and was out the door from his room.

After that he had searched people's minds and found a few others with some sort of illness, he had just wished them to be well and it happened. He was very concerned about this new found ability and was sure not to disclose it to anyone.

He swore to himself that he would never search for anyone to help, never. If someone came into his life, during the normal course of things, and he felt right about it. So be it, otherwise he would distance himself from the rest. He knew that the demands would be over whelming and did not want to be the one that selected who lived or who died.

It was hard enough controlling his ability to influence people's actions/minds and the realization that he was responsible for the consequences that it caused.

★★★

It had been in the second year of his being kept that he found some information on the events that occurred in Grayrock after the trip. He and his friends had been buried with a large ceremony and glitz and glitter. Their deaths were blamed on a cave in of an abandoned government test site in the Laramie Mountains.

The government built three reservoirs on land purchased from the boy's families and two power generating plants were also built. The plants were run by a new company, 'Basin Electric' which was owned by the boy's families also.

Everything was nice and neat, controllable, and contained.

CHAPTER THREE

JAKE SAT DOWN AND PUSHED the button to turn on the TV, the TV quite an invention, it having full PC capabilities was even better. PC's and the Internet were unbelievable, all the data you might want or not 24/7. Between that and the cell phones, I-pads, etc, one could have a mental overload he thought to himself with a chuckle. He picked up the two notebooks that he had gotten from the HR department at work and went through both in about fifteen minutes. He now knew all of the Do's and Don'ts for his department, and the county administration. He pushed a few more buttons and had the TV on line and he searched the last twelve months of the local newspaper. He realized that he was getting some reporter's opinion about what happened, but it gave him a data base of local information to work with. He then went to the local sheriff's site and gleaned a bit more info, he would learn a lot more once he was at work, and had access to the forensic files stored in the active data base.

Jake was at work thirty five minutes early and was not surprised to find the Forensic Lab Director, Dr. Claude Andrews, in his office surrounded by piles of files and papers. He tapped on the glass, that made up the top half of the door, and opened the door and stepped in to the office saying, "Good Morning,"

Dr, Andrews stood up and stepping around his desk put out his hand saying, "Good morning, Jake right?"

"Yes Sir," Jake replied.

"Please find a seat, Jake in here you can call me just about anything, but Sir is not one of them. Outside this building is a different matter of course, I think Doctor Andrews will work best, we will see in time."

Jake moved a few files and sat in the chair across from the Director saying, "Doc, Okay?"

"Yes, that works fine, I put three files on your desk in the Lab.

File One – Case 2013-211 - Active – Highest Priority - Mysterious death of a teenager – seventeen year old AM (African American) male – found on the street dead with foam coming out of his mouth – no apparent injuries - autopsy at ten tomorrow morning – no cause of death yet.

Second File – Case 2009–311 – Young woman found dead in her car - Inactive – Priority - I don't feel satisfied with the findings and case resolution.

Third File – Case 2001-401 – Two young males found dead in an alley behind a tavern on Russell Street - Dead/Closed – Priority – Something is just not correct with everything.

NOTE: All new cases take priority over Second and Third Files.

Your locker is on the wall at the rear of the Lab, there are two Lab coats in it. I've ordered additional coats with your name on them, they will be here in a week or so." He placed a ring of keys on the desk in front of Jake and continued, "There is a key for all of the locks in the Lab, and your locker, on this ring, I have the only other set, that set is locked in my desk and only I have access to them. If you would like to put a second lock on your locker I have no problem with that."

Jake picked up the ring of keys and replied, "I see no need for that,"

The Director nodded and continued, "If you find that you need anything, additional equipment, people, or just stuff to do your job better or faster let me know, and I will attempt to make it happen. On new cases I need regular up-dates verbally each day and written reports, e-mails are ok, weekly. On the others, report as needed. Jake, I really don't want to find out info on our cases from the media, any questions?"

"Only two that I can think of right now, who is doing the autopsy and where, and is it okay if I come in around seven instead of eight thirty?"

"Oh, sorry, Doctor Fox, David Fox, over at the Medical Center on Walton Way. Main elevators down to the Autopsy room, it is in the basement next to the Morgue. As far as the work hours go, suit yourself, your badges and credentials give you access 24/7/365, as long as we get the results in a timely manner and I get at least forty hours."

Jake stood and started for the door saying, "Great, I'll be in the Lab."

He walked about twenty feet down the hall and entered the Lab, he looked around and said to himself grinning, "Home Sweet Home, for awhile." He walked around the Lab slowly looking at each piece of equipment, Atomic Absorption Spectrometer, Gas Chromatograph Mass Spectrometer, Automated DNA Sequencer/DNA Sequencing System, Blood Chemistry Analyzer, Fingerprint Development Chamber, Fluorescence Spectrometer, Thermal Evolved

Gas Analyzer, Automated Solid Phase Extraction System, Electron Spin Resonance Spectrometer, Chromatography Centrifugal System/Chromatography Centrifuge, Microscopes, just about everything he would have thought of needing. The amount of equipment was very, very impressive, he walked to the rear of the Lab, and behind a free standing wall, found his locker and the entrance to a rest room and shower. He put on a Lab Coat and walked to the only desk/workstation in the Lab with a PC, Printer, and Desk Phone.

He sat at his desk and began reading the data in the files that were left for him. In the first file there were copies of the 911 call, from an unknown caller, Emergency EMT reports from the scene and hospital call from the ambulance ride, police reports from the first on the scene, and the first reports from the Detective that caught the case, Detective Julian Brown, his card was attached to the report. There were also specimen jars in sealed/signed/dated evidence packs with samples of blood, foam from the victim's mouth, a gray substance that was marked 'Ground' and a red substance that was marked 'Shoes'.

Jake took a pad out of the desk and made a to do list, Case 2013-211 - Analyze Foam from victim's mouth, Gray substance found on ground and Red substance found on victim's shoes. He cut open the evidence pack for the foam, picking up the vial he got up and moved to the Laboratory Table nearest his desk. He found a sample dish and removed a sample of the foam and placed it in the dish. He got totally engrossed in the processes and his work.

★★★

Jake was distracted by a knocking sound, he looked up from the report he was typing and found Dr. Andrews standing in the Lab doorway.

With a grin on his face Dr. Andrews asked, "You going home or are you working all night? It's five twenty."

"Five – Twenty? He said, "really," not thinking." Going home I guess, just need to send this report on what I've found on Case 2013-211 so far."

"Great, I'll read it when I get home. Have a good evening, Jake, see you in the morning."

"Thanks Doc, see you in the morning."

Jake finished the last of the report and pressed the Send button. He got up and walked back to his locker and placed the Lab Coat in it. He closed the locker door without engaging the lock. He walked out to his truck and got in grinning, he was thinking about the day, "He never checked on me once, guess my report will give him something to evaluate."

★★★

Jake was in the Lab by six thirty and was running some tests on the red substance found on the victims shoes. He was also compiling a list of additional questions, that he added to list from the findings on the foam and gray substances that he wanted to ask Detective Brown. He glanced at the wall clock on the far wall and thought, "its eight ten, and Detective Brown should be in by now." He pulled up the contact list for the Detective squad and finding Det. Brown's extension, hit the Hands free button on the phone and pushed in the numbers.

"Detective Brown, Can I help you?"

"Detective Brown, Ken Smith, Forensic Lab. I was wondering if you have some time to meet with me to go over some questions I have on Case 2013-211."

"Smith, I think that can be made to happen, what's your schedule look like this morning?"

"I've got the autopsy of the victim at ten, sometime after noon work?"

"Is the Autopsy at the Med Center, with Doc Fox performing the cutting?"

"Yes, in the Lab next to the Morgue."

"I'll meet you there around nine forty five or so, we can talk about the case after the autopsy. The cutting might add a few more questions."

"Thank you, see you there." Jake pushed the End button and turned to see Dr. Andrews walking toward his desk.

"Jake, just wanted to stop in and let you know that your report on your activities yesterday was very informative and precise. I like that, and I will say you accomplished a very acceptable amount of work. I have meetings till three today but I would like to meet with you at three thirty to go over a few of the findings you outlined in the report."

"Doc, that sounds doable I have the autopsy at ten and I'm meeting Detective Brown there, we're going to go over a few items after but I'm sure I'll be back for three thirty."

Dr. Andrews had a slight look of surprise on his face but responded, "Very good, see you then." He turned to leave but stopped, turning towards Jake said, "Brown is a good Detective, better yet a good person. You two should hit it off well." He turned abruptly and was gone.

Jake went back to some paperwork, glancing up at the clock thought, "Have about twenty minutes before I have to leave for the Medical Center to be on time." He had used his GPS to find the Medical Center last night and driven the route to get comfortable with the roads. He had also Googled Augusta a bit and found that it was the second city in Georgia founded in 1736 and built to the plans of James Oglethorpe. It was the third city planed by Oglethorpe, Savannah being the first, Saint Augustine, Florida the second and Augusta the third. The city of Augusta was named after the Princess Augusta, the wife of Fredrick, Prince of Wales and Richmond County was named after the Duke of Richmond.

The city downtown was laid out with four main roads going East and West, and the cross streets in the business area and Old Town Area going from 1st street to 15th with other streets mixed in. Just West of downtown was The University of Augusta, it is intertwined with one of the upscale residential areas called 'The Hill.'

Once you get further North West of the city proper, you find the world acclaimed Augusta Club Golf Club home of the Masters Golf Tournament. Jake had driven by the front gate, and glanced up Magnolia Lane, more out of curiosity than anything else. He had played golf on and off for sixty years or so and considered himself a decent player. The only problem were the relationships that went along with the game, he did not really enjoy the loss of acquaintances made during his five to seven year life periods.

For that matter he made every attempt to keep any female acquaintances to a very unemotional level. He had learned quickly that relationships could and would hurt and they also caused many difficulties.

★★★

Jake pulled into a parking space in front of the main entrance of the Medical Center at nine forty. The building looked larger in the daylight, the night before he had not noticed the South Wing that extended to the left of the main building. He walked thru the main entrance and he had not gotten more than five feet in the building before he was approached by a man with his hand extended saying, "Ken Smith?"

Jake shook the extended hand replying. "Yes, and you must be Detective Brown."

"You got it, call me Julian."

"Julian it is, please call me Jake."

"Jake, that works. We have to go over there," Pointing towards the elevators. "Not good to be late, Doc Fox runs a tight ship and he is a stickler for starting on time."

With that they walked towards the elevators, once there Julian pushed the Down button and the door opened at once.

"Well you must be good luck Jake, have to wait for almost five minutes most times."

They stepped into the elevator and Jake pushed the B button on the panel next to the door, the doors closed and the car dropped the eighteen feet to the next floor. The doors opened and they stepped out and Jake was surprised at the cleanliness and brightness of the space around them. Julian pointed to his left and moved that way. They walked to the doorway with a small metal sign above it announcing LAB. Opening the door they found a large man in a white Lab coat bending over a pile of towels laying helter skelter on the floor.

"Need some help there Doc?" Julian asked.

"Well that would be helpful Detective Brown," Doctor Fox replied as he turned towards the voice. He saw Jake and continued, "And you must be Jake, Dr. Andrews called and warned me that you are very sharp. Only one day on the job and you have your boss sold. Impressive, if I don't say myself, Dr, Andrews is hard to impress and you have accomplished that in a very short time."

Julian had stacked the towels on the metal table that was next to the wall before he joined them moving towards the operating table. He had not missed the banter between the two and filed it somewhere in the back of his mind.

Moving over to the operating table Dr. Fox continued with, "Let's get this done, please watch, but no discussion unless I have a question or comment, Understood?"

"We got it, Doc." Julian answered quickly, and winked at Jake when the Doctor turned his head, back to the victim on the table.

The autopsy started with the standard Y cut, removal of organs, etc, but there was nothing out of the ordinary, it seemed.

Jake was quite interested when the throat area was dissected, he had a few ideas about the cause of death but the exam proved none of them out.

Doctor Fox removed his gloves and tossed them into the trash container marked 'Hazardous-Human Waste' saying, "Well, are there any questions?"

Julian responded first saying, "Looked pretty non-descript, nothing stood out as different."

The two men turned towards Jake with a quizzical look.

Jake looked at them saying, "Well Doctor, I really thought there would be more to see when you got to the throat area and the stomach lining. The foam found in his mouth was caused by some mixture of hydrogen peroxide and wheat based dough. The fact that there was no sign of the mixture entering the throat or stomach, it pretty much rules out it had anything to do with the death. It was something done to cause a change of direction to the investigation, which means someone with law enforcement training or knowledge, was involved. I've still got the Mass Spec. working on three different scans based on different search criteria. Hopefully the data will be there when I get back to the Lab. If possible I would like a sample of the victim's Hair, Gall Bladder and the Pituitary Gland. Other than that, I've got nothing to add."

Doctor Fox looked at Julian and said, "You my friend better step up or this man will leave you in his dust." He looked at Jake and continued, "If you would, please keep me in the loop on your findings, I might learn something. Well I'm off to rounds." He turned and as he passed the Lab Tech that had just entered he said, "Take a sample of the victim's Hair, Gall Bladder and Pituitary Gland and get them over to the Forensic Lab – STAT then close him up, Make sure that the recorder is on during the taking of the evidence, and marking the evidence packs, when you are finished close and file the tape, darn, disc, I'm sorry." With that he was out the door and gone.

Julian looked at Jake saying, "How about lunch, we can talk about the case in more detail."

"Sounds good to me," Jake replied.

***

They walked out to the parking lot and Jake followed the nondescript White Ford that was Julian's official car.

***

Dr, Fox sat at his desk picked up the phone and pushed the speed dial for Doctor Andrews.

"Andrews."

"Claude, David, The young man is very astute, I purposely made a incorrect cut during the procedure removing the Gall Bladder, I'm pretty sure that he will somehow bring it up in your conversations. I'm sure he will know that he was being watched closely and mentioning it will be his way of letting you know that he knew. Don't know where he came from but you my friend have a keeper."

"Thank you for the feedback David. I'll keep in touch."

Dr. Fox replied, "Right," then pushed the END button.

***

Julian pulled into the parking lot and into a parking space in the first row, directly in front of the Village Deli. He saw Jake pull into a space in the second row to his left six or seven spaces. He watched Jake get out of his truck and start towards the front door of the Deli. "Confident in himself" he thought, most people following someone to a place they had never been to would instinctively move towards the person they were following. Julian got out of his car and walked to the front door and going in found Jake waiting for him.

"I told the server that there would be two," Jake said smiling.

"That will work, Food is good here and the service is above par."

The young girl picked up two menus and motioned for them to follow her.

Jake noticed that Julian acknowledged four people before they got to their table and he had nodded to two others.

The young lady placed the menus across from each other at a table for four. Once they were seated Jake picked up the menu and glance through the four pages it contained. He looked across the table at Julian and said, "Eat here often?"

Julian laughed replying, "Once or twice a week for over fifteen years. It is one of the local favorites, Jake, if you like, I'll get the first drink after work at another place you should know."

"Sounds good, I will be done for the day around five thirty."

"I'll swing by the Lab around that time."

Just then the waitress walked up saying, "Ready?"

Julian smiled and asked, "Specials?"

She looked at him and smiling replied, "Well Detective, as you know its Tuesday, Meat Loaf Platter, Catfish Platter or Stuffed Peppers, soups are Potato, Split Pea or Onion."

Julian grinned, saying, "Sweet Tea, a cup of Split Pea and Meat Loaf with mashed potatoes and a small salad with 1000 Island on the side."

"Got it," She looked at Jake, pencil ready.

Jake looked up and said, "Emilie, I'm Jake, I'll have a Sweet Tea, a cup of the Pea Soup, a Hot Pastrami on Rye with shoe string fries and a small salad with oil and red vinegar on the side."

She beamed replying, "Got it, be back with the drinks shortly, Jake"

Julian looked at him saying, "Well she's hooked, I haven't seen her smile like that in a while."

Jake just shrugged and glanced around the dining area and commented, "Seems to be quite a different mix of customers. Blue Collar, White Collar and Professionals and most seem to know someone here."

Julian took a sip from the drinks that seemed to just appear in front of them, "Yes, most of the people here have known each other through school, sports, good times and some not so good times. For the most part they are all good people, from good families. There are always a few bad apples but that is anywhere these days, with the drug thing it can happen to anyone or any family."

Jake nodded his agreement and moved his glass as Emilie placed the plates of food in front of them.

Emilie smiled and asked, "Anything else I can get you?"

They both responded, "We're good."

As they ate they discussed the case and some of the people that stopped by to say 'Hey' to Julian. Each time Julian would introduce Jake as the new County Forensic Lab Director. After the first time Julian had looked at Jake saying with a laugh, "Well you are the only one in the Lab."

They finished their lunches and walked out of the Deli, Julian turned to Jake and shook his hand saying, "Enjoyed it, see you around five thirty." He then stepped off the curb and walked towards his car and Jake watched him for a moment then walked to his truck. He was back at the Lab by one ten and found the three samples he had requested on his desk.

Jake sat at his desk and reread the reports he had printed out from the three different tests he had put in action earlier that morning. Having all of the equipment in the Lab on a secure intra-net giving him total access to each device was a really great thing. He had worked with much less in many places.

★★★

Jake walked up to the doorway of Dr. Andrews' office and saw that Dr. Andrews was on the phone.

Dr. Andrews looked up and motioned for Jake to come in and take a seat.

Jake moved the same files he had moved the day before and sat down across from the Doctor.

Doctor Andrews pushed the END button and looked at Jake saying, "Four hours in a meeting, and a thirty minute rehash to get to the same conclusion we discussed yesterday at lunch. Just so everyone is covered, Ahh, the benefits of working in a government agency."

He picked up a paper from his desk, glanced at it, then looked at Jake saying, "I've read your reports on this case, and being you have deduced more about it in one day than we did in a week, how about you let me in on where you think it is going."

'Well, after analyzing the foam I was pretty sure that the foaming at the mouth was a distraction that was caused to send us down the wrong path. I did not list that as a fact in my report because I wanted to see the autopsy to confirm my beliefs. Which the autopsy did do, it confirmed my deduction. It confirmed that the foam was put in place to appear caustic, but was in fact a harmless prop. This was proven by the lack of irritation in the throat or stomach of the victim. The foam was a combination of wheat flour, as a dry base, mixed with hydrogen peroxide. The foam was nothing but the reaction of the hydrogen peroxide destroying the bacteria in the victim's mouth. This accomplished two things – first – cause a distraction/redirection of fact, two – cleansed the victim's mouth of any evidence of inducing a liquid and the liquids make-up. The tests that I ran today confirmed that there were no foreign substances in the throat, stomach or stomach contents.

The inspection of the skin during the autopsy did not find any puncture wounds, injections sites or major contusions or abrasions that would allow the introduction of foreign substance.

I requested a specimen of the Gall Bladder, Pituitary Gland and Hair after the autopsy, I received them and I have a test running on each right now. As you know they all hold residual evidence of substances longer than anyplace else in the body. It is my belief that the victim was poisoned, and these tests will give us the poison used.

I did find it strange how Dr. Fox removed the Gall Bladder, he made the cuts very close to the organ, some if not all of the bile could have leaked out quite easily. I guess everyone has a slip once in awhile.

I am running tests on the other two substances found on, or near the body, Detective Brown has agreed to help me track down the source of them once I have identified them." Jake sat back in the chair.

Dr. Andrews clasped his hands together and leaned forward a little looking at Jake. He glanced at the paper on his desk again and looking back at Jake said, "All I can say is that it appears that you have a good handle on it all and I agree with your procedures and deductions so far. Please keep me informed on the results of the tests and how things go with any of the other Departments that get involved."

"Will do, I'll make it part of my daily report."

Dr. Andrews nodded and turned his interest to a small pile of papers on his desk.

Jake stood and walked back to the Lab. He unlocked the door, locking it was needed to protect the chain of evidence for the samples he had running in the different equipment/devices, and moved over to his desk.

He checked the status of the tests that were running and seeing that they would not be completed for a while, so he walked over to the Lab sink and washed the equipment that had been placed in it. He then placed all of the items in the sterilizer and pressed the Level 2 Sanitize button.

He went back to his desk and sitting down he pulled the keyboard closer to him and began to Google the list of items about the case that bothered him. The Internet and its seemingly endless stream of information and data still fascinated him, he sometime spent hours just Googleing anything that popped into his mind. His thirst for knowledge seemed endless but the answers were also endless. He printed twenty pages of data on the items that just didn't fit well in his mind. After reading the information he separated it in to two piles, usefull and not so much so. He placed the papers in a manila folder and put the folders in the case file he had put together.

★★★

His phone beeped, it startled him a bit, that because he had not given the number to anyone. He pushed the button that engaged the call saying, "Smith,"

"Mr. Smith, this is Joan from the HR Department, just checking up on you. Is everything going alright?"

"Yes, all is well. Everyone has been very helpful. I was surprised to get your call."

"Well everyone can contact you now, I've got you added to the county directory and sent the update to everyone. You should find the updated list in an e-mail that went out earlier today. If you need anything please call."

"Thank you, I will."

"Okay, have a good day."

Jake replied "You also," and pushed the END button. "County wide, well so much for a low profile."

Jake looked at the phone and shook his head thinking, "More knowledge in this thing than the entire library at the Club Library in Washington DC. Heck, more than the entire University he had stayed at gleaning information to support his different Masters programs.

★★★

"Hey Man", Julian called from the Lab doorway, "You working all night?"

Jake looked up and replied, "Done," He closed the file he was working on and stood up from the desk. He reached towards the ceiling with both hands stretching his arms and shoulders, saying more to himself than Julian, "Need to move around more."

Julian laughed replying, "Well let's see if we can exercise our elbows a bit."

"Sounds good," Jake replied walking towards the doorway.

Once they got out in the parking lot Jake asked, "Which way will we be going?"

"Up on the Hill, the place is on Berckman, above the Club, West of here."

"Okay, I'll follow you. I've got to go out off Fury's Ferry Road after."

Julian laughed saying, "No problem, I'll keep it at the legal limit."

Jake got into his truck, and with a wave Julian's way, he started the truck, and pulled behind Julian's car. Jake followed Julian to the entrance to the Calhoun Causeway and sped up to stay a few car lengths behind him as he increased his speed to reach the fifty mile per hour limit. They exited the Causeway on to Washington Road and continued about a half mile to the traffic light Berckman Road. They turned left and drove about three miles up the hill to Surry Center Shoppe's and pulled into the parking lot. Julian pulled into a parking space across from the front of a restaurant named 'The French Market.'

Jake parked in the space next to Julian then he got out of the truck and locked it. He walked towards the restaurant's entrance, alongside Julian. Julian pointed to a white sheet of paper taped on the sidebar window next to the door.

"That's the Specials for tonight, hope you like Cajun food, this is the best anywhere, anywhere that is, other than New Orleans."

"Cajun sounds good to me, haven't had any in quite awhile." He grinned to himself thinking, "Not for twenty years at least."

They walked in and Julian led the way to the bar area, he slid into one of the booths just across from the bar.

Jake was a little surprised that there was no one at the hostess station or at the bar as they walked in. He slid into the booth across from Julian just as someone said, "Detective Brown, Ale, Martini, or Jack on the Rocks?"

"Jack Rocks will do nicely."

Jake turned his head towards the voice and came eye to eye with a Blue Eyed, Blond haired young lady.

"Got it," she replied looking at Julian.

She looked Jake in the eye saying, "Shelly, your new, what can I get for you?"

"Jake, yes I am, and the Jack Rocks sounds' good."

"Got it," came over her shoulder as she moved behind the bar.

Jake looked at Julian saying, "Another place you've never frequented much, I presume?"

"Hardly ever, just about three or four time a week," he laughed.

Before Jake could reply, Shelly was back and placed the drinks in front of them saying, "Detective, just drinks, or dinner?"

"Just drinks for now, Thanks Shelly."

She turned towards Jake and with a smile said, "And how about you, Jake?"

"The drink will do for now Shelly, Thank you."

"Okay, need anything just let me know?" With that she moved back behind the bar.

Julian looked across at Jake and asked, "Not that it is any of my business but where are you living? You mentioned Fury's Ferry Road?"

"Out on Millikin Road off of Old Fury's Ferry Road, in Evans, found a great garage apartment. The owners are a really nice older couple named Ted and Marian Jacobson. They have been very helpful with my getting settled in. My move from Washington DC was uneventful but working outside of the Agency will take a while to get use to." Jake knew he had circumvented at least a dozen of Julian's future questions with one answer.

"So your living out at Teddy's place, they are great people. I guess I've known them for twenty years or more. Teddy was a big supporter of local school sports teams while he was the Site Director over at the Bomb Plant in Barnswell, and Marian was the best teacher in the counties school system. They have had that garage apartment up for rent at least once a year for the last five. You are the first person that they have ever rented it to. That says a lot without saying anything, they always could read people and no one ever met their approval before."

Jake nodded as he sipped is Jack on the Rocks, "Bomb Plant?"

Julian grinned, "Yep, Savannah River Nuclear Facility. Barnswell, South Carolina. At one time they had two or three operating reactors. Now it is mostly used for storage of nuclear waste, they encapsulate it in glass and store it underground somewhere on the site. When they built the storage area they used all out of state people and all of the workers were housed, fed, medical, dental needs and entertained on site. They would bring them in at night and ship them out the same way. At one time Teddy had well over 3000 people working there, it went 24/7/365 back then."

"Interesting, this is just like a small town instead of a city, it seems everyone knows everyone. Is it really that way or is there just a large group that worked at the same monetary and education level that had a lot of interaction professionally and/or socially?" Jake asked as he set his glass on the table after taking a sip.

"I guess it is more like the latter part of that question, most of these people were born here as were their parents, grandparents and so on. Not that it was done intentionally but there has always been a form of Class Distinction or Separation, just always been there and anyone moving in just joined the group that fit them and their life style. Does that make any sense?"

Jake finished his drink and caught Shelly's eye and raised his empty glass and lifted two fingers. He turned to Julian and replied, "Absolutely, I guess I'm just surprised that it still works, the new age of technology has wiped it out for the most part in cities. It kind of makes one feel they are a part of everything and I guess gives people the feeling of belonging, pretty neat."

Shelly set the drinks down and replied, "Me, why thank you."

Julian quickly replied, "Nope the Jack."

She tapped his arm as to scold him, "That was not nice."

Jake came to Julian's aid saying, "Shelly, your way better that just pretty neat, why you're the very best in this place."

Shelly looked a Jake and then Julian, then shaking her head replied, "I don't think it is a good idea for you two to be out together. A girl doesn't have a chance."

They all laughed and Shelly moved back towards the bar. When she tried to step through the opening that allowed access to the serving area behind the bar the man standing on the corner turned and blocked her way.

Shelly said, "Excuse me. Please."

The man did not move.

She said it again, this time her voice sounded a little shaky.

The man turned and looked at her saying, "Sure, you finished brown nosing with those cops? Someone else might like some service, you know."

Jake turned and began to get out of his seat to see who was talking but before he could get out of the booth Julian was out and standing next to the man that had been talking. He looked up at the man's face saying, "Do you have a problem Mr. Mendoza? I'll be very happy to help you out, very happy."

Mendoza looked down at him with a big smile replying, "I bet you would Detective Brown, I bet you would." He turned and waved toward one of the tables by the window to another man that had just walked in. "Sorry we can't chat, important business to discuss." With that he turned and walked to the table he had pointed at and shook the hand of the man that had entered and stood there. They both sat down and began talking, ignoring the rest of the people in the restaurant.

Julian moved back to the booth and sat, his eyes never left Mendoza and the man he was sitting with. He picked up the fresh drink that Shelly had brought and downed most of it with one gulp.

Jake got up and stepped over to the bar and asked Shelly for another round, turning to his left to go to his seat so he could get a good look at the two men sitting at the table. He slid into the booth and looking at Julian said, "A friend of yours?"

Julian snapped his head around to look at him to reply sharply, but seeing Jake's face just sat there for a moment before he replied, "Yes, one I have been trying to put in a cell for years. Mr. Tyrone Mendoza - Controls 95% of the illegal drugs in this part of Georgia. From the Georgia, South Carolina, North Carolina line in North East Georgia to Savannah Georgia, on the South Carolina line, on the coast and out to the South, Southeast to Macon. Every time I get close my evidence and or my witnesses disappear or someone in their family disappears, or they get hurt, then everyone gets amnesia. And he just rubs it in our face time after time."

"Big guy, he must be six, five or six at least. Who is the guy with him?"

"Six seven, know him since grade school, he was always big and a bully. The other is the Doctor of the crooked and rich, Doctor Paul Greenly M.D."

"Well, I guess the town's underbelly has shown it ugly head, it is in every town to some degree."

Shelly brought a third round of drinks and apologized about the confrontation that had occurred.

They told her that it was nothing.

She smiled and moved back behind the bar and remained there.

The pair had struck a nerve, Julian vented for almost an hour about the drug problem in the city, that and the problems with Tyrone Mendoza and Dr. Greenly and Jake just let him go.

Jake waved to get Shelly's attention, she glanced over at them, Jake made the motion of signing a check, and she nodded. A few moments later Shelly moved over to the booth and placed the check on the table. Jake picked it up saying, "I got it." He took his money clip out of his pocket and pulled two twenties off of it and handed the bills and check back to Shelly saying, "Keep the change, it was nice meeting you."

Julian started to protest but Jake waved him off saying, "I got it."

They pushed out of the booth and standing next to each other Julian said, "Sorry for the rambling, they just rub me the wrong way, always have I guess."

Jake grinned replying, "No problem, we all have our devils that we live with. Are you okay to drive?"

Julian grinned saying, "Yes, Officer or not, I watch that pretty close. Thanks for asking though."

They turned and walked to the front door and stepping out each moved towards their cars. Jake looked back at Julian and waved as he got into his truck. He thought about the events and conversation in detail during his drive home.

★★★

That night Jake lay in his bed looking up at the ceiling, not seeing, his mind was miles away in the minds of Tyrone and Dr. Paul. He spent hours seeing and compiling data from their memories and future plans.

★★★

The rest of his week went quickly and all at once it was five o-clock on Friday and Doctor Andrews was standing at the Lab door asking, "Jake, staying the weekend?"

42

He looked up and replied, "Guess not, right behind you. Will it be alright if I call Dr. Fox and ask him to recheck something on the body he autopsied?"

"I don't see why not, but I'd wait till Monday morning." Doctor Andrews waved and disappeared down the hall.

Jake closed up the file he was working on and after locking everything he moved around the Lab shutting down equipment. After turning off the lights and locking the door he moved out to his truck, got in, started it, and headed home.

CHAPTER FOUR

J AKE HAD GOTTEN UP AT seven, shaved and taken a shower, after dressing he had made the bed and went into the kitchen and made a cup of coffee. He turned on the TV and watched the news channel. He was surprised when his phone started to ring, he had selected the traditional ring tone, and had to go back into his bedroom to get it. He pushed the correct button and said, "Smith."

"Jake, Julian, Did I wake you?"

"No, just having a cup of coffee."

"Have anything on the agenda for this morning?"

"Nothing special, what's up?"

"I'm heading up to the lake to clean up my boat. I was wondering if you would like to join me and give me a hand with it."

"That sounds good to me, haven't seen the lake yet."

"Great, I'll swing by and pick you up, Teddy's garage, right?"

"Right, you can help finish the coffee."

"Black works for me, see you in about ten minutes."

"It will still be hot, see you in a few." He pushed the END button and placed the phone on the counter. Jake picked up his cup and thought to himself, "Like it or not, it looks like I've made a friend."

He sat in one of the chairs and watch the talking heads spout their option about what was news. He caught the movement on the security screen out of the corner of his eye. He turned to watch a black ford pick-up pulling into the drive, he watched Julian get out of the truck. Julian turned towards the house and waved that way, Teddy came on the screen and shook Julian's hand. He pointed towards the apartment's entrance and with a wave moved off the screen. The buzzer sounded and Jake called out, "Come on in," as he rose and moved towards the heads of the stairs. He had pushed the button that unlocked the door earlier.

Once Julian reached the head of the stairs he put out his hand to Jake saying, "Trusting guy, you leave the door open."

Jake shook his hand replying, "Not really," and pointed to the security screen and door button.

Julian laughed, "I guess old habits die hard for Teddy."

Jake had moved over to the counter and was pouring Julian a mug of coffee, "There is not anything that I wouldn't have done." He handed Julian the mug and moved to the chair he had been sitting in and retook his seat.

Julian moved over to the second chair and sat down looking around the room. "Quite a setup, feels like home."

"Everything I need and more."

They watched the TV while they finished their coffee and when Jake finished he got up and moved over to the sink. He washed the mug he was using and placed it on the drain tray to air dry. "Be back in a moment," and walked into the bedroom. When he walked back into the room Julian's cup sat next to his on the tray and Julian said, "Ready?"

"Ready," Jake replied.

Julian went down the stairs first and Jake followed, once outside Jake locked the door and followed Julian over to his truck.

They drove for awhile without talking, Jake was sitting back with the sun on his face enjoying the ride and taking in all of the new areas they were going through. They drove for about thirty minutes before they got the first glimpse of the lake.

Jake looked out of the truck window at the vast expansion of water and commented, "Pretty good size, how much electricity does it produce?"

"Well, it supplies some of the power it produces to Georgia and South Carolina, the overflow goes into the power grid. As to how many Megawatts or KW it supplies, that I really don't know. What I do know is, it offers some of the best Striper and Pan fishing in the South East. Do you fish?"

"I've done some, both salt and fresh water, I prefer fresh water though. The fish taste better to me, less fishy than salt."

"Well, if I ever get my boat ready, and some time off, we need to wet a line."

Jake grinned and just nodded.

They pulled into a gravel parking lot marked with a sign, 'Property of the Richmond County Public Safety Department.'

"Didn't think Richmond County came out this far."

Julian laughed, "It doesn't. This plot was left to Richmond County for a search and rescue stepping off point to the lake by an anonymous wealthy resident. If it is ever used for anything else it reverts back to the donor's family. Any member of the County's search and rescue team can keep their boats here. I'm one of the divers on the team."

"And that is supposed to surprise me?" Jake said stepping out of the truck.

Julian looked across the hood of the truck and seeing Jake grinning just shook his head and opened the truck's bed cap and tail gate. He reached in and pulled out a large plastic covered tub onto the tailgate. He pulled a battery out on the bed and picking it up said, "This is all we'll need for right now. He started for the boat dock, with Jake walking next to him, the dock extended about one hundred feet into the lake.

There were six boats tied up to the dock, the largest, of the six, was a white twenty eight footer, with twin 150HP outboards hanging off the back transom. The letters that spelled out 'Richmond County Marine Search and Rescue' glistened in the sun light. Julian walked down the dock and stopped at his eighteen foot TRACKER, it had a 100 HP outboard on the rear transom.

Jake looked at the boat seeing it had two seats, front and rear, trolling motor, live bait well, rod holders and a bright green steering wheel.

Julian set the battery down on the dock and looking at Jake grinned and asked, "Inside or out."

Jake pointed at the boat saying, "Inside, didn't know anyone was going in for a swim."

Julian laughed and stepped onto the boat, reaching over the motor said, "Jake, Pass me the battery."

Jake picked it up and handed it over the tie line to Julian.

Julian placed the battery in the rack and connected the cables, he pointed at a boat lift down a ways from the dock, "Meet you over there. Can you get that tub of supplies from the truck?"

"You've got it."

Julian turned and sat in the first seat and turned the key to start the engine. It sputtered once, caught and idled smoothly.

Jake unhooked the rope and tossed it into the boat saying, "Meet you there." He walked back down the ramp and over to the truck. He opened the truck's door and lifted his work bag out, putting its strap over his shoulder. He hosted the tub off of the tailgate and onto his shoulder and walked over to the boat lift. Julian had pulled the boat onto the lift and was tying it down before he engaged the lift. Jake set the tub down as well as his bag and removed the tub's lid, and as he pulled the assorted cleaning liquids and pastes out and spread them on the work table.

Julian pressed the up button on the lift and the boat was lifted to a level about a foot above the water level. He pressed the second button and the lift moved the boat from over the water, to being over the work area. "Still want the inside?"

"Yep, I've got it." Jake picked up a stiff corn brush, portable vacuum, a container of auto wax, some rags and a bucket with a bag of Tri-Sodium Phosphate, from his bag, and bottle of water in it. He climbed up the lift's ladder and into the boat, finding that the lift held it quite stable. He placed all of his supplies on the boat's seats, all but the corn brush. He started by brushing the six inch rail that went down both sides of the boat that was covered with carpet. Once that was done he mixed a small amount of the TSP with half of the bottle of water. He dampened a cloth with the mixture and rubbed the brushed carpet down with it, folding and refolding it often. With that done he wiped the seats down and then poured the rest of the water into the pail and mixed more of the TSP in it.

He picked up the vacuum and went over the carpet a few times, with that done he moved all of the supplies back off of the boat. As he moved down the ladder to place the supplies on the work table he saw Julian with a scrub brush working on the far side of the boat. The bottom and side of the boat that Julian had finished looked like new. "Looks like new, really good job."

Julian grinned and replied, "I should have taken the inside."

"Maybe or maybe not, I'm not done yet." Jake said as he stepped on the ladder grinning. Once back in the boat, Jake started at the Bow, and scrubbing with the corn brush and TSP mixture worked thru the entire boat. Wiping each washed area dry before moving to another. Jake was just about done when he heard a vehicle pull into the lot.

He looked at the vehicle as it parked and was surprised to see two young women get out, one with a basket on her arm.

One of the young women waved her hand above her head and yelled, "Hey Boo, we have lunch."

Jake heard Julian yell back, "Be right there, Jake, lunch time."

Jake finished the small area that he had left and picked up all of the rags, and the bucket and brush. Then he swung out of the boat onto the ladder and climbed down. He placed the rags, brush and bucket on the table.

Julian stepped next to him and grinning said, "I did not know they were coming but I'm glad they did. Martha is the best cook in Augusta."

Julian didn't wait he just started walking towards Martha and the other woman, Jake followed him about a step behind. When they reached to young women Julian said, "Jake Smith, Martha Stone and Paige Walker, ladies Jake Smith. Took their hands one at a time and replied, "A pleasure to meet you Martha, and repeated the same to Paige.

★★★

Tyrone walked out of the Post Office with a stack of prepaid mailing boxes, and envelopes, with a smile on his face. All was well in his world, he knew in his mind that he was someone to be feared, respected, adored, pampered, obeyed, most importantly obeyed and he had money, tons of money, a mansion, a boat, a plane, workers that were like servants. Yes, all was good, no not good, all was great. He opened the door to his 500S and slid into the driver's seat, he enjoyed the feel of the leather as it surrounded him. He started the car and placing it in gear moved out onto the street and towards his home. He drove about fifteen minutes and pulled off of the main street onto Albacores Drive, it paralleled the river. He had purchased the first three lots, and knocked down the homes that were there, then built his sixteen thousand square foot mansion on all three lots, and had a six foot high two feet thick brick wall built around the complex.

He pushed the button on the dash and the wrought iron gates swung open, allowing him to pull down the driveway to the garage building. He parked in front of the three garage doors, the one closest to the river. Flipping the switch and shutting down the car he got out and walked around the house, and into the door that led to his study, which faced the river.

He locked the door behind him and placed the mailing envelopes and boxes on his desk. He pushed a button hidden under the desk top and the shutters on the windows closed tightly. Tyrone smiled control was wonderful, pushing another button that was concealed as a knob on the desk front. A panel on the wall behind his chair slid open and exposed a recessed safe. The safe was black steel three feet square and three feet deep with a digital panel on the front. Tyrone pushed in the combination digital screen and the door popped open a bit. He smiled as he pulled the door open, and he looked at the contents, it was full of stacks of one hundred dollar bills. The safe held five million dollars in cash, with no record of any of it. "Five Million," he grinned, "Five Million," with twice that coming and going each week.

He pulled twenty two packs of bills out, and placed them on his desk, and sat down with them piled in front of him. He placed two stacks of bills in each of the six large shipping envelopes and the remaining ten packs in one of the prepaid mailing boxes.

He filled out seven shipping labels, one for each, made out to Alisa Mendoza, Your Post Box Inc., Box 1256, Augusta, GA and put them on the box and envelopes. He placed the envelopes and the box in a large leather carrying case, closed the safe and pushed the button to conceal it. Then he pushed the button that opened the shutters and unlocked the doors. He walked out the door smiling as he walked back to his car. "Yes all was great," he thought.

★★★

Martha spread the table cloth over the truck's bed cover and placed four napkins, two at each side of the rear end of the cover, so that they could be reached easily. She placed a pair of covered trays in the center. She turned and said, "Boo, you start."

Jake looked at Julian with a grin and repeated, "Sounds good, Boo, you go first."

Julian shook his head and picked up a plate and fork saying, "That's fine with me, I'm not shy, got it."

Martha laughed and looking at her girlfriend said, "Paige, I guess Boo hasn't told Jake why he's called 'Boo'."

"I guess not, should we elaborate Boo?'

"I don't care. Really, just don't take the fried chicken away."

They all looked at him and he was standing there with a chicken leg in each hand and a grin on his face.

★★★

While they were eating Martha expounded on the story of BOO, she looked at Jake and grinning started, "It was Halloween about ten years ago, Julian, Jimmy and Fox were sitting in his living room plotting on how they were going to go out to the old Jotter's House on Old Walton Way.

The house sits on the hill and the drive winds around a little so you can't see the front door from the street. Mrs. Jotter always gave out really good stuff so all of the kids brave the dark driveway to get it. The house was a little run down and the bushes and trees were very overgrown. Mr. Jotter was too old to do the work and I guess they didn't have the money to pay someone to do the work.

Julian, Jimmy and Fox were planning to hide in the bushes and jump out when a group of us came up the drive.

Well, Julian didn't know that his and Jimmy's fathers were in the kitchen and over heard the plan. They walked past the boys in the living room saying, "You guys stay out of trouble tonight, were going to Rusty's for some pool and stuff." The boys barely acknowledged them as they walked out."

Julian picked up a chicken leg and pointed it at Martha, grinning said, "You really enjoy telling this don't you?"

She looked at him and said, "You bet." She looked back at Jake and continued, "Julian, Jimmy and Fox got to the Jotter house while it was still light, they scoped out the bushes and found the spot they felt was just right. They settled in and waited for the dark to set in and let five or six groups go though. They heard our group starting to walk up the drive so when we got even with them they jumped out and screamed. We all yelled, jumped and ran to the front door of the house with the girls still screaming, Julian, Jimmy and Fox stood on the edge of the bushes and were laughing so hard they were crying. We were all looking back at them and didn't know if we wanted to laugh or go beat them up. Then out of nowhere, two large ghosts jumped out of the trees right behind them, with the most god awful screeching sound. Julian's father had fitted some kind of animal call to an air horn. Julian, Jimmy and Fox jumped and let out a scream and ran towards the door.

The two ghosts were sitting on the drive laughing so hard they couldn't talk or stand. They pulled the sheets off and it was Julian and Jimmy's fathers, they were hooting and laughing as they walked to the front door. "Big bad Letterman," they turned and walked back down the drive way still laughing. The both stopped and turned around and lifted their hands and yelled, "BOO." Well now you know the rest of the story."

Jake was doing his best not to laugh out loud but it was pretty hard not to.

Julian said, "Go ahead, everyone gets one good laugh."

★★★

After they had eaten, they all pitched in and cleaned everything up, Martha and Paige said good bye with Julian getting a big hug from both.

Jake and Julian watched the car pull out of the lot, with a toot of the horn it was out of site.

"Sure looks like Martha is sweet on you, Boo."

"Maybe a little, we've known each other since we were in first grade together. There is a group of about ten of us that have been friends forever. I never know where or when I'll bump into anyone of them. It's like what happened today, I mentioned I was going to work on the boat today in passing to my friend Jimmy last night when he called me about something we have been working on for months. I guess he mentioned it to Martha or Paige after that and surprise, lunch. It has always been that way, one of the things I love about this area, it's comfortable."

"I guess it is, but that would only be for some, there are those that can't, won't, or avoid getting that close to anyone let alone ten people. That ten is in reality is probably twenty five or thirty and they are part of fifty or sixty. I don't believe that any of us know or realize just how many people we touch directly or indirectly each and every day."

Julian stopped and looked at Jake, he studied his face for a moment and said, "Jake, you are a very deep thinking guy, and quick about it also. Remind me to never get in a tight on the wrong side of you."

Jake grinned, "Well, I guess I've got you snowed, let's finish the boat."

"Right, were close. I've just got the transom left, to clean and then a quick wipe down of the bottom with WD-40. It should be about another hour at most."

"WD-40, don't tell me you believe that tale of it attracting fish?"

"Well I figure, why chance it and it makes it easier to clean next time."

"I guess, well, I have about another thirty minutes, then just the clean up." Reaching the lift Jake picked up the can of polish and a few rags. He climbed the ladder and moved towards the bow of the boat, He worked intently on all of the metal surfaces making sure that it all got a coat of wax. When he finished he collected all of the rags and polish and moved back down the ladder. "I'm just about there."

Julian stepped out from under the boat and nodded, "Yep, I'm done, just a little cleanup."

With everything done they packed the truck and were pulling out of the parking lot. Julian looked at Jake saying, "You have about another hour to spare? Something I want to show you."

"Sure," Jake said sitting back in the seat.

Julian drove over the interstate they had taken in the morning, he drove about another ten minutes and pulled into a parking lot.

Jake looked at the side of the building that adjoined the lot and read, 'Harlem Georgia welcomes you to the Laurel and Hardy Museum.' He looked at Julian saying, "For real?"

"For real, only take a few minutes to take a quick run through, but I come back every few months and spend an hour or so here."

The entered the building and paid the entrance fee, a modest fee at that. Julian moved directly towards the rear of the building. He and Jake stepped through a doorway and there on the wall was a ten by ten screen showing the original black and white Laurel and Hardy shows. There were four people sitting watching the show and each of them had tissues out wiping away the tears from laughing so much. They watched for about ten minutes and Julian nudged Jake and moved out of the room.

Jake looked at Julian laughing and said, "That is great."

"Glad you enjoyed, come on I'll get you back home. I just wanted you to see this place, a great place to come when you need a picker upper."

They were in the truck heading back to Jake's place in less than an hour from leaving the boat parking lot.

"Jake, I really want to thank you for the help. The boat looks almost new, that trick of using TSP on the carpet and then a vacuum is sweet."

"No problem I enjoyed it. Now I'm looking forward to getting out and using the fruits of our labor."

Julian chuckled replying, "That will be soon, another few weeks and the pan fish will be on bed. We'll catch us a five gallon bucket full and have a fish fry."

Julian pulled into the driveway and pulled up to Jake's door.

Jake opened the door and stepped out saying, "That sounds good, looking forward to it. See you."

"Thanks again Jake" Julian put the truck in reverse, backed around and drove out the drive.

Jake opened the door to his apartment and took the stairs two at a time. He was looking forward to a shower and relaxing.

★★★

It was around eleven Sunday morning and Jake was sipping on his third or fourth cup of coffee, watching one of the cable news stations. The door buzzer sounded off, He got up and walked to the top of the stairwell saying, "Come in." Looking down the stairs he saw Marian just stepping in the door. She looked up at him and smiling said, "Just me, I've made some Apple Pies and Teddy and I wanted to ask if you would like to share a slice, with some tea, with us."

"Sounds great," Jake started down the stairs smiling at Marian. They walked towards the house and Marian said, "I hope you don't feel that this is an intrusion?"

Jake opened the back door to the house and waved for Marian to enter first replying "Not at all, it's more a highlight of the day, homemade apple pie, my favorite."

Marian smiled a little brighter and walked into the house and into the kitchen with Jake just behind her.

The aroma of Marian's baking filled the air.

Teddy was sitting at the table reading the paper, seeing Marian and Jake enter he stood, placing the paper on the chair left of his seat. He extended his hand to Jake saying, "All is well?"

Jake replied, "Yes Sir, and I believe it is about to get better," pointing at the row of fresh pies on the counters. He had counted eight pies, seemed a bit excessive.

"Yes, I'm quite sure of that," Teddy sat back down and pointed at the seat to his right continuing with, "Have a seat, Jake."

They chatted a bit while Marian fixed the tea and once she had place a slice of pie and cup of tea in front of each seat, she took her seat saying, "First pies of the year, so no complaints now,"

Jake looked at Teddy and then Marian saying, "If it tastes half as good as it smells it will be very special,"

Teddy grinned and said, "I second that."

After Jake and Teddy finished their second slice of pie and had started on their third cup of tea Teddy looked at Jake saying," How is everything going? I noticed Julian Brown stopping by to pick you up. I'm not prying now, just wondering if there is anything we can help you with."

"Teddy, that sounds like prying to me." Marian said quickly.

Teddy turned a little red in the face but before he could reply to Marian, Jake replied, "I worked a few days this week with Julian and we kind of hit it off. He asked me to help him clean up his boat and get it ready for the fishing season. It was fun and a few of his friends showed up with lunch so I also met some nice people. I had not seen the Lake before, so I got to complete two things at one time, the Lake is a good size body of water."

"That it is, 70,000 acres with about half in South Carolina and half in Georgia. It's the largest of three lakes built by the Corps of Engineers on the Savannah River."

"That is a good size lake." He took a sip of his tea and continued, "As far as everything else, all is going great, just getting to know my way around and meeting some new people. Work looks to be interesting and so far all of the people I've met seem nice. I've done a little research and it looks like the area has some of the problems all areas of the country are dealing with. Drugs, misinformation, a general lack of accountability in government, rising costs all around, but it looks like everyone is trying to deal with it and trying to make it better."

Teddy looked a little surprised and said, "That is a mighty good assessment of things for someone new to town. I'm impressed."

Marian reached for Jake's plate and looking directly at Teddy said, "I'm sure that makes Jake feel better. Remember your statement, "We will not be intrusive,"

Jake laughed and said, "Marian I'm sure that Teddy is only trying to make me feel comfortable, just as you are. I did not take it as being intrusive, more an expression of caring. I must say that you both have gone out of your way to make me feel like I belong here and I thank you for it. If I ever feel that I am being intruded on I will let you know."

With that they all grinned and Jake stood saying, "That was one of the best apple pies I have ever had the pleasure to put in my mouth." Looking at the counter he continued with, "Looks like a lot of people will be benefiting for your baking."

Marian smiled replying, "I will be taking all but one of those to Joe, he is a friend that runs a kitchen, on First Street in OLD TOWN, for the homeless and needy. Teddy and I will be taking them down a little later."

"Well they are in for a real treat. Thank you for the pie, tea and company, but I do have a few things I would like to get to before work in the morning. He shook Teddy's hand and gave Marian a hug as he walked out of the kitchen towards the back door.

He grinned as he heard Teddy say, "That young man is way smarter than anyone could imagine."

Just as he opened the rear door when he heard a phone ring, it was a land line with the traditional bell ring. It sounded like it came from behind the closed door to Teddy's library, he heard a chair being pushed back in the kitchen. "Teddy" he thought as he closed the door and walked to his own door.

Jake took the stairs two at a time and once reaching the landing he moved towards the kitchen. Movement on the monitoring screen caught his eye and he shifted his full attention to the screen. He was surprised to see a black Chevy Suburban moving quickly out of the drive. He was more surprised to see a white Federal Government License Plate that read, 'SRS 1', and that it was also stenciled on the Suburban's roof in orange letters.

He went to the refrigerator and got a glass of water with a few ice cubes and sat on one of the stools on the living room side of the counter. He sat there looking at the monitor thinking about the events that just occurred. A phone call, a sudden leaving, a government vehicle, "Strange, very strange" he thought.

He thought about reading Teddy but that would be wrong, Teddy and Marian's business was their business.

If there was one thing he had taught himself was to mind his own business and to use his capabilities only on things that were in his own life. He was very busy over the next weeks, very busy.

CHAPTER FIVE

HE WAS PUTTING A LIST together on his PC of things he wanted to get done during the coming week when the buzzer for the door sounded. He glanced at the monitor and saw Marian standing at the door. He stood and moved towards the landing saying "Come in."

He was moving down the stairs as Marian opened the door, she smiled at him when she saw him. "Jake, I hate to be a pest, but Teddy got called away and, well, we were to deliver my pies to Joe. I was wondering if you would join me while I take them to him. It's just that Joe's kitchen is not in the best part of town and Teddy has always told me that he would prefer that I did not visit that part of town by myself." She put her hand to her face, "Jake, I'm sorry, I was rambling, I guess I feel that I'm intruding, if you have things to do I'll call a cab service."

"Marian, you are not intruding, of course I'll go with you. Give me a few moments to turn things off and I'll be right out."

"Thank you, thank you so much Jake." Marian turned and went out the door and walked towards the house.

Jake went up the stairs quickly and turned off the TV, PC and used the rest room and was down the stairs and backed his truck out of the garage. He opened the rear door and moved to the house and met Marian as she was coming out of the door with a cardboard box. There were four pies in the box, Jake took the box, making sure that he kept it level, moved to the truck and placed it on the floor. He closed the rear door and moved around to the other side and opened the rear door on that side of the truck. He walked back to the house and again took the second box from Marian. He carried it to the truck and placed it on the floor and closed the truck door.

★★★

The drive downtown was uneventful and Jake enjoyed all of the background information on the different buildings that they passed that Marian shared with him. She had him make a turn here and there to point out different buildings and to give him some of the history and stories about each. There was a house where a President of the United States once lived, another that a Mr. Williams from Savannah stayed in, while waiting for his trial for killing someone. The whipping post, that slaves were chained to and dealt the ten, twenty of so lashes as deemed needed for whatever offence committed, whether real or perceived. It still stands old and worn on the corner of Broad Street and Twelfth just before you enter the Old Town area, and carries a curse for all that attempt to destroy it, grave sickness, pain and grief. And the one he found most interesting, a large brick home, three floors with dormers above that, and a full wraparound porch with three entrances. The main entrance had double doors with side rails, in the center of the porch. There also was a smaller single door entrance at each end. It was the best kept property on the street, maybe the whole Old Town area.

Marian explained that there were no signs or outward displays that one could use to explain the buildings use. The only thing that would catch ones eye would be the eight to ten black cars that were parked in the rear lot in front of a four car garage. It was the home of the local FBI office, "It is the second largest FBI office on the East Coast outside of the DC area," Marian explained. "I'm quite sure that is because of the SRS site and Augusta Club."

"Augusta Club?"

"Yes, Teddy has always said that people would be surprised if they knew just how many times Presidents, Big Business and World Leaders are in and out of here, here being SRS and Augusta Club."

"That is interesting stuff."

"Oh, Jake, please turn right at the next block. Joe's place is in the middle of the block, it's a green house on the left."

"Okay, should I park in the street or the drive?"

"The drive will be fine."

Jake saw the green house coming up, he slowed and pulled into the drive. He put the truck in PARK and set the parking brake. He got out and walked over to Marian's door and opened it for her. Just as she was getting out of the truck an elderly man came out of the front door of the house.

Walking around the front of the truck Marian waved saying, "Hello Joe, you look well."

"Thank you Miss Marian, you are looking well also." They met on the sidewalk and Marian gave him a hug. "Joe, I brought you some home baked apple pies, I thought you and your friends might like them."

"Like them? Once the word gets out that we be having Miss Marian's pies there will not be enough seats at the table," Joe said with a big grin on his face.

Marian turned and placing her hand on Jake's arm said, "Joe, this is our good friend Jake."

Joe looked up at Jake's face saying, "Any friend of Miss Marian and Mr. Teddy is my friend and always welcome here."

Jake extended his hand saying, "Jake Smith, Very nice to meet you Joe."

Joe took his hand, saying "Joe Woodsman," and Jake felt a tingle from the man's hand. The tingle told Jake that Joe had something not so right going on, his immune system was working overtime.

Marian reached for the trucks rear door to open it to get the pies out. Jake beat her to it and opening the door said, "I'll get these, just show me where you would like them."

With that he picked up the cardboard box and bumped the door closed with his hip. He followed Marian and Joe into the house, the floor plan of the house had been changed. The room to his left which at one time must have been the living room and the next room would have been the dining room. The wall between the rooms had been removed and there were two posts adding support to the ceiling. There was a homemade table in the center of the rooms with eighteen folding chairs around it. The wall between the large room and what Jake believed was the kitchen, had been modified and had a large opening in it.

Joe pointed towards the table saying, "Jake please set the box on the table up at the end."

"Got it," Jake moved towards the far end of the table and set the box down easily as to not damage the pies.

He turned and moved towards the door saying, "I'll go get the other box."

"Thank you Jake" Marian replied.

Jake moved out the front door and to his truck. He opened the door and lifted the box up and out of the truck, and again bumped the door closed with his hip. He was going up the three steps towards the front door when Marian opened it and held it open so he could enter.

As he passed her she said, "Jake, I have to get my purse from the truck." With that she stepped out of the door as it closed behind her.

Jake was setting the second box next to the first when he heard Marian call out, "Jake!"

He turned and was out the door in just seconds. Marian was standing on the far side of his truck. There were two large young men standing, what he considered way, way too close to her. One of them had his hand on Marian's arm and was saying something that caused the second to laugh.

In four steps Jake was behind Marian saying, "You need to remove your hand and let her go, now!"

The young man grinned, let go of Marian's arm and pointed at Jake saying "You talking to me asshole, you know who I am. You don't tell me shit." The other young man moved a little to his right leaving a space between the two young men.

Jake placed both of his hands on Marian's shoulders and gently moved her behind him. The first young man reached out to grab Marian's arm again and Jake's hand moved faster that one could see and grabbed the young man's hand and squeezed. The sound of the bones breaking could have been heard in the house. The young man screamed, grabbed his damaged hand

and stumbled backwards away from Jake. The second young man lunged forward throwing a punch at Jake's head with all of his weight behind it. Jake grabbed the man's wrist before it got within a foot from his head. He squeezed and twisted at the same time and there were two different sounds, one sounded like a loud pop and the second like snapping branches. Jake gave the man a shove and he landed on his back and slid across the grass and into the street, screaming. Screaming for good reason, his arm broken and his shoulder out of joint, the pain must have been unbearable. The first young man ran to him and helped him get up and they both turned and began to run down the street.

Jake turned and placing his hand on Marian's shoulder asked, "Are you all right?"

She looked up at him and nodded saying, "Yes, a bit shaken though."

They turned and moved back towards the house and saw Joe standing at the door with a shotgun at his side. "Miss Marian, you OK?"

"Yes Joe, Jake stopped them from doing anything," Marian said as they stepped past him into the house.

"Yes Ma'am, I sure did see that, Jake moves like a cat."

Jake took the shotgun from Joe's hand and cracked it open, no shells. "Joe, if you point an empty gun at someone it will get you killed."

"They just punks, the shotgun runs them off."

"Well, maybe, but it is still a bad idea." He placed the shotgun on the table.

"Got to use what I've got. The one with the mouth thinks he can do anything he wants to do. His brother is Tyrone Mendoza, big drug guy around here."

Jake ignored the last part of the statement and looked at Marian saying, "Time to go?"

"Yes, I think I've had all the excitement I can handle."

Jake turned back to Joe and extended his hand saying, "Good to meet you Joe, hope this doesn't cause you any problems."

Joe shook Jake's hand and placed his second over both saying, "Nothing to worry about here. Those two punks will not tell anyone what really happened to them. They will make up a big story up about being jumped or something. They are not going to tell anyone that they got their butts kicked and never touched the guy that did it. I'll be fine,"

Jake had not released Joe's hand while he talked, and when he did the tingle was gone.

Jake and Marian moved towards the door with Joe expressing his thanks and apologizing for the events that occurred.

Jake opened the door and with his hand on Marian's elbow, led the way to the truck. He opened the door and once Marian was settled he closed the door and moved to his door. He shook Joe's hand again and got in driver's seat, he started the truck and placed it in reverse and backed out onto the street.

As they pulled away Joe walked back into the house, noticing that he didn't have the nagging pain in his hip that had been getting worse and worse each week. He would get it checked tomorrow.

In a moment they were passing the business center of town and entering the River Watch Parkway that would take them to Fury Ferry Road.

Jake looked across at Marian and asked, "You OK? You're pretty quiet."

Looking back at him she smiled saying, "I'm fine, I've never been accosted like that before. Thank you for what you did."

"Not a problem, I'm just glad I was there to help. I hope they don't come back and bother Joe."

"Joe did not think they would, I'm sure he knows the area and people best."

"I hope so." Jake turned onto Millikin Road and in few moments was pulling into their drive. He pulled in front of his garage door, put the truck into Park and got out to help Marian get out of the truck and into the house.

Once he had Marian safely in the house he turned and entered his apartment door. He climbed the stairs slowly thinking about the events that occurred this afternoon and was a little unsettled. He guessed that Dr. Greenly was a busy man about right now, with two new patients.

★★★

At eight promptly, Jake picked up the phone and pushed the numbers for Dr. Fox's office, the call was picked up on the second ring. "Dr. Fox's office may I help you?"

This is Jake Smith at the County Forensics' Lab, may I speak with Dr. Fox Please."

"One second please."

There was a slight pause then he heard, "Dr. Fox."

"Jake here, I was wondering if you could do me a favor."

"Ok, what do you need?"

"I need you to reexamine the body in case-2013-211. I need to know if there are any punctures under the tongue."

"Under the tongue, strange request but I'll get it done by noon today. I'll E-Mail a report once I've completed the examination."

"Thanks Doc. I'll copy you on my report if I find anything." Jake hung up the phone and lifted the stack of papers that he had accumulated so far on the case. He looked over at the Mass Spectrometer, it clicked off and beeped that it had completed its task almost like on command.

He walked over and pulled the sample out of the machine and poured the contents into the Hazard Materials container that sat next to the counter. He placed the container in the steam sterilizer.

Jake turned and pushed the buttons that put the Mass Spec's info on the 42 inch overhead screen. He was not surprised at what he read as the report flashed onto the flat screen. The report confirmed that the samples of the subject's gallbladder and hair he had tested were in fact impregnated with Curare.

★★★

Norbert Cain sat at his desk in the rear of the Nome Clinic and Emergency Care Center that sat in the only area that was considered a slum in Nome Alaska. He looked at the envelope that had just been delivered. It had been about fifteen months ago when the last one had arrived and the one before that was twenty months before. This envelope was larger than the other two, he opened it and found six stacks of one hundred dollar bills, each stack having a value of Five Thousand Dollars, thrice the amount he had received the last time. The envelopes were the only thing that kept him and the clinic going. The always appeared in his time of most need. He inspected the envelope again and found the only markings on it, beside the addressee, was a large J in the return address spaces. Norbert sat back and smiled thinking, "Thank you again my friend, thank you."

***

In the basement Lab of the Medical Center Dr. Fox pulled the operating light down and closer to the table, he had the subject's mouth held open with large clamps and had pulled the tongue out and up, it was secured with a large hemostat. With the light and the use of a magnifying glass inspected the area where the bottom of the tongue attached to the lower jaw. He was quite surprised to find one small puncture that was almost totally camouflaged by the damage done by the mixture that had caused the foaming of the mouth.

He stood and thought, "We might all have to step up to keep up with Jake Smith." He looked at the Lab Tech that was assisting him and said, "Close this all up after you take some close up photos of the entire mouth area."

With that he walked out of the room and headed towards his office to send the E-Mail he had said he would send.

***

Jeddah Peon' De Loraine, Administrator – Saint Jacob Parrish Clinic – New Orleans – LA., looked at the envelope for the third time. He turned it over and over in his hands but it did not change, there was the clinic's address and nothing else but a large J in the return addresses space. This was the fifth such 'gift' that had arrived over the past eighteen years, he opened the envelope and shook the two stacks of one hundred dollar bills on to his desk. Twenty thousand dollars, enough to keep him open for the foreseeable future. He sat back, smiled and shaking his head looked up at the ceiling and mouthing 'Thank You'.

★★★

Jake opened the E-Mail from Dr. Fox, and read his report, that was attached as a PDF document. He was not surprised to see the findings confirming his thoughts. He saved the E-Mail to the case folder and opened the report he was preparing for Dr. Andrews. It took him about twenty five minutes to complete his report and he sent it to Dr. Andrews with a request to exhume the body of the victim of case 2009-311. It was less than ten minutes before he got a reply E-mail from Dr. Andrews.

"Jake, please make time for a meeting in my office at 8:15 in the morning to go over your finding and the cause of death in case 2013-311. And your request to exhume the remains of the victim in case 2009-211, it was signed, Dr. C. Andrews, Medical Examiner of Richmond County.

He noticed that Dr. David Fox and the Undersheriff were also requested to attend, "Well, guess I upped the ante a bit."

★★★

Ms. Kessy P. Qualkly of 1364 Pine Tree Court, Old Tree, Washington took the prepaid postage box out from between the storm door and front door where Tom, the postman, had put it. She looked at the box and a smile covered her face, she unlocked the front door and walked into the large room that served as her living, dining, and family room. She placed her purse on the couch and sat at the table with the box in her hands. She looked at it and started to cry, even though she had a smile on her face. She pulled the strip on the end of the box and turned it upside down. The bundles of one hundred dollar bills fell out onto the table top, she cried a little harder. There were ten bundles with each having a value of ten thousand dollars, one hundred thousand dollars.

It was enough to keep her son safe and as healthy as his deformed and twisted body would allow.

This was the fourth time that such a package had arrived out of the blue, with no note or direction other than take care of your son and yourself. The boxes seemed to arrive at the times of her, and her son's most urgent personal need. She looked up at the ceiling and mouthed, "God Bless You."

★★★

Tyrone Martinez sat quietly watching the Doctor placing the air sack over his brother's hand and filling it with just enough air to allow the sack to act as a cushion to protect the cast from any sudden contact. Dr. Greenly looked at Tyrone saying, "Well that will protect it and if he," turning his head to look at Tyrone's younger brother, "keeps it out of harms way. The bones will be okay in about eight weeks, then three to four weeks of therapy."

Tyrone looked at his brother, "You hear that? This is not a joke, mess it up and you might never use that hand again."

"I heard it, I'm not stupid."

"Well Chris, you aren't too damn smart, got your hand run over by a car, bullshit, and your running buddy over there, Jose, two steel bars to replace the crushed bones in his arm. You telling me that he crushed his arm when he is trying to pull you out of the way of the car. The whole thing sounds like a bullshit story to me, just bullshit. The two of you better be on the low for the next few months, I don't want to hear either of your names. You got me!"

"Got it," came out of both of them in unison.

"Thanks Doc," Tyrone said as he turned back to Dr. Greenly.

"No problem, get them out of here, we've got some business to discuss."

"You heard the man, get your asses out of here and remember, keep it low."

Chris started towards the door and looking back at the Doctor said, "Thanks, I owe you."

★★★

Chris and Jose closed the door behind them and moved out to Chris's car without saying anything to each other. It had taken them a while to come up with the story and to convince themselves that it was what they were going to stick with. If anything, the one thing he knew was that whatever they had said, that was what they would have to live and die by. If his brother found out they had lied to him they would both just up and disappear. He looked at Jose saying, "We'll keep it low, but we find out who and where to find that son of a bitch, in time, his ass is mine."

Jose just nodded.

★★★

Dr. Cleo Dice opened the mail box and was surprised to find a large mailing envelope inside it next to the County letter marked 'Last Notice'. Times had turned very hard for the Lake Clinic for the Elderly at 2323 Cold Lake Road, Old Madison, Wisconsin. He had been the Director of the Clinic for the past twenty four years and times had been tough every few years but the last year had been one demand after another, $500.00 here $1,200.00 there, it seemed that even though the bills were not that large, they were becoming over whelming.

He carried the envelope and the rest of the mail into the Clinic and set it all on his desk, hung up his coat and sat down to open up the bad news that he knew the mail had brought him. The notice from the County was $1,345.00 for a past due tax bill. Another was for $512.00 for supplies, all in all there was $7,650.00 due now and $1,365.00 due in six weeks. Not a lot he thought, but he also knew that with all of the cuts in County, State and Federal Funding he was at least $6,500.00 short. He picked up the large envelope and found it strange that there was no name or address on it other than the Clinics. He pulled the opening strip and when the two bundles of hundred dollar bills fell on the desk he sat there staring at them in shock and surprise.

He picked up the envelope again and this time he saw the 'J' in the return address box, he placed his head in his hands. "Thank you, Thank you, Thank you, was all he could say.

***

Dr. Greenly looked at Tyrone saying, "You and I both know that story was just that, a story, you need to keep a close eye on both of them. We don't need a couple of young punks going after revenge and bringing a spot light down on us."

"I know, I know, I will be watching them very closely and so will a lot of other people. What do you think really happened?"

"I don't know but that hand looked like it was crushed by a vice and the arm was snapped like one would break a stick. It would take unbelievable strength to do it, something like a hydraulic press."

"Just have to watch, they will lead me to the cause, Chris will seek revenge and he can't hide much from me. Enough of that, what did you want to discuss?"

"Well I'm about to release a new shipment of 'Take' from the Savannah Lab, about twenty thousand pills, that's five thousand packets of four pills. They will sell for $500.00 a packet to the dealers, and each pill will keep the user high for a day or so. This is to be distributed to the high end of users, not to the street people. This should go to business people, housewives, you know, the ones that control the money. That is $2,500,000.00 cash once it hits the street. On the street they will break down the packets and the value will be over Twenty Million. Once they take the first hit, they will be hooked for life. The second and third packet will cost more and more, we'll stretch it to the highest price that can be maintained. This shit makes Meth look like candy."

"Five Thousand hits will not last very long, if this shit is as good as you say it is, maybe they will last a week at best."

"Right, I will have a second shipment ready to go in a week, twice the amount of stuff, we will need to put a number on it once we see the results of the first shipment on the streets. The second shipment should bring in $5,000,000.00 plus in additional cash. We'll also be shipping the standard base load of five kilo's of COKE with each shipment. My only concern about TAKE is the amount of violence that this shit will cause when they can't get anymore, nothing worse than a new user in need."

"That sounds like a problem for someone else to worry about."

"Right, well keep an eye on those two and let me know what you hear once the shipment reaches the street."

"That I will, any problems with the distribution let me know." With that Tyrone stood and walked to the door. He looked back at the Doctor as he opened the door saying, "If you hear of any other strange injuries let me know." He closed the door and walked to his car.

CHAPTER SIX

J AKE PICKED UP THE FOLDER from his desk and headed towards Dr. Andrew's office for his first official meeting. He stepped out into the hall and saw three people entering Dr. Andrews' office. Might be a bit of a crowd he thought with a grin on his face. Once he reached the office door he saw Dr. Andrews standing behind his desk and the other three people standing in front if it. He tapped on the door frame and Dr. Andrews looked at him with a bemused look on his face saying, "I guess I should have given this a bit more thought."

Jake looked at everyone and said, "I've got the Lab set up for the meeting Doc., If everyone will follow me please."

A look of relief came over Dr. Andrews face and he replied, "If everyone will follow Jake we can get settled and get started." He picked up a few folders and started to move around the desk towards the door.

Jake stepped out into the hall and moved slowly back to the Lab hoping they were all following him.

Jake unlocked the Lab door and stood just inside the door and pointed to the chairs he had set around the Lab table. The chairs all had a clear view of the 42 inch flat screen and there was a blank pad on the table in front of each chair.

The group all entered and sat in the chairs facing Jake and the screen.

Dr. Andrews stood behind the first chair and once everyone was seated he began with the introductions. He pointed at Jake saying, "First I would like to introduce Jake Smith, Senior Forensic Investigator. He pointed at the young woman sitting in the fourth chair saying, "Undersheriff Kay Winslow" Moving his hand towards the next seat "Doctor David Fox and Detective Julian Brown.

We are here to discuss Jake's findings on case 2013-311 and his request to exhume the remains of one Ms. Elizabeth Blanchard, case 2009-311."

The three guests looked at each other then at Jake and back at Dr. Andrews with quizzical looks on their faces.

Dr. Andrews continued, "Jake will go over his findings and then explain the request. Some of this will be heard for the first time by all of us, Jake has supplied me with detailed reports on his daily activities but this will be the first comprehensive report on the total case." Looking directly across the table, he said, "Jake."

Jake pressed a few buttons and a form popped up on the screen, "I've compiled a time line of my activities and findings. I will go thru each in detail and please if there are any questions interject them so everyone maintains a clear understanding of each item."

Turnover of three case files from Dr. Andrews and my review of each.

I first tested all the evidence from the victim and crime scene in case 2013-211. Jake pushed another button and the test results for each item showed on the screen. He went over each part of the report in detail explaining what he was testing for and the findings.

Detective Brown and I attended the autopsy of the victim of case 2013-211 performed by Dr. Fox and Lab attendant Billy Crawford. There were no unusual findings. I requested additional samples of the victim's hair, gall bladder and pituitary gland.

Undersheriff Winslow asked, "Pituitary gland, I've never heard of that being requested before."

Jake looked at her and explained, "The pituitary gland retains the elements that pass thru it for a much longer time than most other organs and hair, even if they are not processed or changed by it in its natural functions. I remembered that from a previous case I worked on in the past, back at the Agency, the report of the element breakdown of the cells from the pituitary gland exposed the true cause of the victim's death.

"Thank you, please go on."

Once I received the additional samples I ran tests on each and found what could have been the cause of death in two of the samples.

I requested Dr, Fox to revisit the victim and do a very detailed search of the inner mouth and tongue for possible puncture evidence. He agreed and after a detailed search there was evidence of a single puncture under the tongue. This was almost totally concealed by the damage the hydrogen peroxide and grain mixture caused. That was why the person that murdered our victim forced it into the victim's mouth after he collapsing on the sidewalk.

After reviewing all of the evidence and the confirmation of my findings I can say without any reasonable doubt that the victim was killed by an injection of CURARE under his tongue.

Julian said, "CURARE, what the hell? I thought that was an old wives tale"

Jake replied, "Yes CURARE, It has been used to kill people ever since the Spanish Conquistadores began invading South America in the 15th century."

Dr. Andrews stood up and said, "Why don't we take a few moments break before we go on, Ok with you Jake?"

"Of course, Jake replied."

The rest got up and started to move around the Lab and some used the rest room. Julian moved over to Jake and asked with a grin on his face, "What other surprises do you have up your sleeve? Don't tell me you found the killer too."

Jake just laughed and replied, Not me, you're the Detective. Not to change the subject but how about a soft drink?"

"Sounds good to me, lead the way."

"Well how about you fly and I'll buy. Don't want to leave the Lab with people here and evidence not locked away. I don't have an evidence locker so I'd have to shoo everyone out and lock the Lab to walk down the hall for the drinks."

"No problem, I'll fly and buy, just so I can hear the rest of the story." He turned and moved off to get the drinks.

Dr. Andrews, Dr. Fox and the Undersheriff were off to one side of the Lab in deep conversation. It seemed that the Undersheriff was explaining something in earnest to the two doctors and was being very emphatic about it. "Hope you like this, only thing the damn machine would give me."

"It works fine."

Dr. Andrews announced, "Okay let's get on with it,"

Everyone moved back to their seats and Jake pushed a button on his computer and a line graph appeared on the screen.

"Okay, once the evidence was clear on how the victim was murdered I started to investigate the why. I took the information on the case report about the victim and started to Google everything we knew about him, school, work history, sports, family, everything. The one thing that came up that I found strange was an eighteen year old that drove a van and spent two hundred dollars a week on gasoline. The job that he was listed as having was medical material currier, but he had a regular drives license not a Class C license. I checked the purchase records from his credit card and all of the gas was purchased either in Augusta, Macon or in Savannah. There was no name that came up for an employer and the only company name on any of the very few checks he deposited was on one, 'Quick Med, LLC. Well, I checked them out and there was little or no information available on them. There was only a box number at a local store that provided a mailing address for any company for a monthly fee. Dead End, or so I thought, the name Quick Med sounded familiar to me and I thought that was strange, being new to the area I know that I had not had any dealings with them. So I knew it had to be something I had read since I got here, well, I went back and started to reread everything I had gotten to this point. Well when I reread the case file on case 2009-311 there it was, it was listed that the victim worked as a receptionist at a call service that provided receptionist services for about ten companies. One of the ten companies being Quick Med, LLC., well, I don't believe in coincidences, and would like to exhume the victim of case 2009-311 to do some testing for a cause of death."

The room was silent for a few moments, the Undersheriff started to say something but stopped.

Dr. Andrews stood and stepped away from the table a few steps and reversed his path and stepped back to the table. He put both hands on the table and looking around at each person in the room spoke, "Ms. Blanchard is from one of the founding families of Augusta, family has been here for over two hundred and fifty years. Having to go to them and ask for their permission to exhume Elizabeth's body is going to have to be done very carefully.

This will go against everything that they believe in, their religion and family status and they will feel it is immoral and a major impropriety."

The Undersheriff stood and glancing at each and then at Dr. Andrews spoke in a very soft tone, "Dr. Andrews, I will call the family to ask for some time to discuss this matter, and I will be happy to go with you to talk to the family. My being close with the family, and having grown up with Elizabeth, and her brother Thomas might help. Being one of the children privileged to be growing up and playing at 'The Club,' while our parents played golf. Well, my being there might help convince them to allow this to happen."

"Thank you, I will take you up on your offer, Kay."

Looking around the table he continued with, "Jake, thank you for a very enlightening morning, you have given all of us new directions and important work to now complete. Please continue to work with Detective Brown and see where it all leads you. Once everyone has gotten on their way I need to see you in my office. Thank you all for coming and if there are any questions about anything, anything at all, please contact either of us. Thank You." With that, he turned and walked out of the Lab to his office.

Dr. Fox and the Undersheriff walked over to Jake and thanked him for his report and hard work on the cases. They chatted with each other as they walked out of the Lab leaving Julian and Jake standing there looking at the screen.

"Jake, you have done one hell of a job. You have accomplished more in a short time then we all did in years. I am sure glad you are on my side of the street."

Jake thanked him and his phone desk beeped, he picked up the receiver saying "Jake."

"Dr. Andrews, please come to my office." The phone went dead.

"That was the Boss, got to go."

"Okay, I'll call you later," Julian turned and moved out in the hall and out to his car.

Jake locked the Lab and walked to Dr. Andrews's office, he was surprised to see the Undersheriff there as well.

Dr. Andrews waved him in and asked him to close the door. "Jake, there is something we need to do, please raise your right hand."

Jake did as he was asked, the Undersheriff looked at him and asked, "Do you swear to protect and serve the citizens of Richmond County to the best of your ability?"

Jake responded, "I do."

She continued, "Under the authority of the Sheriff of Richmond County I now appoint you a Deputy Sheriff of the County of Richmond with all rights and privileges the office holds. You may lower your hand now."

Dr. Andrews said, "Congratulations," he handed Jake a gun, in a holster, and a badge wallet that held his badge. "Now get back to work, after lunch of course."

The Undersheriff congratulated him and shook his hand saying, "Glad you are here and one of us."

Jake thanked them and walked back to the Lab a little dazed, they had taken him by complete surprise.

★★★

Jeb Finley sat at his desk going over the financial data on the small Drug Support Clinic that he was the Administrator of. He shook his head thinking, "Well, another year of scraping by." The County had cut the funding of the support to private agencies again this year and his operating budget, which most of the funds came out of his pocket, looked bleak. A Drug Free World would have to tighten its belt once again the thirty by thirty foot building on Bent Tree Lane in Logan, Kansas had done it before and would do it again.

He heard the front door open and a "Jeb, you back there?"

He stood and moved towards the door to the hall, "I'm here, Jimmy."

He entered the main room of the building to find Jimmy the mailman standing there with a hand full of envelopes.

"Looks like a bunch of bills, Jeb. Sorry."

He took the envelopes from him saying, "Not your fault, you just get stuck delivering them."

Jimmy nodded and turned back towards the door with a "Have a good day, Jeb."

"Thanks." Jeb went back to his desk and put the pile of envelopes in the center of it thinking, "Last week of the month, I sure hope the, I wants, don't exceed the, I haves again."

He walked over to the small table that held his coffee maker and filled his mug, walked back and sat looking at the pile of envelopes. With a grimace on his face he picked up the first and opened it. "Bill number one," he thought, he opened all of the envelopes that looked official, seven bills, and piled all of the sales and advertisements in another. The one large prepaid envelope had no markings so he just moved it to the side to look at the bills more closely. There were two bills that just totally shocked him. The first was a bill for twenty six hundred dollars for his state five year recertification as an approved Drug Rehabilitation Clinic that he had totally forgotten about. The second was for thirty seven hundred dollars for his Federal operating license as an approved Drug Clinic. Without either one of them he was closed for business, and would have to go through the entire accreditation process all over again. They were due in three weeks, "Sixty three hundred dollars and thirty seven hundred in the others, Ten Grand total. All due in three weeks." He leaned back in his chair and looking at the ceiling thought, "I just don't have it, just the thirty seven hundred for the normal bills was going to be a stretch." Most of those bills were double due to his coming up short last month.

Jeb sat there for a moment, in a bit of a daze, without thinking he picked up the unopened envelope and was turning it over and over in his hands. It was the writing in the return address box that caught his eye and he held the envelope still reading it, and rereading it. It read, "You forgot again, J".

He pulled the open strip on the envelope and the two ten thousand dollar stacks of one hundred dollar bills fell on the desk. He picked up a stack with each hand and looking at them said out loud, "You saved us again, Thank You. Thank You, Thank You and God Bless."

***

Teddy and Marian were sitting on the love seat in the sun room that was off of their kitchen, looking out of the tinted glass panels that made up the wall facing the Savannah River. Marian had just told Teddy all of the events that occurred during the visit to Joe's Kitchen.

Teddy was holding Marian's hand, and looking at her and said, "Dear, I'm so sorry that I was not with you at Joe's. I thank God that Jake was there with you and for all he did to keep you safe. I owe that young man a great debt, a great debt for keeping you safe from harm."

"Thank you Teddy, it was quite frightening, I really don't know what would have happened if Jake was not there, Teddy, he dispersed with those two ruffians like they were rag dolls. I, and Joe as well, were shocked into disbelief at how calmly and quickly he disposed of them, and he showed so much concern for Joe's safety and as well as my own."

"Marian, the course of events could have gone very badly, we are all very fortunate at the outcome. I need to thank that young man at first chance." Teddy placed his arm around his wife's shoulder, and they sat back just looking out over the river with each deep in thought.

They had been sitting for a little over thirty minutes when there was a knock at the rear door. Teddy got up and moving into the kitchen called out, "Coming." As he turned into the hall towards the rear door, reaching it he opened the door to find Jake standing there. "Jake, please come in." Once Jake was inside Teddy closed the door and turned to Jake saying, "Thank you," as he put his arms around Jake's shoulders. "Thank you again."

Jake replied, "I'm just thankful I was there, how is Marian?"

"She is fine, a still a little shaken but fine. We were just sitting in the sun room, please join us." Teddy moved back into the kitchen with Jake following him, Teddy pointed to the door way tucked to the left of the counters saying, "Join Marian out there, I'll brew up some tea for all of us."

Jake walked out the door way that he had not taken notice of during his previous visits and walked into the sun room. Marian was sitting in the love seat and started to rise, "No don't get up, please stay seated." He walked over to her and leaned over and gave her a hug. He then took a seat in a brightly covered chair that sat next to the love seat. The view of the river was fantastic and the glass walls allowed just the right amount of heat to permeate the room. "This is a great room." Jake said just as Teddy entered.

"Yes, we both love to just sit and watch the boats and river flow by. It is very relaxing."

Teddy placed the tray he was carrying on the table in front of them saying, "Nuked the water and using tea bags, not quite Marian's way but the one way I don't mess it up, but the cookies are Marian's and I know they will be great."

"It looks good to me," Jake said as he picked up a cookie.

Teddy sat next to Marian and took her hand saying, "Jake, I really can't thank you enough for watching out for Marian, I just would not know what I would do if, God forbid, anything happened to her."

Marian started to say something but her throat tightened and instead she just smiled nodding her head.

Jake took the tea cup and took a sip before replying, "We are all just lucky that it all worked out." Changing the subject he said, "Well it looks like you're going to be stuck with me for a while, the Undersheriff was at the Lab today and Dr, Andrews and she surprised me. They called me into Dr. Andrews' office and she swore me in as a Richmond County Deputy Sheriff."

Teddy sat forward a little saying, "That was quick, most are on probation six months before they formally swear a new employee in as a Deputy."

"I know, we had a meeting about a few cases that Dr. Andrews had given me and after the meeting the next thing I knew I was being sworn in, surprised me."

"Well that tells me that they did not want to take a chance that you might leave the department. Whatever you did or are doing must surely have impressed them. I know Dr. Andrews and for him to act so swiftly, you have really impressed him. Congratulations."

"Thanks just trying to do what is expected."

Marian looked at Jake and asked, "What did you think of the Undersheriff? I've know her since birth, she comes from a wonderful family."

"I was impressed, she asked questions that made sense and knew when to listen and also when to speak, She seems like a very caring person."

Marian looked at him for a moment before continuing, "I don't know what you were meeting about but it's interesting that you came away with the thought she was a caring person."

"Well I can't say anything about the case specifically, but we have to contact one of the older families of Augusta about exhuming a family member that has passed. We are trying to solve the events of that death."

"Interesting, Jake, I'm sure that if Kay can help you in any way she will. If you feel you ever have to get the support or help from any of the founding families here in town please feel free to ask me for assistance, I might be able to help."

"Thank you Marian, I will keep that in mind. I'm glad that you are okay," standing he continued, "but now I will get out here and let you rest."

Teddy stood, "I'll see you out,"

Jake leaned over and gave Marian a hug and then moved towards the door with Teddy a step behind. They walked to the rear door, when they reached it Teddy reached out and took Jake's hand again saying, "Anything I can ever do, just ask."

Jake shook his hand saying "Thanks," then opened the door and stepped out and walked to his door.

★★★

Eric Stedson walked out of the Industrial Food Supply Company Corporate Offices to his truck. They had just informed him that they would no longer be able to provide him with the food stuffs that had expired dates. Something they had been doing for over ten years. They had been told to stop all such activities by the state foods inspector. Everyone involved were upset with this turn of events and the only legal option was for him to purchase the food. They agreed to sell him any food stuffs that were within fourteen days of the expiration date for five cents on the dollar. That was all great but Eric knew that this was still not an option that he could make work. He operated the Mason Food and Shelter in Shelton, Washington totally by donations of money and time. The cost of $1,350.00 a month for the food would take thirty five percent of his budgeted money.

He got in his truck and headed to the shelter, his mind spinning trying to figure a plan of some kind that would keep him in operation. He knew that his small disability check would not be enough to keep him going. Arriving at the shelter he went into his office to find Jessie his most trusted helper sitting there holding what looked like an impeller of some sort.

"Eric, this is from the main hot water pump for the shelter house heating system. Its gone, try as I may I can't fix broken. I'll need about three hundred before the cool weather gets here or we will not have any heat in the shelter. I've closed up the pump housing and filled the system up so we don't let it dry and cause more problems. Need to put this on the top of our To Do list."

"Thanks Jessie, I'll add it to the list."

Jessie stood and walked out of the office saying, "Damn list never goes away."

Eric sat at his desk and saw the envelope that brought his disability check and felt a bit better, He opened the check and found that the amount was reduced from his normal payment, he opened the folded paper that was also in the envelope and it stated, 'Due to Administrative Cost increases benefits have been reduced for the next three months, short falls will be reimbursed in a one sum amount at that time.'

Eric looked at the note thinking, "Three months, what else can bite me in the butt," He sorted through his other mail finding a few more bills and a few requests for money from other support groups in as much trouble meeting needs as his. He set them apart from the stack of his own monthly statements and bills. He somehow would send them each a few dollars.

The last envelope was larger and had no markings on it as to where it came or from who, just the letter 'J' in the return address box. He pulled the open strip and out fell two stacks of one hundred dollar bills. He was shocked, and then it hit him like a bolt, 'J'.

He sat back and said, "I'll be dammed, Thank you my friend, Thank you."

★★★

Jake lay on his bed with his eyes closed and let his mind wander, there were hundreds of alarms he had set over the years that if triggered brought that item to the forefront. It was the list that told him of those from his past that were in need or trouble, the list was long but the data to trip one of his alarms was very tight. It had to be a considerable need, trouble or set of events to cause a trip. He had taken care of the seven that topped the list. He had learned that to help was good but not to help in excess, with excess he had found that those helped held little or no responsibility.

The recent events had taken him by surprise, he really did not like surprises, but some events happened out of normal sequences and hope fully when it happened it was a good thing. All in all he would have to increase his awareness in general, just to be sure the surprises were far and few between events.

Jake concentrated on the two young men that had attacked Marian and it was only a moment that he found their minds. It was like sitting in an invisible bubble listening to a constant flow of information passing by all mixed and garbled. He picked a subject and the information slowed and took form, their Crew was planning a robbery of a convenience store for Friday night, payday and the store cashed checks for all of the locals. Jake 'watched' for about thirty minutes as different things bounced in and around the men's thoughts. He broke off the contact and thought about the information he had learned, he would make contact again sometime Wednesday to confirm the facts before he placed any action in motion.

The two would pay for their actions, to what extent he had not yet determined.

★★★

Jake pulled into the parking lot and noticed Julian's car parked in the rear of the lot, it was parked next to a county box truck. He did not see anyone around the car or truck, and he guessed that Julian was inside for a meeting or as Julian would put it, a conversation.

He walked into the building and stopped by the break room and got a cup of coffee before going to the Lab. With coffee in one hand and a bagel in the other he walked down the hall to the Lab. When he reached the door he balanced the bagel on top of his coffee cup and unlocked the door with his free hand. He walked over to his desk placing the coffee and bagel on it, he then moved around the Lab turning on the different equipment. He walked to his locker and took a Lab coat out and slipped it on, moved to the hand sink and washed his hands and after drying them moved back to his desk and took a seat. He booted up his PC and opened a file on his desk and started to go over one of the reports he had started the day before. He was deep into it pretty quickly and was a little startled by a bumping noise in the hall. He looked up and there was Julian and a county worker pushing a cabinet into the lab doorway.

Jake stood up and grinning said, "You lose something or did I?"

Julian grinned replying, "Thought you could use this." He and the worker pushed the cabinet into an empty space against the wall. It fit like it belonged there.

Jake walked over and shook Julian's hand and then extended his hand to the other man saying, "Jake Smith."

The man took his hand and shook it replying, "Kevin Mc Wattly,' Doo' for short." This guy, looking at Julian, seemed to think you needed a special cabinet, so I put this together for you."

"Well thank you 'Doo'."

Jake looked at the cabinet, and watched Julian flip the door latch open, it had a set of openings that a lock could be set into, and open the doors. The cabinet stood six feet high and five feet wide and a little over two feet deep, there were five shelves with a center brace, each holding two covered trays, each with a latch that could also be locked.

Julian looked at Jake with a grin saying, "I remembered that you couldn't leave the Lab with anyone in here so this, I believe, will allow that. So the next time you fly and I'll buy."

"That my friend, I can do. Thank you both so very much."

No problem, we have to go, work calls. You need to pick up the padlocks for the door and trays, I didn't get them for security reasons. "Julian and Doo turned and left with a quick wave as they went out the door.

Jake pulled out one of the trays and placed it on the table, twenty four inches by twenty four inched and six and one half inches deep. The cover's back end slipped into a slot which when the cover was on and latched made it imposable to open without destroying the tray. "Perfect for evidence containment" Jake thought. He put the tray back on the shelf and closed the cabinet doors, they interlocked so when a lock was in place you would have to tear the doors off to get inside. It was well made and well thought out. "Guess I owe those two gentlemen a refreshment or two," Jake thought to himself.

He went back to his desk and in a moment was deep into the data he was working with.

★★★

"Did the trucks get there yet? Dr. Greenly barked into the phone knowing that they had. The three red dots on the GPS tracking screen had converged as onc but they did not know he had the trucks wired.

"Yes, they are here," was the reply from his man in his Savannah processing building.

"Okay, then get the packages on each of them and call me when they leave. I mean when they leave, not five minutes later."

"You got it. We're loading them now."

Dr. Greenly pushed the 'End' button and sat back in his chair staring at the GPS screen. The first shipment of TAKE was almost on its way. He was waiting for it to hit he streets, he did not know what the long term results of using it were going to be but he knew that the money would come in fast, very fast. He smiled and thought about the ability to take in almost five million dollars extra in two weeks. People were stupid and so intent to self serve their own wants, it was almost too easy.

He watched the first red dot start to move, then the second and third. His phone buzzed, he pushed the connect button saying "Yes."

"They are on their way, each truck was fully fueled and there should be no stops along the way. Each driver will call the moment they arrive at their drops."

"Good, I will wait for their calls. You gave them the scrambled number and drop phones?"

"Yes, once they make the call the phone will be dropped in the nearest body of water."

"Well done." He ended the call and watched the red dots on the screen. He stared at the screen and again thought about the money, it was all about the money.

CHAPTER SEVEN

JAKE TOOK HIS PHONE OUT of the holder on his belt and pushed the contacts button, then scrolled down to Julian's number and pressed the call button.

"Sheriff's Department, Detective Julian Brown."

"Julian, Jake here, how would you like to make a really, really large drug bust today?"

"Well, let me think about that, yes. How big? What's up?"

"Twenty/Thirty Million, street value, so, do you have any friends that are with the State Police?"

"I've got a few, what do you have in mind?"

"It's a long story but to make it simple, I've been checking a lot of gasoline purchases against time and vehicle numbers and I believe that there is going to be a large delivery made today. There will be a delivery going to each of three locations, Brunswick, Macon and Augusta. Due to the time of travel from Savannah the shortest trip will be the Brunswick drop so they need to go down based on that travel time. Nothing can go out on the waves about the take downs until all of the busts are completed."

"Something that big will take a little more push then I've got, we will need to bring the Sheriff or Undersheriff in to make this happen."

"Well you need to do whatever you think is best my friend, this will be your show so you pick the players."

"Thanks, when do you think this going to happen?"

Jake chuckled replying, "The three busts need to happen in about three hours. It should go down on US 95 somewhere around Midway, US 25 around Millen and US 16 between Metter and Dublin."

"Three hours, you are killing me. Let me set up a conference call with the Undersheriff, hopefully the call will take place in about five minutes. Thanks, I think."

Jake went back to putting all of his files and evidence for each case he was working on into the new trays and locking each before putting them in his new evidence cabinet. His desk phone beeped as he sat back at his desk, picking up the receiver he said, "Forensics Lab, Jake speaking."

"Jake, Julian, we've got the Undersheriff on also."

"Jake, Kay, what do we need to happen?"

Jake gave her a brief description of his findings and outlined the events that needed to occur and in what time frame. He gave her the information on each of the vehicles that needed to be taken. There was silence for a moment then The Undersheriff replied, "I will call you both back in ten minutes," and they both heard a slight click.

Julian spoke first, "Well, we soon will know just how much push is available. I can't believe she didn't ask more questions?"

"Well she must think a lot of you to make a jump of faith of this magnitude. Guess we'll see what is to be seen."

"Thinks of me? That's a pile of bull. Let's see what happens, be talking to you, soon I think." Jake heard the phone go quite.

It was just about ten minutes on the dot when Jake's phone beeped, "Jake here."

"Kay here, Jake, Julian is on also, all is in the works. Julian, I told the State Police Superintendent that you needed to be advised on all that was going down. He agreed and you need to meet me in the Operations Center in the basement of the court house. They will have an open feed from each of the three State Police Operations Group Leaders. It is up to you, Julian, to make the 'Go Call' once they have eyes on all three vehicles. Jake, I want you there with Julian, any questions?

They both replied, "None."

"Great, I'll be at the Operations Center in a half hour, I've got to meet with the Sheriff first. See you both there." The line went dead.

"Julian, want me to pick you up?"

"Sounds good, I'll see you in ten."

"Right," Jake put the receiver down and got up and walked to Dr, Andrews Office. He found Dr. Andrews sitting at his desk with a mound of papers surrounding him. He tapped on the door frame and Dr. Andrews waved for him to enter. Jake took a seat and Dr. Andrews set the papers down he had been reading and looked at Jake.

"Doc I'm headed over to the Operations Center in the new Courthouse to meet with the Undersheriff." He then gave Dr. Andrews a briefing on the events that had occurred, mentioning also that all of the support information was in the reports he had sent last night, and asked him if he would like to join the group assembling at the Operations Center.

"Jake, this sounds like very big doings, sure you want me there?"

"Yes, if this turns out to be big, you, the Undersheriff and Julian need to be the spokes people, if it flops I'll step up as owner of the info."

"That does not seem correct, if it is big you need to be acknowledged."

"I will be, to and by, the right people."

Dr, Andrews stood and moving around his desk said, "I'll meet you there, thank you."

Jake smiled and waved as he left the room and headed out this truck, he got in and was on his way. It was only a few moments and he was pulling over to the curb where Julian was waiting.

Julian opened the door and hopped in saying, "Well another nice mess you got me in."

Jake laughed saying, "Yep, buy the way drinks are on me at the Market after work, why don't you see if Doo can meet us. I owe him a few also."

"Hell, after this I might need a few drinks, I've got to make the call for three State Police Operations Groups." He looked deep into Jake's eyes saying, "Have I got anything to worry about here?"

Jake grinned replying, "Nope, just if I have enough money to buy the drinks."

Julian sat back and didn't say another word until they were entering the Operations Center doors, then he said with a grin on his face, "Guess this is what friends are for."

They walked into the room and the first thing that they saw were three 70 inch flat screens on the center wall. Each screen showed a satellite view of the three highways, US 95 – US 16 – US 25, and the subject vehicles movements on each.

Just below the screens sitting at a long table, turned around in their chairs looking back at them were the

Sheriff, Undersheriff, Dr. Andrews, A Captain of the State Police that Julian recognized, one Captain Jonas Walker, and another gentleman in a dark blue suit. There were two seats empty between the Sheriff and the Undersheriff, Jake walked directly to the chair next to the Undersheriff and sat down with Julian right along side of him. The Undersheriff stood and made brief introductions and handed Julian a remote after pressing a few buttons. A screen came up from the floor and it was split into three screens, there were the three Operations Group Leaders on the displays with their names displayed under the picture. The Undersheriff spoke at the screen saying, "Gentlemen, this is Detective Julian Brown. He will be giving you the signal to proceed."

In unison they replied, "Yes Undersheriff."

Julian asked the US 95 Group Leader, "Sergeant Jackson, where are your units deployed?"

"Sir, I've got one unmarked, a pick up, on the side of the road about a quarter of a mile south of the Darin interchange and four cars on the access roads to State Road 99 interchange and another unmarked just passed the 99 interchange. Once the subject vehicle passes the first unmarked just South of Darien, with a Go, we will box in and stop the subject vehicle just passed the 99 interchange."

"Sounds good,"

"US 16 Group Leader, Sergeant Crawford, your teams deployment?"

"Sir, we have a SUV on the side of the road with both passenger side doors open about 500 feet past the East Dublin interchange and four cars at the Dublin interchange and a second SUV on the side of the road 600 feet past the interchange entrance. On a GO we will box the subject vehicle in and hopefully it will all be over in five minutes or less."

"Also sounds good," Highway 25 group Leader Sergeant Adams, your deployment?"

"Sir, we have what looks like a farm pickup on the side of the road 500 feet before the Millen Causeway and two cars on the river access roads mid causeway with two cars at the end of the causeway. On a Go, once they are on the causeway, we will trap the subject vehicle on the causeway closing in and stopping it. It should all be over in two or three minutes."

"All sound good, standby we are not far from this happening."

★★★

Dr. Greenly sat staring at the GPS screen watching the three dots moving steadily along. He was pleased, all seemed well.

★★★

Julian watched the three flat screens the satellite camera continued tracking the subject vehicles movements and the vehicle on US 95 was approaching the Darien interchange. It would not be long now, Julian felt his hands sweating. The US 95 vehicle passed the unmarked car on the side of the road.

"Group Leader Jackson, It's a GO!"

Looking to the other screen he saw that the subject vehicle on US 16 had not made the unmarked vehicle yet.

He looked at the third screen and saw the subject vehicle enter the causeway on US 25.

"Group Leader Adams, It's a Go!

He looked back at the second screen and the subject vehicle was just passing the unmarked on the side of the road but there was a private car moving at what looked like fifty miles an hour in front of it. The subject vehicle pulled out in the left lane and passed the slow moving car. 'Group Leader Crawford, It's a Go! Watch the private car coming up slowly behind the subject vehicle."

Jake sat there and watched each of the takedowns go directly as planned, in moments the vehicle's passengers were on the ground with their hands handcuffed behind them. There were boxes and boxes of unmarked pills in small packets of four pills each in all three vehicles.

Everyone at the table were clapping, they all stopped as each Group Leader came on and reported to Julian. Julian congratulated them and their men for a job well done and signed off.

All of the people at the table were all standing, except Julian and Jake, all of them walked by and shook their hands and congratulated them.

The Undersheriff raised her arms to get their attention, once she had it she said, "There will be a group of news people outside of this room for a debriefing. Detective Brown it is up to you on how you want this to go."

Julian stood and looked at them and said, "Jake and I did our thing, the News people are your thing, Jake and I would like to be mentioned, but the Sheriff, Undersheriff and Dr, Andrews need to be the spokes persons on this. There should be a lot of praise given to the State Police, the Group Leaders and their people are the ones who put their lives on the line today." Julian sat down.

The Undersheriff replied, "Understood, this is big enough for all of us to look very good to the people of Georgia. Please follow my lead once outside, I'd like to get this to the Courthouse's front steps before we expound on the events of today."

She moved towards the door with all but Jake and Julian following.

Jake looked at Julian and grinning said, "You did one hell of a job, it almost looked like you knew what you were doing."

"Ah shucks," Julian said with a laugh.

As they were getting close to the door the Undersheriff stepped in and looking at them said, "Those of us in charge will never forget how professional both of you are, you have made a few people's careers today. Some of them are at the ending of their careers, and some of them are at the beginning of theirs. All of them owe you both, it will never be forgotten."

Before they could respond she was gone, they looked at each other and gave each other a high five.

"It's time for the Market," Julian said walking a bit faster.

★★★

Dr. Greenly sat there staring at the screen in shock, all three red dots stopped, the phone in his hand buzzed, "Cops." He pushed the 'End Button', it buzzed again, "Cops. He pushed the 'End Button' it buzzed again, "Cops." He pushed the 'End Button' again, "Shit, Shit, Five Million Dollars, gone, just gone."

He pushed the programmed button on the phone, "Tyrone. It's gone, all of it, gone."

"What are you talking about?"

"Cops, they got all three trucks. It's all gone, five million of TAKE, gone."

"How the hell did that happen?"

"Don't know, they hit all three at the same time."

Tyrone thought for a moment, "Who knew about the delivery?"

"There were three of us that knew what was coming, but only two knew when."

"Who were the two, you and who else?"

"Jerry in Savannah, the drivers were brought in on different days and times, they did not know when they were leaving."

"Okay," Tyrone pushed the End button and then pressed #@2 and a phone vibrated in Savannah.

"Yo, what's up?"

"Jerry needs to be gone, now! You got it!"

"Got it, it's done." The phone went silent.

***

There was only one light on as the mailman walked up to the front door of Sister Mary's Clinic for Children. He knocked twice but there was no sign of anyone or anything moving around. He was surprised that there were no children or their parents in the main room. Knocked once more and there was no response, he placed the mail in the box next to the door and knocked one more time, a little harder. He shrugged and moved back to his truck and drove to the next drop.

Sister Mary heard the knocking but was on the phone with the health department trying to get the doors open again. "Yes, Yes I know." She told the

New Orleans Health Department's Administrator in response to his statement, "You have to have a working hot water heater for me to allow you to reopen."

"I hope to have it fixed by Monday, but the children need our services. You need to let me open the clinic."

"I'm sorry, this is only Tuesday. I cannot allow you to operate for five days in violation of the law. Please call me when it is fixed or replaced and I will have an inspector stop by. I'm sorry Sister Mary that is the best I can do."

"Thank you," She hung up the phone and looking at her check book balance that read $102.43, placed her head in her hands saying, "Lord, give me the strength to continue."

She remembered the knocking at the door so she got up and walked to the front door. She turned on the main room's lights, even though she wanted to save the cost of using them. She tried to save everywhere she could.

Stepping out onto the porch she had to close the door to be able to get to the mailbox. That because the door had been replaced, and installed opening to the right, instead of to the left. It had been done for free so she would never say anything, "No need to complain when someone is trying to help," she thought.

She moved to the mailbox, and removed the mail and putting it under her arm, she retraced her steps into the main room. She walked over to the table that served as a reception desk and sat down. With the mail in front of her on the table she opened the smallest envelope first, another bill. The second was also a bill and the third, "Repair of the water heater seemed to be getting further and further away," she thought.

She picked up the larger envelope and turning it over looked at the return address box and saw the 'J'. She instantly knew what was in the envelope, instantly. She started to cry, a happy cry, she put her hands together saying, "God be with you, thank you and bless you."

★★★

Julian was the first to get to the French Market so he walked in and over to the bar area and sat in one of the booths. It was only four twenty and there wasn't anyone else to be seen.

Jake pulled next to Julian's car and after locking his gun in the glove box got out and walked to the Market's door. Before he could open the door it opened and Shelly was standing there saying, "Jake, glad you're back, Detective Brown is in the bar area. I'll be with you in a moment or two."

"Great, I think that we will be having Jack on the Rocks to start."

Shelly smiled and said, "Will have it for you first thing." She walked towards the back of the restaurant with a wave.

Jake walked to the bar area and sat across from Julian in the booth. "Ordered, Shelly will be with us in a bit."

"That sounds good, I talked to Doo, and he said he will be stopping by when he gets off."

"Thanks for asking him to stop by."

Julian put up his hand and pointed at the TV above the bar.

Jake turned and looked at the TV, on the screen were the Sheriff, Undersheriff and Dr. Andrews standing on the steps of the courthouse. They were being interviewed by the lead local news reporters.

"Well the show begins." Julian said looking at the screen.

Shelly moved over to the booth with their drinks while looking at the screen. She put the drinks down and pointed at the screen saying, "Something tells me that you two are a part of that."

Jake held up his hands in mock surrender saying, "Not us, we're innocent, totally innocent."

She waved at him saying, "Really," she turned and moved back behind the bar laughing.

They had been watching the news report for a few moments and Doo walked in with a grin on his face saying, "Well, after today I guess I'll need an appointment to talk to you guys. The news has been using your names like free beer."

Julian said, "What are you talking about?"

Doo looked at the TV and said, "You need to have them turn up the sound, every time they show Lab building they mention both of your names. You are now famous, in a way anyway."

Jake shook his head saying, "That is not good, not good at all."

"Well that is what you get when you make the largest drug bust in the state's history. All without as much as a bump or bruise to anyone on either side, good and bad. Yep, Famous as famous is," Doo said sitting next to Julian.

Shelly stepped up to the booth and looking a Doo asked, "What would you like to drink?"

Doo smiled replying, "What they are drinking will be fine, better make it a double and bring my friends here another. Tab is on him, pointing at Jake.

Shelly looked at Jake and he nodded to the affirmative. "I've got it."

"I guess the best thing you can hope for is a bank robbery or a snow storm, something like that might get them off of you guys."

Julian and Jake looked at him and said, "Thanks a lot," in unison.

They sat there for about an hour discussing the events of the bust and Jake thanked them again for the cabinet. He asked Shelly for the tab explaining, "Got to get home, Teddy and Marian asked me to stop by tonight for tea and cake. I sure don't want to miss having Marian's homemade cake."

"I don't blame you," Julian said.

Shelly brought the bill and Jake placed four twenties in the folder and handed back to her saying, "That is good."

He shook Julian and Doo's hands and walked out to his truck.

Julian pointed after Jake and looked at Doo saying, "That is one impressive man, feels like I've known him forever."

"That is a good thing, a good thing," Doo replied.

★★★

Jake pulled into the driveway and up to the garage door. He put the truck in Park turned it off, got out and walked to the rear door of the main house. He knocked on the door and opened it to a "Come in."

He walked into the kitchen and Teddy and Marian were sitting at the table reading the paper. He walked over to Marian and gave her a hug saying, "You alright today?"

"Yes, I'm fine. Thank you for asking, Jake. Would you like some Tea and Chocolate Cake?"

"That would be great."

"Yes it would," Teddy chimed in.

Marian moved over to the counter and put the water on for the tea. She opened the cabinet and took out three cups, saucers and cake plates. She put them on a serving tray and also placed a fork, spoon napkin for each of them. The water started to boil as she placed the tea in the brew basket and placed the basket in the pot after turning the heat off. She carried the pot and a hot plate for it to the table and set it in the middle of the table, next to the cake. She went back to the counter, got the tray and brought it to the table and set it in front of Teddy. "Please get the tea, I'll get the cake. Is anyone for whipped cream?"

"Yes," both Teddy and Jake replied quickly.

Marian smiled saying, "Me too." She moved to the refrigerator and opened the door and took out a bowl that contained the whipped cream. Moving back to the counter she got a large serving spoon and cake server. The server had a serrated edge to cut with and a flat blade that can be used to serve.

Moving back to the table she sat and leaned over and cut the cake.

Teddy took the cake plates off of the tray and passed them to her. Marian placed a slice of cake on each plate and a large scoop of whipped cream on top. She passed the first plate to Jake and the second to Teddy saying, "I hope it's good."

"I'm sure it will be," Jake replied.

They all finished two slices of cake and cream. As Jake placed his fork across the plate he looked at Marian saying, "If I keep stopping by here I'll need to buy larger pants."

Marian just smiled as she collected the plates.

Teddy passed her his plate and looking at Jake said, "You and Julian Brown sure have been getting a lot of air time on the news channel. That was quite the big deal they are now saying that there was over twenty one million in drugs that never reached the streets. All in all, a very impressive, very impressive day's work indeed."

Jake looked at Teddy and replied, "We were very lucky that it all went so well, and there was a new drug found on the trucks. It was analyzed today and it was found that had anyone used it, they would have died within two weeks of not having it."

"That is crazy, why would they want to distribute something that would kill their customers?"

"My guess is that they didn't have the equipment to analyze it completely, all they found out was it was very addictive and cause hallucinations. I'd bet that if it made the streets there would be a few thousand dead people across the state. Somehow we have to have the report on the findings leak out about the long term effects and soon. I'm sure that the dealers/manufactures will try and get another shipment out on the street as soon as they can."

"Quite a predicament you're in, you might try a file folder marked 'Confidential' inadvertently being left where a noscy reporter can find it. Nothing gets out to the masses faster then something that is supposed to be a secret, and can be considered a scoop by the news reporter."

"That is a very interesting idea. Thanks." Looking at Marian he said, "Well that was wonderful as usual,

Marian. I thank you again, and again I must leave with a full tummy and work to do." He stood and shook Teddy's hand and gave Marian a hug, he said "Thank you again," and walked out of the kitchen and out to his place.

CHAPTER EIGHT

FOR THE NEXT TWO DAYS Jake kept a low profile, he had been successful in avoiding the News people, except when he misplaced a confidential file. The information in the file was the lead story on the news that night.

The headline news and TV posts all started with, NEW DRUG, FOUND IN DRUG BUST, FOUND TO BE A KILLER...............

It was carried on every station and in every paper.

The following day a few strange events happened in Washington involving the Vice-President and a Congressional Page and that had taken the spotlight off of the recent local events.

Jake had stopped at the local bagel shop and picked up a dozen bagels and some cream cheese that morning and left it in the break room. It was a thank you, a thank you for everyone leaving him alone whenever they could.

Julian called and asked him if he had anything new on the exhumation order and Jake told him he did not, but he would check on it, but he did have a question.

Julian said, "Shoot."

"Well I looked up where Elizabeth was buried and I drove to the address, but there wasn't any sign of a grave. I even got out of the truck and walked around the entire property and found nothing."

"The address and property? Just where were you looking my friend?"

"Well, the address on the papers I found on the net was, P2, 125 Second Street at the corner of Green Street."

Julian started to laugh, "Sorry Jake, I'm not laughing at you, just the events. Over on First Street is Magnolia Cemetery, it was opened at the same time that the city was laid out by the founding fathers. The paths between the plots are laid out and named exactly the same as the city streets."

Jake shook his head saying, "P2, Plot 2. Damn, never saw that coming."

He could almost feel Julian's grin over the phone, "Okay, I can't be the first person to fall into that quagmire of local knowledge."

Julian replied, "Nope, everyone not from here makes the same mistake. If you want I'll pick you up around four o'clock and we can drive over there and take a look."

"Sounds good, see you then," Jake turned to his PC and typed in Magnolia Cemetery Augusta Georgia on the search page. In a second there was a full page of web sites with info on the cemetery, he opened and read each one of them in turn. "No more surprises," he thought.

He opened a new e-mail and sent it to Dr. Andrews requesting any new information on the exhumation request for Elizabeth's body.

It was only moments before he got a reply from Dr. Andrews, "No new information, have a meeting with the family on Monday." There was no more but no less information stated.

★★★

Julian and Jake pulled through the entrance gate of Magnolia Cemetery and stopped next to the door marked 'Office.' Julian got out of the car and went into the office. He was back in the car and they were moving down Broad Street, some of the graves had very impressive stones. Jake was a little surprised at the one families plot, it had a flag pole and the Confederate Flag flew on it proudly. Jake made a comment about it to Julian.

Julian explained that this was the one few places in town that the Confederate Flag could fly proudly. "There are seven Confederate Generals and some of their family members buried here. This place is all privately owned and operates on all private funds. Each of the families that have plots here pay an equal share of the operating cost, much like the members at The Club."

"The Club, funny how that name keeps coming up," Jake thought.

They found P-2, at the corner of 1st and Greene streets, it was a large plot surrounded by a wrought iron fence that was about two feet high. It was decorated with oval rings of roses spaced every two feet with a 'B' in the center of each ring. There was a Mausoleum at the rear of the plot, Julian stated that there were twelve slots in it with nine occupied. This he knew for he had been here for Elizabeth's internment, two years ago.

"So to exhume the body, one the Mausoleum vaults will have to be opened?" Jake said almost to himself.

"Right, but the opening of the vault makes it seem like it is no big deal when in fact a lot more care has to be taken. It is possible to accidently break the seal on more than one vault if done incorrectly and that would be a violation of the exhumation order."

"Well, I've seen all I needed or wanted to see," Jake said.

"Yes, I'm done. Anywhere else you would like to see?" Julian said starting the car.

Jake glanced at the car's clock, "Its four forty, think it's best to go back to the Lab to get my truck. Feel like stopping for a pizza first?"

"Sounds good, where?"

"Well I've found the box places, anywhere in town where they really make it from scratch?"

"Luigi's at 590 Broad Street, it has been around since 1949. I haven't been there in quite a while."

"Okay, let's go there."

Julian pulled out of Magnolia Cemetery and headed North to Broad Street, and Luigi's. It only took ten minutes to get downtown and Julian found a parking space right in front of Luigi's. Julian and Jake got out of the car and walked up to the entrance to the restaurant. Julian pulled open the door and Jake stepped in, Julian followed and they were standing at the main counter.

A voice came from behind the counter, "Be right with you."

Jake turned to look over the counter and came eye to eye, or rather nose to nose with the young lady, almost bumping, starting to stand up behind the counter.

He said, "Sorry."

She smiled saying, "I'm not, that is the closest I've been to a good looking guy in quite a while."

Julian laughed, and Jake started to get a little red around the collar as he inadvertently stepped back from the counter.

The young lady smiled and picked up two menus and with a glance backwards said, "Follow me." She walked to one of the booths along the far wall and placed the menus on either side of the booth's table. She looked at them with a perfect smile on her face and said, "That Okay, or are you a couple?"

Julian laughed, "That's great, thanks, Janet." He got her name from seeing the small name tag on her collar. He sat in the seat facing the front door.

Jake sat across from him and picked up one of the menus.

Janet placed her hand on Jake's asking, "What would you like to drink?"

Jake looked up at her saying, "Tea, please."

"Got it," she looked at Julian asking the same thing.

Julian replied, "Tea will be fine.

Janet moved away from the booth and Julian looked at Jake saying, "That my friend is trouble, good looking, brownish red hair, green eyes and it seems, very sharp. Trouble, trouble, trouble I tell you."

Jake ignored him and looking at the juke box station at the end of the table replied, "I haven't seen one of these in years."

There was one on each of the booth tables along the wall. Jake flipped the levers that changed the selection of single records. Jake pulled a few quarters out of his pocket and pushed two into the coin slot at the top of the machine. He pushed D-2 and E-4 and Dean Martin's voice filled the place singing "Everybody loves somebody, sometime."

Janet moved back to the table and placed the glasses of tea in front of them. She sat next to Jake and slid really close to him asking, "Have you picked anything that you like, besides a great song and me, that is.

Julian almost spit out the mouthful of tea, across the table, he had just taken.

Jake turned and was again almost nose to nose, "Pizza, pepperoni pizza, a large pie please."

She looked into his eyes and replied, "That all I can get you?"

Jake never broke the eye to eye contact replying, "For now."

She laughed sliding out of the booth saying, "Take your time, I've got plenty, of time that is." She walked away and glanced back after a few steps to see if they were watching her walk away.

They were.

She smiled as she turned her head away.

Julian looked at Jake with a bid grin on his face saying, "Trouble."

Jake looked at him and asked, "How is it you don't know her?"

"Don't know, she might have grown up elsewhere. Ask her where she grew up."

"I don't think so, hope the pizza is good."

Julian just laughed.

Jake put a few more quarters in the coin slot, and Frank came on in the background singing 'New York, New York' as Jake looked around the room. There were tons of photos of New York's Little Italy, buildings, people, restaurants. It was just as he remembered it, from twenty or so years ago, from when he lived there. That was three or four lives ago, back when he was Mike 'Jake' Thompson, when he was an Inspector for the Federal Marshall service.

Another Dean Martin song came on just as Janet was setting the pizza on the table. She moved back to the waitress station and returned with a pitcher of Iced

Tea and refilled their glasses. She smiled at Julian and asked, "Anything else I can get you?"

"I'm good. How about you Jake, need anything else?"

"No, I'm good, the pie looks good."

"Jake, I like that," Janet said as she glanced at Jake and walked away.

Jake looked at Julian saying, "Thanks buddy."

Julian grinned as he picked up a slice of pizza and tried to take a bite. "Damn, that is hot."

Jake grinned saying, "That was punishment for your wayward ways." He slid a slice of the pie onto the plate Janet had set in front of him. He waited for the end of the song and put few more quarters into the coin slot. He played 'I left my heart in San Francisco' by Tony Bennett, and one more oldie by Frank Sinatra and B1, Dave Brubeck Quartet. He picked up the slice of pie and took a bite. Looking across at Julian said, "That is good pie, very good pie."

Julian nodded his agreement, he couldn't talk, because his mouth was full of pizza.

Janet came back to the table and sat next to Jake again saying, "Pizza done okay?"

Jake nodded his head in agreement. He swallowed what he had in his mouth and wiped his face with a napkin. "The pie is great, I was wondering, do all of your customers get such personal service?"

Janet smiled and looked him directly in his eyes replying, "Not really, only the very special ones."

"Really, how many of those do you have?"

"How many, right now? Hum, Well, I guess it's up to one right now." She replied, placing her hand on his sleeve.

Julian laughed saying, "Hey, I'm still here"

Jake and Janet laughed. She turned and walked back to the waitress station.

They finished the pizza and drinks, Jake waved to Janet and made a signing motion with his hand.

She nodded and turned to the station keyboard to total their check, once completed she walked to the booth and placed it in front of Jake.

Jake picked it up and saw what she had written on the back of the check. Janet Anders, 706-555-8890, off Tuesday, Thursday and Sunday evenings. ☺

Jake placed twenty five dollars on the table and put the receipt in his pocket. It did not go unnoticed by Julian.

They both got up and Julian and Jake both waved at Janet as they walked out to the car. Once they were both in, and locked their seatbelts, Julian started the car and pulled away from the curb. He was pulling into the Lab parking lot before he said anything. "She was very nice, a little showy but nice." He parked next to Jake's truck and put the car into Park.

Jake opened the car door replying, "Correct, but I bet most of it is all show."

Julian replied, "My bet also, has a great personality, and not really pushy. If she was, she would have asked for your number, not given you hers."

"Correct again my friend.

"Talk to you tomorrow." Jake closed the car door and got into his truck.

Julian waved as he backed out of the parking space and pulled away.

Jake started the truck and backed out of the parking space, and then he pulled out of the lot and drove home.

***

Tyrone and Dr. Greenly sat there, with a drink in their hands, trying to understand what happened. They both agreed that it was inside information that lost them their shipment. Tyrone believed that he had eliminated the inside source in Savannah but he would keep a very close eye on who and when someone made the move to take the empty space.

Dr. Greenly looked at Tyrone saying, "One of my people picked up on the job your brother's crew is planning for the end of the week."

"Job, what job, what the hell you talking about?"

"He is planning to hit the convenience store on Gordon Highway Friday. Its payday and that place always have a bunch of cash on hand."

"Well, that shit is not going down, don't need that little shit and his boys bringing us any heat. I told him to lay low, he don't understand anything. If you know, that means a lot of people do, such a dumb shit."

"Well, you need to make that all go away, enough of that. I pulled a sample of the new batch of TAKE and ran some more tests, that damn news report was correct. Everyone that would have taken it would have died a short time after. I disposed of all of it and it will take another three weeks to replace it. A second batch of COKE went out yesterday to replace what was taken. I cut it another ten percent to recoup some of our losses. Our street people are nervous about handling our new stuff. You might need to convince a few of them that they need to do as they are asked, when they are asked. Once a few are convinced the others will fall in line."

"Sounds good, I will have a very long and public talk with a few, a talk that will make an impression on everyone. The first thing I need to do is straighten up that ass of a brother of mine."

Dr. Greenly nodded and finished his drink saying," You need to do what needs to be done and quickly."

★★★

Tyrone asked, "What is planned for this week, brother?" He sat looking at his brother and his ever present running buddy, Jose, listening to the babble that his brother expected him to believe. He picked his hand up and pointed his finger at his brother saying, "Do you really expect me to believe that crap? Do you know what 'Stay on the low means?' Let me ask you this, if I heard about your planned job don't you think that everyone else has to? Are you that stupid? I'm telling you again, lay low, do you hear me?"

"Yes, but I need to make some money too."

"Shit, you need money? Fine I'll give you some money. Stay low, I don't need you or your boys screwing up all I have going now. You got that?"

"I don't want your money, and they ain't boys, I will work it out and, Yeah, I got it."

"You better, next time I will not be the one talking to you, and your boys. Now get out of here and stay low."

The two of them stood and walked out without even looking at him, and the door slammed loudly.

"Stupid one and stupid two," he thought to himself.

★★★

Dr. Andrews and Kay pulled out of the gate at the Club and neither spoke for awhile, once on the causeway

Kay looked at Dr. Andrews saying, "That was very stressful for all concerned. Don't you think?"

"Just being in that place for business instead of relaxation is stressful. And yes, bringing up a loved one's death is never easy, and asking permission to exhume that loved one. Well, stressful might be an understatement."

"Yes, if they agree to the exhumation, I'm sure that they have concerns about the media and how they will be treated in the news. They beat on them quite hard when she died, especially about the fact that she did not work for one of the family businesses."

Stopping at a red light Dr. Andrews looked at Kay saying, "So am I, if it ends up that the company Elizabeth worked for is somehow intertwined with this drug business, the media will have a field day."

"Yes, I've thought about that, even if the fact is, she worked for a phone reception company that handled many companies indirectly and none directly. They will make it sound like she was directly involved in the drug business."

Dr. Andrews pulled into the Sheriff Departments parking lot and parked in the space marked, 'Visitors'. Once he put the car in Park and turned it off he turned to Kay again, "Do you have any ideas on what direction we should take now?"

"We need to finish the investigation, and that includes tests on Elizabeth, so we can nail these animals that are poisoning our young people. We just have to figure a way to do it without bringing the Blanchard family into it."

"Well, I agree, and I think that you and I need to meet with Detective Brown and Jake to see if we can complete the investigation without bringing the media into it."

"Yes, I will send an e-mail to them and ask them to meet us at my office in the morning. Is that okay with you?"

"Yes, that will be fine." With that she opened the car door and stepped out. With a wave she moved towards the building's entrance.

Dr. Andrews started the car and placing it in drive pulled out, and drove to his office.

***

Kay was sitting at her desk half reading a case report, she had just sent the e-mail about the meeting in the morning, when her cell phone started to beep. Pressing the Call button she said, "Kay."

"Kay, this is Thomas Blanchard, I've talked to the family and if it can be done tactfully we will allow the exhuming of Elizabeth's body. If there are any papers that need to be signed, have them sent to my office and I'll sign them and have them returned to you."

"Thank you Thomas, we will handle it in the most sensitive way possible. Please give the family my very best."

"I will, thank you."

Kay held the phone for a bit then pushed the End button and put it back in the holder. She thought about what needed to be done and tried to come up with some way to get it done without it being publicized. She truly hoped that there would be some solution arrived at during their meeting in the morning.

★★★

When Jake pulled into the driveway he saw Marian standing by the rose bed in front of the house. Seeing the basket at her feet, he guessed she was doing a cutting, collecting flowers for the various vases in the house.

Hearing the truck Marian turned and waved at Jake, Jake waved and pulled in front of his garage door. He got out of the truck and walked around the house meeting Marian halfway to the front. He took the basket saying, "I've got that."

"Thank you Jake. I've made some fresh tea and I have a slice of apple pie or two around, please come in and have a cup."

"Thank you Marian, I would enjoy that. Is Teddy around?"

"Oh, he's down at the boat house. When we get inside I'll run down there and tell him we're having tea and see if he wants to join us. Is that alright with you?"

"Of course, Boat house, didn't know you had one of those."

As she opened the house door she replied, "The boat house and dock is down on the river's edge, it is built almost under the garage. Teddy has two boats that he keeps in it, at one time he used to fish a lot. He got tired of going fishing alone so now he just keeps the boats as a hobby. I guess you can't see the boat house from your window."

"I'll have to ask Teddy if he can take me down there to see it."

"He'll be thrilled to do that, he misses fishing I think."

Jake set the basket on the counter and sat in one of the chairs.

Marian picked up the phone and tapped in five numbers, there was a pause "Teddy, Jake is here and I'm making tea, will you be joining us?"

Another pause, then she continued, "All right I'll set out three cups." She hung up the phone and turning towards Jake smiling said, "He'll be right up."

Standing and moving towards the counter said, "Great, let me help setting the table."

Marian put her hand on his saying, "No need to do that, I will get it."

Jake was startled when he felt a slight tingle from her hand. He placed his other hand on hers asking, "You okay?"

She looked up at him replying, "I have been feeling a little tired but I'm sure it's nothing."

Jake held her hand a few moments more and the tingle disappeared, she looked at him for a moment with a small smile on her face, she turned to reach for the cups.

Jake said, "I've got those," then he took the tea cups from the counter and set them on the table.

Marian busied herself preparing the tea, cutting and placing a slice of pie on three plates she had taken out of the cabinet. She placed the plates in the oven for a few moments to warm the pie.

She was just setting the plates on the table when they heard Teddy coming in the back door.

"Well, something smells good in here," Teddy said as he walked into the kitchen.

"You bet, apple pie," Jake replied.

"Ah, my favorite."

"Teddy, you told me last night my Apple Crisp was your favorite," Marian said as she took her seat.

"Well at that time it was, this is a different time, so this is my favorite. Sound right to you Jake?"

"No arguments from me on any count, especially if it concerns Marian's cooking."

Marian blushed, saying, "You two are impossible."

They looked at each other with smiles on their faces and nodded their agreement.

★★★

Jake followed Teddy to the left of the garage, and down a path that led down the hill that he had not noticed, between the trees. It took them a little less than five minutes to reach an opening along the river's edge. Teddy turned right and Jake turned to follow him and that was when he saw the boat house. The building looked like it was built into the hill side not on it, the roof was almost totally covered with tree branches making it almost impossible to see from above. The dock was covered also and extended out from the left side of the building into the river about eight feet. It had an extension that turned up river from the end of the dock and the opening of the boat house.

Jake said, "Nice," almost to himself.

Teddy just smiled and did not reply. He walked over to the rear side door of the building and pushed some buttons on the numbered keypad that was next to the door frame. There was a click and Teddy twisted the door handle and opened the door. He looked back at Jake and said, "T and M, opens it every time."

Jake looked at the key pad and realized it only had numbers, no letters, just numbers. Stainless steel, with raised numbers that show no wear, so they always look the same, no matter how much use they got, Smart.

They both stepped in and Jake realized that the boat house was much bigger than he had thought. Teddy pushed two buttons on the switchbox that was next to the door and the front of the boat house began to rise. The opening was the size of a three car garage door, there were two boats up in slings with a walk in front and between of them. The closest boat was a sixteen foot center console with a trolling motor in front with two outboards on back, a hundred horsepower and forty horsepower. The second was a twenty six foot cruiser with an inboard engine. Its shell was all highly polished mahogany with brass fittings, a classic.

Jake looked at the boats and moved down the walkways, he walked up and back twice on both sides of each boat before saying, "Teddy, they are magnificent, they look new but I know that this one," placing his hand on the cruiser "has to be forty years old."

"Forty two actually, It is my favorite. Nothing like just moving up and down river in the evening in that, nothing."

"I have to say that they both are just wonderful examples of craftsmanship. You can't find anything like it today."

"Jake, anytime you want to use them please do so, they both could use a little use. Marian and I don't get out in them much anymore."

"Teddy, if it is okay with you how about I invite Julian Brown to join us for a day of fishing?"

Teddy brightened up and responded, "You fellows don't want an old guy like me handing around. You just feel free to use them."

Jake replied, "That is nonsense, I'll talk to Julian about it. If we can, will Saturday morning work, say 7:30?"

Teddy grinned replying, "That would be a wonderful thing, wonderful."

"I'll pick up some gear and away we will go."

"Gear, nonsense," he waved his hand towards the rear of the building and there hanging on the walls were a dozen rods and reels, fish nets, just about anything you might need. "Please use whatever you need, anytime."

"Great, lets head up to the house, I've got to meet Julian at the French Market at seven o'clock, gives me forty minutes to get there."

Teddy looked at his watch and saw that it was six twenty, on the dot, not a second before, nor a second after. He followed Jake to the path and noticed he did not wear a watch.

CHAPTER NINE

J AKE FOUND JULIAN IN THE Lab break room when he got
to work the next morning, "Hey, you lost?" he asked
as he entered the room.

"Nope, I'm just getting an early start on the day.
Hope we get somewhere on all of this today."

"Well, if Dr. Andrews and the Undersheriff called a
meeting I'm pretty sure it was not just to see our bright
eyed faces first thing in the morning."

Just as Julian was going to answer the Undersheriff
walked into the room saying, "That is correct, good
morning gentlemen."

Julian looked around saying, "Gentlemen, Is she
talking to us?"

Jake swallowed his sip of coffee and replied, "Must
be, no one else here."

The Undersheriff shook her head and filling the cup
she took out of the cabinet with coffee said, "Let's go see
if Dr. Andrews is ready for us." With that she turned
and walked out the door.

Grinning Jake and Julian refilled their cups and
followed her to Dr. Andrews' office. They heard her
say, "Good Morning Doctor."

Dr. Andrews looked up and seeing the three of them replied, "Good Morning. Jake please open the Lab, we'll use the table in there for this."

"Yes Sir." Jake turned and moved to the Lab door, unlocked it and waved his hand at the light switch and all of the lights came on. He held the door open as they all entered and moved to the table. They all took a seat and after looking to see that the door was closed Dr. Andrews looked at each of them in turn saying, "Kay and I met with the Blanchard family yesterday about the exhuming issue. Kay, would you please explain the outcome of the meeting?"

She folded her hands in front of her and looking at them said, "We meet with the head of the Blanchard family and explained all of the details that were relevant to the need to exhume Miss Elizabeth's body. We of course did not divulge any of the facts pertaining to the case at hand. The family called me about two hours after the meeting and agreed to allow us to do the exhumation. Their only request is that it be done in a way that will cast as little exposure on the family as possible. The media will make a very big deal out of this, very big, if they can, Blanchard family business sells papers and news time. The facts will have little to do with what they report and the family will be forced to relive this whole mess if it is not done correctly. I need some help making this happen and also keeping the fallout to a minimum."

Julian sort of lifted his hand saying, "Understood, Jake and I made a visit to the cemetery and looked around a bit. Elizabeth is in one of the vaults in the Blanchard Mausoleum. So there is no need for a backhoe or workers with shovels, so a limited number of people need to be there. That should make it a little more controllable."

Kay replied, "That sounds good, so how do we do this?"

Dr. Andrews looked at Jake saying, "Any ideas on how we should proceed?"

Jake sat there for a few moments before replying, "By law we need the Medical Examiner, or his appointee, the Sheriff, or his appointee, and a family member, or an appointee and a witness present, also someone that is authorized to open the Mausoleum. Then there are the persons that move the casket to a hearse and transport it to the Lab unload it, reload it and transport it back to the vault. That is at least seven people that will have full knowledge of the events that take place. With many more that will be witnesses to some, or all, of the actions concerning the transporting to and fro."

They all nodded their heads in unison with agreement to the facts outlined.

Jake continued, "Well, If the Medical Examiner's office is represented by me, The Sheriff's department by Julian, the Family by Kay and someone gets authorization for one of us to open the Mausoleum. Well, the whole thing can be done with just the three of us being involved, I will take the samples I need for testing on site and we can have the whole thing done in less than an hour with the casket never leaving the Mausoleum."

Dr. Andrews looked at each of them saying, "I can make all of that happen, but my concern is that when the information comes out in a courtroom, it could be misconstrued as tainted evidence. A Defense Prosecutor will have a field day with it and a lot of people will look bad."

Jake replied, "Yes, that could happen if the results of the tests, and the events leading up to there being attained, is presented as the prosecution's primary support documentation. I believe that the tests and the findings can be presented along with everything else put forth in the case. It will just be another piece of the Prosecution's support evidence. If handled correctly Elizabeth's name will never have to be divulged in court."

Kay looked at Dr. Andrews and standing said, "I've got to meet with the Sheriff and the Blanchard family. This is something that needs to be done face to face."

Dr. Andrews nodded replying, "I agree, I will contact those that I need to also." Looking at Jake and Julian asked, "When will this be accomplished?"

Julian replied quickly, "In the morning at 7 AM, if all approvals are in place."

"Plan to have it done," Dr. Andrews and Kay stood and walked out of the room talking in low tones leaving Jake and Julian sitting there looking at each other. Jake spoke first "You noticed he did not say if." Slapping his forehead he continued with, "Another fine mess you've got me in."

They both laughed.

★★★

Tyrone Mendoza sat at his desk looking at the five prepaid mail boxes he had just filled with one hundred thousand dollars each. He was smiling as he thought of them being delivered to his box at the Your Post Box Service Inc. located in the local Federal Building's lobby. Many of the services that called the building home had been relocated to the new County Administration Complex. The Your Post Box Service was started by a US Postal Service employee that had lost their job due to cutbacks. He opened the post box service as his way of competing directly with the people that fired him. The service was mostly used by Attorneys and most of the boxes were small, but there were a few boxes that amounted to small rooms. Totally in the open but yet totally not traceable and the greatest thing was that the building was one of, if not, the best secured building in the city.

With this mailing he would have well over fifty two million dollars safely being protected by the Federal, State and County Law Enforcement Departments. The same enforcement departments that chase their tails round and round while trying to lock him up for all his street businesses. They were protecting his retirement fund, he laughed to himself just thinking about that fact.

★★★

Teddy and Marian sat in there sunroom looking out on the moon's reflection on the river, it was very peaceful. There were slight house noises that every house ended up having as it aged. They sat holding hands, and each deep in their own thoughts, reviewing some of the current events that had changed their lives. Teddy Asked, "Tea?"

"Yes, that would be nice."

Teddy stood and moved into the kitchen, he put water on and placed two cups and saucers on a tray. He put the tea in the brewing basket and when the water came to a boil he poured it into the cups and placed the baskets in each cup. He picked up the tray and moved back into the sunroom. Placing the tray on the table he retook his seat next to Marian. "I know it has not been more than a few months but Jake has made an impact on things around here."

"Yes, Teddy but there have been a few things that I just cannot get correct in my mind. I spoke to Joe today, you know he has been under the doctor's care for the last few months, and he told me that he got a clean bill of health from the doctor a few days ago. All that seemed to be going wrong are now gone."

"Well that sounds like great news, nothing strange to me."

"Well I haven't said anything but for the past two months I've been feeling a bit poorly."

"Why haven't you told me?"

"I did not think it was anything. Getting back to my thoughts, well yesterday Jake helped me bring in the basket of flowers and he held my hand for a moment or two and as funny as it sounds, I could feel the trouble leaving me."

"Marian, are you saying that Jake had something to do with those events? He is a healer?"

"Yes, no, I don't know. I know it sounds strange and Lord knows if that is what it is, I feel blessed."

"Marian, You know that I don't believe in any of that, this can never be discussed, if it got out, true or not, we would never see Jake again, It would be the end of his life as he knows it, you know that."

"I know, it is something that I will keep to myself, it's just a feeling."

"You and I both know that a feeling will cause more trouble than the truth every time."

***

Jake sat up a little straighter, one of the many alerts he had out there was sounding off, loudly. He forced himself to relax and he closed his eyes and let the information flow to him. Teddy and Marian's discussion flowed through his mind, word for word. He sat there and thought about each word that had been said. He got up and walked to the refrigerator and opening it took out a soft drink. He took his seat again and thought about just how sharp Marian was to pick up on those two events and put it all together. He waited for a few hours to make sure that Teddy and Marian were asleep.

He opened his mind and entered Teddy and Marian's minds to the area that deals with current events, he did not look at anything else but the facts discussed by them earlier. Jake pulled all of the information, memories, thoughts, and discussions surrounding his actions and the perceived results, he then replaced them with memories of having tea and watching the river. He wiped them clean.

He sat up and told himself, "Watch yourself, that never should have happened, don't get so comfortable."

He was unsettled now, he reviewed all of the events of the past two months in detail, he went over everything being very detailed. There was nothing that was incorrect, he felt a bit better.

All of his alerts were pushed up a notch, he was not happy about this. He was at the turn of events that normally did not occur until he was into his third or fourth year. He need to be more carefully, way more careful.

He went into his bedroom and undressed, brushed his teeth and pulling back the covers climbed into bed.

He lay there with his mind darting from one series of events to another at blinding speed. About ten minutes into his attempt to sleep another alarm went off. It was Tyrone's brother's thoughts that set off Jake's alert alarm system. Tyrone's brother was putting things in motion to over throw his brother. It was a stupid plan that would not fool anyone with street knowledge. Jake now had the way to close the events that occurred at Joe's, the boy would never bother anyone again. He closed his eyes and the information seeped into Tyrone's mind, slowly at first, then at a very, very quick rate. Tyrone was asleep he began to toss and turn, he yelled out, "Son of a Bitch."

★★★

Jake met Julian at the Lab at 6 AM he went into the Lab and collected all of the equipment that he might need. They stopped at a chain food store on Gordon Highway for coffee and a breakfast biscuit. They watched the Undersheriff's car go by, "Better get going. Let's get this done," Julian said standing.

Jake was up and headed for the door almost before Julian had it out of his mouth. He opened the door and followed Julian out the door and into the car. Julian pulled out onto Walton Way crossing Gordon Highway and was right behind the Undersheriff as she pulled into the cemetery. They followed her to the Blanchard Mausoleum and parked twenty feet behind her. They all got out of the cars and walked up to the door of the Mausoleum, the Undersheriff took a key out of her pocket and unlocked the door. The first thing she did

137

was set up the video camera that would tape everything they did and said.

Julian walked thru the opened door and carrying the bag of tools he had brought, everything he could think of to allow him to open the vault. He moved to the specific vault and Jake was right next to him, "Looks like we can pull the casket forward once the vault is open."

Julian nodded and replied, "Yes, but what then?"

From behind them the Undersheriff said, "Well it might be a good idea to pull it on to this." She was pushing a table like device into the door, "Some help here?"

Jake moved quickly along side of her and pushed the device up to the vault. The Undersheriff turned a wheel and the top of the table device moved up to the correct height. Jake stepped on what he believed was a brake on the front wheels and moved around to the closest point to the vault front.

Julian inserted a very large screwdriver's tip into a small slot at the bottom of the vaults door after he used a work knife to make a cut around the entire outer edge. He looked at Jake saying, Ready?"

Jake nodded and pushed a large suction cup onto the front of the vault door. Julian pushed the tip in and pressed down hard.

Jake pulled at the suction cup and there was a pop as the seal was broken, the door moved towards them. Jake grabbed it and lifting it off the table, placed it on the floor out of the way. They both grabbed the casket through the open end of the vault and pulled. The casket moved out on the holding table with little resistance. It was less than ten minutes from opening the vault to having the casket on the table.

Jake inserted the hand crank into the first lock and turned it until it stopped, he continued until he had opened all of the locks. He looked at Julian and the Undersheriff saying, "It might be a bit strong at first." He pushed the top of the casket open and placed a bar to insure that it would remain open. He moved to the end of the table device and turned the wheel until the casket was at waist level. He put four sample jars on the table and the other instruments he would need. He opened the blouse and taking a scalpel reopened the Y cut made by the Medical Examiner for the original opening of the body. He spread the chest open and cut a small section of the gall bladder and placed it in one of the sample jars. He did the same with the hair, liver and lungs, then sealed each with yellow evidence tape and signed each. He took one more jar out and with a small scalpel he scraped the inner ear and placed the samples in the jar, closed it and signed it. Once completed that he placed the jars into his case. He then used a large clamp device to close the chest, he then re-buttoned the blouse.

Julian assisted him in closing the top and used the hand crank to engage all of the locks. Jake turned the wheel and the table was raised to the vaults height. The two of them pushed the casket back into the vault and Julian moved the table device. He then moved over to help Jake lift the cover back into place. They put it in place and Julian held it there while Jake used a hand pump to draw the air out of the vault. Once the vacuum held it in place Julian took a tube of glue/sealant and put a layer around the cover.

He turned to look at the Undersheriff and Jake saying, "That got it."

The Undersheriff looked at her watch saying, "Fifty five minutes from going in to going out, Great Job. Now let's get out of here."

"You bet, meet you back at the Lab," Julian said as she walked away.

She waved over her head as she got into the car, started it and pulled away.

Jake and Julian put their stuff in the car and got in, "That seemed to go as planned," Julian said as he started the car.

Jake looked around and replied, "Yes, let's get out of here. Someone is coming down the other drive."

"You got it," Julian pulled out and in moments was back on Walton Way. "Think that was someone looking for us?"

"Don't know but why take a chance."

Julian pulled into the Lab parking lot and pulled next to the Undersheriff's car and parked. He looked around and not seeing anyone that looked out of place said, "Let's get inside, you've made me paranoid."

Jake opened the car door and grabbing his bag got out and moved quickly into the building with Julian right behind him. Walking to the Lab was surprised to see the door open. He stepped in to see the Undersheriff and Dr. Andrews sitting at the table, they both looked at him with looks of concern on their face. Moving towards the table he asked, "What's up?

Dr. Andrews began to speak, "I don't know if this is related to what was done this morning but there were two young men found hanging upside down with their throats cut from ear to ear across the street from Magnolia Cemetery while you were in the Mausoleum."

"Wow, sounds bad but I can't see how it could be connected, bet it had something to do with drugs," Jake said as he sat down. "Sounds like Tyrone took care of his problem," he thought.

Dr. Andrews and the Undersheriff stood looking at Jake and Julian, who was just sitting at the table. The Undersheriff lifted the camera out of her bag saying, "I'm heading to my office to write this up while it is fresh in my mind. Need to have it correct just in case we all get called into court about it all. I will also meet with the Blanchard family head and let him know that all is done. Thank you both for being so professional, again."

Before they could reply she and Dr. Andrews walked out of the door of the Lab.

Jake looked at Julian, "Well, I need to get to work on those samples."

"I can take a hint, call you later. I better get over and see what the story is on those two kids found dead."

"Drugs I'll bet," Jake repeated.

"Yep," Julian walked to the door and waved as he left.

It was not long before Jake had every device in the Lab working on the samples, spinning, turning, heating up, cooling down, and almost endless amounts of movement. Now it would just be a matter of time before he had his information.

He was reading the last of the reports when a voice came across the Lab, "Hey man what are you doing still here? Its midnight and you set all of the alarms off."

"Really, well I'm leaving, sorry for the hassle."

"No problem Doc, whatever you need. Just close all of the doors when you leave, the system will reset itself."

Jake sent his last e-mail on the findings to Dr. Andrews and closed everything down and turned everything off as he left the building.

***

The next morning Jake was sitting at his desk going over his findings on the samples he had run the day before, for about an hour when Dr. Andrews leaned into the doorway saying, "Jake see you at ten in my office, Please."

"You got it Doc, Do I need anything?"

"Just you will be fine."

"I'll be there."

"Eight ten, time to get coffee and to check a few things out further," He thought. He grabbed his mug and headed for the break room. As he was walking into the break room one of the administration assistants was pinning a poster onto the bulletin board. She turned to leave, and seeing him smiled and said, "A fun time downtown this weekend." She did not wait for a response and walked down the hall towards the central administration area.

Jake walked over to the bulletin board and looked at the poster, 'Taste of Augusta, Saturday - Sample foods from over fifty local restaurants. Event times 10AM till 2PM, samples two, three and four tickets, Tickets $1.00 each.'

"That could be a fun thing to do, it was wonderful in New York," he thought. He moved to the counter and filled his mug with fresh coffee. He walked back to the Lab and passing the door to Dr. Andrews office he noticed Dr. Fox in with Dr. Andrews, the two men were in such an intense discussion that they never noticed his passing.

Back in the Lab he sat at his desk, he was entering data on his PC when the desk phone beeped. He looked at it with a questioning look, "That doesn't happen much, must be the lady from HR again," he thought. He picked up the receiver saying, "Lab, Smith." A man's voice answered, "Mr. Smith, my name is Alan Jefferson, and I'm with the Witherspoon Institute,"

Jake froze, 'Witherspoon Institute,' he had not heard from anyone there verbally in over eighteen years, at least eighteen years. Anytime he needed to move he would just call the number and leave the name and new location and somewhere he would be for a day or two before the change. Once he reached that location a large envelope would be left for him under the current name, that of who he was, with all of the new documents and history reflecting the new him.

"Yes," he replied,

"I need to talk to you face to face. There is a large Butterfly statue on the river walk trail between the open air theater and Saint Paul's Church, 9:00AM Saturday morning. Have a good day."

Jake held the receiver, just staring at it. "Twenty five hours six minutes to wonder, wonder, ponder, and guess. He knew that anything he came up with had a 99% of being wrong. Just as it had been the last time he was contacted by the Witherspoon Institute, in any other way than the phone number burned into his memory, of Washington D.C., the Institute founded by the one and only Dr. Tim Witherspoon of Laramie, Wyoming.

Jake tried to busy himself with reading and rereading the Mass Spec reports on the samples he had run. His eyes read it but his mind was not acknowledging it. His internal clock said it was 9:50 and time to see Dr. Andrews, he got up and walked towards Dr. Andrews' office.

***

Jake tapped on the door frame of Dr. Andrews' office and Dr. Andrews waved him in pointing towards the second chair in front of his desk. Dr. Fox stood saying, "Hello Jake, hope all is well."

"Dr. Fox, thanks all is well. I hope all is well with you also."

"Yes, thank you." Dr. Fox retook his seat as Jake sat down.

Dr. Andrews put his hands together at the finger tip, as if praying, looking first at Jake and second at Dr. Fox. He leaned back a little, and looking at Jake said, "Jake, Dr. Fox and I have just spent a little over two hours discussing your job performance over the past three months.

In that time you have gone from Probationary Lab Technician to Sr. Lab Technician, Probationary Sheriff's Deputy to Sheriff's Deputy, all of which is amazing.

We have gone over some of your reports, test findings and results, and the reports from the State and FDA certification technician's reports on the operation and status of all of the equipment in our Lab. Their reports tell us that the equipment in the Lab has more run hours on it, since the last inspection then the previous year."

"And they have not seen such complex tests requested on any other equipment anywhere except at the main lab at the CDC in Atlanta." Looking directly in Jake's eyes he continued with, "Young man, they have six PHD's and eight techs running that Lab," Dr. Fox added.

Jake looked at them both and replied, "What did I do wrong?"

"Wrong. Wrong." Dr. Andrews stood and sat back down continuing with, "Nothing, all you did, according to the reports, is out work fourteen people in a lab that has done very little in over a year. Jake we are just profoundly amazed and thankful."

Dr. Fox repeated part of the last, "Amazed."

Jake just sat there looking at the two men not knowing what to say.

Dr. Andrews looked at Jake and Dr. Fox, he rubbed his face with his hands and leaning forward addressed them both, "Well, I've made up my mind on where we go from here. As of now, Jake, your position with this County will be three fold. You will hold the position of Deputy Sheriff, Sr. Forensic Lab Administrator; you may hire whoever you need, and Assistant County Corner. I will make sure that all of the appropriate paperwork is completed with the assistance of Dr. Fox."

Dr. Fox stated, "With pleasure."

"Jake, does that work for you?"

Jake stood and extended is had to Dr. Andrews saying, "Yes, if it works for both of you it most certainly works for me."

Dr. Fox stood and shook Jakes hand after Dr. Andrews. Dr. Andrews looked at Jake and finished with, "I will attempt to put this all in a job description, with some additional job background info, so you can have something to work with. Now go close whatever you are working on down and take the rest of the day off. I will see you on Monday. That is an order, no arguments"

"Yes sir." He stood and shook both men's hands and looking at Dr. Andrews said, "Can we meet at nine Monday? I have some findings that I want to rerun over the weekend if the results are the same we should discuss them."

"That will be fine, nine works."

"Thank you," Jake turned and walked back to the Lab.

He sat at his desk turning off his PC and pulled his phone from the holder. He pushed Julian's number and waited for him to pick up.

"Hey man, what's up?" Julian asked.

"I just got the rest of the day off. Can you get away for lunch? I can meet you at the Market."

"You bet, but let's try someplace else today, meet me at Sixth and Watson, on the corner of Sixth and Watson, at eleven forty five."

"Sounds good to me, see you there. Oh, by the way, are you up for some fishing on Sunday morning? Teddy was showing me his boathouse and boats and he would like to join us."

"Sunday sounds good to me, talk to you about it at lunch."

"Great, see you in a bit." Jake pushed the END button and then pushed the button for Teddy's phone.

"Hello Jake," Teddy answered.

"Teddy, how does fishing sound for Sunday morning? Julian Brown will be joining us."

"Jake, I would love to but Marian and I have a previous commitment, maybe we can do it next week?"

"Okay, I'll see if we can go next Saturday morning."

"That will work for me. Thank You."

"Great, I'll let you know if anything changes." Jake pushed the END button and put the phone back in the holder. He stood and glanced around the room making sure that everything was off. Seeing that all was good left the Lab and walked out to his truck. He got in and started it, pulling out of the lot to find Sixth at Watson.

***

Jake pulled into the lot and parked a few feet away from the only other car in the lot. He had driven half way around the block after finding the place, he had turned onto Watson off of Sixth and there were only a few parking spots on the street. The parking lot was off Sixth behind the restaurant. He sat there for about ten minutes until Julian pulled into the lot and parked next to him. He got out of the truck and walked around to meet Julian in front of the truck. Julian put his hand out and Jake took it saying, "Good to see you."

"You bet," they walked around the corner and entered the front door. A young lady said, "Two?"

Jake replied, "Yes."

She turned and led them to a booth on the front of the building and placed menus on the table, one on each side.

Jake slid in facing the entrance and Julian slid in the other side saying," The fried chicken is really good."

Jake never opened the menu that was left for him, just pushed it towards the middle of the table replying, "Okay, I'm sold."

The waitress stopped at the table saying, "Drinks?"

They both replied, "Tea. Thanks."

"You got it," she replied turning and walking away.

"Nice place, never would have known it was here if you had not given me directions," Jake said looking at Julian.

"Yes it is, I like to get here every once and awhile, there aren't as many people that know me here."

"Ah, someplace to hide, I get it," Jake said with a laugh.

"Right," Julian replied. He continued with, "I've got to go to the pistol firing range after lunch, I need to get recertified. Want to come?"

"Yes, I've never been there and I guess I have to be certified also."

"We can make that happen."

The waitress returned with their drinks and asked, "Make a selection?"

Jake looked at her saying, "Fried Chicken, mashed potatoes and green beans."

Julian said, "Same for me. Some more tea would be great."

"Got it, be right back with the tea."

A short time later the waitress returned with a tray of drinks and food. She placed the tray on a fold out rack and placed the plates of food in front of them and refilled the glasses with tea. She left the pitcher of tea on the table and turned and walked away.

They both picked up a piece of chicken and Jake took a bite and looking at Julian said, "This is good, really good. You were right again."

Julian did not say anything just waved a chicken leg Jakes way with a smile on his face.

They finished eating and were finishing their drinks and Jake looked at Julian saying, "Teddy can't make it for fishing on Sunday, next Saturday works for both of us."

"That sounds good to me. Meet at your place at eight?"

"I'm sure that will work, Teddy would like to put some run time on his boat."

Julian grinned saying, "Well, now I really have something to look forward too, getting to see Teddy's boathouse, boats and fishing spots. Win, win, win."

"You bet, done?"

"Yep," Julian went to pick up the bill to pay but Jake stopped him saying, "My treat, I think I got a raise today."

Grinning Julian said, "A raise, Okay, you can get this and also tell me about the why, how and how much later."

"Jake laughed replying, "Can do."

★★★

They pulled into the Richmond County Sheriff's firing range parking lot and Jake was surprised at the amount of cars and trucks in the lot. He pulled next to Julian's car and parked his truck. He got out and walked around to the passenger side and opened the door. He opened the glove box and took his pistol and badge case out, putting the badge case in his pocket and hooking the gun to his belt. He took the magazine out and rocked the pistol to eject the shell in the chamber. He put both in his pocket.

Julian opened his car's trunk and lifted a green canvas bag out of it and put the strap over his shoulder and walked over to Jake.

Stepping up to Jake he said, "Some extra ammunition, didn't think you had any with you."

"Nope, thought I could get some here."

"Used to be able to get all you wanted, but now you are on your own. Budget cuts."

"Darn, I would think if there was one thing the public would want is for their weapon carrying defenders of justice to be able to hit what they shoot at."

"You would think so. Let's see if we can get a lane and scorer so this all counts." He stopped and looked at Jake saying, "You never said, you any good at this?"

'Fair, hit what I shoot at, most times."

Julian laughed replying, "We will see, we will see."

They walked into the building and towards the counter, out of the group of men standing at the end of the counter a voice rang out, "Please put your bullet proof vests on, Julian Brown is in the house."

All of the men laughed and the man behind the counter moved towards Julian and Jake saying, "Detective Brown are you here to give these losers a lesson on the art of gunmanship?"

Julian waved to all of the men replying, "Some people just can't be taught, they are hopeless."

All of the men laughed.

The counterman placed his hands on the counter and asked, "Julian, what can I do for you?"

"Stan, need a lane and spotter, we both need to be certified."

Jake could feel the demeanor of the man change to an all business mode.

"Yes Sir, Lane three and four, I will have Jimmy and Jack spot you both. The standard set? Three sets of three at 20 feet, twenty five feet and thirty feet and one set of five rapid firing at twenty feet?"

"You got it."

"Need any practice time?"

Julian looked at Jake and Jake shook his head from side to side indicating none needed. "Nope, set the line, I'll go first each set."

Stan nodded and moved away to talk to the spotters.

Julian moved towards a door in the rear wall and Jake followed.

The range had twelve firing lanes with target holders that moved back and forth on cable to the designated distances from the spotters up above.

Julian stepped into lane three and placed his bag on the shelf in front of the firing station. He took a box of nine millimeter ammunition and placed it on the shelf on lane four for Jake. He then placed one on his shelf. He turned to Jake and said, "We will shoot each stage and place our weapons on the shelf once each is completed and the scored calls back the target. Once we start keep the ear protection on at all times, the green light at the back of the firing lane will let you know when it is safe to fire. Good?"

Jake grinned, saying, "Good."

Julian moved back to his lane and the green light came on, he put the ear protection on and opened the box of shells and loaded his pistol.

Jake put his ear protection on and stood one step back from his firing position.

The cable moved a target out to the twenty foot mark, and the six inch bulls eye target moved back and forth for a second, and then was still.

Julian raised the pistol and snapped off three shoots with a ten second interval between them.

The lane light turned red and the target moved back upwards to the spotter.

The green light went on in the back of Jake's firing lane. He stepped up to his lane's shelf and loaded his pistol. He stepped into his firing position, raised the pistol and snapped off three shots, with a five second interval.

The target moved up to the spotter.

They alternated firing periods until they were done, when both firing lanes red lights came on and stayed on, they both took off the ear protection and hung it on the hook provided.

Julian stepped over to Jake saying with some surprise in his voice, "I think you got me."

Jake cleared his weapon and looked at Julian saying, "Nope, it was even, I was a little off on the rapid fire, four black and one half black. Same as yours, all the rest were black in each set. You my friend are very good, very, very good."

"Me, what was that you did, first time in six years anyone even got close to me. Glad you are on my side, very glad," he laughed as he turned and repacked his bag.

Once they had everything packed up and the brass policed then moved back into the other room and Stan. They walked up to the counter and Stan stood there with a look on his face. He looked at Julian and said, "You did not introduce me to your friend."

Julian looked at Jake and back to Stan saying, "This is my friend Ken Smith, Jake to his friends, he is the Richmond County Sheriff's Department Forensic Lab Manager, Deputy Sheriff and Assistant Medical Examiner.

Jake looked at him and started to say, "I didn't,"

"I also have friends in high places, Undersheriff called."

Jake just shook his head.

Stan put his hand out saying, "Jake, it is my pleasure to meet you, you ever want to shoot, please stop by. It will be on the County, same as Julian, I don't have the pleasure to see shooting like that very often, and Mr. Julian always a pleasure."

Jake shook his hand saying, "Thank you, nice to meet you also."

Julian and Jake turned and were walking out when they both heard Stan say, "Both of them had 'Ten perfect scores, ten I tell you."

Jake opened the door for Julian, and grinned, saying under his breath, "Another fine mess you got me in."

They both laughed as they walked towards their vehicles.

CHAPTER TEN

J AKE PULLED HIS TRUCK INTO a parking space on James Brown Boulevard, 9th Street, and walked up to the Open Air Theater on the River. He walked down the steps until he reached the beginning of the walking trail that led to Saint Paul's Church, The trail followed the river's edge and had a few spots that were marked as 'Kodak Moments'. The large Butterfly statue was one of these spots, due to the twists and turns of the path you could not see the entire trail.

Jake knew that it was eight fifty so he started walking along the trail, he did not see anyone else anywhere around. In a few moments he saw the Butterfly statue, but his view was partially blocked by a large tree trunk that extended out over the river.

As he got closed he saw a man standing next to the tree, behind the statue, looking out at the river.

Jake stepped up to the man and the man put out his hand saying, "Mr. Smith, Alan Jefferson."

Jake took his hand and gave it one shake, before he could reply Alan Jefferson said, as he handed Jake a five by five envelope, "This is self-explaining. Please have a wonderful day." With that he turned and walked back down the trail towards Saint Paul's Church. In just moments he was out of site, gone, like he never existed, except for the envelope Jake held in his hand.

Jake looked at the envelope, turning it over and over in his hands. There were no markings of any kind on it, just a clasp on the back. "Just like before," he thought. He put it in the inside pocket of the red flannel over shirt he was wearing over a white Augusta golf shirt he had purchased last week. He turned around and walked back the way he had come. He got back to his truck, after stopping for a cup of coffee and a sugar coated donut to go. He got into the truck and placed the coffee in the cup holder and the donut on the dashboard. Taking the envelope out of his pocket, he opened the glove box, and placed it in it and closed the glove box. He picked up the cup of coffee and took a sip, thinking, "I will take care of that later." He finished his coffee and donut listening to the truck radio letting some time pass, and trying not to think, thinking about what you can't change will make you crazy, he truly believed that.

★★★

Dr. Paul Greenly sat back and looked at Tyrone saying, "That was one hell of a way to take care of that problem."

"Well, it got taken care of, that son-of-a-bitch was just a day away from trying to off me. Was going to take over, show the world how it should be done. Stupid ass, what he did do is showed the world what happens if you fuck with me."

"I guess it got the signal out, everyone is working hard to not shake the tree. Well, the first shipment of 'TAKE' hit the streets last week, sold out in three days.

They are screaming for more, next shipment will be sent out Monday, at twice the price."

"That shit isn't going to kill anyone is it? We don't need a mess of murder charges flying around."

"No, I changed the mix and all is good, this shit keeps them high for four or five hours at a time. Have you gotten the money drops from last week yet?"

"Got half, rest will be at my place today. I'll get yours to you this evening around seven."

"That is what I like to hear. I will let you know about the meeting next month with the South American guys. Go make us some money."

Tyrone stood and looking down at Dr. Greenly with a ugly look on his face said, "You make the shit, I'll make the money. You take care of your business I'll take care of mine." With that he turned and walked out of the room.

An uneasy feeling came over Dr. Paul Greenly as he watched Tyrone leave.

★★★

Jake got out of his truck and walked down Ninth Street to the intersection with Broad Street and looked Westward towards the area that the Taste of Augusta would take place.

Broad Street between Tenth and Twelfth Streets was quite wide, in each direction there were two lanes for traffic and diagonal parking on each side of the traffic lanes. The police had already placed no parking signs on the right side of the street in both directions, and red cones limiting traffic flow in the right lanes only on both sides of the street. This left the equivalent of four lanes in the center for the vendors and visitors.

It looked like people were everywhere setting up tables, booths and banners. Jake saw one of the ticket booths at the end of the block and walked towards it. There was an older gentleman with a 'Volunteer' button with his name above it, Tim, on his shirt tending the booth.

Jake said, "Good morning Tim,"

"Well, a good morning to you, young man. How many tickets can I get you?"

"I'll take twenty-five dollars' worth, please."

"You got it," and Tim started pulling the tickets off of one the large rolls of tickets hung on a section of pipe. Once he got to ticket number twenty-five he tore them off and handed them to Jake.

Jake handed him a twenty and five dollar bill saying, "Thank you Tim."

Tim grinned saying, "You're welcome, come back for some more, soon."

"I'm sure I will." Jake walked across the traffic lane and stepped inside the boundary marked off for vendors and visitors. He was looking at some handmade book markers when he heard "Jake, Jake, over here."

He turned around looking down the row of tables and saw Martha and Paige waving at him from three tables down.

He waved and started to walk towards them. Once he got to their table they both gave him a hug saying, "It is so good to see you," almost in unison. "It's great to see you both, what are you all about today?"

They both stepped aside and pointed to the banner hanging behind the table and said, "Kids Care."

He looked at the large banner hung behind the table. It read **'Kids Care - It's Important! Important to You and Them'** in large bold red letters. A smaller banner read, **'Needed Items - New Clothing, Shoes, Sneakers, School Supplies, Sport's Equipment, Tutoring, Mentoring and just plain Help'**

On the table were two large boxes marked donations and a stack of pledge sheets next to each. The pledge sheets listed everything on the banner, also a place for Name, Address, Phone Number and E-mail address.

"Well that about sums it up." Who's program? What can I do to help?

Martha put her hand on his and gently pulled him around to the behind the table saying, "Stand here and smile for starters. We'll think of some other things as time passes. This is a program that Paige and I put together to try and help local children."

Jake smiled saying, "That is great program, I think that BOO needs to be back here also."

"Don't worry he will be, he just doesn't know it yet," Martha said laughing.

Jake stood behind the table and talked with numerous people that stopped at the booth for an hour or so and he slipped a few twenties in each of the collection boxes when Martha or Paige wasn't looking. There was a break in the people and looking at both of them said, "Okay, I'm going to take a walk around to see the other booths and get something to eat. What can I bring you back?"

Paige said, "If the French Market has a booth a Shrimp Poor Boy would sure taste great."

Martha nodded her agreement.

"I'll see what I can do." With that Jake started to walk down the row of tables again. He found the French

Market booth at the corner of Eleventh and Broad Streets, Shelly waved and said, "Jake, How are you?"

"Hi Shelly, I'm good and about to get better," pointing to the platter of Shrimp Poor boy sandwiches. Each was cut in half and the small sign next to the platter read, 'two tickets'.

She laughed asking, "How may I help you?"

"Please give me four of the sandwiches."

"Four, you must be hungry."

Jake laughed and replied, "Yes and no, these are for some friends about ten tables back that way," he pointed back towards the way he had come.

Shelly put the sandwiches in a bag with a few napkins, she turned to him saying, "I hope you enjoy."

Jake took the bag after putting nine tickets on the table saying, "One for the excellent service." He turned and headed back to Martha and Paige's table.

A big "Thank you," followed him across the street.

He lifted his hand and waved backwards over his shoulder. It took just a few moments and he was back in front of the 'Kids Care' table. He handed the bag to Martha saying, "This is just what the Doctor ordered."

"Jake, thank you so much, let me get you some tickets."

"Not needed, enjoy. I'm going to see what else I can find to taste." He turned to his left and started walking the other way. He walked back to Tenth and turned right and walked around to the South Bound lane of Broad Street, and turned to go north. He stopped at the third booth and was looking at some handmade belt buckles. Jake heard someone behind him say, "Mr. Jake." He turned around and standing a few feet away was Stan from the firing range and a young lady.

"Hello Stan, good to see you."

"Mr. Jake just wanted to say hello, this is my friend Sally."

Sally blushed to a light pink and said, "Mr. Jake, nice to meet you."

"Miss Sally, it is my pleasure."

"Thank you, Stan let's go, we might be bothering Mr. Jake." With that she grabbed his arm and started to move away.

Stan said, "Have a great day." As Sally guided him into the crowd of passer bys Jake heard him say, "Ten perfect series, ten I tell you."

***

Julian parked his car and getting out looked East on Broad and was amazed at the number of people already on the street moving from table to table. "Wow, great crowd already," he thought.

He crossed the street and started walking eastward towards Martha and Paige's table. He was stopped after only passing five or six tables by a uniform officer that he had known since high school.

The officer put out his hand saying, "Julian, congratulations on the promotion, well deserved my friend."

Julian shook his hand while looking at him saying, "Promotion? What promotion are you talking about Tommy?"

"The one on the front page of the morning paper, there is a photo of you and the new Forensic Lab Manager, or should I say Assistant Medical Examiner. It announced the promotions that you both just received. Mr. Smith to Assistant Medical Examiner and you to

Commander of SIU, the Counties Special Investigations Unit and liaison to the Georgia State Patrol."

Julian was a bit unsettled, he said, "Thanks," and walked away really not seeing anything thinking, "Promotion, what the hell."

He was so preoccupied that he was walking past Martha without seeing her or Paige.

Martha stepped up behind him and reached out to touch his arm saying, "Julian, Julian where are you going?"

He stopped and turned around and seeing Martha, and Paige in the background said, "Sorry, Just got some information that has taken me by surprise."

"What information?' Martha asked.

"Well, I was just told that there is an article in the paper this morning announcing that Jake and I were promoted."

"Really, Jake was here earlier and he didn't say anything."

"Well, if he didn't read the morning paper he wouldn't know, just like I did not know. That is until Tommy Jameson just told me."

"Well, come over here by the table, promotion or not you are still going to help."

He grinned and nodded his head saying, "Of course."

They walked to the table and in moments Julian was in deep conversation with a few of the masses of people that were now passing the table. Martha stepped back towards Paige and told her about everything Julian had said. Paige turned and walked to Julian and reaching him put her arms around his neck and kissed him on the cheek saying, "Congratulations, what were you promoted too?"

Julian looked at her and said, "To what? I really don't know."

Paige said quickly, "Mind the table, I will find a paper and be back." She was gone, and not visible, into the crowed in a moment.

Martha stepped close asking, "Where did Paige go?"

"To find a morning paper, said she would be right back."

There were three people standing at the table looking at the pledge sheets.

Martha said, "Let's get them before they walk off."

★★★

Jake turned back to the table and after a few moments continued to walk down the row of tables. He tried a sample of cookies from one table, some escargot from another and was just going to purchase a drink when he heard, "Well, Good looking it is sure good to see you. Thought you dropped off the end of the earth or left town."

Jake turned and standing very close was Janet from 'Luigi's Restaurant' with a big smile on her face. They were almost nose to nose and she said, "Well for the second time I'm very close to a good looking guy and no contact made. Ah, an opportunity missed is an opportunity lost."

Jake put his arm around her waist and pulled her close giving her a big hug. Then he removed his arm saying, "Not missed, nor lost."

Janet was surprised at his actions and was speechless for a moment, something that did not happen often.

Jake stepped back away from the table and she stepped back also, "Well, where are you headed Miss Janet?"

She grinned at the Miss Janet and replied, "Well, I am working at our table a ways up there, and need to get back," turning to her left pointing north on Broad Street.

Jake stepped next to her and they both started walking north, Jake put his hand on her back as he tried to direct her around a few people standing still and talking.

She turned to look back at him, and putting her hand on his arm, saying, "Thank you, I like someone with a good sense of direction."

Jake laughed replying, "I have a real good sense of direction, but it is the arriving that worries me."

They both laughed and nether removed their hands from the other.

"Janet, are you working or playing? Working I hope."

They both looked at the man who had just spoken.

The man was about fifty and about six feet tall with wavy black hair with streaks of gray scattered through it. He had a smile on his face and a plate with a slice of pizza on it in his hand.

Janet said quickly, as she moved quickly around to the back of the table, "Working Boss, got a customer right here. He needs one of everything."

Jake stepped up to the table and the man set the plate on the table and extended his hand out to Jake saying, "Tony, Mr. Smith, my pleasure."

Jake shook his hand saying, "When did we meet?"

"Never, you're in the paper this morning, congratulations on your promotion to Deputy Medical Examiner."

"Sorry did not know that, thank you."

Janet said, "Congratulation," and moved around the table quickly and gave him a kiss on the cheek. She quickly moved back behind the table and placing a slice of pizza, a cream puff and a container with a stuffed shell in it, in a bag. She put a napkin and plastic fork in the bag also. "That will be six tickets Sir," she said with a big smile on her face.

Jake placed eight tickets on the table saying, "Two for the wonderful service."

Tony grinned saying, "She gets off at three, please come pick her up and get her out of my hair."

Jake looked at him smiling and replied, "The things you have to do for friends, Okay Tony, I'll be back at three to take her off your hands."

Janet put her hands on her hips saying, "Well, do I get a say in this?"

They both looked at her saying, "No."

Jake picked up the bag and grinning moved away from the table, he was a few tables away and he stopped and looked back, Janet was looking after him and seeing him turn around, smiled an even bigger smile and waved. Jake stepped away and was out of site. Jake walked along the row of tables looking at each and the wares that they displayed. When he got to Twelfth Street he turned right and right again so he could see the rest of the tables on the northbound side of Broad. He saw Julian's car parked on the north side of the Twelfth and Broad, so he walked over and placed the bag of food from Luigi's on the trunk. He opened the bag and spread the food out on it. He was unwrapping the slice of pizza when he heard, "That is an official department vehicle not a table."

He turned around and was eye to eye with a uniformed officer, the man stood at least four inches taller than Jake.

Seeing Jake's face the officer stepped back saying, "Sorry Sir, Didn't recognize you from the rear, Sorry."

Jake did a quick sweep of the man's mind and replied, "No harm no foul Sergeant Keller, none at all. I'm sure Detective Brown appreciates your keeping an eye on his car."

"Yes Sir, have a great day."

"Thank you Sergeant," Jake turned back to his slice of pizza. Jake had taken his first bite when he heard a girl's voice say, "Daddy, that's what I want, that's what I want."

He turned and saw a girl, ten or eleven he guessed, pointing at his slice of pie. The little girl's father was saying, "Okay, Jill, but we have to wait for mommy."

Jake said "Hi Jill, do you like pizza?"

The girl replied quickly, "Yes Sir, a lot."

Jake reached into his pocket and pulled the rest of his tickets out and handed them to the little girl's father saying, "Luigi's table is just on the other side about ten tables down." He looked at the little girl and continued, "There is a pretty lady at the table, her name is Janet, tell her that Jake sent you and you love pizza." He looked at the girl's father saying, "I hope you are all hungry, food is great."

Jake looked up at the woman that walked up to them, he smiled saying, "Hello Undersheriff."

"Hello Jake, I see you have met my family, my husband Steve and my daughter Jill."

"Yes I have, just gave them directions to the best pizza on the street today."

Steve put his hand out saying, "It's my pleasure Jake, I've heard many good things, and often."

Shaking his hand Jake said, "Thanks."

The Undersheriff took Jill's hand in hers and said, "Well let's go get some pizza." With that she stepped out to cross the street, making sure she checked the traffic each way first. Her husband stepped up beside her and took her hand.

Jake heard the little girl say, "Mr. Jake said we have to see Janet for the pizza." Grinning Jake turned back to his food and finished his slice of pie thinking, "Walked less than three blocks and met eleven people that I know, happening way to fast I think." He ate the stuffed shell and the cream puff, putting all the papers in the bag he walked over to a waste container and put it in. He then walked over to a ticket booth and purchased another twenty dollars worth of tickets before starting back along the row of tables.

★★★

"Mr. Jake, Mr. Jake." Joe called out from behind his table.

Jake stopped hearing his name and turned towards where the call had come from, he saw Joe waving at him from behind a table a few sections further East.

He walked over to Joe's table and shook the hand extended across the table towards him saying, "Joe, how are you? You're looking well."

"Thank you Jake, things are good, real good, thank you for asking. Miss Marian is good?"

"Yes, she is fine, she was shook up, but she is fine."

"That is fine, now I feel way better, way better about it, I was very worried over her, she be a good lady."

"Joe, I will tell her that I saw you and how you asked after her," Jake shook his hand again and moved away from the table with a wave of his hand. As he passed it he put a twenty in the box marked 'Donations'.

He began moving along the tables again and stopped at one that was selling soft drinks, he smiled at the young girl behind the table saying, "A Diet Pepsi please."

She placed a cup on the table saying, "Two tickets please."

Jake handed her the two tickets and picked up the cup and continued moving along the tables.

CHAPTER ELEVEN

TYRONE TURNED ONTO BROAD STREET from North Tenth Street and crossed in front of an oncoming car causing the driver to slam on the breaks. He looked at the driver saying loudly, "You best slow down, hear," in an ugly voice. The driver just pushed the buttons that raised the windows and locked the doors.

Tyrone laughed and walked into the crowd of people, just pushing those that did not move. He moved to the westward lane of Broad Street and began to move along the tables. He saw Julian standing behind one of the tables and walked past not acknowledging him. He walked across Eleventh Street and continued just pushing people out of his way. He was in mid step when a hand grabbed his shoulder and spun him around and he heard, "You just knocked my wife down, you ass hole."

Tyrone struck out before he stopped turning, he felt his fist crash against the man's jaw. The man went down and Tyrone turned and started kicking him. The man was knocked out from the punch and could not move away from the kicking.

The next thing Tyrone knew he was flying through the air and crashed into a parked car.

Sergeant Keller reached down and helped the man up from the ground, he was now standing right next to the man that had yelled at Tyrone, when he saw the kicking he grabbed Tyrone and threw him towards the street.

Sargent Keller moved across the street placed his knee into Tyrone's back and grabbed Tyrone's wrist and twisted his arm behind his back placing a handcuff on it. He reached around and grabbed Tyrone's other wrist and pulled it behind his back and placed the second cuff around that wrist.

Sargent Keller grabbed Tyrone's hair and lifted him to his feet reading him his Miranda Rights. "Do you understand these rights that I have read to you?"

Tyrone looked Sargent Keller in the eye saying, "You just signed your death certificate."

Sargent Keller laughed saying, "I'll take that as a yes and you now have an additional charge of threating a law enforcement officer."

There were now four uniform officers standing around keeping the crowd away from Sargent Keller and the man that had been punched and kicked.

Sergeant Keller pushed Tyrone towards one of the uniforms saying, "Please book this trash, I will file the required papers. Charges are Assault and Battery and Threatening the life of a Law Enforcement Officer."

The Officer grabbed Tyrone's arm and moved him towards Tenth Street and a waiting patrol car.

Jake was standing across from Sergeant Keller and Tyrone watching the events unfold, he turned to check on the man that had been punched and kicked, he was nowhere to be found. A few of the bystanders said that he had grabbed his wife by the arm and just left. Jake had gotten the man's name, 'Johnny Poles' and his wife 'Fanny' but nothing else.

Julian saw the Officer walking down the street with Tyrone in handcuffs and he started to walk westward quickly to see what had happened. He saw Jake standing in the street talking with a group of uniformed officers.

"What's up? He asked as he got closer to the men.

Jake could feel Julian approaching, he turned saying, "The perpetrator punched a man and was kicking him while he was unconscious on the ground. Sargent Keller arrested him and sent him to be booked."

Julian looked at the uniforms and asked, "Any of you see this?"

"I did, happened just that way."

Julian turned towards the voice and looked at a uniformed officer, it was Tommy Jameson, he nodded saying, "You need to get down to Central and fill out a 'Five,' it needs to be very detailed."

"You got it Detective, sorry, Commander," with that he turned and walked towards a Patrol Car parked on Tenth Street.

Everyone started to move away and Jake and Julian walked back towards Martha's table.

Julian shook his head saying, "What sucks is with no one to sign a complaint Tyrone will back out on the street in less than an hour. The threat will be dismissed as just a heated rant."

"What if we find Johnny Poles, he should sign the complaint."

"Never happen, he knows Tyrone and will distance himself real quick."

Jake nodded but thought, "Tyrone will be getting his, soon. Well, Commander Brown what's next?"

"We will see, Assistant Medical Examiner Smith."

They both chuckled as they walked towards the 'Kids Care' table.

★★★

Martha looked up and saw Julian and Jake getting close to the table, once they reached it she said, "You both look like the cat that got the canary. Please take over for a bit, I've got to go find a restroom.,"

They nodded and she was gone like a flash.

They talked to many people and many of them filled out Pledge Cards and also pushed bills into the donation boxes.

It was about an hour before Martha and Paige reappeared carrying a white box that was about a foot square and ten inches high. Behind them were about a dozen uniformed officers and the Undersheriff and her family.

Martha yelled "Surprise" as she placed the box on the table. All of the others yelled, "Congratulations."

Paige opened the box and took a cake out of it and placed it in the middle of the table. She took packages of plastic plates and forks out of the bag she had been carrying then took a serving knife out of her purse and began slicing the cake into small slices.

Jake and Julian were shaking hands and saying thank you to the Officers and friends that surrounded them.

The Undersheriff shook their hands and gave them a hug saying with a laugh, "We are off duty."

It ended up with about twenty people gathering around, Paige and Martha started handing out slices of the cake, with a fork. The crowds just moved around the group with an occasional 'Congratulations' being called out.

The festivities lasted about thirty minutes and the group drifted away with many 'Congratulations' being repeated. Julian and Jake were standing well behind the table trying to disappear, they both were little embarrassed over all of the attention. Martha and Paige stood in front of them talking to the people that were still stopping by.

There was a lull in the people and Julian said, looking at the three of them," How about drinks at five? They are on me."

Paige replied quickly, "Love to but I have a date, we are meeting at Sheehan for drinks at four."

Martha said, "I'm in, free drinks with Julian paying." Oh yeah!"

The three of them looked at Jake.

"Well, I have to pick up a friend at three, I'm sure that we can make it."

Julian grinned saying, "Okay, Paige is it alright if barge in on your date and we all meet at Sheehan's at four?"

"That will be fine, I'm meeting Charles, and he is pretty flexible and knows almost everybody that will be there."

"Great, four it is," Julian was grinning as he turned to Jake "Do I know your friend?"

Jake replied, "I think so."

"Okay, I have a few things I need to do so I'm off, see you all at four."

Paige said, "Me to, see you at four.

They both moved into the crowd and were gone.

Martha looked at Jake grinning and asked, "Well, are you going to keep your friend a secret?"

Jake replied, "Her Name is Janet Anders, she works at Luigi's and she is originally from North Augusta. That is about all I know about her."

"Janet Anders, I remember an Anders that played aggressive field hockey for a few years in high school. Might be her, I'm looking forward to meeting her." She looked at her watch saying, "Its two thirty, better get this shut down."

"Okay. What do you need done?"

"There is a box under the table and we just need to put the pledge papers, banner and the donation boxes in it, and we're good to go."

Jake moved the cloth covering the table and pulled a large cardboard box out and put it on the table. He turned and took the banner down, folded it and put it in the box. He took the pledge papers from Martha and placed them in the box on top of the banner. They both looked around and everything was in the box.

Jake picked it up and asked, "Where to?"

"I'm parked on tenth, up a ways towards Green Street."

"Okay, let's go."

Jake and Martha walked to Tenth and turned right towards Martha's car. It took only a few moments to get to the car and Martha opened the trunk. Jake placed the box in the trunk and closed the lid.

"Okay, see you at four at Sheehan's. That is on Mont Sano?"

"Yes," She moved to the driver's door, and as she got in said, "See you at four." She started the car, and putting it in gear pulled away from the curb.

Jake waved as she pulled away, he turned and moved briskly back towards the festivities.

***

The snow mobile moved down Glacier Street, until reaching West Eleventh Street, and pulled over a mound of snow that was almost ten feet high. Juneau had had almost twelve feet of snow in the last seven weeks. The driver pulled it up to the door that was really on the second floor of the structure. Better known to the locals as the winter front door, once the snows began to accumulate the lower door is sealed shut.

The door opened and a tall thin man stepped out with a mug in each of his hands, steam rose from each mug in a white vapor.

"Vincent, cup of hot chocolate, bit of Bailey's for taste?"

The driver shut down the machine and pulled off his snow mask saying, "Sounds good Harry."

Vincent took the mug and after taking a sip said, "That is good." Looking over the other man's head said, "Harry, noticed the roof has a bit of an odd tilt to it."

Two small heads popped out of the doorway and they said in unison, "Hi Mr. Vincent."

Vincent grinned at them replying, "Hey kids, better get back inside, it's cold out here."

The both said, "Yes Sir," and disappeared.

Vincent looked at Harry again saying, "Harry, How many you and the Mrs. caring for now?"

Harry grinned, saying, "Twelve, found three last week living in a cardboard box back off the old Coach Road. The parents, if you can call them that, just dropped them off with a few sandwiches and headed south. They were darn close to freezing up. Hope I don't ever meet them so called parents, would not be pretty."

"I agree, you and the wife doing okay, like I said, the roof looks to have a strange tilt to it."

"Yep, it will last till spring, with the trapping, fishing and hunting we'll all be fine, Mrs. has a few 50 pound sacks of flower and one of rice in the cupboard. It will make do, has to, no other options. We will need to replace most of the house come spring or find someplace else to move to. After the thaw most of the exterior will need to be stripped and a new heating system put in. We'll make it work for the kid's sake. The only thing keeping the law away is it's to damn cold for them to come bother us."

Vincent finished his hot chocolate and handed the mug back to Vincent saying, "Well here is your mail, anything I can get you? I can always swing by after my run if you need anything from the Post."

"Thanks, we're fine, thanks for the asking though."

Vincent started the machine and with a wave was gone.

Harry looked at the envelopes and laughed, they were sale papers from the two department stores in Nome. "Fat chance of us ever seeing the inside of them, let alone buy anything." He looked at the box and put it under his arm and went back inside.

He walked down the stairs to the kitchen and placed the box on the table and looked at his wife Anne saying, "Vincent said hello and thanks for the hot chocolate."

She smiled and continued to kneed the bread dough she was working on. She looked over at him and asked, "What's in the box?"

"Don't know, haven't opened it yet."

"Who is it from?"

"Don't know that either." He picked up the box and turned it over and over, in the return address box there were two Ute symbols and a 'J'. One symbol that symbolized prosperity and the other symbol symbolized long life and good health.

He looked at his wife with excitement in his voice saying, "It's from Jake, Jake, I tell you."

"Vincent, you sure, we haven't heard or seen Jake in fifteen years."

He pulled the tab on the end of the box and a folded sheet of paper fell out. Vincent unfolded the paper and read out loud, "Vincent, use this slowly and it will serve you, Anne and the children for a very long time. I know you understand what I'm saying. Kiss Anne for me and keep helping the children, I'll never be far away. 'J'."

Vincent dumped the contents of the box on the table, and counted the stacks of hundreds, "Gosh darn, $200,000.00 dollars."

Anne moved to the table and placed her hand on Vincent's shoulder saying, "Vincent, we are blessed."

He placed his hand on hers replying, "Yes, that we are."

★★★

Jake stood at the corner of Tenth and Broad just watching everything slow down and the vendors breaking down there tables. One by one the vendors loaded their boxes, bags and other equipment into trucks or cars and moved away. His internal clock told him it was two forty five, he moved towards Luigi's table to see if he could help them breakdown in anyway. He got there just as Tony was attempting to lift one of three large coolers into the back of a truck.

Jake grabbed one end of the cooler, ignoring the, "I got it, I got it," from Tony and placed his end on the truck bed. Tony pushed and the cooler slid all the way to the back of the truck bed.

Jake turned to grab the end of the next cooler and Janet was holding the handle on the end.

She said, "Got it."

Jake lifted his end and put it on the truck bed and Janet pushed it alongside of the first. She ended standing close to Jake once again, he grinned and turned towards the last cooler.

Tony had the end of the cooler and said, "Well if you help get this in the truck you two can stand there and look at each other all night."

Jake picked up the end of the cooler and placed it on the truck bed alongside the second cooler. Tony pushed it in and lifted the tailgate, locking it in place. Jake picked up the last box and placed it on top of the coolers.

Tony put his hand out saying, "Thank you."

Jake shook his hand and replied, "No problem."

Tony looked at Janet and said, "Okay, you are off the clock, see you tomorrow. Jake will you drop her off to get her car at the restaurant later?"

"If that is what the lady wants, that is what she will get."

Tony laughed saying, "You keep that attitude and she will have you crazy in a week."

Janet said, "Hey, I am standing right here."

Tony and Jake both laughed as Tony opened the door to the truck. He got in and started it and waved as he pulled away leaving Jake and Janet standing in the empty booth.

"He seems like a really nice guy."

"Yes, he is. He helps everyone he can, almost to a fault," Janet said as she bent over and picked up a stray piece of paper. She walked over and placed it in a trash container and walked back to Jake looking up at his face saying, "Well, what's on the schedule now Mr. Jake Smith?"

Jake put his arm around her waist replying," Miss Janet, we have been invited to meet some friends and have a few free drinks to celebrate a couple of promotions. Does that suit you?"

"Why yes it does, suits me fine,"

He laughed and started back towards his truck, with his arm still around Janet's waist.

They walked to the truck, in took about fifteen minutes and neither of them said anything, but Janet did move closer.

When they got to the truck Jake unlocked it and opened the passenger door stepping to the side and waved his hand towards the seat saying, "Your coach awaits."

"Janet stepped in and sat on the seat saying, "Thank you kind sir."

Jake closed the door and moved around the front of the truck and got into the driver's seat.

Janet looked at him saying, "Where are we meeting your friends?"

"We are meeting them at Sheehan's Pub at four."

"Great that gives us almost thirty minutes to get there. That is enough time to stop by my car so I can change my blouse, if that is okay with you?"

"No problem." Jake started the truck and pulled away from the curb and drove towards Luigi's.

While he was driving Janet moved closer to him, close enough that both their hips and upper leg were touching.

Jake looked at her and she had a smile on her face, he also had a smile on his.

Five or six minutes passed before they got across town to Luigi's and once they arrived Jake pulled into a space right next to Janet's car. There were only a few cars in the spaces due to the time of day.

Janet got out of the truck and walked around both vehicles to get to the passenger side of hers, she opened the door and got in.

Jake watched her move around the vehicles and get into the passenger's seat of her car, he saw her moving around but could not see what she was doing.

Janet pulled the back of her blouse over her head and discarded the blouse, she pulled the clean blouse, that she had had folded on the consol, over her head. She put her arms into the sleeves and pulled the blouse down to her waist. As she got out of the car she straightened the front and back of the blouse to make sure they were even. With that done she closed the car door and locked it as she turned to retrace her steps to the truck and got in.

Jake was surprised to see her in the new blouse but tried to not show it. He looked at her saying, "That was quick."

She smiled and slid closer saying, "One must always be ready for any event that comes up."

"I see that, planning, planning, and more planning."

They both laughed.

Jake pulled out of the parking space and drove to Sheehan's Pub.

CHAPTER TWELVE

T HEY WERE ALL SITTING IN a room off of the main dining room but still only ten or so feet from the bar. Karin, the bartender, had brought the first round of drinks and a few bowls of snacks. There were three tables that seated four and being set at an angle allowed everyone to be close enough to talk without having to raise their voices.

Julian, Charles, and Jake had stepped outside to look at a new Rod and Reel that Charles had just purchased.

Martha, Paige and Janet were sitting at the table to the right of the archway to the extension room off the main dining room.

Paige's phone stared to chirp and she pulled it out of the holder and pushed the Call button saying, "Yes?"

She listened for a few moments then replied, "Hold on for a moment." She looked at Martha and Janet saying, "I've got to step outside to take this."

They both nodded and Paige moved out of the room and towards the front door.

Martha looked at Janet saying, "I remember you a little from eighth or ninth grade, you were a great field hockey player, and then it was like you disappeared."

"Well, things happen and you need to do what you have to. My mother was always ill but during summer break after eighth grade she was sent to Georgia Central Hospital in Milledgeville."

"My God, Georgia Central? Back then that was a hell hole."

"Yes that it was. My brother, sister and I were kept in a home in Milledgeville for about three months. That was before they put us in three different foster homes in three different towns."

"What about your father?"

"Well he kept in contact but he did not make enough to be able to support us so the state wouldn't let us live with him."

"When did you all get back together, or did you."

Janet took a sip of her drink before replying, "Well after three years the state released my Mother and gave her a subsidized apartment in North Augusta. The three of us moved back in with her but we never got close again. My mother died a few years ago but I see my brother and sister every holiday and maybe a few other times a year. I guess I pretty much stayed on my own and just a little remote from the kids at school."

Martha waved Karin over, and ordered herself and Janet a second drink saying, after Karin moved away, "Janet, no one should have had to go through that alone. I'm so sorry."

"No need to be sorry, things like that happened to a lot of people back then. Different time, different way of life, things have changed a lot, some for the good and some for the not so good. "Janet picked up her drink and finished it just as Karin brought the second round.

Martha put her hand on Janet's saying, "Well, I'm glad to have been able to re-make your acquaintance."

Janet looked at Martha saying, "Thanks." Looking up she saw Jake, Julian, Paige and Charlie moving back to the table. They had the Undersheriff, her husband and daughter in tow.

Julian said, "Look who we found wandering around the parking spaces on the street."

The Undersheriff said quickly, "One drink, then we will get our table so I can feed these guys."

Julian nodded and waved for Karin.

Jake stepped over to the table Janet was sitting at and sat next to her saying, "Everything okay? You look a little troubled."

Janet smiled putting her hand on his replying, "Everything is good, just thought about some things that weren't all that good, but all is okay now."

Karin walked up to the table saying, "Need anything, drinks, and/or appetizers?"

Jake replied first after looking at Janet's glass, "I'll have another Jack Rocks and a refill for everyone. Do you have a sampler platter of appetizers?"

"Not on the menu but I can have them put something together for you."

"Great, a platter for each table, thanks Karin."

Julian reached over and gave Jake a light push on his shoulder saying, "Beat me again."

Jake grinned and replied, "That's okay, I'll hold back when the bill comes."

Everyone laughed at that, the Undersheriff said, "Told you he was smart."

They all laughed louder and Julian just grinned.

★★★

Tyrone walled out of the central police booking area and was met by his Attorney. The man looked at him saying, "Well, I have everything covered, Monday all of this will be wiped clean like it never happened. Please don't have any interface with anyone that was involved with this in any way."

"Right, but I will interface with them someday." He walked away from his Attorney without another word and once he was outside of the building he realized that his car was still downtown. He looked around and waved to a cab that was waiting across the street. The cab pulled around and after getting in told the cabbie, "Tenth and Broad."

The cabbie replied. "Yes Sir." and pulled away from the curb. It was just about ten minutes when the cab pulled up to the curb at the corner of Tenth and Broad.

Tyrone flipped a twenty over the seat back towards the driver as he opened the door and stepped out. The cabbie called a "Thank You" as he pulled away and drove down Broad Street, Tyrone watched him for a moment then turned and walked up Tenth to his car. When he got there he got in and burned the tires as he pulled away from the curb and headed for his house. He was pissed and his mind was working on a plan to find and pay a debt to one Sergeant Keller and Officer Tommy Jameson and how they would pay.

***

Paige took the paper out of her purse and pushed it in front of Jake saying, "Well you both look so handsome. Don't you think Martha?

Martha picked up the paper and looked at it and handed it to Janet asking, "What do you think?"

Janet looked at the photo and looking at everyone said, "Well, I guess they will do, got to work with what you have."

Everyone busted out laughing and the good natured jabs began.

Jake and Julian just grinned and made a big fuss when Karin walked over with a tray with the platters of appetizers and drinks.

Once everyone had their drinks the Undersheriff stood and tapped on the table saying, "I want to congratulate both Commander Brown and Assistant Medical Examiner Smith on their promotions and I know that the County and City are just a little bit safer than they were." She lifted her glass and everyone did the same, "The Best."

Everyone else repeated "The Best."

She took a sip of her drink and placed the glass on the table, she looked at her husband and he nodded and stood. Looking at everyone said, "Thanks for allowing us to intrude on your fun, but we are getting a table and having dinner. With that the Undersheriff, her husband and daughter turned and walked back into the main dining room and the hostess joined them and took them up the stairs to the other dining room.

They all tried the different offerings on the sampler platters and the conversations drifted from one subject to another.

Martha looked at her watch and surprised to see that it was six forty five, she nudged Julian saying, "If we are going to make it to your Aunt's as you promised we better think about leaving."

He looked at his watch and was also surprised, he looked around at everyone saying, "I hate to break this up, but I saw my Aunt downtown today and she asked me to stop by and do a few things for her, and I told her I'd stop by around seven tonight. Well, it's about seven."

Jake looked at Julian saying, "No problem, I have this. Do what you need to do, I'll talk to you tomorrow."

Julian looked at him, "You sure?"

"Get, I got this."

Julian and Martha said their goodbye's and were gone.

Paige and Charlie chimed in, "Jake we have half of this."

"No, Janet and I have it covered."

Paige replied, "Next time it is on us. If it's okay, were going to get along also."

"No problem, thank you again, for letting us meet you and turn you're date into our party."

They both laughed and Charlie replied, "It was a blast and now I have a reason to be pretty much guaranteed another date."

Paige punched him in the arm saying, "Like you need a reason or a guarantee."

They both laughed, and with a wave headed for the main room and the restaurant's exit.

Karin walked up to the table with the bill in her hand and said, "Looks like you are the winners."

Janet said, "Absolutely."

Jake took the bill and took some bills out of his pocket and handed it back to Karin saying, "That's good, thank you for the extra service, we all appreciated it."

Karin took the bills and said, "Thank you very much. Look forward to seeing you both again." With that she was gone.

★★★

The postal truck pulled into the parking lot on the corner of Washington Avenue and Philip Street in the Faubourg Livaudais District of New Orleans. The driver looked at the small sign hanging by a black chain link rope, "The Children's Place for Care, Ms. Pearl De Florins, RN."

He walked up the brick walk and when he reached the door knocked twice, waited a few moments and knocked again. He heard a voice that sounded like a happy laugh, "Coming Sugar, I saw your truck pull in." He stepped back to avoid the door when it opened, and it did open almost with a flourish.

The large woman standing there all in white had a big smile saying, "I sure hope you brought some good news today, been pretty down low lately."

"Well Ms. Pearl, I have some envelopes, one from the Tax people and one from the Health Department, and a prepaid box for you. Don't know about the box but those from the Tax and Health Department people is never good news."

A small frown came over her face replying, "Yes, yes, they been pushing hard lately, don't much care the good we be trying to do."

"Well you have a good day, see you tomorrow."

"Thank you, have a blessed day and be careful."

"Thank you Ms. Pearl, you also," with that he turned and walked back to his truck.

Pearl watched him until he was back in his truck thinking, "Good boy, we was lucky to have got him through the fever years ago." She turned and walked back into the clinic. "Yes it is a clinic, no matter what those people out there says," she thought.

The old building had been serving her well over the past twenty years or so but the Tax and Health

Departments have been trying to shut her doors for over a year now. The Tax people changed the zoning or something, they want more than ten thousand dollars and the Health people be telling her, "Ms. Pearl you need to have separate bathrooms and the examining rooms need exhaust fans and you don't have enough hot water and on and on. She sat down behind the old desk that served as her office and opened the envelope from the Tax people first, the paper read, "Final Notice Remit $10,235.00 within sixty days or the listed property will be seized and sold at auction." She placed the paper back in the envelope and placed it in the IN basket and picked up the next from the Health Department. She opened it and took the papers out and began to read them, "Final Notice, All Medical services being provided must cease at once until the property is brought up to code for spaces used for the offering of Medical Services. Please contact this office at once with the intent of compliance."

She looked at the papers for a few moments longer and thought, "Well. They might be shed of me." A tear rolled down her cheek as she thought about the eight children now in her care. They would be taken and placed in Social Services and be lost in the system for ever.

She wiped the tear away and opened the remaining envelopes, mostly bills of one sort or another. She put them on the ever growing pile in the IN basket feeling more and more helpless. It was a feeling that she had been fighting off for over a year, she looked at the ceiling and said a small prayer.

She picked up the box that had come with the envelopes and turned it over and over, the only markings were her address. She pulled the tab and opened the end of the box, a sheet of paper was folded over and placed next to the wrapping covering the contents. She pulled the paper out and unfolded it and began to cry. The paper read, "Dear Ms. Pearl, God Bless, use this a little at a time and continue to do what you do, for those that need. 'J' She turned the box on end and the stacks of hundred dollar bills tumbled out from the brown paper, that covered them, on the desk. Still crying she placed the stacks in equal piles and sat there in amazement, $200,000.00 dollars.

"Yes, I will Mr. Jake, yes I will, they can't stop me now. God Bless."

***

They were standing in front of Sheehan's and Janet looked at Jake and asked, "What now Mr. Smith."

"That is up to you, I know we have been picking on stuff all day, but are you hungry?"

"A little, don't need a lot but a little something would be nice," Janet replied.

Jake asked, "Are you up for Chinese? I found a great place for takeout on Fifteenth."

Janet placed her hand on his arm saying, "That sounds good to me, and if you don't mind, can you drop me off at my car and I'll follow you to the Chinese Take-Out place."

"That is no problem, we I can do that."

"Great, Jake, it sounds like the Chinese Take Out place isn't far from mine, we can go there and eat."

"That works for me."

She grinned asking, "Not too much, too soon, it is our first date?"

"First date, sure seems like we have always been hanging out together." Jake stood and helped her get up.

"Yes it does."

They walked out of the restaurant and to Jake's truck.

Jake opened the door for Janet, and she slid in saying, "Thank you."

He moved around to the other side of the truck and opened the door and got in.

Janet moved next to him and he turned and gave her a quick kiss on the lips and turned and started the truck. She did not say anything until they were parked next to her car, she got out and walked around to Jake's window and reached in and gently pulled his head towards her and kissed him. She turned and walked around her car and opened the door saying, "I'll follow you" got in and started the car.

Jake pulled away, keeping a watch on her car in the mirrors. It wasn't long before they were parked across from the Chinese takeout.

Jake opened the truck door and got out, he walked around the truck and stepped close to her car and opened the car door for her. As she got out he leaned over and gave her a quick kiss.

She got out saying, "That was nice," and started across to the takeout restaurant.

Jake moved next to her saying, "Which, the kiss or the opening of the door?"

She opened the door to the restaurant with, "Both."

They walked up to the counter looking up at the overhead display of food and prices.

The counter man asked, "Yes, you would like?"

Janet replied, "Wonton Soup, Spare Ribs, and Pork Lo Mein for two." She looked at Jake asking, "Miss anything?"

He grinned, saying, "Add two shrimp egg rolls, and that will do it."

The counter man pushed the keys on the register and looked at Jake saying, "Nineteen fifty six,"

Jake handed him a twenty as he glanced over watching Janet who was standing across the room reading the newspaper article that was framed and hung there.

The man handed him the change and moved back to the cooking area, he called out the order in what Jake thought was Chinese. The other two workers moved even quicker and things started to sizzle and the aromas were great.

Janet touched his arm saying, "Everything smells wonderful, if it tastes half as good as it smells it will be great."

"It is very good. Do we need to get some soft drinks or beer?

"No, I've got some at the house."

The counterman moved towards them with two bags of food saying, "Thank you, come back, thank you."

Jake picked up the bags and replied, "We will, thank you."

Janet walked over to the door and held it open for Jake.

Jake said, "Thank you" as he stepped through the door.

With a big grin Janet replied, "My pleasure."

They moved to the truck and Janet opened the passenger side door and Jake slid the bags onto the seat.

Jake closed the door and opened Janet's car door, she got in saying, "Follow me. We'll go up to Walton Way and go right, we'll stay on Walton Way to the top of the hill and turn right onto Milledge Road. Three blocks down is Battle Row, we'll make a right and then a left into the second drive on the left. Got it?"

Jake grinned saying, "I got it."

Janet started her car and seeing Jake was in his truck pulled away, out of the parking lot onto Fifteenth Street. She followed the path she had told Jake and in a little less than ten minutes they were making the turn off of Battle Row.

Jake pulled into the drive, it was gravel and lined with very large trees. He pulled next to Janet's car and turned the truck off. He sat for a moment looking at the house in front of him, more a cottage than a house he thought.

He got out of the truck and walked around and got the bags out of the truck and walked up the brick path to the front door where Janet was standing.

"Well, this is home sweet home," she said putting the key in the front door lock. It clicked and she swung it open, reached in and flipped the light switch, she stepped aside allowing Jake to enter.

Jake stepped in and glanced around, the cottage consisted of one very large room that was the kitchen, dining and living room all in one. There were two archways, with one going off to the left and the other to the right.

Janet took one of the bags from Jake and moved towards the kitchen counter, it separated the kitchen area from the living area. She placed the bag on the counter and Jake put the second next to it.

Janet turned to him saying, "Well, let me give you the nickel tour before we settle in." She walked to the middle of the room saying, "This is the living room, and that table covered with books in the corner is the study," she pointed to the area six feet away "That is the kitchen." She walked over to the archway on her left and pointing through it said, "This is the Laundry Room." She took him by the arm and walked to the other archway and reached around the wall and flipped a light switch. They took a step into the hall and she pointed at the first door saying, "Bathroom" pointed to the second door "Bedroom."

She stepped back into the living room saying, "Sit where you like, I'll get some plates, silverware and glasses out."

Jake sat on one of the stools at the counter and watched her take out everything and place it on the counter. She opened the refrigerator asking, "Soft drink, tea or beer?"

"Tea will be fine, anything I can do?"

"Please turn on the TV, see if there is anything you want to watch."

He got up and walked over to the table in front of the sofa and picked up the remote. He pushed the Power button and the Flat screen on the wall powered up, it was on the History Channel. He did not change he channel, he placed the remote back on the table and sat back down.

Janet sat next to him and opened the containers of food and put a fork in each.

They both put some of each item on their plates and she spooned the soup into the bowls. They ate for awhile and Jake looked at her saying, "This is a very nice place, it seems isolated yet it's in the middle of everything."

"Well, it used to be the cottage for the house help for the main house, it is just up the hill a bit. You can't see either from the other and can't be seen from the road. This Estate in owned by the Norris family's trust fund, they have been good friends for a long time. They were kin to my father in some way, and they gave me a lease on this place for ninety nine years. I pay four hundred a month and all utilities, with an automatic cost increase of three percent every two years. It's all managed by some firm in New York City, and I have no idea why I just told you all of that."

"It's my magnetic charm," Jake said with a grin.

She laughed and gave him a soft punch in the arm.

They finished eating and Jake helped her clean up and dried the dishes and silverware. They moved to the sofa and sat close together watching the TV.

CHAPTER THIRTEEN

J AKE OPENED THE GLOVE BOX and took the envelope from the Witherspoon Institute and just stared at it for a few moments. He put it in his pocket and got out of the truck, walked to his door and unlocked it. He was just about to enter when he heard, "Jake, it's Marian."

He turned and Marian was standing just outside of the rear door of the house, he walked over to her saying, "Something I can do?"

"No, I just wanted to congratulate you on your promotion and invite you to dinner later. I'm making fried chicken and such. Teddy and I would be pleased if you can join us."

"Of course, I would love to. Will seven be okay?"

"That would be fine, I'm sure Teddy will be back from his meeting at the Club by then."

"Great, I'll see you then, and thank you." Jake turned and walked back to his door, opened it and took the stairs two at a time.

Jake picked up one of the counter stools and carried it over to the window that over looked the river. He sat on the stool and leaned against the side wall, there were a few dozen geese floating slowly along the far riverbank.

Jake picked up the envelope and he slid his finger under the edge and pulled. The envelope flap opened and Jake blew at the open edge, this allowed him to see one sheet of white paper. He pulled the paper out and it was folded over only once. He looked out on the river thinking, "Just how much will this small piece of paper change the world."

The last envelope from the Witherspoon Institute had shortened a conflict and ended a government.

Jake opened the paper and there in red ink were a list of names, he read and reread them. He knew what was expected and also knew that he was the only one that could make the needed events occur. He closed his eyes and let his mind go blank for a moment, then a plan for each name began to develop. He stood up and put the stool back in place and walked into his bedroom. Lying on the bed he lay on his back and stared at the ceiling, he allowed his mind to travel.

***

Jake opened his eyes and sitting up shook his head a little, he swung his legs off the bed and got up and walked into the kitchen area. It was six thirty five and he would have to leave in a few moments to have dinner with Teddy and Marian. He was looking forward to the dinner, when he traveled for a long period of time it consumed a lot of his energy. He had set a lot of things in motion in the past few hours, things that would change the country, all would change, change under the direction of the Witherspoon Institute. There would be less than a dozen people aware that what was happening was a very well planned course of action being directed and positioned by the Institute.

His attention was drawn to movement on the security flat screen, he watched Teddy's black SVU come down the drive and pull in front of the last garage and pull in. In a few moments he watched Teddy walk up to the house's rear door and enter.

★★★

Jake waited five minutes and then headed down the stairs, "I can almost smell the chicken cooking from here" he thought. Reaching the house he knocked on the door and opened it and stepped into the hall, Teddy was just coming out of the door from his study.

He put his hand out saying, "Congratulations Jake."

Jake took his hand replying, "Thank you Teddy."

Teddy grinned, "I understand you will need a larger business card."

"I guess, the ink hasn't really dried on the first ones they gave me."

"Well, from what I hear you are doing everything expected and a lot more. Your name is coming up in a lot of the right places."

Marian call from the kitchen, "Are you two going to stand in the hallway all night?"

They both grinned and Teddy replied, "No dear, were on the way."

They walked up the hall and stepped into the kitchen, the food smelled wonderful and Jake knew it would taste even better. He followed Teddy, as he moved across the kitchen to stand next to Marian, Teddy gave her a kiss, saying, "Dear, everything smells just wonderful." He moved over to the table and took his regular seat.

Jake gave Marian a hug saying, "What he said."

Marian smiled saying, "Hope it tastes as good as it smells."

"Can I get or do anything?"

"Not a thing, please have a seat everything is almost ready."

"Okay." Jake sat down, and looking at the dishes on the table thought the only thing that was missing was the chicken. He saw cucumber salad, okra and tomatoes, turnip greens, fresh cut French fries and a pitcher of Sweet Tea.

Marian carried a platter of chicken to the table and placed it in the center, she turn and walked back to the oven and took a platter of cornbread out and brought that to the table as well. She placed it next to the chicken and sitting down said, "Well, I believe that is everything."

Teddy said, "If it isn't on this table it isn't needed. Thank you my Dear."

Jake chimed in with, "Yes, thank you Marian."

She looked at them and said, "Enough of that now, help yourselves before everything gets cooled down."

Teddy started by taking a portion of each item and passing the platters to Marian, one at a time. She in turn would do the same and pass them to Jake.

Once they had the plates full Teddy reached over and took Marian's hand and bowed his head saying, "Thank you lord for what we are about to enjoy and bless those at this table. Amen."

It was quiet for while they ate except for the soft music filtering in from the sunroom. The music was mostly big band music with an occasional vocal mixed in. The soft tones of the music, and the singer's voices seemed to fit the mood very well.

Jake finished his second helping of chicken and sat back a little saying, "I'm stuffed, Marian you are the greatest."

She smiled and replied, "You're not too stuffed to miss out on Apple Pie are you?"

Teddy and Jake both said, "Never," at the same time. They looked at each other and laughed, Jake said, "Great minds think alike,"

Marian laughed as she got up from the table and moved over to the stove. She opened it and lifted the pie out of it. Turning walked back to the table and placed the pie in front of Teddy saying, "Teddy, please cut the pie while I clear the dishes."

Jake did not ask, he stood and started piling the dishes saying, "I've got this." He walked over and put them on the end of the counter, he scraped them into the trash container and placed them in the wash sink.

Marian moved to the stove and after filling the tea pot at the sink, put it on the grill rack and turned on the gas to boil the water. Teddy had gotten up and gotten the tea cups, saucers and spoons and placed them on the table.

By the time the tea had seeped Jake had the dishes washed, rinsed and in the drying rack. He sat down just as Marian started putting the tea in each cup.

She placed the pot on a warmer plate and sat down saying, "We make quite a team, everything almost cleaned up and we still have desert to enjoy."

Teddy and Jake nodded, they did not reply because they had their mouths full of pie.

When they were on their second cup of tea Teddy looked at Jake and said, "Congratulations on your new position, or should I say additional position?"

"Both I guess. When Dr. Andrews called me in and he and Dr. Fox explained everything, I really did not know what to say. The whole thing really took me by surprise."

Teddy continued, "Well you have impressed a lot of people in a very short time and you and your friend Julian Brown have made a lot of people look very good, some across the state. I guess I can tell you what was told me earlier today, it is going to be on the morning news. The Sheriff is announcing that he is retiring do to health issues as of the end of the month. After all the positive coverage surrounding the drug bust that you and Julian completed, yet gave all of the accolades to others, is allowing him to exit on top. He is appointing the Undersheriff the acting Sheriff to finish his term of office."

Jake did not respond right away, he processed what he had just heard and the questions jumped out at him. "Well, I am very glad that he is going to be able to exit on a high note. I really don't know him, most of my involvement has been with the Undersheriff and I'm very happy for her also. Teddy if I may ask, how did you get all of this?"

Teddy sat back a little and looking directly in Jake's eyes replied, "The members of the Club are very involved in most of what happens in Augusta. There is not much that goes on without one of the members being involved in some way. That is about all I can say about that."

"Okay, I think I understand." Jake looked at Marian saying, "Once again I cannot thank you enough, everything was wonderful once again. If it is okay I'm going to go and put the finishing touches to a report I will be going over in the morning with Dr. Andrews."

Marian placed her hand on Jake's arm saying, "Of course, congratulations and thank you for all you do."

He gave her a hug and with a quick good bye was out the door.

★★★

Jake pulled into the parking lot of the Lab and parked in the space that had been marked with a white sign that just had his last name across it. It was next to the space marked Dr. Andrews, he looked at his sign and thought, "Didn't take Dr. Andrews very long to get that done." He locked the truck and entered the building and proceeded to the Lab. He unlocked the door and walked over to the Mass Spec and saw that the screen was flashing 'Done'. He walked over to his desk and sitting down pressed the keys and brought up the reports that he had programmed into the different equipment on Friday before he had left to meet Julian.

He worked on his findings and completed the reports that he would discuss during his meeting. He printed a hard copy of the three sets of findings that made up his completed report. Stacking all of the papers he put them in a manila folder, standing he put it under his arm and walked out of the Lab, locking it, and walked towards the break room for a cup of coffee.

Standing in front of the counter he placed the folder about three feet away from the cup he would be pouring his coffee into thinking, "No Monday morning snafus." He poured the coffee without any problems and with the cup in one hand and the folder in the other walked back towards Dr. Andrews' office.

Dr. Andrews saw him as he walked past the office window and waved him in to the office, he pointed at the chair that Jake had been sitting in on Friday.

Jake took a seat and placed his coffee on the floor and opened the folder saying, Morning Doc, hope the weekend was good."

"Yes, it was fine. What do you have?"

"Well, I've run three sets of tests. One set on the evidence that was collected from Elizabeth's remains, one on the Curare taken from our other case and one from the Cocaine recovered in the drug bust. I've taken the different evidence samples from the three cases to the molecular level and compared them against each other.

After doing that I've come up with the following conclusions.

First, after doing a detailed set of tests on her Cerumen, it proved without a doubt that Elizabeth was killed with an injection of Curare."

Dr. Andrews asked, "Ear wax?"

"Yes, it will give a lot of information if the correct tests are run. As you know it really isn't wax, it is viscous secretions from the sebaceous glands and the apocrine glands."

Dr. Andrews nodded agreement.

Jake continued, "The tests also prove that exactly the same Curare was used in both cases. There was a puncture just behind her left ear, at the time of death that area was covered by a bruise. At that the time the bruise was explained away as having occurred during her falling and hitting her head.

Second, on the molecular level I was able to prove the exact same water was used in making the Curare in both cases. Exactly the same water, one hundred percent positive test results."

"So, based on the findings, both subjects were killed by the same person using the same poison?"

"Yes, that is what the evidence is telling us."

The third set of tests that I performed on the Cocaine also proved that the plants and flowers that were used to make it grew in the same water as that used to make the Curare. This proves beyond any doubt that the deaths were directly connected to the drug trade. If we can find the Curare, we find the killer and provider of the drugs being distributed across the state."

"So we can safely inform Elizabeth's family that she was killed, also that the evidence collected during her exhumation has provided us with the proof to put her killer away for life. That evidence will also be used to cause damage to the illegal drug trade across the state. This saving lives of maybe hundreds of people?"

Jake realized that Dr. Andrews was trying to ease all of the pain Elizabeth's family had and still endures. He looked at Dr. Andrews and responded, "Yes Sir, I believe that would be the right thing to do. I think that you and the Undersheriff should provide that information to the family."

Dr. Andrews sat back in his chair and said, "Please send me all of the data on the tests and your report. I will be calling the Undersheriff now, Jake thank you."

Jake stood and said, "Doc, I'll get that information to you with in the next half hour." He turned and exited Dr. Andrews' office and walked back to the Lab thinking, "A certain Doctor will soon be getting his just rewards."

★★★

Master Sergeant Kareem Washington awoke from a fitful night of sleep that had been full of dreams and horrific events. All of them were just out of his full memory but he could almost feel them. He shook his head and walked into the latrine and splashed water on his face. The cool water somewhat cleared the thoughts from his mind, he dried his face and folded the towel and placed it on the rack, exactly in the center. He put on his cover and headed off to his duty station, he was responsible for the maintenance and operation of the helicopter known as Air Force One.

★★★

Dr. Andrews pushed the numbers and the Send button, and heard the phone on the other end click a few times and then the Undersheriff's voice came on the line saying, "Undersheriff Winslow."

"Kay, this is Claude Andrews, have a moment?"

"Of course," Even though she was up to her eyeballs in responding to the announcement by the Sheriff that he was retiring at the end of the month. "What can I do for you?"

"I need to talk to you about Elizabeth, Jake's report is finished. We just spent the last hour going over it, and we need to have a meeting with Elizabeth's family."

"I'll be in your office within the hour." The phone went dead.

★★★

On the other side of the country one Carmine Diaz, a known bulk only drug dealer, and the controller of SNAP Card fraud, across the entire state slept. He had been up for a 20 hour period overseeing a large transfer of a shipment from Mexico and was still in a deep drug induced sleep. He dreamed about killing, killing a Bitch for all the evil she had done and was still doing under the guise of helping his people. She was an important Congresswoman but she could be touched, greed always gave people a way of getting to you. This Bitch was not only greedy for money but more so for power. He sat up and said out loud to no one, "Today, today, Bitch, you die."

***

The Undersheriff pulled her car into the parking lot and parked next to Dr. Andrews' car, turning off her car she stepped out and pushed the button locking it. She walked into the building and walked directly to Dr. Andrews' office, entering she said, "Claude, I hope this is good news."

Dr. Andrews looked up saying, "Hello Kay, Yes it is. Please have a seat."

Once she was seated Dr. Andrews open one of the many files he had scattered across his desk. Picking up the first sheet of paper he looked at the Undersheriff saying, "Elizabeth was murdered, she was murdered with the same poison used in the previous case, exactly the same poison. From the evidence extracted during her exhumation there is proof that she was the victim of an attempted drug cover up. If any of the poison is found or recovered we can prove without any doubt that it is the same. The poison and the Cocaine were made using the same water supply. This has been proven with 100% reliability and with a 0% chance of being disputed in any case of law."

"Claude, this will give the Blanchard family closure, finally after all of this time. The family will be so relieved, so very relieved. Is there any way we can keep this out of the public eye to prevent the media from opening all of the old wounds?"

"Yes, Jake has a plan on how to use the information to insure a conviction but will limit the exposure."

She sat back and thought a moment, "Claude, I will contact the family and set up a meeting for us to meet with them. It will need to be Wednesday some time though,"

Dr, Andrews replied quickly, "Wednesday?"

"Yes. With all this stuff concerning the Sheriff, tomorrow is booked solid for me."

Dr. Andrews leaned forward a little saying, "I'm sorry I don't know what you are talking about"

"You did not hear the news this morning? The Sheriff has announced his retirement effective the last day of the month and recommended that I be made the acting Sheriff to finish his term."

Dr. Andrews looked a little befuddled for a moment hearing the news, he pushed back from his desk, stood and moved around it saying, "That is wonderful, congratulations." He put his arm around her continuing with, "That is going to be fantastic for everyone in this City and County."

"Thank you, I did not know how you would react to the news, I know you and the Sheriff have been friends for a long time."

'Well, we have been acquaintances for a long time, friends, not so much. You will have my total support and I'm sure that of the County Coroner as well."

"Thank you, I've got to leave but I will call about the meeting, again thank you. Please give my thanks to Jake also."

★★★

The traffic all over the city was snarled and bumper to bumper, horns blared and tempers flared. The George Washington Bridge is down to one level and the Cross Bronx was still under construction. The rush hour was far from being that, a rush hour, it was more like a wait hour, over the entire city.

Minister Kareem Jackson looked out the window of his parish hall, on the corner of Edgewater Avenue and 149th Street, at Jackie Robinson Park. He watched a few young men playing basket ball and two others playing catch. He wondered if he would be here much longer, the building needed to be repaired in so many ways. He was now having almost daily visits from the different city inspectors informing him that the violations were adding up. He also knew that the 'Improve the plight of Blacks' group was pressuring the city to close him down, knowing that it would almost surely force him to sell the building to them. They had been buying everything up under the guise of helping the people of color while fattening their wallets.

He turned towards the sound of someone knocking on his rear door that headed to the alley that ran on the right side of the building. He opened the door and found the postman standing there with a stack of envelopes and a few boxes.

The postman said, "Hey Padre, sorry about the back door, but I was on the other side of the alley and you're the only one with anything on this side. It saves me the hassle of getting on 149th Street."

Taking the boxes and other mail replied, "No problem Jerry. Thanks."

He watched as Jerry walked back down the alley and closed the door when he turned out of site, then walked to his office. Once there he sat at his desk and leafed through the envelopes not opening any of them. He looked at the boxes and knew what was in two of the three boxes. He picked up the third and saw a 'J' in the return address block and started to laugh thinking, "My man Jake, said he would be watching out for me, yes he did.

He thought about his meetings with Jake, there were five of six of them. Each one after something went bad in the neighbor hood, a robbery, fight, a shooting, anything bad. Always had a plan, always, and they always worked, cleaned up the neighborhood and made people feel good about the place. He opened the box and stood there staring at the pile of money and the note. "Jackson, don't let them win, 'J'."

He grinned thinking, "No Sir, they ain't winning."

★★★

Jake's phone beeped, he took it from the holder on his hip and pushed the Call button saying, "Smith" without looking at the display.

"Hey Smith, how busy are you?"

Jake smiled, it was Janet. He replied, "Not too busy to talk to you, something I didn't do?"

Janet laughed saying, "Nothing I can think of, are you busy for lunch?"

"No plans, what are you thinking?"

"We've got some really good Meatball Parmesan sandwiches for lunch, and I can join you anytime after 1:00 o'clock. The lunch crowd will be mostly gone by then."

"Well, I think you need to set a few of those sandwiches aside for us, I'll see you at 1:00."

"Great, see you then, miss you."

The phone went dead.

Jake grinned and put the phone back in the holder and thought, "Damn, I need to be very careful. Janet is the first lady, I've let get close in twenty years, damn, very careful."

***

Jake placed the evidence containers back into the evidence cabinet and locked the doors. He walked over to the Mass Spectrometer and slid the samples in the holders, with that done walked back to his desk and sat in front of his PC. He programmed the tests he wanted run and set all of the parameters. He knew it would take an hour and a half for the tests to run, time for lunch. He secured the lab and headed for his truck.

***

Janet and Jake were finishing their sandwiches and just chatting when the TV on the wall flashed and beeped loudly.

'Bulletin,' 'Bulletin,' Bulletin,' flashed across the screen. The commentator began to speak, "The following report is of ultimate importance. The President and his family have been killed in a crash of the Presidential Helicopter Air Force One. The Vice President has been rushed to the Whitehouse under very heavy security. Please stand by we will announce further developments as they come forth."

Janet looked at Jake with shock on her face saying, "My God, the President and his whole family. Do you think it was an assassination?"

Jake replied, "I don't know, they did not give enough information to make any assumptions. We will have to wait for more information."

Tony came out of the kitchen with a dazed look on his face saying, "My God, My God, This is so much worse than Kennedy, so much worse." He walked to the front door and turned the Open/Closed sign to Closed. Walking back he stopped and looking at Janet said, "We need to clean up, I need to close and get home to the family."

Janet slid out of the booth and leaned over and kissed Jake on the cheek saying, "I'll call when I finish here."

★★★

The TV flashed and blared, 'Alert, Alert, Alert.'
The talking head on the TV came back on with a camera shot sweeping across the wreckage and

destruction left by the helicopter's falling to the ground. He was saying, "Air Force One, the President's helicopter had hit and crashed between two homes and exploded, and resulting fire, had set both homes on fire. There were three people in the homes injured by the fire and flying debris, all serious enough to be hospitalized. Federal Investigators have sealed off a two block area and are sweeping for evidence and any parts of the helicopter. It appears that the crash was caused by a mechanical malfunction. We repeat, the crash of the President's helicopter appears to be from a mechanical malfunction. We will be back as soon as we have additional information."

***

Turning away from the TV they looked back at each other, and Jake said in response to Janet's comment, "Sounds good, I need to get back to the Lab, this might turn out to be a even worse emergency, let's hope no one takes credit for causing this. If that happens, all hell is going to break out." He walked to the front door and pulled it open, pushing the lock button as he closed it behind him.

It took him less then fifteen minutes to get to the Lab, and entering the building, he found everyone standing in small groups, by the TV's that were scattered around the building talking in low tones.

Jake hurried to Dr. Andrews' office and found him on the phone, seeing Jake pass the window Dr, Andrews waved at Jake to enter.

Jake stood in front of Dr. Andrews' desk waiting for him to finish his call.

Dr. Andrews placed the phone down and looked at Jake saying, "Don't take this wrong, but Thank God it appears the crash was caused by an equipment failure and not a person or group. Had it been a person or group there would be riots in the streets in every city in this country. As it is, there is still unrest and the massing of crowds of people in the streets, one small spark and this will explode into blood in the streets. We need to be on constant vigil, it could go bad at any moment."

"Yes Sir, should we all stay here?"

"No, it might be better if we were not all in one place. Keep your phone handy. Give Commander Brown a call and see if all is well."

"Commander Bro...., Julian, yes Sir." Once he stepped into the hall he pushed the button on his phone to connect to Julian.

"Brown."

"Julian, Jake, we are all heading home, the thought is it will be better if we are dispersed instead of in one central place."

"Good idea, we have every available officer on duty, moving around but keeping a low profile. Don't want anyone thinking we are pushing, this could get out of hand very quickly."

"I agree. Any place you need me to be?"

Somewhere close to downtown, but not downtown. Does that make sense?"

"Yes, I'll be five minutes away."

"Thanks, hope we don't need to move on this."

"Me to, I'll be in touch."

Jake locked up the Lab and while walking out to the truck got a call from Janet.

"Hey."

"I'm off and heading home."

"Okay if I join you? Julian would like me to stay close."

"That works for me. I was wondering how I'd get you back to my house."

"Hah, like that would be hard to do. I'm sure a simple 'Come on over' would work quite well."

With a laugh Janet replied, "I guess. I'll see you there in a bit."

Jake grinned saying, "See you in ten minutes."

Jake pulled into the driveway and was not surprised to see Janet's car. He pulled next to it, putting the car in Park and turning it off, he got out and walked up to the door.

Janet opened the door before he could knock, or ring the bell, she put her arms around his neck and gave him a big kiss. She stepped back saying, "We have all afternoon to be together."

Jake grinned replying, "Yes, unless something happens."

She took her hands from around his neck and grabbed his hands pulled him into the cottage saying, "Time is a-wasting."

At three ten Jake's phone started vibrate, and chirp. He said, "Work" as he picked it up, He pushed the Call button saying, "Jake."

"Jake, this is Kay Winslow I need you to be in my office at four sharp."

"I will be there. Do I need to bring anything?"

"Just your memory," The phone went dead.

He placed the phone back on the table and turning towards Janet said, "I've got to leave at three thirty. I have a meeting with the Undersheriff, soon to be Sheriff, at four."

Janet put a frown on her face saying, "Darn."

★★★

The Undersheriff had called for a meeting in her office at four o'clock sharp. She had called Julian, Jake, Dr. Andrews, and the SWAT Commander requesting their presence. It was three forty and they were assembling in the lobby, Jake and Julian were surprised to see the SWAT Commander there. Dr. Andrews walked into the lobby and did not hesitate, or say anything to anyone. He nodded towards them but continued towards the Undersheriff's office, and the others followed without saying anything.

The door was open to the office and Dr. Andrews walked in and took the seat directly in front of it. The others entered and stood around him facing the desk and the Undersheriff.

"Kay, we are all here."

She looked at him and then at each of them before replying, "Sergeant King, what is the status on the streets?"

"We have every officer on the street, walking two block cross patterns, we have them walking alone so it does not look like we are taken over. There are large groups of people at most of the intersections. They are milling around a lot but there hasn't been any violent incidents reported. We are doing everything to prevent any of our actions from being misinterpreted and causing a riot."

"Please keep a constant and open display of officers on the streets for the rest of today and all night. Thank you. Please let me know if anything occurs, anything."

King replied, "Yes, Undersheriff." He turned and walked out of the room.

The Undersheriff looked at Dr. Andrews, Jake, and Julian saying, "Thank you for allowing me to use you all a bit. Sergeant King now feels that he and all of his people are special, being I spent my time first with him and his challenge today."

Everyone nodded their understanding.

The Undersheriff sat in her chair and continued, "The events that have occurred will have this country in turmoil for at least three to four weeks. Every Law Enforcement Agency in the country will be on high alert for at least a month. We will also be on high alert for that time. The fear is that the entire country will be dealing with race riots and violence. But that is not what I called you all here to discuss. Not knowing what was going to happen today I made an appointment yesterday to meet with the Blanchard Family today. I would like to keep that appointment, they have asked for all of you to be there."

Dr. Andrews leaned forward in his chair and replied, "I think that we need to do that also, as bad as the events of today are there is very little that we can do that we are not now doing."

Jake and Julian nodded their agreement.

The Undersheriff stood and said, "We can go in my car, Julian will you drive?"

He nodded yes.

They all followed the Undersheriff out of the building to her car. The Undersheriff and Julian got into the front seats and Jake and Dr. Andrews got in the back. The Undersheriff looked at Julian saying, "The meeting is at the Club."

Julian pulled out of the lot and headed to the Club, when he pulled into the Club's drive the security guard stepped in front of the car.

Julian stopped and pushed the button to open his window.

The guard then walked around to the driver's window. Once it was down the security guard looked into the car and seeing the Undersheriff said, "They are waiting for you all in the grillroom Ms. Winslow."

She looked at him saying, "Thank you."

The guard stepped back and waved Julian forward.

Julian drove down the drive and pulled into the parking lot just to the right of the main entrance and parked in the first space.

Once they all got out of the car they moved towards the front door. It was opened and one of the staff welcomed them and looking at the Undersheriff saying, "The Blanchard's are in the small library on the second floor, please follow me."

They followed through the foyer and across the hall to the stairway that led upstairs. The climbed the stairs and were led down the hall to the left and through the duel open doors into the library.

The Blanchard family, father, mother, and two adult children, were all sitting at the main table, that took up the middle of the room. Tommy stood and moved over to Kay and said, "Thank you for coming. We would have understood if you rescheduled with all that is going on."

"No Tommy, you all have waited long enough for the truth about Elizabeth."

Tommy moved back to his seat and waved them to the open chairs saying. "Please take a seat."

In a few moments they all were seated and Kay said, "Dr. Andrews will you please give the results of the findings of your office please."

Dr. Andrews looked around and said, "First I would like to introduce the young man that made all of this possible." Pointing at Jake he continued saying, "This is Kenneth 'Jake' Smith. He is the Lab Manager and the Assistant County Medical Examiner. It was at his request that we asked for your permission to exhume Elizabeth and his findings that have giving us the truth. The findings are as follows."

He opened the file he carried and read the findings, conclusions and facts about Elizabeth's death.

He talked about fifteen minutes without a sound in the room. Once he paused and closed the file, each of the Blanchard family thanked him and sat again still and silent. Tommy looked from one to the other and then back to Jake and Julian saying, "You have done this family a great service, one that will not be forgotten, nor go unrewarded."

Jake replied quickly saying, "There is nothing that needs to be rewarded Sir, just knowing that you and your family now know the truth is reward enough."

Julian continued with, "That is correct we did what we are paid to do, and are glad that we now have the means to do it better."

Tommy looked at them and said, "Well, thank you, you have brought us closure on something that is very important to us. Now please join us in the grillroom for some refreshments."

The Undersheriff started to protest but Tommy stood saying, "We will not take no for an answer, please. He waved his hand towards the door, and his family stood and started out the door talking softly amongst themselves.

The Undersheriff stood and kind of shrugged her shoulders as if to say, "Oh well." She moved towards the door with Dr. Andrews next to her.

Jake reached out and touched Dr. Andrews sleeve asking, "Restroom?"

"Once we are down stairs we will go to the right that leads to the grill room. If you turn left the rest room will be the second door on your right."

Jake nodded saying, "Thank you."

When they reached the bottom of the stairs they all went right, Jake turned left and walked to the restroom. The others walked into the Grill room and there was a table set for them and each took a seat. The server asked each for their drink preference and was gone.

Tommy looked at the group saying, "Dr. Andrews, "I would like you, Jake and Julian to be my guests here at the club Sunday. Please let me know if that works for all of you, I realize that the current events have put a burden on everyone, all the more reason to relax a little when one can."

★★★

Jake opened the door and stepped in to the men's restroom and he walked to the first stall, entered and locked the door. He heard someone entering and he swore that it was Teddy's voice he heard saying in the Old Tongue, "Blood Bound, Sir Knight." The Other voice repeated in the Old Tongue, "Blood Bound, Sir Knight."

The two voices then started to talk about the day's events.

Jake froze, "That was the end of the Knights of Templar greeting when one met another."

It was something he had learned many years ago, and the person he had learned it from had told him it while on his death bed. He revealed that he was a Knight Templar, Sr. Eric of Garth, and swore Jake to an oath, the oath of a serf to a Knight, on his life, to share a message that he also told him in detail, to any other Knight Templar that he should ever meet.

"What did he step into," he thought. He stood still and it was only a few moments when the voices faded as they moved out of the room through what must have been a second door. Jake finished and walked out into the room. He looked around and saw no second door in the direction that the voices had gone, "Strange" he thought.

He left the room and walked back the way he had come thinking about the Greeting. The greeting shared for over 900 years when any members of the Knights of Templar met.

"The Cross is covered with Blood."

"So it is, the Cross is covered with blood, in the caverns so deep."

"The cavern walls are seeping the blood of our Brother Knights, those lost protecting the Cross."

"Blood let for the Cross, Sir Knight, now and forever."

"As well it should be, now, and forever, Sir Knight."

"I stand and fight for the Cross at all costs."

"We, The Brotherhood of the Knights of Templar, stand and fight for the Cross at all costs."

"Blood Bound, Sir Knight."

"Blood Bound, Sir Knight."

He turned at the stairs and walked into the grillroom and to the open seat at the table everyone was sitting.

There were no other Members or guests in the room. He took his seat and it was almost like magic, a server appeared and was asking what he would like. He ordered some sweet tea and the lunch special, he did not know what it was but he was sure it would be great. It seemed like a second had passed when the tea was placed in front of him.

Everyone was chatting softly about this or that about the events of the day, Julian nudged Jake and leaned closer saying, "We have been invited to play with Tommy this Sunday, breakfast at eight thirty and tee time when we are ready. You up for that my friend?"

Just then the server brought out their food and placed the plates in front of each of them. The food smelled wonderful and Kay said, "Well the food has not gotten anything but better, and that is saying a lot." She looked at everyone saying, "The kitchen was always a five star, now it is even better."

Everyone nodded agreement and were quietly eating their meals.

Jake looked at Julian and after a moment replied, "That sounds good to me, I have to go buy some clubs, a bag, balls, tees. You know, golf stuff and I can make that happen tonight."

Julian grinned and looking across at Tommy Blanchard saying, "Sunday would be good for both of us, if that offer is still open."

"Of course, I'm looking forward to it. We will meet here in the Grill Room at eight thirty you can use my locker in the locker room. I'll have them make space so you are not cramped, just ask for Blue when you get here. I'll let them know to expect you both."

Tommy looked at Dr. Andrews, "Doctor?"

Dr. Andrews grinned, saying, "Thank you, maybe the next time."

He looked at Kay and added, "Kay, You are also invited if you would like to play. I remember when you used to beat me on a regular basis."

Kay laughed a little and replied, "Thank you Tommy but I'll pass, I have some things that I've promised my children that I would do with them."

"That is someone with their priorities in order." Tommy looked at his wife saying, "Something I needed to do more of. Right my Dear?"

"She smiled replying, "A few years ago, Yes, Sometimes it would have been better Tommy, sometimes."

Kay looked around the table saying, "We really need to go. Thank you for the time and your hospitality Tommy. They all exchanged thank you's and good bye's and the four of them walked out to the car.

CHAPTER FOURTEEN

THE CONGRESSWOMAN AND HER HUSBAND got into the back of their limousine, and once seated she picked up the phone and beeped the driver.

He picked up the phone saying, "Yes Congresswoman."

"You need to stop by the Support for Mexican Americans March at the Civic Center before heading for the airport."

"Yes, Congresswoman, Do you want me to contact your security and let them know?"

"No. They'll find us at the airport."

"Yes Congresswoman." He started the engine and pulled out of the driveway.

She turned to her husband saying, "No reason we can't stop for a few moments, I can get some good publicity and also pick up a gift from the Chairman of my re-election campaign. He has a check for the balance that was left after paying for the re-election bills, three million, seven hundred thousand and change. Security doesn't need to see that."

He just smiled.

It took about twenty minutes to get to the Civic Center and he pulled up to the crowd at the front entrance. The crowd parted leaving a wide path to the doors.

The driver got out and walked around to the passenger side rear door and opened it for the Congresswoman.

She got out followed by her husband. They both turned and waved at the crowd as her Campaign Chairman walked towards them from the front of the building. He had just reached them when the glass entrance doors exploded from gunfire. The four of them were hit with almost too many hits to count. The impact of the bullets pushed the Chairman and Congresswoman into her husband and the Driver. The rain of bullets continued, now striking the people in the crowd randomly. The sidewalk was covered with dark red pools of blood and the limousine was riddled with over two hundred bullet holes and splattered with blood.

Carmine Diaz and three of his enforcers stepped through the broken glass still firing the automatic weapons. The same weapons he had bought from the US Agents in Mexico just months before.

The car full of the Congresswoman's Security Guards slid to a stop behind the Limousine, The Guards were cut down before they got a shot off, they and the car were hit by over a hundred bullets in just seconds. The sound of sirens could be heard getting closer.

Carmine Diaz raised his hand saying loudly, "We go." The four of them jogged around the corner of the building into the parking lot. They climbed into the Tahoe that was waiting for them. In just moments they were out of site, before the police ever reached the massacre.

There were thirty four people killed, twelve wounded and out of all of the remaining hundred people that were there, when asked about the events their responses were all the same, no one saw anything.

It was less then fifteen minutes from the event happening before live streaming of the death and devastation was being shown on every TV, PC and Tablet screen across the Nation. The TV stations switched back and forth from coverage of the President and his family's death, and the massacre of the Congresswoman, her husband, Election Campaign Chairman, four Security Guards and thirty four citizens.

★★★

Jake and Janet were walking out of Everything Sports at the mall when his phone started to vibrate and beep. He set the golf bag down and pulled the phone out of the holder. He pushed the Call button saying, "Julian."

"Jake, have you heard about California?"

"No, been in a store at the mall for about a half hour."

"There had been a massacre, Congresswoman and forty people killed. The weapons used are from that Fast and Furious crap in Mexico."

"Do we need to come back in?"

"No, just wanted to let you know so you can be a little more careful, if that is possible."

"Thanks, I'm headed someplace off the grid, no use taking any chances, any spark is going to grow into something we don't need."

"Yep, I'll call if there is anything happening." The phone went dead.

Jake put his phone back into the holder and picked up the golf bag and looking at Janet said, "Well looks like you get to eat some of my cooking tonight. Anything special you would like?"

She grinned replying, "Nope, surprise me."

"Thanks." He opened the rear door of the truck and placed the golf bag and the bag he was also carrying on the seat. Janet opened the other door and placed the two bags she was carrying on the seat also. She closed the rear door and opened the front and got in. Jake slid into the driver's seat and started the truck, looking at Janet said, "I'm going to stop at the food store, do you mind waiting in the truck? Have too much stuff in here, all in the open."

Janet slid close replying, "Not at all, just don't be gone too long."

Jake laughed and pulled out of the parking space.

"What was the call about? Sounded important,"

Jake glanced at her saying, "More bad news, figured we would see the details on the news when we got to the house."

"Okay, I can always wait to get bad news."

★★★

Jake pulled into the driveway and pulled up in front of his garage, he and Janet got out and he opened the door to his place. They put all of the bags of stuff he had purchased on the steps and then he opened the garage door and pulled the truck in. He closed the door and joined Janet at the foot of the stairs. He picked up three of the bags and the golf bag and headed up the stairs. Janet picked up the remaining bags and followed him.

Jake placed the bags with the food items he had just bought on the counter and the other on the floor. He turned and took the bags from Janet and placed them on the counter also. He put his arm around her waist and pointed to the flat screen TV saying, "This is the living room," he turned back to the counter saying, "The kitchen," turned halfway to the stairs and pointed at the two doors in the hall saying, "bathroom and bedroom."

She moved out of his arm and over to the counter and started to take the items out of the bags. He stepped next to her saying, "Nope, you need to go sit in the living room and take control of the TV so we can see what is new on the events of today."

She leaned over and kissed him on the cheek saying, "Yes sir."

She walked into the living area and sat in front of the TV. She picked up the remote and turned the TV on. The screen was filled with the image of dead bodies and pools of blood. There was a small photo of the Congresswoman in the corner of the screen and the talking head was saying something about a check made out to the Congresswoman, for over three million dollars, being found at the scene.

The screen flickered, and the devastation of the crash scene of Air Force One and the damage it caused flashed on the screen. The talking head was saying that the failed part from the engine that caused the crash was found. The country was in mourning, the deaths on each coast affected everyone.

The fact that both tragedies were directly caused by the government itself, was being exploited by the US News Media, and the Foreign News agencies as well. Maintenance cuts due to budget reductions and selling of arms to our enemies and lack of drug enforcement the key subjects of discussion.

Janet stared at the screen saying almost to herself, "How awful, all those people dead, and the President and his family dead."

Jake was putting the two peppers and two onions, he had cleaned and sliced, into a Dutch Oven where he had also put six tablespoons of olive oil, one tablespoon of garlic, one teaspoon of dried oregano, and a pinch of salt and pepper. He had hand rubbed the oregano over the Dutch oven releasing the flavor. He also had two lengths of sweet Italian sausage frying in a pan with olive oil. He had two hard crusted sub rolls to complete the sandwiches. He looked up and replied, "Just so long as no one takes credit and causes a country wide riot."

Janet stood and walked back into the kitchen area saying, "Wow, something smells great."

Jake smiled saying, "There are a few beers in the refrigerator and a pack of diet Pepsi. If you would get them out please, I'll have a Pepsi."

Janet turned and opened the refrigerator and took out two Pepsi's and placed them on the counter. She opened one of the cabinets and found glasses, she placed two of them on the counter and opened the freezer and put ice in each. She popped the tabs and poured the Pepsi into the glasses, over the ice.

Jake put the sausage, peppers and onions on the rolls and placed the sandwiches on plates next to some Potato Chips.

He picked up the plates and Janet picked up the glasses, they walked into the living room and placed the plates and glasses on the end table between the chairs.

They sat in the chairs and started eating as they watched the events unfold on the TV Screen.

Jake sat looking at the screen, but his mind was thousands of miles away in California reading and writing in Carmine Diaz's mind. The day's death toll was not over yet, not yet. He scanned for a few moments more, and found who he was looking for, he put the thoughts he needed, where he needed too.

★★★

Carmine Diaz carried the weapons out to his car and placed them on the rear seat next to the box of ammo. He was going to meet the biggest drug supplier on the West Coast. He had sixty million dollars in gold in the trunk of the modified SUV, to be traded for a sixty foot box truck full of uncut marijuana with a street value of over one hundred fifty million dollars. He had seven of his best men going on the buy to protect him and his sixty million in gold. He guessed there would be at least five of six with El Loco Grande and all would be heavily armed. He was sure the plan was to just kill him and his men and take the gold and drugs. A win, win!

This was to be his biggest score of the year, of the year! He would double his yearly take with this one buy, double it. He had set up the buy quickly, for it had to occur this evening, he knew that all of the law enforcement personnel in the state would be involved with security. The earlier events insured that.

His phone barked, he pushed the Call button saying, "When."

The voice on the other end said, "One hour, state park thirty miles out on Fifteen East."

He put the phone down and walked over to the door to the garage, he opened it and yelled to the men playing cards. "Let's roll, carry all the heat you got."

He turned and walked back out to the car and got in the front passenger seat, he checked the sawed off shotgun and was satisfied with the seven double buck shot loads. He checked his forty five and the two extra magazines, loaded and ready. Carr opened the driver's door and got in saying, "Where we going Boss?"

"Just drive out on Fifteen East."

"Yes sir," he started the car when the other two men got in the back seat and pulled out into traffic. In five minutes he was on Fifteen rolling east at Seventy miles an hour.

Carmine said, "Keep it under sixty five the limit is sixty. We don't need to get pulled over Asshole."

"Right, Boss."

Carmine looked out the rear window and the second car was right behind them, the driver was keeping four to five car lengths between them.

They were about twenty miles out on fifteen and the traffic had disappeared. This pleased Carmine, no cars, no witnesses.

El Loco Grande had his driver pull behind the body of the parked truck making the car invisible from the road. He had six of his other men spread out hidden with automatic weapons watching and ready to do whatever had to be done. His other car was four miles down the road watching for the buyer. They would follow and kill all with the buyer, once he had possession of the gold.

Carmine saw the car parked on the side of the road with one person sitting in the driver's seat with a cell phone to his ear. He pushed the Call button on his phone and when it was answered he said, "Plan dose."

The turn off for the State Park was coming up and his driver slowed with his directional signal on. The second car pulled into the right lane and kept going till it was out of sight. His driver said, "They pulled onto the road and are coming up slow." Carmine just nodded. The driver pulled into the Park and after going just a few hundred feet pulled into an open field.

Carmine saw the truck and told his driver to pull up in front of it. He saw the car parked behind the truck, he pulled the slide on his gun checking the load in the breech. A second car pulled in behind his and six men got out. El Loco Grande got out of the car and so did Carmine. They walked towards each other and El Loco Grande waved his arm and all of his men came out of hiding and began to walk towards the cars. There were now eleven armed men against Carmine and his three men.

Carmine spoke first saying, "Ah my friend, I see you are still concerned about security. That is good, I also have concerns. That is why I have all of us covered by automatic weapons at this very moment. If I die, we all will die."

El Loco Grande turned almost a complete circle and saw the men in the woods with heavy automatic weapons. He smiled at Carmine and walked closer with his hand out stretched saying, "My friend, here are the keys to the truck, we move the gold and I will be gone."

Carmine stepped to the back of his SUV and opened the trunk, he pointed in it saying, "Have your men move the gold, I will have one of mine check the truck. Okay?"

El Loco Grande replied, "Of course, of course."

The men all started to perform the work to move the gold and check the trucks contents.

There was a sudden humming sound and out of nowhere a large black helicopter appeared and the mini guns on both sides of the chopper exploded with rapid fire. Every square inch of a five hundred by five hundred foot area was hit with a bullet in less than two minutes. Nineteen dead in one sweep, the chopper dropped closer to the ground, the rear door of the chopper opened and four men dropped to the ground and ran to the SUV. The chopper set down and six more men got out and in less than ten minutes the gold was loaded and secured. The chopper lifted off, and hovered about one hundred feet above the truck for a moment before both mini guns opened fire, a full minute burst, the truck's fuel ignited. The box trailer's aluminum walls and ceiling was shred into hundreds of small scraps of metal. The fire spread quickly enveloping the drugs and a large plume of gray smoke spiraled upward.

The chopper turned and was gone. The smoke from the burning truck would get someone's attention, sooner or later.

★★★

"Jake, Jake are you okay?" Janet had her hand on his arm.

"Sure, sorry just zoned out in thought."

"Well, I don't know what you were zoned in on but from the expression on your face, well, it did not look good."

Jake reached across and gently pulled her across to his seat saying, "Well it is time to make up for ignoring you."

Janet moved over onto his lap and put her arms around his neck saying, "What a wonderful idea,"

★★★

The TV flashed, 'Bulletin.' 'Bulletin,' 'Bulletin.'

Jake looked at the screen as photos streamed by of a field and the remains of cars, people and the burned out shell of a large truck. The talking head was saying, "The bodies of nineteen men have been recovered. The bodies are riddled with gun shots, at least twenty wounds each. The burning shell behind me is what is left of over one hundred and sixty million dollars of illicit drugs. There is no trace of who, how, or what caused this devastation. The weapons found at this site have been tied to the massacre that occurred earlier today involving the Congresswoman and her party. These are the same weapons sold by US Border Agents to Mexican Drug Cartels in the FAST and FURIOUS Scandal.

Janet said almost to herself, "Nineteen more dead, this is a day that will be remembered for a long time."

Jake looked at her replying, "Yes, but will anyone learn from it?"

She just shook her head from side to side acknowledging the negative.

They both turned towards the beep from the security flat screen hanging by the stairs.

Jake lifted Janet up and placed her in the other chair as he got up saying, "Coming."

He walked over to the screen and saw Marian standing in front of his door. He pushed the button unlocking the door while saying, "Marian, please come in."

Marian opened the door and stepped into the entrance area. She looked up at Jake and said, "Jake, I've made some Apple Pies and Teddy and I were wondering if you would like to join us for tea and pie?"

At that moment Janet walked up next to Jake and looking down at Marian saying, "Hello."

Marian smiled replying, "Hello," looking back at Jake she continued with, "Of course that invitation also includes your friend."

Jake looked at Janet and back at Marian saying, "Sounds good, about ten minutes okay?"

"That will be wonderful, see you in a bit," with that Marian turned and moved out the door.

Janet looked at Jake saying, "What do you think?"

"I think we are going to have some of the best Apple Pie in Augusta, and you are about to be introduced to two wonderful people that have made my life a bit easier and are concerned about me." Stepping away towards the bedroom continued with, "Hope you make the grade." He ducked out of the way of Janet's hand as she tried to hit his arm saying, "Make the grade, Why you, you …."

He turned and scooped her into his arms pinning her arms and kissed her saying, "Well, I am quite a catch."

She laughed, kissing him and saying, "Well yes you are, but so am I."

Giving her a slight squeeze said, "You are very correct, on both counts."

She pulled her arms free and wrapped them around his neck pulling him close and gave him a long kiss which he returned.

She laughed saying, "The ten minutes is almost up."

Jake grinned, saying, "Lucky for you."

"Maybe, but maybe not, we'll see a little later."

"Promise?"

"Promise!"

They both laughed and turned towards the stairs, a few moments later they were walking into Marian's kitchen.

As they walked in Teddy and Marian were sitting at the table, they stood up as Jake and Janet walked towards them. Jake looked at Marian first saying, "Marian this is my special friend Janet. Janet this is my dear friend Marian and turning towards Teddy continued with, "and her Husband Teddy, who is also my dear friend."

Janet gave each a hug saying, "Jake has told me a lot about both of you, you both are very special to him."

Marian beamed a bit saying, "Please take a seat." Looking at Janet continued saying, "Is tea okay? I can make some coffee if you would prefer that instead."

"Oh tea is perfect, thank you. Is there anything I can help you with?"

"No, no, I've got it. Jake bring Janet into the sunroom, we'll have tea in there."

"Yes, Marian," he looked at Teddy saying, "We'll follow you."

Teddy grinned and moved across the floor towards the door to the sunroom. Jake and Janet followed and Janet seeing the room said, "Oh, I love this room, it's perfect."

Almost in unison Teddy, and Marian from the kitchen, replied, "Thank you, we love it also."

Janet turned and moved back into the kitchen saying, "There must be something I can do to help."

Teddy and Jake took seats and hearing the two women chatting looked at Jake saying, "Marian's sold and so am I. Jake she seems like a very, very nice young woman."

"Thanks, I think so also."

"So are we still on for Saturday morning?"

"We sure are, barring any more unexpected events that is. Julian and Kay are doing everything they can to keep everyone from over reacting. The people on the streets seem to be looking for something to light the fuse."

"It's a shame that the country needs to walk on eggshells just to appease fifteen percent of the people. And what makes it worst is it's the same fifteen percent that costs over sixty percent of the public funds to support them. Oh well, I'm looking to be on the river about nine tomorrow. I'm really looking forward to it. It's been awhile."

Jake looked at him for a second before replying, "That sounds fine, I'll be talking to Julian a little later, if anything changes I'll give you a call."

"That is great."

Marian and Janet had walked in and taken a seat and she said, "Jake, I hope you and Julian are as ready as Teddy is for this day of fishing. He had been in that boat house more in the last two weeks than he has been in the past three years. He and I have been to the store a few times just to get the needed cooking items needed to fry up the Bream and Red Bellies that you are going to catch. Teddy has convinced me that you will be catching enough to feed the eight of us twice."

Jake grinned, replying, "Eight?"

Marian smiled saying, "Eight, Teddy, Me, You and Janet, and Julian and his friend Martha and Paige and her friend Charlie. Teddy and I met them during the Taste of Augusta, at their booth for Kid's Care. They are very nice, and caring, young women that are truly trying to make things better. Janet and I were discussing Saturday in the kitchen and she agreed to call them and invite them to join us. Teddy, I've also asked Janet to pass an invitation to Paige's friend Charlie to join you fishing. I hope that is okay?"

"Of course, wow, that gives me a reason to use the big boat, that's great." He looked at Jake continuing with, "Hope they will be making power tomorrow, if not there will not be enough water to get into a few great spots. I'll have to make a few calls and see." Teddy was referring to the Power Company generating electricity, when they did make power, the lower river basin's level goes up about eighteen to twenty four inches.

Janet passed the cups of tea around and Marian passed a plate with a slice of her Apple Pie on it and a napkin to each.

They all sat quietly enjoying the tea and pie watching the river flow by, with the occasional boat or log bobbing in the current.

Jake sat there with Janet's hand in his, but his mind was thousands of miles away, deep in two minds, switching between the two. He stayed in contact for over fifty minutes, sculpturing future events.

★★★

Tyrone looked across the desk at Dr. Greenly with a look that expressed his dissatisfaction and contempt. "Okay, what is the deal? When is this all going to happen?"

"It is going to happen in two weeks. With all that has happened our friends want to wait until the President's funeral, and all of the fallout, is over. We will be meeting at the old Wilson Farm you know the place where we have been storing the materials to make and cut the drugs. It's in the middle of nowhere and safe and we have night access to the Jenkins's County Airfield that is only a few minutes from the farm."

"All that sounds good, I guess. What are our numbers?"

"We deliver sixty million in cash and they deliver sixty million of raw cocaine. That we convert and cut threefold, and then we sell it for at least one hundred ninety million dollars on the street. That my Friend is a Hundred and thirty million dollar profit in three to six weeks."

"Six weeks? We have never moved that much stuff in six weeks."

"We will this time, I've been in contact with people in Alabama and South Carolina, they will be buying fifty million each the first week,"

"Alabama and South Carolina, you sure we are covered? The word on the street is that they both are pretty fucked up operations."

"We're good I tell you, it will be cash up front. We're covered I tell you, covered."

"We better be!"

***

Jake and Janet had walked back to his place and were sitting at the kitchen counter having a glass of ice tea. Jake was on the phone with Julian and they were discussing all that was going on around the city.

Janet was on the phone with Martha discussing the events for Saturday and discussing Paige and Charlie. Martha was sure that they could make it.

Julian said, "All was quiet for the most part but we still have a very large police presence on the streets. We don't have more than two officers together but there are six officers on any three blocks in any direction of downtown."

"Well that should work but you will not be able to keep that up for too long."

"True, but we need to make sure we get to Monday without something blowing up."

Jake agreed, and then he told Julian that he would have breakfast on the counter at seven thirty and not to be late. "Breakfast at seven forty five, and we will be on the river at nine. The fish will be waiting."

Julian laughed replying, "In fear, total fear. See you in the morning."

"See you."

Janet was finishing her call with Martha and when she was finished Jake handed her a second glass of tea saying, "I need to walk down to the boathouse in a bit. I'd like to pick out the rod and reel that I'll be using tomorrow."

"Okay if I join you?"

"Of course you can."

They sat for awhile quietly both in their own thoughts and Jake finished his drink and stood and walked to the sink. He washed the glass and placed it on the drain rack that sat next to the sink. Janet stepped next to him and placed her glass in the sink. Jake picked it up and washed and rinsed it. He placed it next to his and turned towards Janet and put his arm around her waist saying, "Share and share alike."

She reached up and kissed him on the cheek saying, "Always, now, about selecting that rod and reel for tomorrow."

He put his arm around her and turned towards the stairs saying, "We are off to the boathouse."

They walked down the path and in a few moments they were at the door to the boathouse.

Jake stood in front of the pushbutton keypad and punched in 20,1, 14, 4, and 13 he turned the handle and the door swung open.

"How did you know the code?" Janet asked.

"Last time we were here Teddy said, "T and M always works."

"Wow, and you remembered that and the numbers that each letter stands for. I'm impressed."

Jake just shrugged and stepped into the boathouse, turning on the lights as he did.

Janet followed him and stopped when she saw all of the equipment displayed on the rear wall of the building. "Wow, looks like a sports store."

"Yes, Teddy has quite a selection to choose from." He walked over to the wall and picked one of the Shakespeare Ugly Sticks with a spinning reel on it. He pulled a section of line off and pulled it as to snap it. It popped after he increased the pressure to what he knew to be twelve pounds. "Ten pound test," he said, almost to himself, "That will work." He placed the rod and reel on an open hook next to the door, than moved over to the largest tackle box, of the three that sat on the table in the far corner. He took a six by six plastic tackle case out of his pocket. He opened the large box and selected four black and yellow beetle spins and put them in his case. He picked four claw hooks, size six, and four split shot lead weights and put them in the case also.

Janet stepped towards him and handed him a light tan canvas fishing vest saying, "You can put that stuff in the pockets of this."

Jake took the vest from her saying, "Great, thanks." He turned back to the tackle box and took an inch and a half red and white bobber, which he put in a second pocket. He took a small plastic bag out of his jeans pocket and put it in the small chest pocket of the vest.

Janet asked, "What is that?"

Jake grinned saying, "It's like hollow angel hair pasta soaked in WD 40. You break a small section off and slide it on the hook's shank, above the barb."

"WD 40, what is that about?"

Jake grinned, "Well, WD 40 is mostly fish oil it lets the fish find the lure quicker."

He crossed her arms in front of her chest saying, "That sounds like cheating."

Jake laughed replying, "Not really, there are no rules in sport fishing, but there are when you tournament fish."

"Well, I still think is cheating, the fish doesn't have a chance."

Laughing Jake replied, "They sure do, getting them close is one thing getting them to bite is another."

"Okay, I guess you're correct, and we do want to have fish to eat."

Jake just smiled and walked over to the hook that the rod and reel were on, he hung the fishing vest on the hook also. He turned back towards Janet saying, "Okay, ready to go back to the house?"

"Sounds good to me," She walked towards the door and placed her hand on the mahogany deck of the boat saying, "This is class, pure class."

"Yes, that it is that it is."

They stepped out of the boathouse and Jake pulled the door closed, it clicked as it locked.

They walked back up the path and back up to his place.

***

Janet was watching the news and they were going over the schedule of events for the funeral for the President and his family. It was to start on Thursday and continue until Saturday when bodies would be buried.

She was so engrossed in the entire spectacle of events that she paid little attention to the news snippet about them finding a Master Sergeant who had taken his own life. The report explained that they felt he killed himself out of grief over the death of the President and his family who he had met numerous times. They went on to explain that there had been over two dozen suicides in the last day and all were believed to be out of grief and despair.

Jake sat down next to her just as the talking head completed his report on the deaths. "I guess there will be a lot of people confused and distraught for the next few weeks. Many saw the President as the person that would have them taken care of for the rest of their lives."

Janet looked at him before replying, "A lot did, mistakenly so, but a lot did. What do you think the outcome will be of all of this? You know the realization that the government is not everyone's panacea."

"Well, I don't know what is going to happen long term but this country has some very trying times ahead of it, for everyone. A lot of what has been done over the past few years needs to be changed, fixed or done away with. That is my opinion only of course."

Janet nodded and turned back to the talking head, he was repeating the story about the suicides. They were starting to spin the news to favor one sides' opinion of what needed to occur next by the new President.

Jake smiled almost to himself fully knowing that all of the events had not occurred yet.

They sat there for a few more moments then Janet pushed the off button saying, "Enough of all of that, big day tomorrow, we need some rest." With that she stood and pulling Jake by the hand headed for the bedroom.

★★★

Jake was in the kitchen getting things ready for breakfast and was peeling potatoes and slicing them in one eight inch thick slices. He then placed each of the slices in a bowl of cold water. He glanced at the security flat screen and saw Teddy walking out of the rear door of his house. "Must be going down to the boathouse," he thought.

He opened the package of crusty white bread and took out five slices, and then he picking up a juice glass he pressed the open end into each slice to make an inch and a half hole in each. He placed the bread on a plate and set it next to the stove top grill.

"Well its seven twenty five, Julian should be here soon," He took four plates out and set them on the counter and placed a knife, fork and napkin next to each.

Janet walked out of the bedroom drying her hair with a large white towel and a second wrapped around her, saying, "Morning love."

Jake looked at her smiling, replied, "And good morning to you." He noticed Julian pulling up to the front of the garage on the flat screen, "Julian is here, the food will be done in about fifteen minutes."

"Oh, I'll be out in a few," she turned and disappeared into the bedroom.

The door buzzer sounded off, Jake stepped over and pressed the button unlocking the door and said, "Doors open, come on up." H stepped back to the stovetop and placed a quarter stick of butter in the pan and turned the heat to low.

Julian came up the stairs right behind Martha, saying "Hey, well I smell something cooking."

Jake replied, "Yep, bacon, eggs coming up. Get a mug, coffee maker is on the counter."

Martha said, "Sounds good."

Jake placed the slices of bread on the grill and let is set for a few moments, he turned them over and then cracked an egg into the hole in each slice. The sliced potatoes he had spread out on the grill were browning nicely, he shook a little salt over them, then placed a few extra slices of butter on top of them. Jake turned the bacon asking, "Bacon crispy or on the chewy side?"

He heard two "Crispy" and one "Chewy." He separated the bacon into two groups of eight slices. He preferred his on the chewy side and was a little surprised that Janet did also. After placing two sheets of paper towels on the counter he took the eight slices of chewy bacon and placed them on the paper towels.

Picking up the spatula he slid it under the first slice of bread/egg and flipped it over, he did the same to each in turn. Picking up a plate he placed one of the slices on it and four slices of bacon. He opened the oven which he had on warming, and placed the plate in to it.

He picked up the second plate and did the same thing. Placing two more sheets of paper towels on the ones already there and put the remaining bacon from the grill on the sheets. Jake put the remaining bread on the remaining two plates and also the bacon. He took the plates out of the oven and placed potatoes on each of the four plates, grabbing two he placed them in front of Julian and Martha. He moved back and made up the other two plates and placed one in front of Janet and one at his place.

Moving around to his seat and sat down saying, "Well I hope you enjoy this, a wonderful old Italian lady in New York taught me how to make it. It is called, Eggs in a Basket." The moment it was out of his mouth he knew that he never should have said it.

"New York, When did you live in New York," Julian asked between bites.

"I never lived there," he lied, "I worked a case there for a few months when I was with the Agency."

Julian let it go but Jake knew that it would come up again somewhere down the line.

"Jake this is great," Martha said as she reached for her coffee cup.

"It sure is," Janet chimed in.

"I'm glad you are enjoying it, all fair in love and war, I cooked now everyone else cleans up, sounds really fair to me."

They all laughed and Martha stood up and moved around the counter saying, "I'll wash, Julian you dry. Janet you and Jake need to put everything where it belongs."

Jake and Julian both replied at the same time, "Sounds like a plan."

Janet looked at them and said, "You two are spending too much time together."

They all laughed as they moved to almost form a production line from the sink to the cabinets. They had everything done in short order and they all moved down the stairs and out the door.

Jake, Janet and Martha were standing just outside of the door watching Julian walk over to his truck.

"Janet, Janet?"

Janet turned to find Marian coming outside her back door and walking towards them.

"Hello Marian, "Janet replied.

"Hello Janet, Martha, I was wondering if you two young ladies can give me a hand once the boys go off?"

Martha and Janet both replied, "Of course we will."

Hearing the sounds of car they all looked towards the drive. It was Paige and Charlie in Paige's car.

Julian was walking back from his truck with a rod, reel and tackle box, he turned and seeing Paige's car lifted his hand with the rod in it in a wave.

Paige parked and Charlie was out of the car first with his rod and reel securely in his hand. He said, "The fish are a waiting, point me towards the river."

Everyone laughed including Marian.

Jake pointed towards the path saying, "That is the way, I saw Teddy head that way about an hour ago."

Janet leaned over and gave Jake a kiss saying, "Have fun and bring back lunch."

Jake grinned saying, "That is a deal." He turned and started towards the path saying, "Gentleman the fish await."

The three of them walked down the path towards the boat house and Julian asked, "Jake will there be enough room in Teddy's boat."

Jake replied, "Plenty, You'll see in a moment," and stepped up to the door and stepped through. Julian and Charlie stepped into the boathouse and Charlie placed his hand on the deck of the first boat saying, "Wow, this is sweet, I mean really sweet."

Julian just stood looking at it.

Teddy stood up in the rear of the boat saying, "Thank you, she is my baby. I've had her for over twenty five years and she runs like new. Come around this way and I'll stow your gear. Jake I've put yours and my gear on board already."

Jake stepped over to the boat and stepped in saying, "Thank you, anything I can do?"

"Nope, we are all ready to go."

Julian and Charlie stepped on board and Teddy hit the switch to open the door to the river. He turned the key and the motor came to life, it ran with a low grumble and very smoothly. He pressed a button and the four bumpers moved away from the boats sides, putting the lever in reverse the boat began to move slowly out of the boathouse. Teddy gave it a jolt of gas and the boat cleared the boathouse and the dock that extended out into the river.

Charlie watched the door come down and remarked with a big smile on his face, "Mr. Teddy has done that before."

Teddy just grinned. He pointed the boat upstream and gave it some more gas and it moved swiftly and smoothly into the rivers current. "I think we will start at Deep Step, if we don't have any luck there we can move further upstream. How does that sound?"

Julian looked at Charlie and they both said, "That sounds great," Julian continued with, "They are making power today, we should have no problem getting into Deep Step."

Teddy just nodded but never looked away from up river, the air moving by them smelled fresh and clean. A whiff of honey suckle carried on the wind as they passed a large growth on the river bank. Teddy looked totally at peace.

Julian looked at Jake and Charlie and grinning said, "I smell fish."

They all laughed.

A few of the home owners that were out in their back yards waved as they passed by, a few yelled hello and called Teddy by name.

He looked at those in the boat and said, "They must remember the boat, and associate it with me. I guess there aren't too many like this one left."

Julian replied, "This is the only one of this type I have ever seen on the lower lake and/or the upper lake. If I had seen one I'm sure that I would remember it." Placing his hand on the mahogany boards that made up the decking he continued with, "They just don't make boats like this anymore."

Jake and Charlie both said, "That is for sure."

Teddy moved the wheel and directed the boat out of the way of a section of tree trunk that was slowly down river in the current. Teddy pulled the throttle back slowly slowing the boat, he turned to his left into the mouth of Deep Step and took a path in the center of body of water,

Jake was standing next to Julian and he turned towards him and asked, "Is this natural? There doesn't seem to be enough flow, it looks more like a large backflow."

"Yep, that is exactly what it is. When they are making power there is plenty of water, when they aren't you will see hundreds of stumps poking up out of the water. This boat would be a bit to big to maneuver when the water is at that stage. When the Corps built the damns they cut all of the trees to the ground right down the center here to allow access at all stages but at the low stage you can only fish the bank zone with a small flat bottom."

Jake just nodded because it was something he had seen many times before in many places.

Teddy moved the boat slowly to the rear of the back water and shut it off, he used the trolling motor to turn the boat around and stopped. He looked at everyone and said, "Okay, string them up, first fish boated doesn't have to clean fish."

All four of them grabbed their rods and in moments they were casting into the clear cool water. Jake flipped his line towards the bank and retrieved it slowly over the weed bed at a steady rate. His lure was about six feet from the bank and a Bream shot up and hit the lure and dove back into the weeds. Jake popped the rod upwards and started reeling faster. The Bream darted back and forth, Jake guided it alongside the boat and lifted it into the air. He grabbed it and set the rod down and unhooked the fish saying with a laugh, "Well, I guess we know who isn't cleaning fish."

The others tossed comments back and forth as Jake placed the fish in the live well. Teddy moved the boat slowly along the bank stopping whenever they found a honey hole. Bream stayed in groups in pockets of deeper water normally where a small stream entered the main body of water. There could be twenty or more in such a spot, when one was found it was called a honey hole.

They had been fishing for about an hour when Teddy asked, "Anyone thirsty or hungry, I've got some soft drinks and snacks."

Jake set his rod down replying, "I'll have a diet soft drink, I need a bit of a rest from catching all of the fish." He had a big grin on his face as he turned away and dug into the cooler.

Julian and Charlie laughed, Charlie said, "There is always one in every crowd, catches three fish and he thinks he's a pro."

Julian added, "Yep, you're correct, always one."

They placed their rods down and Charlie said, "The least you can do is hand us a cool drink."

Jake flipped a can to each of them and looking at Teddy asked, "Are you ready?"

Teddy was grinning as he said, "Sure." He looked at Julian and Charlie saying, "Well, he did catch the first one and at least five more. I guess we have about thirty in the well, another twenty and we should have enough for lunch."

They all laughed.

Julian pointed across the expansion of water towards the far side saying, "There is a large honey hole over there just a few yards from that big pine."

Teddy turned the boat away from the bank and headed across the water to the other side. He said almost to himself, "What a great day."

Jake, Julian and Charlie all tapped their cans of soft drink together saying, "You bet."

Teddy turned the boat slowly putting it parallel to the bank, he set the trolling motor into reverse moving the boat a little against the waters flow. It moved slowly towards the spot that Julian had pointed out. They all cast their lines towards the spot and in seconds all four had a fish on their line. They cast each of their lines a few more times as the boat moved across the hole. Teddy used the trolling motor to move the boat back to the other side of the hole and let it began to drift across it again. They made a few more passes and caught another twenty-two fish.

"Well that is about it, we caught eight Red Breasts, six Crappie and the rest were Bream. A very good day on the river I'd say." The others all agreed.

Teddy hooked his lure to the lowest guide ring on the rod and turned the reel until the line was tight. The others did the same and placed the rods on the boats floor and took their seats. He looked around and seeing all seated with their flotation vests on, he pushed the switch and the motor came to life. He moved the boat back into the center of the body of water and pushed the throttle forward and the speed picked up. Once he was back in the river he moved to the center and gave the motor more fuel. The air flowed over them and they again enjoyed the freshness and the aromas of the water, flowers and the smell of someone's freshly cut grass.

When the boat house came into view Teddy reached under the wheel housing and pushed the button to open the door. He backed off on the throttle and turned the boat sideways and as it got close to the entrance he increased the speed and pulled out of the current and into the boat house. Jake stepped onto the deck and pushed the button to engaged the hoist and lifted the boat about three inches. With the boat stable the others climbed out carrying the fishing equipment. Jake reached over the side of the boat and lifted the live well out onto the deck after removing the hoses for the pump that kept the water in the live well fresh. He picked the live well up again and walked out onto the deck that ran along the boat house and into the river. When he moved back into the boathouse he stepped around Teddy. Teddy was washing down the outside surfaces of the boat with pressure from a hose. When he was done with that he pushed the button lifting it totally out of the water.

Julian and Charlie wiped down the rods and reels after taking the lures off and after tying a rubber band to the end of the line. Then he turned the reel's handle, it wound the line tight. Then they stretched the rubber band over the reel's handle securing it so the line would not unwind.

Teddy stepped out on the outside deck and found Jake with Janet standing next to him, already busy with the fish. He had the plywood cleaning board that Teddy kept hanging on the boathouse wall, across the top of the sink and the faucet running into the tub. He was using one of the tablespoons that Teddy had hanging on the boathouse wall also, to scale the fish. He cut the head off of the fish using a diagonal cut from the back of the head to the belly. Then he cut the belly open and pulled the entrails out, flipping them over the rail into the water and putting the fish in the tub.

"Looks like you've done that before," Teddy said stepping up next to Janet.

She looked at Teddy saying, "And he does it so quickly."

"Yes he does, not that I'm surprised. I don't think there is much our man Jake can't do well." Teddy said as he placed his hand on Jake's shoulder.

Julian and Charlie stepped out on the deck and Julian asked, "Want me to get the rest Jake?"

Jake stepped back and with a flourish handed Julian the spoon and knife saying, "I thought you would never ask."

They all laughed and Jake and Janet stepped out of the way.

Janet pointed to two five gallon pails saying, "One with soapy water and one with fresh, so you can wash your hands. I've got fresh towels also."

Marian walked up with a two gallon stainless steel pail saying, "The fish go in here and when all of them are cleaned. One of you strong young men can carry it up to the house for me. Martha and Paige are busy up there getting everything ready."

Charlie reached out for the pail saying, "That is my job."

★★★

Sergeant King stood in front of his squad leaders taking their reports for the area of the city that was their responsibility. All seemed to be quiet with nothing other than the normal minor disruption or two. He picked up the phone and called the Undersheriff to give her his hourly report.

The phone was picked up on the second ring, "Undersheriff Winslow."

"King here, all precincts have reported in and all seems to be normal. We have had a few disruptions but nothing out of the ordinary."

"Thank you, Sergeant King, please keep me informed, things should defuse once the work week routines start in the morning."

"Yes, I believe that also. We will remain diligent and I'll report back in an hour unless something occurs before that."

"Thank you Sergeant." Undersheriff Winslow pressed the End button and set the phone down on her desk.

★★★

Marian picked up another fish and placed it in the bowl of milk, then flipped it over. She then picked it up and dipped it on the tray of ground corn flour on both sides, then placed it in the deep fryer of peanut oil with the others. It floated on one side for two minutes and flipped over to the other side and fried for two more minutes.

Marian used the slotted spoon to remove one the fish and placed it on the platter next to the others. She had seven more to finish the frying of the fish, Martha was putting the coleslaw platter on the table and Paige set the platter of hush puppies next to it.

Charlie was placing the soft drinks on a platter with a bucket of ice, he looked at Jake saying "Diet okay?"

"Sure, do you have enough ice?

"Sure do."

Marian walked over to the table and placed the platter of fish in the center saying, "Time to eat."

The eight of them sat and Teddy said grace.

The platter of fish was passed around and each took two fish, it was followed by the plates of coleslaw and hush puppies.

"These are wonderful," Janet said after the first bite of one of the hush puppies.

The men nodded but did not stop the process of taking the fish off of the bones to reply.

There was a lot of Wow's, this is great, and many accolades to the cook, the plate of fish made another trip around the table along with the hush puppies. Everyone did a lot of eating and a little talking. Teddy took a drink from his glass and looking across the table said, "What a wonderful day, great fishing, great food and good friends, it just does not get better than this!"

Julian grinned replying, "That is for sure, just don't let anyone leave before the dishes are done and everything is cleaned up. Miss Marian yours, and Mr. Teddy's job is to sit right there and supervise the cleanup."

Martha, Paige and Janet all agreed, and at that Charlie stood and started to scrape all of the bones on to one plate. Charlie looked at them all saying, "I'd do dishes every night if I could eat like that each night.

Martha looked at Paige saying, "Make sure you remember that for future use."

Charlie rolled his eyes saying, "I forgot, they never forget anything."

Everyone started laughing and Charlie blushed, a bright red as Paige patted him on his shoulder saying, "Only what we want to young man, only what we want to."

They all chipped in and the clean up was done in a flash.

Julian, Martha, Paige and Charlie made another round of thanks with a few hugs and were gone.

Julian stepped over to Jake saying, "Meet you at the Waffle House on Washington in the morning. We can leave my car there and just take one to the Club."

"Sounds like a plan, see you there."

With their goodbyes said, they walked back to Jake's.

Once they were upstairs Jake looked at Janet saying, "When I take you home I'm going to swing by the Lab for a bit. I left a few tests running when I left and I want to clear the equipment. I don't want it to sit there another day."

"That sounds good, I do need to get home and do a few things myself." She stood and walked towards the bedroom saying, "Might need some help packing my stuff." She disappeared threw the doorway.

Jake replied as he moved towards the doorway, "I'll help with that."

***

Jake moved around the Lab removing specimen plates and containers from the different equipment thinking, "Well it's only Ten thirty." He didn't get Janet home until ten and their good bye lasted almost another two hours. He grinned to himself as he cleaned up and reset the equipment and started a few more programs,

It was about eleven when he pulled into The Club's drive, he saw Teddy's SVU and two other high priced rides parked next to it as he pulled into the parking lot. He pulled into the second space and locked the door of the truck as he got out. He saw Teddy walking towards him from the Club's front door.

"Jake, glad you made it," Teddy said putting his hand out towards Jake.

Jake shook his hand saying, "Hope I'm not late."

"No, no, you are right on time, let's go inside. There are a few people I think you need to meet and speak to."

Once inside the building they walked down the hall and Teddy opened a door and motioned with his hand for Jake to enter first.

Jake noticed that there were none of the help in view or bustling around doing all that needed to be done. He entered the room and was surprised to find an elevator, he noticed that it only had a down button.

Teddy stepped beside him and pushed the button, he did not say a word. The door opened and they both stepped into the elevator and the door closed. It moved down and when it opened Jake was surprised again, there was a small rail car, like a mini subway car. It seated four, Teddy opened the door and waited for Jake to get in then sat across from him. Teddy reached above the door and pushed a green button, the car lurched a little and moved away from the platform. The car ran quietly for about five minutes in almost total darkness, the tunnel began to lighten and the car pulled up to a platform of sorts. The platform was about eight feet wide and ten feet deep, it abutted a white concrete wall with a dark gray door. There were two men standing on the platform, back by the door. The car stopped and the door opened, Teddy looked at Jake pointing at the platform and saying, "Sir Knight," he spoke in the Old Tongue.

Jake stepped out on the platform and the two men walked closer, standing next to Teddy, they said in unison, "The Cross runs red."

Jake replied, "So it does, the Cross is covered in blood, in the caverns so deep."

"The cavern walls are seeping the blood of our Brother Knights, to protect the Cross, now and forever," they replied.

"Blood let for the Cross, Sir Knights," Jake said.

"As it should be, now, and forever, Sir Knight," they replied.

Jake looked directly in their eyes, saying, "I stand and fight for the Cross at all costs."

"We, The Brotherhood of the Knights of Templar, stand and fight for the Cross at all costs." They stood taller.

Jake said, "Blood Bound, Sir Knights."

The three men replied, "Blood Bound, Sir Knight."

Jake spoke quickly, "Sir Knights, I am but a serf in the service of My Lord Sir Eric of Garth, who has joined our Brothers of the past."

One of the men walked over and opened the door and held it open for them to enter. Jake stepped through the door and almost stopped from the sights before him. He thought, "If I did not know better I would swear that I'm in a Castle in Europe." Before him was a room with stone block walls, hand strung chairs and a table with pottery urns and stone mugs. The floor was covered with the skins of bears, tigers and the heads of Boars were mounted on the walls.

The men took seats at the table and one of them poured what looked like red wine into the mugs. Teddy looked at Jake saying, "Tell us your tale Sir Knight."

Jake stood next to the open chair that the other Knight had placed a mug in front of. "Brothers, Sir Eric gave me this quest of fact to be given to the first Knight of meeting, once confirmed that he was so. Sir Eric's quest is, "On the Isle of Oak, in the new world, there lay the world's worth of the Brotherhood. From the gate, on the new world side, of the seven levels of naught, one must face the true home of the Cross. Walk eighty six paces towards the Cross' home, turn to the rising sun, sixteen paces more, go, then twelve paces down, there lay a door to the Brotherhood's worth. The Guardian's sword must be inserted, turned thrice to the favored, lifted once then twice to the weak. The door will rise and the riches of the Brotherhood can be saved."

Jake sat down and lifted the mug and took a large swallow of the wine, it was sweet yet tart at the same time.

The three Knights sat there looking at each other, their faces frozen, not a sound to be heard, nothing.

Two minutes passed and Teddy stood and looking at Jake said, "Sir Knight, you have done well, you will forever be known as Sir Jake of Garth, after your sponsor Knight, to all of the Brotherhood. Now, will you please come with me, I must take you to your leave and then return to meet with my Brothers."

The other two Knights stood and placed their right arm across their chests saying, "Blood Bound, Sir Knights."

With that, Teddy standing his side, Jake crossed his arm and they replied, "Blood Bound Sir Knights."

Teddy and Jake moved out of the door on to the platform, Teddy closed the door and moved to the car and opened the door. Jake got in and sat facing the direction they would be traveling. Teddy got in and sat facing him, he reached up and pushed a blue button and the car started to move, they did not talk during the ride back.

Once the car stopped at the platform Teddy opened the door and stepped out, Jake followed him. Teddy opened the door to the building and waited for Jake to step through. Terry stepped in beside him and placed his hand on Jake's arm saying, "We all thank you, and we know that you will not speak of what occurred tonight. You will be known across the Brotherhood. Once back in the Club can you find your way?"

Jake nodded saying, "I can, and all is safely stored in my mind and will never be revealed."

Teddy nodded his head and moved into the elevator, once back at the correct level and in the Club he turned, facing Jake, placed his arm, with a closed fist, across his chest saying, "Go with the Cross." Teddy turned and returned the way he had come not waiting for a reply. The door closed on the elevator and there was nothing but silence.

Jake walked to the front door and let himself out, he saw no one but could feel someone watching him. He walked to his truck thinking about the events of the last hour or so. To him, it all had been very, very surprising, and after all of his years it took a lot to surprise him. It had been nothing like what he had expected it to be. He glanced to the North, the direction the car had traveled, to see if he could locate the building they had traveled to. His line of site was blocked by trees and assorted bushes as well as the dark of night.

CHAPTER FIFTEEN

JAKE WAS SITTING IN HIS truck when Julian pulled into the parking lot of the Waffle House, he got out, once Julian parked and got out of his car, they shook hands and Jake said, "Just put everything in the back seat."

Julian nodded and opened the car's trunk, he reached in and lifted his golf bag out, he then placed it on the back seat of Jake's truck. Next he moved the hanging bag with an extra change of clothes and the bag with his golf shoes and some extra golf balls.

Looking at Jake he said, "I can't think of anything else, clubs, shoes, balls and tees. What do you think?"

"Sounds like everything, everything but a golf swing."

"Hey, I've got one of those, and it used to work fairly well."

Grinning Jake said, "Well, we will soon see. It's been a few years since I've played eighteen so it might get ugly out there."

"Right, just like at the firing range, are you going to shoot at Par or Under?"

"Well in the day I could hang around Par, now, I don't know.

Laughing Julian replied. "That is just what I thought. Did I ever tell you the story of how I won the City Amateur?"

"No, but I'd love to hear that story. Is it true?"

Julian laughed again, "Yes, it's true."

Jake opened the truck door and got in behind the wheel saying, "Think it's safe to leave a Department car here?"

Julian opened the passenger side door and slid in replying, "Yes, I let the desk Sergeant know that I would be leaving it here. He'll have a patrol swing by every hour or so."

Jake started the truck and pulled out of the lot replying, "That should work, things seemed better when I drove through down town last night. Not quite as many people milling around, and the officers were doing a good job of not standing out."

Julian glanced at him and replied, "I noticed the same conditions earlier this morning, I pretty much canvassed all of downtown around six. Hopefully all will remain calm today and tonight."

Jake just nodded, feeling Julian's eyes on him.

Jake pulled into the drive and was greeted by the ever present security guard. He put his window down and was about to explain why there were there.

The guard waved them forward saying, "Have a great day Mr. Smith, Mr. Brown."

Jake said, "A camera, forgot to bring a camera."

Julian replied, "Have no fear, I have this and so do you," holding up his phone said, "These takes as good or better photos than my Cannon TX."

Jake grinned replying, "Sometime I forget that a phone is a lot more that a Phone."

Jake pulled into the second space in the lot in front of the Clubhouse and turned the car off and opened his door. By the time they both got out of the truck, and opened the rear doors, there were two men in white caddie suits standing next to the rear of the truck. Jake said, "Good morning."

One of them replied, "Good morning Sir." He stepped to the truck's door and began to lift the golf bags out. He looked at Jake saying, "We'll have these out on the range. There will be a cart waiting when you come out of the Club, to drive you over. Please leave your shoes on the floor outside of your locker. Jerry will have them looking like new in no time."

Julian asked, "Is Mr. Blanchard here yet?"'

The second caddie replied, "Yes Sir, I believe he is waiting for you both in the Grill Room. Please see Blue once you enter the Clubhouse." With that both of them walked off with a golf bag on their shoulder.

Jake and Julian picked up their bags from the truck seat and closing the doors walked towards the main entrance of the Club. Julian reached for the door knob but the door opened and the gentleman that opened the door smiled saying, "Mr. Smith and Mr. Brown, pleasure to see you again, please follow me to the locker room. I will let Mr. Blanchard know you have arrived."

They both responded, "Thank you Blue."

He just smiled and walked towards the locker room with them in tow.

Blue showed them the two lockers they were to use and excused himself to announce them to Mr. Blanchard.

They sat on the bench in front of each locker and took their shoes out of the bags and changed from their street shoes to their golf shoes. They then took their shirts and pants out of the bags and hung them up in the lockers, then placed the bags on the bottom of the lockers.

Just as they closed the locker doors Blue stepped into the room and seeing they were ready said, "Please follow me."

They walked past the door that led to the elevator and subway Teddy had brought him to, then to the location where they discussed Jake's quest.

The three of them walked through the clubhouse and into the Grill Room, Tommy Blanchard stood as they entered and when they got to the table he shook their hands, and waved for them to take a seat, in turn saying, "Jake, Julian so good to see you, glad you could make it. If it's alright with you, we'll have something to eat and go to the practice area for a bit. Would you like to play the Par Three Course first, or the full Eighteen?"

Julian replied, "Second, maybe we'll be a little loose by then."

"Great, please give James your order, whatever you would like. James looked at each of them saying, "Juice, coffee, tea?"

Tommy Blanchard ordered first, "Tomato juice, Coffee, two eggs over easy, home fries, white bread toasted well and a small plate of sliced melon."

"Yes Sir." James looked at Jake and Jake said, "Grapefruit juice, two poached eggs on white bread toast, home fries, and I will also take a small plate of melon."

James said, "Yes Sir," and turned towards Julian.

"Orange juice, two eggs over light, grits with cheese, white bread toasted well and I will also have some melon."

James said "Thank you," and was gone.

Tommy glance out of the expansion of windows and said, "It looks like it will be a wonderful day."

They both agreed and as they turned back toward the table, their juices were in front of them, and pot of coffee and cups were in place.

Jake looked at the two men and closed his eyes for a moment and had a few good thoughts.

"They have made quite a few changes out there over the past few years, but from the Member's tees it is still enjoyable and playable. I hope you will enjoy today, it should be a lot of fun."

Jake was not surprised that their food arrived and was placed in front of them with them hardly noticing.

As they ate the coffee pot was warmed twice and the food was some of the best Jake had ever eaten. It was breakfast but what a breakfast.

When they finished they all stood and walked towards the locker room, they washed their hands and in moments were in a cart fitted out to carry eight people. In just a few moments they arrived at the practice facility.

Jake looked at it and then Julian saying, "This is unbelievable."

"Yes it is my friend, yes it is."

The three of them hit six or seven shots with each club and then they walked to the practice green to hit a few putts. They putted for about fifteen minutes and Jake was done. He walked over to his bag and placed the putter in it. He unzipped one of the pockets and took two balls and a few tees. He took his wallet out of his pocket and put it in one of the large pockets on the side of the bag.

Tommy and Julian walked up and Tommy asked, "Are we going to walk or ride?"

Julian replied quickly, "Walk." He looked at Jake and Tommy with a questioning look on his face, "Okay?"

Jake laughed saying, "You got it buddy, and wouldn't miss the opportunity."

Tommy laughed saying, "Nine out of ten say walk, unless there is a physical reason not to."

Tommy looked at the caddies saying, "Bud, you're with Mr. Smith, Cat, you're with Mr. Brown and V you're with me."

Bud moved over next to Jake, Jake put out his hand to Bud saying, "It's Jake."

"Yes Sir Mr. Jake."

Cat stepped up to Julian saying, "Cat." Julian put out his hand saying, "Julian."

"Yes Sir, Mr. Julian."

V just moved over and picked up Tommy's bag saying, "First is open Mr. Blanchard," and started to walk away.

The other two followed in a single line and Jake, Julian and Tommy walked next to each other chatting about the first hole.

They walked onto the first tee box and Jake looked down the fairway seeing it sweep to the right in a slow arc around the snow white bunker that guarded the right corner of the fairway.

Tommy flipped a tee in the air and it came down pointing to Julian, "First." He flipped it again and it pointed to himself, "Second." Looking at Jake said, "Last but not least."

Jake said, "I'm good with that. Show us the way Julian."

Julian grinned replying, "Two sixty with a left to right fade."

Tommy grinned saying, "Oh, this is going to be fun."

Julian teed up his ball and took two practice swings, he took the club back and came through at a controlled pace. They watched the ball rise and turn from left to right and bounce in the center of the fairway. Cat took his club and said, "Just like described," with a grin on his face, Julian looked at Jake and grinned even more.

Tommy said, "I'm impressed." He teed his ball up and with no practice swings brought his club back and through in one continuous motion. With a click the ball rose and moved from right to left and flew Julian's by ten yards. V took Tommy's club and coughed when they all looked at him he shrugged his shoulders with a small grin on his face.

Jake took his club from Bud, Bud said, "They're pretty good." Jake nodded and stepped onto the tee box. He teed his ball up and stepped behind it looking down the fairway. He looked at Bud asking, "That about two eighty to fly the trap and end up within a wedge to the green?"

"Yes Sir."

Jake stepped up to his ball and took a full swing with a very high finish with his hands. The ball clicked and rose as it passed over the trap on the right side of the fairway, it landed twenty yards in front of Julian's ball and stopped on the right side of the fairway. This gave him a direct shot to the green. He handed Bud the club saying, "Even a blind hog finds an acorn once in awhile."

Bud, laughed out loud, that drew a stern look from Tommy.

Jake saw that and stepping next to Tommy as they walked down the fairway, "Not his fault, I was showing off for Julian. He meant no disrespect."

Tommy looked at him and after a second grinned replying, "No harm, no foul. That was a great shot, play the second a little left of the flag."

"Thank You." With that Jake moved over next to Julian saying, "Good shot. Is this place just unbelievable or what?"

Julian nodded saying, "It's like being in an outside church, only without the crowds, great shot by the way."

"Thanks."

They stopped a few yards behind Julian's ball and Julian looked at Cat asking, "About one forty?"

Cat replied, "One forty three, best target would be six or seven feet right of the flag, it will move left once it lands. Just don't put too much zip on it."

Julian reached for his eight iron, putting his hand on it pulled it out of the bag. Cat moved away about six yards to Juliann's right and back a few yards.

Julian took his stance and took a practice swing, looked at the flag and took his swing. The ball rose off of the club face and landed on the green about ten feet right but pin high. It moved about a foot towards the flag and stopped.

All said "Good shot."

Cat filled the divot with the grass seed/fertilizer mixture in had in the white canvas bag he carried slung across his shoulder,

Tommy and V moved to his ball, and Tommy pulled a club out of his bag with no discussion. He lined up and hit his shot very quickly, with only one quick look from his ball to the flag and back, the ball landed three feet from the flag and rolled past it by six feet. "Good shot," came from all of the others.

As V fixed Tommy's divot Jake and Bud walked up to his ball, "Gap wedge," Jake said, when he was standing next to his ball.

Bud took the club out of the bag and handed it to Jake saying, "Right five feet and short of the pin two feet. She'll roll up close."

Jake never answered, he took his stance and swung the club in one continuous motion back and though. The ball jumped off of the club face and looked like a homerun ball looking for the fence. The ball landed two feet short and five feet right of the flag, it rolled towards the hole and stopped three inches from going in.

Bud said, "Great shot Sir, great shot."

Jake replied, "Thank you."

Julian stepped over to him as Bud fixed Jake's divot saying, "What a great shot." Grinning continued with "Hope you make the putt."

Tommy over hearing the conversation laughed and added, "That is a 'Gimmie' even here. Great shot Jake."

Jake grinned and replied, "Thank you." He walked onto the green and to his ball, he tapped it in and leaned over and picked it up. He looked at Julian and winked.

V took the flag out of the hole and placed it on the fringe away from the lines of play.

Julian marked his ball and wiped the loose grass on it off. He replaced it and removed the marker and looked down the line of his putt. Cat also looked at the line from both sides. Julian looked at him saying, "What do you think?"

Nine feet down hill, it will move right to left six inches. If it misses the hole it will go five feet past."

Julian looked at Jake with a big grin on his face saying, "Just what I always wanted, this putt, on this course, in a need to make position, just to stay even with my companions."

He took his stance over the ball and stroked it as softly as he could with an even stroke. The ball moved down the incline at a even pace at first then it started picking up speed, it hit the back of the hole and popped up about an inch and dropped back into the hole.

Cat said almost to himself, "What a putt."

Jake slapped Julian on the shoulder saying, "Just like a pro, never a doubt."

Julian just replied, "Right."

V stepped over to Tommy's ball and bent over to look at the line of Tommy's putt, he did not say anything until Tommy looked at the line and looked at V saying, "What do you think?"

"It will fall left to right two balls."

"Yes, that is what I see also." He took his stance and softly stroked the ball on its way. It traveled the six feet in a slow arc of two and one half inches and hit the back of the hole and dropped in. Tommy looked up at Jake and Julian saying, "Three birdies on this hole is the exception, not the rule, Gentlemen, great golf."

The three of them moved off the left rear of the green towards the second tee box, a long par five that stretched out and away two hundred and twenty yards before turning and running down a long hill to the left, this at the fairway bunker that stretched twenty yards along the far edge of the fairway. Off the left side of the fairway was a steep drop off into deeply wooded and weed covered slopes that ended at a small creek on the low point. In the fairway the drop was almost a hundred feet down to the green, and the green has three defined levels and has large bunkers protecting the front and sides of the green.

The caddies were walking a few yards behind the three of them, talking softly to each other, safe to say a few dollars would pass hands today. At the tee box the caddies handed there man his driver and moved down the fairway on the left side to have a clear view of the balls landing.

The men kept the same rotation since they all had the same score on the previous hole. Julian teed his ball up and stepped behind it visioning the flight he wanted it to take. He glanced at Jake saying, "Two forty right to left to the left side of the fairway just past the left end of the bunker. With that, he took his stance and made a clean even pass at the ball, it clicked and flew off the clubface rising in a right to left flight landing in the middle of the fairway and bounding another thirty yards and landing just about where he said it would go. He picked up his tee and said, "Next."

Tommy grinned and teed his ball up on the far left side of the tee box, took his stance and made a smooth even swing at and through the ball. With a click it shot towards the right side of the fairway in a high turning arc, it landed in the middle of the fairway and bounced twice and stopped five yards to the left of Julian's ball but almost even with it. He picked up his tee and stepped out of the teeing area, he did not say anything but he was smiling.

Jake moved to the extreme right of the tee box and leaned over and teed his ball, he glanced at Julian and smiled. He took a strong deliberate swing and it sounded like a gunshot. The ball flew off the tee in a straight line until it almost reached Tommy's ball and then turned left. It bounced in the middle of the fairway forty yards past Julian and Tommy's balls and rolled another eight yards.

Jake picked up his tee saying, "Got that one."

Julian and Tommy were still looking down the fairway in disbelief, Tommy turned to Jake saying, "That is the best drive I have ever seen on this hole, Pro or Amateur, astounding."

Jake did not look at them and stepped off of the tee box a little embarrassed saying, "Thanks."

As they moved down the fairway they remarked on the weather and brightness of the flowers and shrubs. It truly was a great day. When they got to Julian and Tommy's balls it was determined that Julian was away by a foot or so.

Julian took his Five Metal out of the bag, he took the cover off of it and handed the cover too Cat. He looked at Cat asking, "Left front, just left of that front bunker?"

Cat nodded and stepped away.

Julian hit the shot just a little fat and the ball flew almost to the bottom of the hill leaving him about a hundred and five yards to the flag.

Tommy said, "That will work." He moved to his ball and took out his Three Iron out of the bag. He waited until Cat had stopped moving around fixing Julian's divot and once that was done he took his stance over the ball. He took another great swing, even though it was from a downhill lie, and the ball flew in a right to left arc landing on the upper tier of the green. The flag was tucked in the back of the second tier, for Tommy to get to the flag he might have to chip his ball off the green's surface.

Julian said, "Nice shot."

Jake had already moved to his ball, he looked at Bud and asked, "What is it to the hole?"

Bud replied, "Two thirty six, two twenty eight to carry the bunker."

Jake took his Six Iron out of the bag, Bud just stood there, Jake looked at him saying, "I've got it."

Bud moved away not really knowing if Jake meant he had the shot, or he had the club he wanted. Two twenty eight carry off a downhill lie with a Six Iron was one hell of a shot, he did not remember when he had ever seen it done.

Jake took his stance and looked from his ball to the pin and back, he would have to take a little off the Six Iron and bring the shot in from left to right and land soft. He took the club back with a little outside in motion and the ball shot off the face towards the bunker that guards the left side of the green. It rose and began to turn slightly and landed four feet from the flag.

Julian and Tommy looked at each other, then at Jake, with them both saying at the same time, "What a great shot."

Julian continued with, "Sure you don't want to do this for a living?"

Jake grinned saying, "It Comes and Goes, but it sure is fun when It's in the Comes mode."

They walked down the hill and just enjoyed the company, when they got to Julian's ball they all moved to the right of the fairway to get out of his site path. Cat handed Julian his pitching wedge saying, "One eleven to the flag."

Julian nodded and took his stance over the ball and hit a smooth wedge to within three feet of the flag.

Jake and Tommy said, "Great shot."

Cat repaired the divot and walked over to the other caddies. The three caddies moved to the right rear of the green and placed the bags down. This, after they took the putters out for their player, V also took out Mr. Tommy's sand wedge. They looked at each other and V said, "I know Mr. Tommy will shoot Par or maybe one or two under but this guy Jake, hell, he looks like he could shoot 61 or 62. He's the best ball striker I've ever seen. And Mr. Julian looks like he will be right there with Mr. Tommy."

The other two nodded their agreement. They moved back onto the green and Bud reached for the flag looking at Mr. Tommy. Tommy had both his putter and sand wedge in his hands, if he putted his line would need to go over the fringe about six inched for a foot or so. It was that or to chip the ball over the fringe and hope to stop it close to the flag or in the hole. He motioned to Bud to pull the flag and handed V his sand wedge saying, "Better odds with the flat stick."

V nodded confirmation and moved away.

Tommy stroked the putt with a firm but light stroke it rolled onto the fringe and came back onto the green barely moving. It hit a very slight slope and picked up speed, it caught the left edge of the hole and spun to the right four inches and stopped. Tommy stepped over to the ball and tapped it in for his birdie. He took the ball out of the hole saying, "A bit faster and I'd still be away."

Julian replaced his ball and removed the marker saying, "That is just what I needed to know."

Jake laughed replying, "Such confidence."

Julian grinned and took his stance over the ball and hit it dead center with no delay. He picked the ball out of the hole with a grin on his face saying, "Need to hit them firm to keep the line."

Jake shook his head replying, "Thanks for that," Looking at Tommy he asked, "Isn't that considered offering advice? That's two strokes isn't it?"

Tommy laughed replying, "Not really but a very nice try."

Julian broke out with a chuckle.

Jake placed his ball down and removed his marker saying, "Gentlemen please, a little decorum."

Tommy, Julian and the three caddies burst out laughing, all at once.

Jake stood over the ball and sank his Eagle putt even with all of the laughter around him. He bent over and took the ball out of the hole and flipped it to Bud saying, "Please keep that one separate."

Bud nodded and cleaned the ball and put it in his pocket.

★★★

They were standing just off the tenth tee enjoying a cool drink from the food cart, the cart was almost five yards long and the server wore a large white cook's hat and was dressed all in white. There was a roast and a ham on the carving station in the center of the cart and different breads and rolls, along with all of the condiments one could want. The bartender was also the Cart's driver and was happy to make them fresh Iced Tea with a touch of Jack while their sandwiches were made.

So far the day was perfect, they all had played very well so far and were enjoying each other's company.

The caddies were standing off to one side, closer to the Cabins, enjoying the soft drinks and sandwiches that Mr. Tommy sent over to them. Bud looked at V and Cat saying, "Well, Mr. Julian and Mr. Tommy are three under Par and Mr. Jake is six under Par so far.

Some of the shots that I've seen today, well they have been almost unbelievable, I've seen some of them made before, but never all in one half round of golf by one player."

Cat took a sip of his soft drink and replied, "During the last few holes I believe Mr. Jake backed off a little, showing respect for his playing partners."

V nodded and added, "I think there were two or three holes that he backed off just a little. Best damn player I've ever seen. Everything is effortlessly accomplished, best muscle control I've ever seen."

Both of the other two nodded as they finished their lunch and kept an eye on Mr. Tommy to see when he was ready to resume play.

★★★

The stood on the twelfth tee box and looked over the creek at the green, Julian looked at Tommy and Jake saying, "Toughest one hundred forty five yard hole in the game of golf."

Tommy nodded replying, "Yes, on Sunday it looks a lot smaller and the wind seems to blow more erratic." He was making reference to the final day of the tournament held each April or May.

Jake looked at Bud and Bud said, "One forty seven, slight breeze from the right towards us," Jake reached into the bag and pulled his Nine Iron. The flag was setup directly behind the small bunker between the green and the creek. Jake had had the honors on the tee for the last five holes, and never seemed to take much time making his decisions. He teed the ball at the cut level and stood over the ball following the path from the tee to the hole with his eyes. He knew that it was 80% of his Nine Iron and the breeze would not really affect his shot. He brought the club strait back and through with just the correct force. The ball left the tee and never wavered from the flag, is dropped onto the green five feet past the bunker and rolled strait as a die into the hole. Jake just raised his hand with the club in it towards the sky.

Julian, Tommy and the caddies all let a loud yell out that they might have heard at the clubhouse, and began slapping Jake on the back. It took about five minutes for things to calm down Jake shook each of their hands and said he would like to take a photo of the entire group. This he did with him in the picture and with him out of the picture.

Jake looked at Bud and asked, "Please save that one also."

"Yes Sir Mr. Jake." He was up to four saved balls, so far.

Julian teed his ball up and looked at Jake saying, "That is one hell of an act to follow."

Jake and Tommy laughed and Tommy said, "Never been back to back hole in ones on this hole, ever."

Julian grinned replying, "I'm sure." He took his stance over the ball and looking once at the flag took the club back and through and the ball jumped off the clubface with a click. It rose steeply and dropped down from the apex of the flight, it dropped on the green two feet in front of the flag and rolled past the hole with in two inches of going in. It stopped three feet behind the flag.

"That was one great shot Julian, a great shot." Tommy said loud enough for all of them to hear.

Jake placed his hand on Julian's back saying, "That was close my friend, very close, great shot." Julian took a small bow saying, "thank you, thank you very much."

They all laughed again.

Tommy took a club and then teed up his ball up, looking at Jake and Julian said, "Nothing like a little pressure." He took his stance, and addressed the ball, placing the club behind the ball. He took a practice swing, looked at the flag and made his swing, slow but with force. The ball jumped off the club and flew at a lower trajectory moving from right to left. It landed on the green and rolled directly towards the hole, missing by less than an inch. Tommy's ball stopping two feet from the hole just a little left of Julian's.

The three caddies clapped their hands and V said, "I've never seen three better shots to this green ever, by anyone at anytime."

Cat and Bud said, "We agree" in unison, Cat also said, "Unbelievable."

The three golfers nodded their thanks and stepped off towards the bridge over the creek to the green. They all stopped to look at, and read, the commemorative plaque mounted on it. Julian looked at Jake saying, "Makes you feel a bit special. Doesn't it?"

Jake replied, "Yes, it does my friend. Yes it does."

The Tommy and Julian moved on to the green holding their putters, Jake stepped over to the hole and picked his ball out of it.

The caddies moved to the left rear of the green where the path was to the next tee box. Bud, Jake's caddie, stepped on to the green and over to the flag, he pulled it, and took Jake's ball from him, placing it into his pocket with the others Jake had asked him to save.

Jake moved off of the green and stood watching Julian and Tommy mark their balls. Tommy stepped away so as to not distract Julian as he checked his line of putt from both sides. Julian moved back to his marker and set his ball in place behind it, picked up the marker and took his stance over the ball. He moved his eyes from the hole to his ball and back. His putter moved back slowly and made the transition forward in one fluid motion. The ball rolled true and dropped into the hole. Julian pumped his fist in the air.

Tommy and Jake both said, "Nice putt," at the same time.

"Thank you," and moved off the green next to Jake, Jake, with a grin, gave him a fist bump.

Tommy walked around the hole, checking his putt from all sides, then placed his ball behind the marker. He took his stance and made one practice putt out and away from his line. He took a second look at the line and moved his putted back and through in one smooth motion. The only sound was that of the ball dropping in the hole."

Jake and Julian stepped onto the green, and once Tommy stood from picking his ball out of the hole, shook his hand and congratulated him.

Bud looking at V and Cat said, "Three players, four under on number 12, unbelievable, just unbelievable."

"Never seen it before, and probably never again," Cat responded.

V just shook his head saying, "Best I've ever seen. He picked up Tommy's Bag and started for the next tee. The other two followed his lead, both still talking about what they had just experienced.

Tommy looked over towards Jake and Julian saying, "That will be hard for people to believe."

Jake replied quickly, "Tommy, all that happens here stays here, correct?"

Tommy looked at him and replied just as quickly, "If that is your wish, it is so. I will talk to the caddies and make it so."

Jake looked at him for a second before answering, "Thank you."

Julian just nodded and punched Jake in the arm softly saying, "Thanks, I didn't want anyone to know how bad you beat me anyway."

They all laughed a bit. Arriving at the tee the three of them stood looking at the fairway and the way it turned to the left marching towards the unseen distant green.

Tommy looked at them and with a grin asked, "Anyone up for a friendly wager?"

Julian grinned and replied, "Depends, what's on your mind?"

"Five dollars each, all goes to the lowest scorer on this hole, the money goes to the player's favorite charity."

Jake said quickly, "I'm in."

"Me to," Julian replied.

Tommy looked at Jake saying, "You Sir have the honors."

Jake stepped backwards on the tee and teed his ball up.

The others stepped further back as Jake pulled his driver out of the bag. He looked at Julian saying, "Well on Sunday they turn it around that corner and leave an iron shot left to the green. Guess I'll give that a try, all for a good cause."

He stepped behind the ball and picked a spot on one of the trees on the far side of the fairway. He took his stance and looked from the ball to the spot and back, his swing was stronger than any of the others and when the club hit the ball it sounded like a gun shot. The ball left the club and started out moving right, away from the fairway, it climbed higher as it turned left. They never saw it come down in the fairway because it went past the tree line, on the near corner, that blocked their view.

Julian looked at Tommy grinning and said, "Gee, hope that stopped turning before it reached the creek."

"Me to," Tommy quipped as he pulled his driver out of his bag.

Jake looked at them, grinning to himself, saying, "Shouldn't say anything until you ball is on the ground out there." He handed his club to Bud.

Julian stepped on the tee box, teed his up his ball and stood behind it for a moment looking down the fairway, then took his stance. He looked down the fairway and then back at his ball, he pulled his driver back and moved it through the ball with a little more force than he had been. The ball flew straight at the corner, rising and turning slightly to the left. It bounced just past the middle of the fairway at the turn and rolled out of site.

Jake said, "I don't think that will reach the creek, great shot."

"Thank you, I really thought I went after that a little too much." He handed Cat his club saying, "Missed it," Cat just laughed.

Tommy teed his ball up and looked at both of them saying, "I truly have to say that you two are the toughest I've ever played with. And also this is the most fun I've had out here in a long time." He took his stance and took one quick look towards the corner, he moved the club back and around his body. The finish of the swing was as smooth as any he had ever made. The ball rose and turned in the direction that both of the others had taken but on a bit lower flight path. They saw it land just short of where Julian's had then it shot forward and out of site.

Tommy handed V his club as he walked by, the caddies seemed to be moving a bit faster. Julian noticed it and remarked on it once they were out of ear shot.

Tommy looked at Jake and Julian saying, "I believe that there might be a bit of wagering going on. The caddies will sometime do that when they think that the golfers are pretty evenly matched."

Jake and Julian laughed and Jake said, "I hope they are better at it then we are."

Julian added, "Does that mean I have to try harder now?"

They all laughed as they moved towards the fairway.

They walked towards where the fairway turned and as they got closer they saw all three caddies standing in the fairway, V and Cat were standing about two feet apart, Bud was forty yards in front of them, he had a huge smile on his face.

Jake looked at the others saying, "Not hard to see who made money on this one."

They all laughed.

V looked at Tommy saying, "Two hundred twenty one to the flag, two hundred fourteen yards to the middle, one hundred eighty two to the creek and one hundred eighty-five to carry it."

Tommy pulled his four highbred out of the bag and stepped closer to his ball.

Julian and Jake moved down the slope closer to the creek, the caddies did the same, to watch the shot.

Tommy took a practice swing and then reset his feet, he moved back and through the shot hitting it solid. The ball rose, riding the slight breeze that moved towards the green, it landed on the left front of the green and rolled all the way to the back left fringe. It stopped thirty feet from the flag.

"Good shot," came from each of the other players.

Julian moved to his ball and looking at the shot to be made, he reached into this bag and took out his Three Iron. He took his stance and choked down about an inch on the grip. He felt the breeze move from his right cheek, forward a little, he shifted his weight side to side then settled in to his stance. He took his swing and as soon as the club hit the ball he spun the club muttering, "Got you."

The ball landed on the right side of the green and rolled to the front, just inches from the front fringe, sixteen feet from the flag.

"Great shot," came from all again.

Jake moved up to his ball, Bud said, "One eighty one to the pin, seven yards behind, sixteen to the front. If it starts down in front of the flag it will move all the way to the creek."

Jake pulled his eight iron and wiped the face with the towel on the bag. He stepped around and took his stance. He looked at the flag and back to his ball, he took the club back and through and the ball took off in a perfect arc.

They all watched the ball's flight and when they saw it hit the flag and careened into the creek, there was a united gasp.

Jake handed Bud the club and looking at the others said, "Stuff happens."

They all walked to the green in silence.

Jake walked towards the right side of the green and when he reached the bank of the creek he turned and said, "Wet."

He walked back six or seven yards and took a new ball out of his bag, he pulled his sand wedge and standing facing the green held the ball out at shoulder height. He dropped the ball and it rolled about a foot and stopped. He looked at the lie and shook his head a little.

Bud said, "That is probably the only thin spot on this entire course."

"Yep."

Tommy stood by his ball marker looking at the line of the his putt, trying not to stare at Jake and his difficulty.

Julian marked his ball and moved towards the left side of the green, to make sure that he was out of Jake's line of site.

Jake looked at Bud and said, "Please go take the flag out."

Bud did not respond, he just started walking towards the green. He walked onto the green and lifted the flag out of the hole. He then moved off to the left side of the green and stood there perfectly still.

Jake looked at the hole and took his stance while staring at it, his gaze did not waver as he took the club back and came through the ball. The ball jumped off of the club and landed on the green and rolled up and in.

Bud let out a loud yell, he then put his head down saying, "Sorry Mr. Tommy, sorry."

Tommy and Julian moved towards the right side of the green to meet with Jake as he moved towards the hole to get his ball. One hand slapped his back and the other shook his hand all the while saying what a fantastic shot that he had just made.

Jake said, "Thank you, thank you, I believe that is a birdie gentlemen, it is now your turns."

Tommy and Julian laughed and moved back to their ball markers, with Tommy looking at V saying, "V, again, that was one of the best shots I've ever seen. I think that makes five or six wonderful shots."

V responded, "Yes Sir, Some of the best I've ever seen also."

Tommy stood over his ball and looked from the flag to his ball and back, there was at least twelve feet of turn, from left to right, and it dropped four or five feet. Speed was the most important if you hit your line, if you missed either the ball could end up further away from the flag or in the creek. Tommy lined up his putt twenty feet left of the hole, he stroked the putt softly. The ball moved slowly along the ridge of the high point of the green and when it was parallel with the hole it started to turn right moving down the slope. The ball picked up speed and tracked directly towards the hole, it hit the back of the hole and popped up four of five inches. It came down and hit the back edge and rolled five feet back towards the center of the green and stopped.

Tommy moved to the ball quickly and marked it saying, "Wow, that could have gone bad quickly."

Julian replied, "Yes, it sure could have, hard to believe it could pick up that much speed."

Tommy grinned saying, "That's why I marked it quickly, it might have started moving again."

Julian moved behind his ball again and took a last look, he stood over his ball and looked at the hole and back to his ball a few times. He reset his stance and moved the putter back and through, the ball rolled directly at the hole and veered off and stopped four inches from the hole. He walked up quickly and taped it in saying, "Got you." He walked over to Jake and shook his outstretched hand.

"Great two putt my friend," Jake said.

Tommy replaced his ball and walked all the way around the hole checking the line of his putt. He moved over his ball and looked from the hole to his ball once more and set himself. He moved the putted back and through and the ball moved on a line about an inch above the hole. Just at the end as the ball slowed it turned to the right and dropped in.

Jake and Julian said in unison, "Great putt."

Tommy took the ball out of the hole and turned to them saying, "Thank you" as he shook each of their hands.

★★★

Tyrone sat at his desk looking out at the river watching a log slowly past by, he saw it but didn't. His mind was bouncing from item to item and event to event that occurred over the past few months. He kept coming back to the day of the Taste of Augusta. "That damn cop threw me like a rag, like a damn rag. Need to make that right, soon. Damn cop will pay for making me look so bad." He started to plan just that, some place dark and lonely, no one around. "Yep, Sergeant Keller, your time is coming." He stood up and walked to the door and looked up the river, looking but not seeing.

★★★

Walking towards the sixteenth tee one of the many preset alerts went off in Jake's mind. He stopped for a moment and lifted his hand to his temple looking down at the grass. In less than a second his mind replayed every thought that Tyrone had thought, including his plans.

Julian looked back at Jake saying, "You okay?"

Jake looked up replying, "Sure, all is well." He moved up to the tee and took his eight iron out of his bag. He looked at the green, the flag was just a few paces off the back but almost at the center line, turning to Bud he asked, "Different pin placement, never saw that one on TV?"

"Someone must have taken a new page out of the pin book, I've only seen it there a few times. If you're short it will roll all the way back to the bottom left, a little long and it will go off the green, right of the flag more than four feet it will roll all the way to the bottom also."

Jake grinned replying, "Sounds like it needs to be high, soft and straight."

Bud grinned back saying, "Sounds right."

Julian and Tommy were standing next to Jake and had heard the exchange between the two of them.

Julian looked at Tommy saying, "Sounds like a piece of cake, a hundred and sixty two yards, high, soft and straight, Yep, a piece of cake. "Jake my man, you're up."

Jake reached down and teed his ball, he stepped up to it and swung the club back and through, making it look effortless. The arc of the ball was very high and when it landed behind the hole it hopped and drew back stopping just a few inches from the hole. He spun the club in his hand and pushed it into his bag looking at Bud and winked.

Tommy looked at Julian saying, "High, soft, and straight, nothing to it."

Julian replied, "Right, nothing to it," as he teed up his ball. He pulled his six iron and took his stance over the ball. He swung with no hesitation, in an attempt to mimic Jake's swing. His ball landed short of the hole and rolled past the flag and off of the green about a foot.

"Good shot," came from Tommy and Jake.

Tommy teed his ball and stepped up to it and took his stance, he moved through the ball and the click of the ball being struck was clear and sharp. It moved a little right to left and landed high on the green twenty five feet short of the flag. It released and rolled along the high right side of the green, rolling slowly and reaching the back of the green it turned left and trickled down the slope and stopped six inches from the hole.

Cat looked at Bud and V saying, "Three best tee shots I've ever seen on this or any golf hole." They both nodded their agreement.

Jake, Julian and Tommy shook each other's hands and they turned and started walking to the green and their balls. Jake loked at Julian saying, "I'll need to call in after the round, hopefully all is well."

Julian nodded and replied, "I need to also."

V and Tommy walked across the green, reaching Tommy's ball V pulled the flag, and Tommy, taking his putter out of his bag, tapped in the putt.

Jake marked his ball and V put the flag back in the hole and stepped away.

Julian stepped behind his ball to check the line of his shot, he had sixteen inches of first cut and three feet to the hole. The shot would move six inches left to right in the last foot and a half. It was totally a feel putt or chip. Cat looked at him and Julian asked, "What do you see?"

"Well, if you chip it, you need to carry it on the green and hit it with dead hands, no spin, for it to keep the line. If you putt it, it will break seven inched moving from left to right. Both shots need the correct speed or you'll have twelve feet back. I think the putt is the safest of the two shots."

Julian nodded and stepped over to his bag and stood there for a moment with one hand on his putter and the other on his wedge. He pulled the putter and looked at Cat saying, "Please pull the flag."

He moved over his ball and took two more looks at the shot and line, settled his feet and gripped and re-gripped his hands. He took a short breath and moved the putter back and threw. The ball moved slowly thru the first cut and looked like it wouldn't make the green, it moved onto the green and amazingly continued to roll towards the hole. The ball made its final half roll into the cup almost like it was slow motion.

Jake said, "Wow!" Almost to himself but it was loud enough for Tommy and all three caddies to reply, "Wow, Unbelievable, Great shot, Great.

Julian stepped over to the hole, and picked his ball out of it, with a big grin on his face. "I thought I left it short, really, I did."

Jake stepped on the green with his putter and replied, "Well I hope I leave mine that short."

All of them laughed a little as Jake placed his ball in front of his marker and picked up the marker. He wasted no time and stepped over the ball and with a quick glance at the hole shifted his shoulders and tapped the back of the ball and it dropped into the hole.

The six of them moved towards the seventeenth tee box, the players in one group, and the caddies in another.

V, Cat and Bud were in deep conversation and Bud was very animated in whatever he was saying. They got very quite as they approached the tee and their golfers, they tilted each bag towards their player allowing them to easily remove the club of their choice.

Jake pulled out his three wood, taking the cover off of it, flipped the cover back on the bag. He moved to the left side of the tee boxes and teed his ball. He teed it a bit lower than normally, and took his set up to allow him to move the ball from right to left. Bud had mentioned that the flag was on the left front today so a shot in from the left side of the fairway would be the best. Jake stood over his ball and adjusted his stance a few inches narrower, He took a full turn and moved through the ball smoothly, it jumped off the club face and rose as it went down the right side of the fairway and slowly turned towards the left. It bounced once and rolled another twenty feet, stopping just seventy yards from the green. Jake stepped over to his bag and handed Bud the club and just grinned.

Tommy and Julian hit their drives with both landing in the fairway, Julian's taking a left to right flight and Tommy's a right to left flight. They both ended up forty yards behind Jake's ball.

As they walked up the fairway Tommy told them about the plans to replace the large pine tree that was lost during an ice storm a year ago. He explained that the Club had been working with a farmer in North Carolina grooming a tree that resembled the lost tree almost exactly. It was a eight to ten month process to ready the tree for removal and transport to the Club. He explained that once it was in transit they would prepare the spot where it would be planted. The Club's specialist had been treating the spot to insure that the tree would have a very high percentage of taking.

Julian could not pass up the opportunity to say, "I bet that will be a costly event."

Tommy grinned saying, "Well, it will cost a bit more than the Magnolia for the drive."

Jake was walking a few yards to their left in deep thought, he was scanning Undersheriff Winslow, Dr. Andrews and Dr. Fox. All seemed to be quiet with only a few minor events occurring on the streets.

"Fore," Julian said as he stopped at his ball, Jake had passed it and was ten yards past it.

Jake looked around and started stepping backwards, he grinned saying, "Sorry, thought you hit it better than that."

Julian chucked replying, "Yep, missed it a bit." Julian's and Tommy's drives were almost two hundred and eighty yards from the tee, well longer than that of the average golfer.

Cat looked at Julian saying, "One hundred and eight to the pin."

Julian pulled his sand wedge and stepped over the ball. He set his feet and moved through the ball and it flew high and landed softly just on the green front and released up to less than two feet from the hole. He looked at Jake saying, "Darn, missed it."

Jake and Tommy both laughed, and the caddies chuckled.

Tommy moved over his ball and was just about set to make his pass at the ball when a squirrel darted out on the fairway and right over Tommy's ball and threw his legs. Tommy stepped back and watched the squirrel reach the other side of the fairway and dart up a pine tree. Tommy looked at V saying, "That was a first, should be a last."

V just nodded thinking, "Will that will be the last squirrel ever seen on this course."

Tommy moved back over his ball and looked at the hole and back to his ball, he made his move through the ball. The ball flew at the green moving right to left, a slight puff of a breeze came up and the ball seemed to hit a bit of a wall and dropped into the bunker guarding the right front of the green. Tommy looked at V and flipped him his club. He stepped up to a spot even with Jake's ball and looked from bunker to flag and back, it was obvious that he was not happy.

Jake stepped up, and over his ball, looking at the hole. He had a sixty degree wedge in his hand. He made his pass at the ball and it flew sixty yards high and seventy two yards towards the green. It landed on the green eight yards past the hole and spun back hitting the flag pole and dropping in the hole.

All six men yelled at the same moment.

Julian almost ran to Jake to congratulate him with Tommy right behind him.

They walked up to the green chattering with accolades flying back and forth.

When they got to the green Jake walled to the hole and took his ball out and flipped it to Bud saying, "One more."

Bud was grinning and replied, "Yes Sir, My pleasure."

Tommy walked over to the trap and saw that his ball had popped out of its pitch mark and was on a slight upgrade. The flag was about twenty-two feet from the trap, he pulled his sand wedge, looked at it and put it back in the bag. He pulled his pitching wedge an stepped into the trap. Turning his feet he dug in about a quarter of an inch with his stance to the left of the flag. He opened the club's face and gripped it firmly, released it and re-gripped it softly. He took a very up right back swing and a full follow through, it sounded like what a dropped melon would sound like. The sand and ball exploded out of the bunker, the ball dropped on the green and released right up to the hole stopping two inches from going in.

Jake and Julian both said, "Great shot Tommy, great shot."

Tommy, as he moved out of the bunker, replied, "Thank you, thank you, came off better than I thought."

V put Tommy's club in the bag and stepped into the bunker with a rake to smooth and tidy it up thinking, "First one today, amazing."

Julian re-marked his ball and took his stance over it and stroked it firmly, directly to the back of the hole and in, making it look easy.

The three of them moved the fifty feet to the last tee box and stood looking up the fairway to where it turned to the right towards the hidden green.

Jake reached over and pulled his driver from his bag saying with a slight laugh in his voice, "No guts, no glory."

Bud aid, "Two sixty to the traps, two eighty-five to carry."

Jake nodded and teed up his ball on the extreme right of the tee box, and took a semi practice swing. He glanced up the fairway, back to his ball and took a strong, firm smooth swing. The ball shot to the left side if the fairway and continued to rise as it approached the traps, flying over them and landing a good fifty yards past them.

Tommy stood there looking at the ball finally saying, "Jake, that is the best drive I've ever seen on this hole, better than any person that ever played here, Amateur or Professional."

Jake said softly, "Thank you Tommy."

Julian and Tommy both had their drives land in the middle of the fairway leaving clear shots to the green.

The caddies were already thirty yards ahead of them walking up the fairway. Cat was saying, "Bud, your guy can set a new record today, one that will never be beat. Not in our lifetime. Par gives him fifty eight, birdie fifty seven, even a shot at a fifty six if he holes it. Yours and his name will be forever displayed in the clubhouse, Mr. Tommy asked us to not discuss this outside of the round, easy to do. No one would ever believe what we have seen today, and I believe that Mr. Jake backed off on three or four holes."

Bud looked at them replying, "Hey don't forget Mr. Julian and Mr. Tommy, with a par each it's a sixty two and a sixty three and with the way they have been playing it could be better than that."

Julian got to his ball first and Tommy's was a yard or so in front of him.

Cat said, "One sixty one to the flag, uphill by sixteen feet."

Julian pulled his Seven Iron, and set up for a little less fade and a little higher flight. He wanted the ball to land soft with little release.

He made the swing and watched the ball follow his imagined ball flight exactly, it landed with one bounce and settled seven feet from the hole.

Tommy said, "Great shot," as he stepped up to his ball. He pulled his seven iron and set up for a slight draw. He wanted to bring the ball in high over the right bunker and for the ball to hit and roll out five to six feet.

Tommy took a smooth and deliberate swing, he watched the ball start towards the bunker and turn just as he had planned with it landing on the green and releasing seven feet towards the flag, He would be left with a five foot putt slightly uphill with a little right to left line.

Julian grinned, saying, you got me, great shot."

Tommy replied, "Thank you."

They both turned to watch Jake's second shot.

Jake pulled a nine iron out of the bag and stepped over to his ball, he took his stance with the ball just a little forward, and moved through the ball very firmly but smoothly. The ball flew very high and landed eight feet past the flag and rolled back three inches in front of Tommy's ball. He looked at Tommy with a grin saying, "Looks like I'm going to get a teach."

Tommy replied, "Yes, but I don't think that is really necessary my friend,"

Julian just laughed walking up to Jake and slapping him on the back said softly, "Thank you, this is a day I will remember for the rest of my life and to spend it with a great friend makes it very special."

Jake started to reply but Julian waved him off and walked over to Tommy.

When they reached the green Julian pulled his putter and Cat set the bag down and moved on the green and pulled the flag. He stood behind Julian's ball for a moment and moved to the first cut and placed the flag down.

Jake and Tommy marked their balls and moved out of Julian's sight line.

Julian looked at his putt from behind and then stepped over his ball and stroked his ball. The ball moved at the hole and just missed going in and stopped two inches past the hole. Julian stepped up and tapped it in. He moved off the green and stopped standing next to Cat.

Tommy looked at his putt from both sides and stepped over the ball. He stroke the ball and watched it move directly towards the center of the hole and drop with a clunk.

Tommy picked up his ball and moved over to stand next to Julian as Jake stepped over his ball.

Jake looked at the hole and back to his ball, without hesitation made the stroke and watched the ball follow Tommy's line and drop in the hole with another clunk.

Julian, Tommy, V Cat and Bud all started clapping. Tommy said Sir, congratulations you have just set a new course record, a record that I don't believe will ever be beaten, a fifty four."

"Thank you, but please don't overlook that both of you shot sixty nine, that my friends is out of sight golf. I'm proud to have spent the day with you both." He turned towards the caddies and said, "I want to thank you for making this a special day, I don't believe that any group of caddies will ever carry for three golfers that shoot one eighty two total for eighteen. You all make this a very special day." He walked over to them and shook each of their hands. He then walked over to Julian saying, "You owe me a drink."

Tommy chimed in with, "Guys, the drinks are on me." He looked at the caddies saying, "The three of you will join us as soon as we get back to the clubhouse in the grill room for a drink to celebrate, I will have a photo taken of the six of us, then you are off to complete your work." Tommy knew that allowing them to join them in the grill room would place them in the Caddie's Club history. It will be talked about for years and years.

The three of them, grinning, replied, "Yes Sir, Thank you Mr. Tommy.

Julian, Jake and Tommy walked up the hill to the door to the Grill Room kidding each other about the play on the eighteenth, their drives, iron shots and putts were all discussed.

Just as they reached the door it opened, Blue said, "Hope it was a good round gentlemen."

Tommy stepped through the door saying, "It was great Blue, I will need a camera, please."

"Yes Sir, in just a moment," he started to say something as Bud walked towards the door.

Tommy saw what was occurring and said quickly, "Blue, Bud, V, And Cat will be joining me, us, for a drink. We have to celebrate something very special today Mr. Jake set a new course record today. A record that I believe will stand for a long, long time, if not forever."

Blue held the door for the three caddies to enter, and had a look of astonishment on his face. It was the first time that he could ever remember that a caddie was in the Member's Grillroom. Yes, this day would be remembered, and talked about, by Members and Caddies alike for a very long time.

The six men stood at the bar, and the bartender served Tommy, Jake and Julian first and then the three caddies.

Blue appeared with a camera and Tommy had the caddies kneel in front of him, Jake and Julian with Jake and Bud in the center looking at Blue.

Blue said, "Smiles please."

That was not a problem for them at all, they had the biggest smiles already, smiles that couldn't be hidden even if they wanted to. Blue snapped five shots of the group and then four more of just Jake and Bud, then four more of just Jake.

The caddies finished their drinks and shook each of the players hand once again with many comments of praise. They walked towards the door and to their surprise Blue beat them there and held it open for them saying, "Thank you Gentlemen."

Yes, it would be a day not soon forgotten.

***

Tyrone picked his phone up off of his desk and pushed the Call button as he lifted it to his ear saying loudly, "Yes!"

"Tyrone, it's me," came the voice of Dr. Greenly, "The visitors from South America, they have moved up their visit. I need to see you tonight."

"I'll be over at seven thirty, have some scotch, good stuff," he pushed the End button not waiting for a response.

"Moving the meeting, well I guess that is good," he thought. "They would make well over a hundred million in less than six weeks according to Dr. Greenly."

***

Stepping back in to the Grillroom and moving to the bar, Julian lifted his drink and took the last sip looking at Jake and Tommy said, "Well, this has been a wonderful day but Tommy we will have to take a rain check on playing the Par Three course. We, Jake and I, have to get to a meeting that both of our bosses have called. I cannot thank you enough for the invitation, experience and company. You have been the most gracious of hosts."

"I understand, thank you both for being my guests, this is the most fun day I've had in a very long time. I look forward to us doing it again soon, very soon I hope. You should find everything you need in the locker room. Again, thank you."

Jake and Julian shook his hand and walked to the locker room, Julian spoke softly saying, the Undersheriff wants to meet with us in an hour. Something from the State Police, a problem that they have asked for our help with."

Jake just nodded and stepped into the Locker room just in front of Julian, moving to the lockers that they had placed their clothes in earlier. Jake was not surprised to find his shoes shined and his clothes pressed. He took his new clothes into the shower area and undressed in the dressing area of one of the individual shower stalls and rinsed off. Stepping out of the stall he dried off and redressed. He could hear Julian a few stalls to his left, deeper in the room.

Once back at his locker Jake folded and placed his clothes and golf shoes in his ditty bag, Julian was also placing his stuff in his tote bag.

Almost like magic Blue appeared and asked, "Would you gentlemen like a Tea of Soft drink to go?"

They both replied, "No thank you." They picked up their bags and followed Blue to the club's front door, which he opened and held for them. "Gentlemen, it was a pleasure to serve you and thank you for making Mr. Tommy smile so much, it's been a long time since he has had that much fun."

Jake turned to Blue and put his hand out saying, "Thank you Blue, you helped make this a day to remember always." Julian also said his thank you and offered his hand.

Blue shook Jake's hand, and then Julian's saying, "Thank you, my pleasure."

They both turned and walked over to their vehicle and they found their caddies standing at the rear of the truck. Cat and Bud had placed Julian and Jake's golf bags, and clubs in the bed of the truck. Jake opened the rear door of the truck and they both placed their bags on the seat. Jake closed the door and they both moved to the back of the truck towards where Bud and Cat were standing.

Bud handed Jake a small bag saying, "The balls you asked me to keep for you, and I've taped a tag to each with a brief outline of the events that took place." He then put out his hand saying, "Sir, it was my pleasure to be part of today, at your request no word of this will be discussed off of these grounds, but when alone I'm sure V, Cat and I will marvel at the events of today. The three of you put on a show that I believe will never be equaled."

Jake shook his hand an replied, "Thank you Bud, Maybe we will get out here again, if so I will request that the same team be assembled, it was fun." He turned and shook Cat's hand, Julian shook both of the men's hands and he and Jake turned and got into the truck.

Jake started the truck and slowly moved down Magnolia Lane with the clubhouse getting smaller and smaller in his rearview mirror.

CHAPTER SIXTEEN

J AKE POURED HIMSELF HIS SECOND cup of coffee and picking up the cup he moved over to the window overlooking the river and sat in the tall chair he had placed there. He had a small table just to his right of the chair that held the half of breakfast sandwich that he had made earlier.

Jake sat down and taking a sip of coffee he watched a small boat move slowly along the far bank with the occupants casting their lines close to the Lilly pads that lined the bank. He was looking at the scene but not really seeing it, his mind was thousands of miles away. He visited place after place and person after person, something he did often, tweaking his web of alarms that follow him every day.

He sat almost in a trance-like state as he viewed all of the events that were coming together regarding Tyrone Mendoza and the good Dr. Paul Greenly. Based on the meetings he had sat in with Julian, the Undersheriff, the State Attorney General and the Commander of the GBI, time of reckoning was coming. A payback of sorts, payback for all of the wrongs that had and were being caused across the city, county and state by the poison being distributed by the Doctor and Tyrone's network.

The sound of his door buzzer interrupted his thoughts, he glanced at the security screen and saw a delivery van in the drive and the driver was standing at his door.

"Be right there," he called as he moved off the chair and towards the stairs. Looking at the security screen he noticed the driver was holding a box, it looked to be about a foot long and half as wide and tall, but it just did not look right.

When he reached the door, at the foot of the stairs, before he turned the knob he glanced at the twelve inch flat screen he had installed on the wall. When the door was open it was hidden behind it, but until you opened the door you had a close up look at who, or what, was on the other side of the door.

Something did not look just right, it looked like the driver's hand was in the end of the box. Jake did a quick scan of the man's mind, all of his thoughts were in Spanish, and were not the thoughts of a delivery driver.

The driver's thoughts listed the complete schedule of the who, how and when, Jake, Sergeant Keller, Office Tommy Jameson and Julian were to be killed. There was a kill squad loose in Augusta, sent by one Tyrone Mendoza and his drug supplier.

Jake watched the screen as he took control of the man's mind rewriting his thoughts, he watched the man remove his hand from the box then turn and walk back to the van. Jake now had full control of the man's mind, he knew his wants and fears. The man started the van and turned around and drove up the driveway, making a right at the street and pulled over to the side of the road then up over the curb onto an empty lot. The driver sat there hearing things dropping on to the van, thump, thump, and then a large snake landed with a louder

thump on the short hood of the van Looking through
the windshield the driver's eyes were wide with fear.
Catching a bit of movement out of the corner of his eye
he snapped his head around. He saw two more snakes
slipping through the window opening. He let out a gasp
and pulled the trigger of the pistol he was holding, the
bullet shattered the window and the shot sounded like
an explosion in the confined space. The large snake on
the hood began to slither through the windshield and
was ready to strike at his arm. He turned the pistol and
fired again taking the head of the snake off, but also
shattering his arm. He felt a sharp pain in the groin,
looking down there was a snake that had struck him on
his upper thigh. In total panic he turned the pistol on
himself and pulled the trigger to kill the snake that only
he could see. The bullet tore through his artery and the
blood shot out onto the trucks floor in large spurts. The
gun fell out of his hand into the large puddle of blood
that was forming on the floor of the truck. The thoughts
of snakes filled his head as his life left him.

★★★

The delivery van pulled into the dirt alley and up to
the small cabin that sat alone in the most run down part
of the former business district. With the new highway
and shopping mall on the bypass just one mile away the
business district, which had only be made up of five
stores on each side of the street, had been abandoned.
The same had happened in many small towns across the
state and county, not just in Arizona.

The cabin door opened and a large man, almost seven feet tall, stepped out. He was joined by a pretty woman that stood almost two feet shorter than the man.

The van driver stopped the van and stepped out onto the scrub grass and weeds that were trying to survive in the poor soil and a lack of water. He nodded towards the couple saying, "Rock. Penny, I have a package for you." He opened the side door of the van and reaching in lifted a white package off of the floor. He turned and walked up to the man he had called Rock and handed it to him.

Rock took the package saying, "Thanks David."

"It's what I do, hope you both have a great day." He turned and returned to his van, got in and backed around and turned towards the street, completing a perfect K turn, and in a moment was gone.

Rock looked at the package on all sides and turned towards his wife saying, "Penny, this is from Jake, Can you believe that? It's been over fifteen years since we've seen or heard from him?"

"I think it has been longer than that, the kids were still here when he was around, now they are all gone. Darn, it's been six years since the last one left home."

Looking at the package and then Penny, Rock said, "Well let's get inside and see what this holds."

They moved into the cabin and walked to the kitchen table, each taking a seat Rock pulled the wrapping off of the box. An envelope was tapped to the top of the box with Rock & Penny written across it.

Penny removed the envelope and opened it by slipping her finger behind the fold over flap. She found one sheet of paper folded over in three folds. Lifting the first fold and then the second she looked at the sentences that filled half of the sheet. She looked at Rock and then back at the paper and began to read out loud. "Dear Rock and Penny, I hope this will cover yours, and the children's, medical bills with some left over to make things a little easier. It is the least that should be done after all both of you have done for the needy in Waverly over the past twenty years, both children and adults.

You have been putting everyone else's needs first for a very long time, what is in this package is from me to you, a gift, please do not slight me by using it in any way other than for what I have asked. I am asking you both to use this gift to make your lives a little bit better, now and over the next years."

It was signed, 'Your friend Jake.'

Penny placed the paper on the table and dabbed her eyes with one of the napkins from the table.

Rock picked up the paper and read it again, then again. He placed it on the table and opened the package, he stacked the bundles on bills two high and next to each other, they stretched almost the length of the table. Twenty thousand in each stack, with twenty-four stacks, added up to four hundred and eighty thousand dollars.

Rock stared at the stacks of bills and then Penny and shook his head saying, "We've lived on less than ten thousand dollars a year for the last eight, maybe ten years. What in the world will we do with all of this?"

Penny looked at his and replied, "Rock, we will do exactly what Jake has asked us to do, exactly. This is our salvation Rock, Jake has given us the gift of peace of mind for both our children and ourselves."

Rock reached across the table and took his wife's hand saying, "Praise the Lord and God bless true friends."

★★★

Jake reached out to Sergeant Keller and Officer Jameson putting them on full emergency alert, they would not know why they were so paranoid but they would react the proper way. Next he called Julian.

"Hey, what's up?" Julian asked as he brought the phone up to his ear.

"We have a big problem, there is a hit squad in town and the people on the list to be visited are you, me, Sergeant Keller and Officer Jameson."

"What, how do you know that? When is it supposed to go down? What…"

"I just had a visit from one of them a bit ago, and I was moving to interview him but he broke away and jumped in the van he was driving and sped out of here. What I did get was that the other two men are driving in white vans with 'Delivery' on the side panels in red lettering. They are very heavily armed and very intent on completing their mission. One is on the way to Sergeant Keller's home, and the other to Officer Jameson's home. You need to get people moving but I'm sure they are monitoring the police band."

"Okay, I'll get word to the men on the street and have cars at each of the homes in moments without the radio. You call Keller, I'll call Jameson?"

Jake replied, "Got it, I'm heading to Keller's home, it's only a few minutes from here, I'm on the way. Watch your back, might be more of them."

"10-4, I'll be in touch.

Jake opened the door and stepped into his garage, getting in his truck and he was moving up the drive quickly as the garage door closed. Passing the white van he looked at the driver, it looked like he was taking a nap. He tried to find the other two shooters with his mind, but nothing came back, he set alerts for anyone's thoughts of violence and Jameson and Keller.

It took Jake just a little over five minutes to reach the street that Sergeant Keller lived on. Turning onto the street he saw a white van turning onto the same street three blocks down the street, it turned towards him. Looking at the street numbers he knew that he was only five or six houses away from Keller's home. He passed it and pulled over in front of the house next door. He looked at the truck's floor and concentrated on the man in the white van moving towards him. The man's plan was to pull into the drive and spray the house with gunfire from the automatic rifle he was carrying. He then would kick in the door and search and kill anyone in the house that was not dead already.

Jake waited until the van was turning behind him and opened the door and moved quickly alone the street side of his truck. The van driver was opening the van's door and had the rifle in his hand. Jake stood up and shouted, "Police, drop your weapon!"

The driver raised the rifle, pointing it at Jake, seeing the movement Jake pulled the trigger of his pistol three times quickly. The man's head exploded and two large red spots appeared on his shirt. He fell to the ground just as a police cruiser pulled into the driveway, and the two officers in it jumped out with their guns out. Sergeant Keller came out of this house with his service revolver out in front of him.

Jake yelled, "Clear, guns down, Clear." As he walked up the drive making sure that he held his gun out to his side in plain view. The officers all holstered their guns as Jake picked up the rifle, cleared it, and placed it on the hood of the van. He walked around to Sergeant Keller saying, "You okay?"

"Yes, okay, felt something wasn't right, just didn't know how wrong it was. Thanks for the call, gave me time to get the family out of the house and safe. Any word on what's going on with Jameson and his family?"

Jake lifted his phone to his ear as he pushed the Call button saying, "Checking now."

Julian's voice came on saying, "We got him, when he saw one of our cars he stopped the van he was driving and started shooting. Luckily he didn't hit anyone before we got him, stopped him a half block from Tommy's house. We were lucky, how did you made out?"

"We got him just as he pulled into the driveway, he had an assault rifle which he pointed at an officer and when ordered to drop his weapon he began to raise it to fire. No one was hurt and all at the Keller house are safe."

"Great, please tell Sergeant Keller there will be heavy police surveillance 24/7 in his area for awhile."

"Got it, I'm heading back to check out the first shooter from here, then I'll be heading downtown."

"Okay, I'll meet you at your lab in about an hour."

"Great, need to have a car go by my place and yours for awhile, I'm concerned for Teddy and Marian."

"Got it, I'm having them pass by Janet and Martha's on a regular basis also, you never know."

"Thanks see you in about an hour."

Jake told Keller what had happened and what was going to happen.

Keller thanked him again and went to be with his family after talking with the other officers that had arrived.

Jake walked over to the body and leaned over it saying, "Officially, he is dead. Have them send and ambulance and tell the Coroner's office that the scene was cleared by me. I will have a five on your Sergeant's desk in an hour or so."

"He heard a "Yes Sir" as he walked back to his truck.

It took him a few moments to get back to the first white van, he pulled to the side of the road behind it and noted the plate number and that it had South Carolina plate. He walked to the driver's door and opened it and leaned over the body and took the pistol from the puddle of blood. He walked around the front of the van and opened the passenger door, he was not surprised to find an assault rifle on the floor with its muzzle on the floor and the butt on the seat. The placement would have made it easy for the driver to pull it up and fire out any of the windows. The patrol car he had called in and requested pulled up with lights flashing.

Jake stepped in front of the van and over to the police car carrying the pistol and rifle. Looking at the Officer driving he said, "Kill the lights, an ambulance is on the way, shooter is pronounced dead on the scene. He died from self inflicted wounds. I'll have a Five on the Sergeant's desk in about an hour, if anyone drives in here and turns around and leaves get the plate number."

"Should we stop them?"

"No, just note the plate and make and model of the vehicle. If they pull into that drive," he pointed at Teddy's driveway, "Follow them and check out their credibility. Be careful they could be heavily armed. You have my authorization to use deadly force if needed, clear?"

He got a loud, "Yes Sir."

Jake got back in his truck, followed the curb around the circle and headed downtown, his mind was working overtime.

He picked up his phone and pushed the button for Janet and was glad to hear her voice, "Thank you for calling, been thinking about you all day."

"And hello to you to, thinking about you also. Is everything okay?"

"Yes, just a lot of police activity, you have anything to do with that?"

"Yes, I'll call you a little bit later, Please stay at home, better if you don't go out for awhile. I'll bring the food and the drink."

"Well, what do I need to have here?"

"Just you, talk to you." Jake pushed the End button and at once was totally engrossed in his thoughts.

★★★

Julian moved from the holding area in the jail building towards the exit that would take him out to his car parked in the Sally Port. Reaching the door he opened it and stepped out onto the driveway, while talking to the Sheriff on his cell. He was giving her a quick update on the killing squads and the events that had already occurred.

He turned and took a step towards his car when the shot rang out. The bullet whizzed by his head and splattered on the concrete wall blowing out a three inch hole. He fell to the ground pulling his pistol and rolled towards his car. A second shot hit the driveway about six inches from his head and splattered small bits of concrete at Julian and his car. Julian had caught sight of the shooter just as the second shot exploded into the drive. He rolled onto his knees and fired up into the lone tree that stood twenty yards from the wall that surrounded the Sally Port. The tree was the only point high enough to allow a clear site path to the exit door and most of the Sally Port.

The shooter's head snapped back and the man and his rifle fell out of the V in the tree trunk that the shooter had used as a firing platform.

Julian saw the body bounce off of two large limbs like a wet bag before it was out of sight behind the wall. A dozen officers streamed out of the door onto the drive with guns drawn. Julian yelled, "Get some men out on the Gordon Highway side of the wall, make sure you are careful, might still be alive and he is heavily armed, Move it, Move It, Move It!"

★★★

Julian moved over and picked up his phone saying, "Sheriff, you still there?"

"Yes, what just happened, I heard shots being fired."

"Yes, there was another shooter. He just tried to take me out, firing from the tree on the Gordon Highway side of the Sally Port wall. I will call you back with a full report once this is contained."

"Okay, you and your people remain vigil and remain very, very careful."

"Yes, that we will do!" He pressed the END button.

★★★

The men scattered and as the door to the Sally Port raised four men ran out with their guns at the ready. They moved around the wall and saw the shooter lying in a heap eight feet from the base of the tree trunk. One of the officers ran to the shooter and reached out and pulled the man's shoulder to turn him over to confirm his condition.

The body turned over slowly and the gun in the shooter's hand discharged three shots in a rapid series of mini explosions, two of the officers went down.

★★★

The other two fired until their pistols were empty and smoking in their hands. The shooter's body bounced as each round struck it.

★★★

Julian heard the shots from the other side of the wall and ran towards the door out of the Sally Port.

★★★

There were seven officers with Julian standing over the body of the shooter, once the body was examined there were a eleven hits confirmed, in total, one from Julian's pistol and five from each of the others.

Thankfully the two officers that were shot did not have fatal wounds, both would be out for six or seven months, but alive.

Julian took out his phone and pushed the button to call Jake,.

Jake pushed the CALL button saying, "Jake here."

"There was another one, tried to get me leaving the jail, high powered rifle from the tree on the other side of the wall. Two of ours got hit, but they will be fine."

"I'm about five minutes away."

"Nothing here to see, I'll meet you at your Lab in ten."

"I'll be there in five, see you there," Jake stepped down on the gas a bit harder and took the turn heading to the Lab at about sixty miles an hour.

★★★

Tyrone walked into the old municipal building with three of his men and entered the office of the private Postal Service. He showed his identification and he and his men were led to the storage room that was his postal box. The employee unlocked the door and stepped away back the way he had come.

Tyrone stepped into the room and looked at the stack of boxes against the wall. He was a little shocked but hid it from the men with him, "Never show uneasiness, shock, fear to any of them," he thought.

Each of the men picked up three of the boxes and Tyrone picked up two, they made six trips out to the SUV, Tyrone stayed with the SUV, and the money, after the first trip. Fifty-six boxes in all were removed and placed in the rear of Tyrone's modified SUV. The boxes held sixty million dollars in clean cash, untraceable and in small enough bills to be used without causing any suspicion.

Tyrone knew that there were boxes missing, at least a million dollars worth, it was totally unaccounted for, just gone.

If that got out it would not be a good thing, not for anyone, his only savior was he was the only one with that knowledge. No one, not even the good Doctor had a count of what was supposed to be there. He would have to spend a lot of time finding out where it went after their meeting, no one gets in Tyrone's pocket, no one.

★★★

Jake pulled into the parking lot and pulled his truck into the parking space with the small sign with his name on it. He jumped out and hurried into the building and to the Lab. The fist thing he did was check all of the tests he had run on the open cases he was working on. He compiled the information and inserted it into the reports he had written and were waiting for the test results to prove or disapprove his findings.

Once complete, he E-mailed the reports to Dr. Andrews and Dr. Fox, he was now up to date on all of the cases and the support data for each. The cases were, for the most part, normal and he had not found any questionable data.

He sat at his desk and ran the all of data he knew about the kill squads through his mind. He was very surprised that Tyrone had kept almost all thought about the operation out of his mind. He knew that there were only three shooters all with their specific targets, all to die with the most additional damage to people and property.

"Hey man, you look like you're a million miles away," Julian said as he moved towards Jake's desk from the door.

"Jake looked up and replied, "Nope, just a few miles down the road. I was just going to type up two 'Fives' for the recent events and my involvement. I'm sure that there are two Sergeants that would really like them to clear up a few details."

Julian grinned saying, "Yep, they get a little nervous when there are people killed, yep, a little nervous. I've got one to fill out myself, a copy to the file and a one to the Undersheriff within the next hour, at her request."

Jake replied, "Well, you can use that terminal on the desk next to the back wall."

"I guess, better to get it done and over with, then we can discuss all that went down." He walked over to the second desk and took a seat and pressed the buttons to bring it to life. In just a moment he was totally engrossed in the report, and all of the details he knew were required.

Every once in awhile he would look up and watch Jake working on one of the pieces of test equipment crammed into the lab. The amount of equipment had almost doubled since Jake took over the Lab. It was very rare that there was not at least three or four devices running at any time of the day or night. There were now four computers tied to the equipment network and also four printers. This of course did not include the PC and Printer that Jake had on one of his desks just for the recording and printing reports. Every morning there were four stacks of reports that he had to review and compile into detailed reports for Dr. Andrews and also for Dr. Fox. The ability to set the samples into the equipment, and program the different tests he needed done, and be able to be doing something else let him get twice as much done in a shorter time.

Jake looked over at Julian and asked, "You close to being done?"

Julian pushed the last button on the keyboard and raised his hands saying, "Done."

Jake's PC pinged.

"I sent you a copy of my report also. Don't want you to feel slighted." Julian said with a grin spreading across his face.

Jake shook his head saying, "Sure you don't want me to check the spelling?"

Julian laughed replying, "That would be okay but why waste valuable time."

Jake stood and stretched his arms above his head and looking at Julian said, "How about some coffee?"

"Sounds good, let's go over the events of this morning."

"Great idea," Jake started for the door with Julian right behind him.

They were sitting at the only one of the tables in the break area that was positioned next to one of the large windows overlooking the parking lot. They had both scanned the lot and the vehicles in it before they sat down.

Julian took a sip of his coffee and asked Jake, "What made you suspicious of the delivery man this morning?"

Jake looked over his cup at Julian and then looked out the window then said, "I got one of those feelings, just one of those feelings. I didn't open the door right away, asked him to show his credentials. When I saw on the flat screen that he wouldn't put the package down to pull out his papers, well, I just knew. Does that make sense to you?"

Julian nodded his head saying, "Completely, sometimes all we have is a feeling that can stand between living and dying."

Jake continued, "I guess when I opened the door and grabbed him, he answered a few quick questions, then he spooked, broke away and ran back to the van and sped off. I got my truck out as quick as I could and followed him. He was only two or three hundred feet from the drive when I found him pulled off the road. There was blood all over the driver's window so I just continued to Keller's and just call it in. When I turned onto Keller's street I saw the subject vehicle coming down the street from the other direction. I pulled to the curb in front of the house next to Keller's and lifted some papers so the Perp would think I was local. He did, passed me and pulled into Keller's drive, he never looked back. I slid out of the truck and moved low along the truck's side and when the Perp opened his van's door and stepped out with the assault rifle at the ready I stood and announced who I was and for him to drop the weapon. He started to bring it up to fire, so I fired three times. One in the head, two in the chest and the Perp went down. I moved to the Perp and cleared the weapon after announcing to the others that it was all clear and to holster their weapons. All did what they were trained to do and I pronounced the perp dead and went back to the first Perp and his vehicle."

"All sounds like a open and shut case and a justified shoot to me. I'm sure all of the other reports will confirm what went down. What killed the first perp?"

"Well, when I got back to the perp's van I found him with five self-inflicted gunshot wounds. He had shot himself in the arm, foot, left leg, the other leg and groin, the groin shot cut the artery and he bled out. Doubt if it didn't take less than fifteen minutes for it all to occur, recovered two weapons, a revolver and assault rifle. He must have gone nuts."

Julian sat looking out the window for a moment before replying, "Drugs will make you do strange things."

CHAPTER SEVENTEEN

JANET AND JAKE HAD JUST finished eating and were sitting watching a replay of the swearing in of the Vice President as President, this of course was for show. The Vice President had been sworn in within an hour of the death of the President.

Jake's phone began to chirp, he picked it up and pressed the SEND button saying, "Jake."

Jake, Julian, the Undersheriff just called to relay a question from Tommy Blanchard. He would like you and I, with Janet and Martha of course, to join the members of the Club for dinner Friday evening at eight' o clock. Appetizers, drinks and dinner will be served in the Member's Dining Room, dress is business casual, which I believe is a Sport Jacket and tie for us and a dress for the ladies. The Undersheriff also said it would only be the four of us with the Members. She said that she could hear the earnestness in Tommy's voice."

Jake put his hand over the speaker and looked at Janet asking, "Do you want to go to dinner at the Club Friday evening with all of the Members that are in town?"

She grinned and replied, "Yes."

Jake moved his hand and replied to Julian, "Okay with us, how about you and Martha?"

"Were in, Martha said she wouldn't miss it for anything."

"Okay, Janet and I will be the ones in green and white. Green for the color of my gills and white for the color of my skin."

Julian laughed replying, "Right, like you could be rattled. I'll call the Undersheriff and let her know. See you tomorrow, have a good night."

"Night," Jake pushed the END button and placed the phone on the end table. He reached over and put his hand on Janet's saying, "Well I guess were going up town."

She squeezed his hand saying, "I'm excited, I've never heard of anyone getting invited to have dinner in the Member's Dining Room."

Jake leaned over and kissed her on the cheek saying, "That is because you are special."

★★★

Jake sat down in his desk chair, with his cell in his hand, and pushed the button to call Julian's cell, and when he heard Julian's voice say, "Brown," he said, "Julian, need to see you, how about lunch?"

"Okay, its ten-thirty now. How about a pie at Luigi's at eleven thirty?"

"Sounds good to me, see you then." He pushed the END button and turned back to his PC and refreshed the page he was looking at. After pressing the PRINT button he scrolled over to the second screen he had open. He read the description under the photo that covered over half of the page and pressed the PRINT button again. The printer hummed and the pages slid onto the tray.

There were twelve pages in all that printed. Jake picked them up, read them, and then added them to the stack of papers he already had in the manila folder on his desk.

Hearing a moderate buzzing he stood and moved over to the Automatic Chemistry Analyzer whose buzzer was signaling that the tests Jake had programmed in to it were complete. He lifted the pages of the reports, and glanced over them before adding them to the other pages in his folder.

Jake looked at the tray on the Gas Chromatograph Mass Spectrometer and saw the last report that he had requested. He added the report to the file, and held the file in his left hand as he walked out to his truck. He had twelve minutes until he was to meet Julian.

★★★

Jake found Julian sitting in the first booth, closest to the door and away from the others in the restaurant. He moved into the booth and slid on the red leather seat, all the way till his back was against the wall saying, "Julian, glad you could make it." He placed the file on the table against the wall.

Julian grinned a little saying, "It did not sound like I had a choice my friend."

Just as Jake was going to respond Janet stepped up to the table and placed a large cheese pie on the stand in the middle of the table. She took two tall glasses of iced sweet tea off of her tray and placed them alongside of the plates she set on the table. She then leaned over and gave Jake a kiss on the cheek saying, "My treat love." Before he could answer she was gone.

Julian grinned saying, "Nice service if you can get it."

Jake grinned saying, "Special service, that is for only for special people." The grin disappeared and he continued, "Once we have the pie we need to talk about something that is going to be occurring shortly."

Julian sensed the change in Jake's demeanor and nodded.

They both took a slice of pie and placed it on the plate Janet had left for them. They ate and chatted about this and that but nothing that was very important.

Jake picked up his glass and tipped it towards Julian saying, "Happy Birthday to Stephanie Kwolek."

Julian picked up his glass and clinked Jake's asking, "Stephanie Kwolek?"

Jake laughed a little then explained, "Stephanie Kwolek is the inventor of Kevlar, that which all bullet proof vests are made. She saved hundreds of lives with her discovery of the polymer that Kevlar is made of."

Julian toasted her again saying, "I don't know how or why you know that but, God bless her."

Jake tapped his glass against Julian's saying, "God Bless."

They finished their pie and Janet stopped by and cleaned up the table and refilled their glasses.

Jake slid the folder in front of him and flipped it open and placed his hands on the papers saying, "My friend, one of the biggest drug meetings concerning the Southeast is going to happen in less than two weeks. It is going to go down in Jenkins County and will involve the largest drug dealer in Georgia and his supplier from South America. My guess is there will be eight to ten million in cash and the direction of all future drug trade in Georgia, Alabama and South Carolina."

Julian looked Jake directly in the eyes and asked, "Jake, how in the world do you know that?"

Jake tapped the papers under his hands replying, "It's all in here, I've tested everything from paper, dirt, drugs, credit cards, jet fuel purchases and orders, interviews, phone records, everything. I've followed everything that Tyrone Mendoza and Dr. Paul Greenly have done for the last six months. I believe that I can pinpoint where they make, cut and package the drugs and where they ship them from."

"Wow, do you have any doubts?"

"None, with the facts and data I have in this folder I can prove every statement made so far and a lot more."

"What do you have in mind as far as an operation?"

"Well, I have a lot in mind to make this happen, you will need to involve FDA, FAA, State Police, Locals and us. First we need to get the Sheriff to buy in and throw all of her support behind this. If we do it right we can cripple the drug trade for a long time, here and in a lot of other places."

"Well do you want a meet with the Sheriff tonight?"

"No, lets meet with the Sheriff tomorrow around one and set the parameters of the plan before we get anyone else involved. There is no reason to take a chance of messing up the dinner we're going to tonight at the Club."

"Got it, speaking of that, I've got to get going to make sure I clear my plate for that. I'll confirm a meeting with the Sheriff at one tomorrow and tell her the reason for the meeting will be self explanatory once we get together." Julian slid out of the seat and shook

Jake's hand saying, "See you tonight. We'll meet you and Janet at the Club, quarter to eight."

"I'm looking forward to it, my friend."

Janet saw Julian going out the front door so she moved along the isle and slid into the booth next to Jake saying, "Hey good looking, you here alone?"

Jake put his arm around her and replied, "Not anymore." He leaned over and gave her a kiss on the cheek. He gave her shoulders a squeeze asking, "Is seven-thirty too late to pick you up tonight? We are meeting Julian and Martha at seven forty-five at the Club."

"That will be just about right. I don't want to be late, not even one minute, this is not something to put on a front and be fashionably late for. I am so looking forward to this Jake, it's a once in a life time for us common folk."

"Well, then I better get going, there are a few things I need to finish and a few tests to get started."

Janet slid out of the booth and Jake followed, they exchanged a kiss and Jake walked out of the door onto the street. He glanced right and left, not seeing anything out of place walked over to his truck. It was only moments and he was pulling into the Lab's parking lot. He spent about an hour setting different tests in place, that after setting the test parameters in the software program. The tests would be done by eight in the morning, based on that he would have plenty of time to confirm his earlier findings before the meeting with the Sheriff.

Jake locked up the Lab and walked out to his truck and headed home at six o' clock.

★★★

Tommy Blanchard walked into Billy's office with carrying a cardboard box in both hands with a big smile on his face. He placed the box on the corner of Bill's desk saying, "It just arrived by bonded overnight courier from New York."

Billy stood grinning and saying, "Well, let's see what eighty three hundred can buy."

Tommy picked up the letter opener and using the tip cut the tape on the ends and top of the box. He carefully opened the flaps and lifted the object, wrapped in bubble wrap, out of box.

Billy moved the box to the floor and Tommy placed the object in the center of the desk. He carefully started removing the layers of wrap, there were six layers of wrap. Once the wrap was removed he could see that the object was in a velvet suede blanket like wrapping.

Billy leaned closer murmuring, "Well protected."

Tommy glanced at him and nodded to the affirmative, he returned his attention to the wrapping. He slowly removed it and lifted the object out of the wrapping and held it at arm's length. He and Billy both said, "Wow" at the same time.

The object was a commemorative plaque, a plaque like no other. The plaque was shining like a jewel under florescent lights. The base was oval shaped, with the oval having a diamctcr width of twenty four inches, made out of Diospyros Celebica, (Macassar Ebony). A deep black wood with dramatic blond streaking, it is one of the rarest and most expensive woods in the world.

There were golf tees inserted around the outer perimeter of the base centered two and a quarter inches apart. The tees were made out of Osyis Wightiana,

(Sandalwood Burl) from Tanzania, also very expensive and rare.

There was the Club emblem, in Silver and Gold, in the upper center, and a silver insert about three inches high and eight inches wide just below it. It had the number 54, in raise gold lettering, center top.

The first line read Ken (Jake) Smith – The Club's Low Net Round Score,

The second read – Round shot playing with Mr. Tommy Blanchard (69) and Mr. Julian Brown (69), both being from Augusta, Georgia, U.S.A,

The third line read - Caddies for the group were Mr. V, Mr. Cat, and Mr. Bud.

Around the silver insert there were eighteen golf balls attached to the tees and below the first nine tees, across the upper half of the base, there was a one inch silver disc with the score shot for that hole, #1 - Birdie, #2 - Eagle, #3 - Birdie, #4 - Par, #5 - Birdie, #6 - Par, #7 - Par, #8 – Birdie, #9 – Birdie.

The other nine tees were along the lower perimeter of the base and each had a silver disc just above each with the score shot for that hole, #10 – Birdie, #11 – Birdie, #12 – Double Eagle, #13 – Birdie, #14 – Birdie, #15 – Eagle, #16 – Birdie, #17 – Birdie, #18 – Birdie.

Billy and Tommy stood there looking at the plaque almost in a trance, the plaque almost glowed, and it held your eye like a rare jewel. The buzzing of Billy's phone broke the spell cast by the sheer beauty of wood's sheen, he picked it up saying, "Yes."

The conversation lasted for less than a moment.

"Yes, that will be fine." Billy placed the phone down and said, "Everything is ready for tonight, there will be almost eighty members in attendance."

"Great, I think we will have a few very surprised visitors tonight, very surprised," Tommy said still holding the plaque in his hands.

Billy pointed to the plaque saying, "You might want to have Blue bring that up to the member's dining room."

Tommy pulled it a little closer replying, "I will take it up and make sure it is hung properly. It is the least I can do." He picked up the velvet suede wrap saying, "I'll see if Carrie can make a shroud for the plaque that we can use to cover it with when confidentiality is needed."

"That would be wonderful, and also very fitting. I'll have Facilities send someone up to hang it." With that, Billy picked up the phone and pressed the buttons for the Facilities Department.

Tommy walked out of the office and towards the dining room, he had his phone in his hand and was saying, "Carrie please meet me in the Member's dining room.

★★★

The Former President and former Secretary of State were having an argument about the formal dinner that was going to be held by the new President, they both needed to be in attendance at the request of the North Korean President.

The two of them were once again arguing about something trivial, they were arguing about who would walk into the dinner affair first. They spent most of their time together arguing about something, anything, but never when out under the scrutiny of the public eye.

They had been invited to cocktails at four at the Korean Embassy, the evening of the dinner that the Korean President/Dictator was to have with the President of the United States. It was the first invitation to anyone from the outside to visit the Embassy in over eight years, quite a big thing. It would be a huge feather in their caps to be the first to be invited and attend such an event at the Embassy.

The event would reinforce their status as the movers and shakers in world politics and strengthen the Past Secretary of State's advancement on her march to the Presidency.

***

Jake carried the dark blue sports coat out of the bedroom and placed it on one of the kitchen chairs back as he moved towards the fridge. He turned and looked at the security screen at the sound of the beep, the beep was sounded by the new sensor he had installed above the garage door, the sensor sounded when anything moved towards or away from the house. He saw Teddy's SUV moving up the drive.

He opened the fridge and took the carton of milk out and placed it on the counter, he took a glass out of the cabinet and poured himself a glass. Opening the fridge he put the carton back on the main shelf in the fridge.

Jake moved over to check himself out in the full length mirror, putting on his jacket, the pale blue shirt and light tan slacks were a soft contrast to the dark blue of the jacket. The tie he had selected was one with one inch wide blue, yellow and tan strips. "Well, not GQ but respectable," he said to his reflection. He walked back to the counter and picking up the glass finished his drink. He rinsed the glass and set it in the drain.

He removed his jacket as he moved down the stairs, it took just a few moments and he was driving out of the drive way. It took him just under fifteen minutes to get to Janet's house. He pulled into the drive and stopped at the end of the walk. Getting out of the truck he walked up to the front door, knocked once, and opened the door and walked in to the hall. Janet called out, "Be there in two."

"Ok," he sat on one of the counter chairs.

It might have been two minutes but it seemed like a few seconds when Janet walked out of the back hall and into the living room.

Jake stood and said, "WOW, you look fantastic."

Janet beamed a little replying, "Really? I hope so."

Jake looked her up and down with a grin on his face, her red hair was loose and draped over her left shoulder. The dress she was wearing was a soft tan with clam collar and a twisted waist with knee high pleats extended down from the twist that seemed to flow when she moved.

Fantastic, just fantastic," Jake said putting his hand out to her.

Janet blushed a little replying, "Thank you Sir." She stepped over taking his hand and gave him a kiss saying, "We better leave so we aren't late."

Jake said, "OK, moving towards the door he continued with, "Do me a favor, lock the door from now on please."

Janet stepped through the door replying, "Yes my love."

Jake did not reply he just moved to the truck and opened the door for Janet.

Once she was settled in Jake closed the door and moved around to the driver's door and got in. In just a moment they were moving onto the main street and towards the Club.

Jake pulled into the Club's drive and pulled up to the parking area, he was surprised to see it full. Blue was standing at the front door and waved for Jake to stop. The truck stopped at the door and Jake opened the window, "Blue, looks like a full house."

Blue grinned and replied, "Yes Sir." Moving around the truck to get the door for Janet he continued, "Mr. Jake will you leave your truck here, one of the valets will park it for you. You will find Mr. Julian and Miss Martha just inside the door." He opened the door and Janet stepped out of the truck, she turned and put her hand out to Blue saying with a big smile, "I am Janet."

Blue took her hand replying, "My pleasure Miss Janet."

Janet turned and walked around to Jake's side and in a moment Blue opened the door and stood to the side looking at the young woman standing just inside the door saying, "Mr. Jake and Miss Janet, please show them to Mr. Julian and Miss Martha."

Once they were in the door Jake saw Julian and Martha standing with Tommy and another gentleman. The young lady led them to the group and announced them softly, Mr. Jake and Miss Janet." She quickly moved back to the door.

Tommy put his hand out to Janet saying, "Tommy Blanchard."

Janet took his hand and replied, "Janet."

Tommy turned to Jake and nodding towards the other gentleman said, Jake this is Mr. Billy P......"

Billy put out his hand and said, "Billy, please, just Billy." He turned to Janet bowing at the waist a bit and said, "Miss Janet, my privilege."

Looking at the four of them he continued with, "You will be meeting quite a few people tonight, it is not expected that you remember all of the names. We all just want the four of you to feel welcome and comfortable."

He turned to tommy and said, "Tommy, I'm going up, please bring your friend up in a few moments please."

Jake and Julian shook hands and Martha and Janet gave each other a slight hug and Martha whispered, "I'm so excited." Janet replied, "Me to."

Tommy looked at them and said, "Both of you ladies look wonderful," Turning to Jake and Julian saying, "Lucky guys. Well if you are ready we can head upstairs."

They all nodded and replied, Yes."

Tommy turned and walked to the stairway and saying, please excuse my back ladies but if you do not take offense I will proceed up first. He turned and walked up the stairs and turned and waited for them to reach the landing.

Once they all reached the landing Tommy nodded to the two men at the doors to the dining room. The seeing the nod they opened the doors and stepped aside. Tommy walked in front and once in the room walked to the head table, he held the chair out for Janet. Once she was seated he motioned to the next chair for Jake, he skipped one chair and pointed to the next for Julian, Julian stepped back a step and allowed Martha to pass. Tommy smiled and moved the chair out for Martha and waited until she was seated. Julian took his seat and Tommy moved to the center seat and sat down.

Jake, Janet, Julian and Martha looked at the tables and acknowledged Teddy sitting at the center front table.

Billy stepped to the center of the room, in front of the table facing the eighty Gentlemen that sat at the other tables.

"Gentlemen, welcome to this special Member's dinner. I know that many of you have come a long way on short notice and without knowing the reason this meeting was called." He turned to one side and he pointed at Tommy continuing with, "Mr. Tommy Blanchard requested this meeting and I will allow him the privilege to introduce his guests and the reason for this meeting."

Tommy stood facing the men said, "My fellow members, I would like to introduce my friends." Turning to his right he put his hand out towards Julian and Martha saying, "Mr. Julian Brown and his lady Miss Martha."

There was a polite clapping of hands.

Tommy turned the other way and lifted his hand towards Jake and Janet saying, Mr. Ken 'Jake' Smith and his Lady Miss Janet.

There was another polite clapping of hands.

Tommy looked out at the men and continued, "Gentlemen I have invited you and my friends here tonight because I have one unbelievable event to announce to you and the other a proposal that needs your approval.

Turning towards Jake Tommy asked, "Jake will you please stand."

Looking back at the group Tommy said a bit louder, "Gentlemen, please meet the holder of The Club's Low Net Score and new Record Holder, Mr. Ken 'Jake' Smith. Gentlemen our new course, and Club, record is '54'.

There was silence for a moment and then the walls vibrated with the applause.

Tommy moved to the wall the entrance door we on and stood next to whatever it was hanging on the wall and coved with a red velvet cover. Tommy removed the cover and the plaque shown like it had a life of its own. He said, "There will be drinks and appetizer's served for a half hour and then we will have dinner."

He moved back to the table and shook Jake's and then Julian's hand, there was a line forming behind Tommy and each and every member took their turn to shake Jake, Julian, Martha and Janet's hands in turn.

The waiters moved around the room with plates of every hot and cold finger food one could think of, and others delivered drinks to order.

Teddy shook Jake's hand and then Julian's saying, "From the info on that plaque both of you had a wonderful day, I think that is Tommy's best round also. Congratulations gentlemen."

Billy tapped a spoon on his glass to get everyone's attention, looking around the room he said, "Please take your seats, you will find a menu with tonight's offerings, Standing Crown Roast of Beef or Pheasant Under Glass. A server will be around to take your requests, and while we are waiting for our service Tommy has the second part of his announcement to complete. It will need your Yea or Nay vote, mine is Yea. Thank you. He moved his hand towards Tommy.

Tommy stood up and began, "I hope all of you have met these very special friends of mine, they are not only dear friends but they have performed at the very highest level in their professions. Jake and Julian have and continue to serve the city, county and state and all of the persons that live here. Based on my personal knowledge of these two men I make the following motion to all of you.

I propose that Mr. Ken 'Jake smith and Mr. Julian Brown be accepted tonight as Members of this Club with all of the respect, and personal accommodations this membership carries with it, and that they will never be assessed, billed, or be requested to make any remittance for any of the Club's offerings. I know this is unprecedented but I request this motion as strongly as my being allows."

There was not a sound in the room, Teddy stood up and raised a glass saying "Yea." It was followed by what sounded like one mighty voice, "Yea."

Billy raised his glass and said, "So be it."

Jake, Janet, Julian and Martha must have looked strange sitting there with their mouths open and staring at each other. Jake stood and moved to the space left open by Tommy's chair being removed, Julian moved to his side.

Jake raised his hand and the men all quieted and were looking at both of them. "Gentlemen, Julian and I could never say what this, what you have just done, means to us. We give you our word on our souls and hearts that we will never say or do anything to bring any shame or disrespect to this Club or any of its members. If there is ever anything that either of us can do to help or assist any member all that needs to happen is to ask. Thank you"

The room almost exploded with the sound of the clapping, the only thing that got everyone seated again was the servers bringing out the meals.

Teddy and Billy walked to the table and shook their hands giving them there best and welcoming them into the Club.

There was another hour of food, drinks, shaking of hands, congratulations and welcome to the Club statements. Teddy stopped by and asked if the four of them would like to stop and have desert with him and Marian. They agreed and said they hoped to be able to leave within the hour. Teddy assured them that that would be possible.

Almost to the minute the last ones standing in the room were Tommy, Billy, Jake, Julian Janet and Martha. Billy looked at them and asked, "Can you please follow me, there is something you need to see, before you leave." With that he turned and walked towards the door and they followed. They walked out the door and down the hall a ten or twelve paces, Billy opened a door and motioned for them to enter. It was the member's formal dressing room. There were one hundred and fifty wood lockers around the perimeter of the room and in many rows lockers in isles. Billy moved across the room and stopped at the third locker, engraved on the front was Jake Smith and under it Julian Brown. He opened the locker and pointed at the green jackets that hung there. All we ask is if you are in the clubhouse and on the first floor, other than the Grill Room, please wear your jackets at all time. To play just call the Pro Shop and tell them when you would like to Tee off. Ladies, no disrespect, but ladies, other than members, are not allowed on the second floor unless accompanied by a member, or it is a very special event." With that he turned and left the room.

Jake looked at Julian and asked, Need to try it on?"

Jake grinned saying, "I'm sure it fits."

Jake replied as he closed the locker said, "Time to go."

They all nodded and followed him out of the room and in a few moments were driving towards Teddy and Marian's for desert.

★★★

CHAPTER EIGHTEEN

THE PAST SECRETARY OF STATE and the Past President were just about to leave their townhouse for an early dinner when there was a knock on the door. The former Secretary of State grabbed the knob and twisting it, opened the door, to her surprise she was looking directly into a badge.

"Federal Agents, you are under arrest."

Shocked, she glancing to her right and she noticed that the two Secret Service men that formed the security guard for her and her husband were standing stiffly off to the side of the walk. They were being talked to by another man that was talking quite loud, and pointing his finger at each in turn.

The Past President stepped forward saying, "What is the meaning of this, who, who do you report t..................."

A second Agent stepped alongside the Past Secretary and took her hand and moved her hand and arm around to her back saying, "You are under arrest, you have the right to an Attorney, if you cannot afford one, one will be appointed by the court. Anything that you say, can, and will, be used against you in a court of law."

The Past President started to protest again and to his surprise a second Agent stepped in and took his arm and pulled it behind his back making the same statement to him as the other Agent had made to his wife. The Agent forcefully put the handcuffs on his wrists.

The Past President raised his voice saying, "What is this all about? I demand to know."

"That will be explained once we get to the Federal Building."

Both were led out of the townhouse and ushered into two unmarked black cars, each of them being placed in one of the cars with two Agents. An Agent sat on each side of them and another Agent driving, also in each car, one of the Secret Service Agents that had formed the security detail was seated in the front passenger seat.

The cars pulled onto the main street and in moments were in route to the Central Federal Building. At the Building there were eight Agents waiting at the entrance to the high security level and there was a group of three people from the Attorney General's Office. They stood off to the side and spoke in low voices to each other. It was apparent that the taller man in the gray suit was in charge. The other two were doing a lot of head nodding and what seemed to be fake smiles crossed their faces in flashes.

The two black cars turned into the security tunnel, the first one stopped and the three occupants of the back seat got out and were rushed past the two groups and into the holding area. The car pulled away and the second car pulled up and stopped, the three occupants in the rear seat got out and were also rushed past the two groups.

The group of Agents formed a human wall across the entrance walk and moved slowly towards the building, this causing the three from the Attorney General's office to follow the path that the two groups from the cars had taken.

The former Secretary of State and former President were seated in an interrogation room with two Agents standing a silent watch. They had been instructed to remain silent, they listened.

The door opened and the two guards stepped out, the Chief Justice of the Unite States walked into the room and closed the door. He stood across from them looking down at each one by one. The former Secretary started to speak, he cut her off. "I am here to make a Statement of Opinion, and it will also include a Statement of Fact. Do you understand what I am saying?"

The both nodded to the affirmative.

He continued, "You will no longer be given the respect of being spoken to with the respect that your former offices demand. Everything said and done in this room is being recorded, visually and verbally. There are three copies being made each second with one being in a secure lockbox in a remote location." After a pause he started as if from the beginning, "You are being charged with High Treason, under Article III section 10 of the Constitution of the United States of America. Both of you have lost your careers, reputations, family name, assets, respect, everything, everything will be gone and your public and private lives are over."

The former President started to speak and the Chief Justice held his hand in his face stopping him before he could even start.

"We have been informed that a packet is being delivered to the six largest distributors of news, across the world, to the general public in the morning. One packet was sent to us eight hours ago to allow us to take you into custody so that you would not be harmed by the masses. We are very sure that when the packets are opened and the contents exposed to the peoples of the world, your lives will not be worth very much. A copy of the packet we received was sent to CNN - U.S., The Sun – England, The Washington Post – U. S., The New York Times – U. S., The Bild – Germany, and The Yomiuri Shim Bun – Japan. There are Documents, verified to be original, factual, and beyond reproach, CD's, Tapes and Live Video with proof that both of you conspired with the Saudi's, ISIS and Iraq Leaders, in regard to the attack on Benghazi which resulted in the death of US Ambassador, Christopher Stevens and US Foreign Service Information Officer, Sean Smith and destruction of the U.S. Government Compound, on September 11, 2012 and other things.

We have the telephone conversation from the day before the attack, between the two of you, discussing the upcoming attack and possible death of both of these men and others. The conversation clearly displays the cavalier attitude you both had about the whole thing.

Let me quote you," pointing towards the former secretary, "The loss of two or three of them, on the compound, is a small price to pay, just think of what we will end up with," and your response to this former President was, "Yes, your right, it really doesn't matter what the outcome, our friends will be very generous, very, very generous. Any losses incurred are a small price to pay for such large gains."

After a slight pause he continued, "We have copies of the transfer of large amounts of funds into your accounts and the transfer of holdings from Saudi Arabia, ISIS leadership, and Iraq to different companies and accounts of yours. In the morning you both will be the most disgraced people in the world, the world. Do you understand?

They both were white and shaking with fear, they just nodded.

The Justice continued, "You will be held in protective custody, in solitary confinement, for your own good throughout this entire matter. You will be found guilty and maybe, just maybe you will not be sentenced to death. A formal sentence that cannot, and will not, be challenged in any court for any reason. If you are not, you will spend the rest of your lives in solitary confinement in a Federal Prison. If I were you, I would not get my hopes up. All of your holdings will be picked apart page by page, e-mail by e-mail, conversation by conversation, every event and movement either of you have made in the last twenty years. Your daughter will also be investigated, at this time there is no connection between her and your actions, I hope for her sake it stays that way. Your case will be placed in the hands of my court and will be handled at its discretion as allowed by the Constitution which you so casually ignored and so easily disrespected. There will be no loop holes or public hearings on TV, no army of lawyers in suits, none of the things that make our legal system seem like a joke at times. I personally guarantee that you both will be prosecuted to the fullest extent of the law. I hope you both understand what I've said and you're retribution to this county for payment due to the ramifications of your actions will be extreme. Your child will be investigated and if she has any involvement she too will be prosecuted."

With that he turned and walked out of the door with only a nod at the Agents, that entered the room when he opened the door, that had been and would continue to, stand guard over them.

The three representatives of the Attorney General's Office stepped into the room and the tallest placed a folder on the table saying, "Jed Smithson, Attorney General's Office, Chief Attorney." Placing his finger on the folder continued, "This is an outline of the proceedings that will be occurring, you will have little to do. You will be the first ever tried solely by the Supreme Court and it's Justices. The only defense you will be allowed will be one opportunity to address the court. This will occur at the end of the trial/hearing before the sentence is declared. There will be no opportunity to file for a retrial you will be found guilty or not guilty. I will leave this folder for you to read, you will be given thirty minutes in this room together and them you will be processed and placed in separate cells where you will remain until all proceedings are complete. You will be transported separately and in a covert manner. You will not be allowed visitors until the events are concluded. To the world it will seem you have vanished. The Chief Justice will release a statement to the public and the world once the furor of the data released in the morning diminish."

★★★

Jake pulled up as close as he could to the garage door and Julian pulled beside him. They all got out of the vehicles and walked towards the house's back door. Julian stopped and turning to Jake said, "This all seems like a dream, never in my wildest dreams did I ever think I would be a member of The Club. Jake my friend, Thank you, being your friend is a privilege and an honor and not without excitement. I'm done, no discussion."

The three of them looked at Julian and Jake replied, "Bull."

They all laughed as the door to the house opened and Teddy looked out at them saying, "The tea is on the brew, come on in."

They all entered the house and Teddy ushered them through the kitchen and into the sun room. Teddy had moved the chairs to form a U and added a table so that all would have a clear view of the river. The moon light glistened off of the water as it slowly moved by, making the view almost mystical. They all took a seat leaving the first two for Teddy and Marian.

Marian entered saying, "Hello everyone and congratulation Jake and Julian, what a wonderful turn of events. The Club is in a better place with both of you as members. I am so happy for you both." She moved around and gave them and the two girls a big hug. "I'll get the tea."

Both Janet and Martha stood quickly and followed her into the kitchen, they were talking so fast it sounded like a breeze through the leaves of a tree.

Teddy rolled his eyes and laughed softly, Julian and Jake joined him. Their eyes all swung towards the river as a small boat passed slowly with a running light on the bow.

"Hope he is keeping a keen eye out, would not be hard to miss seeing a log in the dark," Julian said almost to himself. Jake and Teddy both nodded agreement.

Janet walked in carrying a tray with six small plates, with a freshly made cinnamon swirl on each, and five additional swirls on a larger plate. She placed the plates in front of each seat and the larger one in the center of the table. Martha followed her with napkins, mugs, spoons, and forks which she placed next to the plates that Janet had set down and the milk, sugar in the center of the table. Janet walked back into the kitchen with both trays and returned just in front of Marian. Marian moved around the table pouring the tea and once finished took her seat next to Teddy. "I hope you all like cinnamon swirls, I thought I'd make something different."

Julian replied, "I love them, and I cannot remember anything that you have ever served that was not just wonderful." The others all nodded their agreement.

They drank their tea and silently watch the moon light sparkle and bounce off of the slight swells caused by the water's current.

★★★

The leader of Democratic People's Republic of Korea walked into the formal dining room, and moved to the head of the large ornately carved table. He picked up the crystal carafe that sat on an ornate stand and poured a drink of Soju. Soju was the finest Korean Rice Vodka that was served neat, the cup was made of solid gold and was inlaid with silver and gems that formed the image of a brightly colored dragon. He grinned as he toasted himself as he brought the cup to his lips, for there was no one else that he would toast. He walked to the window and looked out at the gardens that flowed from the palace to the white wall that surrounded the rear of the palace grounds.

He watched the guards finish securing the four men, that had insulted him and his family that very morning, to a makeshift rail made out of three inch bamboo. The rail was about forty eight inches high and the men's arms were over the rail and behind their backs. Their feet barely reached the ground. The guard looked up at the window and Kim raised the cup and then brought it down quickly.

The four guards drove the swords that they held at their sides, deep into the men's bodies. The bodies slumped forward with their heads forward with their chins almost resting on their chests. Kim raised and lowered his cup again, the guards swung their swords again and decapitated the four men. He turned away from the window just as the servants were placing his lunch on the table. He smiled and moved back to the table and took his place at the head of the table. He would have a lunch comprised of foods prepared and served to Royalty for hundreds of years, Royalty, he liked that.

He would start with a cup of Bosin, a delicacy, dog soup, one of his favorite soups. He enjoyed picking the main staple and having it pulled out of the arms of some lower person he might see on the street or in the square.

Before him were Gujeolpan and Sinseollo, meals he enjoyed time and time again. The Gujeolpan was served in an octagonal dish with elaborate carvings and in set with gems. It was divided in eight side sections that surrounded a larger center section. The outer sections were filled with different cooked items, such as carrots, mushrooms, beef, pork, bean sprouts, leeks, onions, etc. The larger center section was filled with miljeonbyeong, paper thin wheat flat cakes, that were filled with the items from the outer sections and eaten entirely. When served correctly the dish looked like a beautiful flower.

The Sinseollo was served in a large round silver vessel about six inches deep with a hole in the center. The center was filled with burning embers that keep the meal hot throughout the entire meal. The Sinseollo consisted of flesh from Farm Raised Pheasant, Grain Fed Beef, Corn and Grain Fed Pork and Natural Organic Vegetables cooked in a very rich broth. All foods his people had never had, nor ever would, if he had his way. He looked at the meal spread before him thinking, "This food prepared only for Korean Royalty, yes Royalty."

He picked at each meal for over an hour and finished with a pot of Poricha, a Barley Tea, and sweet pastries.

He poured himself a full cup of Soju and moved off to his office/study, once reaching it he sat in the leather high back chair and stared at the TV screen and watched the world news scrolling past. His eyes closed and his head rolled to the side as his heart stopped. The cup fell out of his hand and onto the floor splashing the Soju on the white rug and the cup splitting with a loud click.

★★★

Julian walked into the Lab Building and down the hall to Jake's lab, for the meeting. He saw the Sheriff's car in the parking lot as well as Dr. Andrews and Dr. Fox's cars. He turned into the lab and saw Jake sitting at his desk holding a stack of papers. "Sure hope that's important."

Jake turned and grinned replying, "It is to someone." He placed the papers in the folder in front of him and closed the folder.

Julian sat in the chair next to the desk and asked, "Is everyone here?"

Jake nodded to the affirmative replying, "Yep, Dr. Andrews said he would call when they were ready to start. I gave him a snapshot of what we were going to talk about so he wouldn't be surprised totally."

"Good idea. How about getting some coffee?"

"Sounds good, I'll bring the files, Dr. Andrews will probably grab us as we go by his office."

Standing Julian replied, "Good idea."

They both walked out of the lab and down the hall towards the coffee area.

As they were passing Dr. Andrews office Kay Winslow stepped out into the hall and the others were standing around Dr. Andrews' desk.

Jake and Julian both said, "Sheriff."

"Gentlemen, we can start the meeting in about ten minutes, rest room and coffee break."

Jake nodded and said, "Understood."

She turned left towards the restrooms and they continued to the break area. Once there they got a cup of coffee each, Dr. Fox joined them and shook both their hands saying, "Good to see both of you."

Dr. Fox poured three cups of coffee and put them in a cardboard holder, the three of them walked back to Dr. Andrews' office.

Dr. Fox placed the holder with the coffee on the desk and lifted one of the cups and handed it to the Sheriff and then one to Dr. Andrews. He took the last one and took the seat he had used earlier.

The Sheriff nodded to Dr. Andrews and he turned to Jake saying, "Jake, tell us what you have."

Jake placed his folder on the desk and after opening it, took five stacks of papers out. Each stack was held together by a two inch metal clip, the stack was five smaller stacks that were held together by large paperclips.

He handed each of them a stack saying, "What I've giving you is my report on twelve unsolved deaths and a description of the drug business and perpetrators plaguing the city, county and the state." Looking at Dr. Andrews he continued, "Way back when I first started here you gave me three cases that bothered you for me to check out when I had time. Well we solved the first one and we thought the second. We did exonerate one of the victims totally, which was a very good thing, but there was a lot about these cases and many of the other open cases on the books that just did not fit.

I have proof that the twelve cases that I have listed are all connected in one way or the other. All of it reflects back to the drug network that has grown and prospered over the past four years here and across the state."

The sheriff said, "Only twelve?"

Jake looked at her and continued, "Twelve that I can prove that were done by or ordered by the same two men without a shadow of a doubt. The same two men responsible for 85% of the drug trade in the state." Jake pointed to Dr. Fox's stack continuing with, "I have reports that will prove that eight of the victims were killed by doses of Curare, all from the same lot of the poison. It was all made in the same place in South America with the exactly the same ingredients and with exactly the same chemical makeup of all of the components. The other four were victims that were killed at the order of either of the two men in charge. Two in Savannah and two in Augusta, those in Savannah were killed right after the last drug bust that was orchestrated from here. I have copies of cell phone records and text messages that contain the order to have the killings completed."

Dr. Andrews looked at the group saying, "Twelve cases solved at once, amazing."

The Sheriff looked at Jake saying, "Without a doubt."

Julian lipped over the page he had been reading in the stack of reports and glancing around the room said, "Why do I think that that was only the tip of the iceberg."

Jake let a slight grin pass over his face and replied, "Correct my friend, correct."

Dr. Fox tapped his stack of papers saying, "Only one third of these reports are to confirm the data and events you have explained so far. I have never seen some of these reports, did not know we had the equipment to run them. I'm not surprised mind you. I've never seen them before because we never had anyone that knew enough to request or input the data to get them. I am confident that each of the findings will be not only correct but beyond most people's ability to understand them and well beyond reasonable doubt."

The sheriff nodded and looked at Jake saying, "Okay, let's hear the rest."

"Right, well we have and had a major drug problem, twelve murders, and a kill squad rooming our streets all at the orders of Tyrone Mendez and Dr. Paul Greenly. These events assisted by one Juan Mortises, better known as 'El Caapo Morta,' The Master of Death, the largest Drug Lord in South America and Mexico. We eluded the havoc the death squad could have spread across the city, but the heart of all of that death and pain still beats.

Greenly and Mendez are going to have a meeting and drug buy in four days. Sixty Million dollars will be changing hands for enough drugs to infect the users across the state for three months or more."

The Sheriff sat up straight in her chair saying, "In four days? What do we need? Where? How?"

"Tyrone has the money ready and Dr. Greenly has everything set for the meeting in place. The meeting and transfer will occur in Jenkins County, the drug lab and storage building is in a field off of Brown Road. Brown Road is across Route 25, it is a four lane at that point, from the Jenkins County Airport. It is all red dirt which allows a lookout, placed in a fire tower, to see any vehicle movement on the road. It can be seen due to the large cloud of dust that gets kicked up as the vehicle moves down it."

"Jenkins County? That's in the middle of nowhere. Why there?" Julian asked.

Jake looked at him and continued, "First, The building is less than a quarter of a mile from the airport. It is close to being half way to Statesboro and the highways it makes available.

Second, It's in the middle of nowhere with great safe access to and from Augusta and its highways, and all the fresh well water needed for their processing. So there is no large utility bill that would cause unneeded attention."

"I thought that that airport was only a small county airport, mostly for use by crop duster and the like," Dr. Fox mused.

Jake looked at him and then the others responding, "All of the State's County Airport runways were lengthened and resurfaced just a few years ago at the order of the state's outgoing Governor. They are all now a mile long and plenty wide enough to handle larger planes, such as a G-550."

The Sheriff said, "G-550? Why do you think that?"

Jake picked up one of the papers he had in his stack and responded to the questions. "First- One Juan Mortises owns a shiny new G-550, which is ninety six feet five inches long with forty three feet of interior cabin space. It holds over forty one thousand pounds of fuel, that's roughly five thousand one hundred gallons that allows it to travel over six thousand seven hundred miles in any direction at Mach 0.87. Cruising at 41,000 to 51,000 feet

Second - The most interesting facts are it has the capability to land on a runway of less than twenty eight hundred feet and take off with in fifty nine hundred feet, that with a full load. Much less distance is needed if not fully loaded. It can be in Jenkins County in fourteen hours from South America, leave at Seven PM and land at Eight AM the next morning.

Also there was an order placed by Dr. Greenly for fifty one hundred gallons of jet fuel to be delivered to Jenkins County Airport by nine AM in four days."

The Sheriff coughed, more to get everyone's attention than need, and then said, "All of that is enough for me, Jake, what do you need me to do to get this going?"

Jake picked up a two copies of a second sheet of paper and handed one to the Sheriff and the other to Julian. He picked up his copy and said, "I've outlined a plan that hopefully will make this action successful. There will be a lot to get done quickly and discreetly, Sheriff, you will need to get a lot of clearances and agreements, Jenkins County, State, and Federal agencies, FAA, FDA, Border Patrol, CIA and FBI. They all will want to run this, but they can't, Julian needs to be the lead and most active in the planning and direction of the operation. The hardest thing to get, I believe, will be the hand held rocket launcher, and a person authorized to use it, that I feel is required."

Julian looked at him and asked, "A rocket launcher?"

Jake nodded saying, "That plane cannot leave the ground."

They all looked around and Dr. Andrews replied, "I agree."

The rest motioned their agreement.

The Sheriff stood up with the papers in her hand and said, "I'm heading to my office, I need to ruin a lot of peoples weekend, starting with the Governor and Superintendant of the GBI." With that she left the office and headed towards her car.

Dr's Andrews and Fox looked at Jake and Dr, Fox said, "We will be here if you need us or the support of either office. We will be going over the reports to make ourselves comfortable with the findings so we can support you in any way needed."

Jake nodded and looked at Julian and said, "We can use my lab to discuss what is about to happen,"

Julian stood saying, "Sounds good." With that he moved out of the office into the hall with Jake right behind him.

When they got to the Lab they sat at one of the open tables facing each other with the files in front of them.

Julian asked, "Well, where do we start?"

Jake opened his file folder and pulled a page out of the stack and handed it to Julian saying, "That is an outline of everything that needs to be done and a timeline. I've giving this a lot of thought and we need to catch them all with the drugs and money. If we cannot do that then we need to at least destroy the drugs and money. It is going to be very hard to catch them in the remote building due to that dirt road. The dust will send a signal even if we were to travel the road on a bike."

Julian was looking the paper over as Jake spoke and placing it on the table he looked at Jake and said, "Plan one sounds like it might work but plan two I know will work. From what I see here you really don't think that the good Doctor and Tyrone will ever leave that building alive no matter what we do."

Jake nodded his acknowledgement and replied, "'El Caapo Morta,' The Master of Death' will not let them survive the meeting. From some of the info I've collected I'm sure he knows that along with distributing and selling of his drugs the good doctor has been selling a drug of his own making. That allowed Tyrone and the Doctor to make an extra five to ten million a month. The drug causing a great loss of revenue to 'El Caapo Morta,' and with no additional expenses, just provided profits to them."

"After looking at your plan two, it is plain to see the need for the rocket launcher. Well, it looks like some of us might be spending a few nights in the woods around an airport."

Jake grinned, saying, "Yep. We are going to have to come up with something for the locals to do somewhere else so they don't get in the way or get hurt. That Drug Lord is going to have his people armed to the teeth."

Julian leaned forward and said in a much lower voice, "Are you planning to let them get on that plane and then blow it?"

Jake did not respond right away, he put all of the papers back in the folder and picking it up moved over and placed it on his desk. He turned and looked at Julian and replied, "What will be, will be, the events of the time will dictate the outcome."

Julian tilted his head a bit and replied, "Okay, I'm good with that."

They both turned at the noise at the doorway. An officer was standing at the door and said, "Turn on your TV, you will not believe what is going on."

Jake reached over and pushed the button on the remote that turns on the large TV hanging on the wall. A news reporter was talking at ninety miles an hour, "Again, The Sun - London has released a special issue revealing tapes, recordings, photo's and many other documents that prove that the Former Secretary of State and her husband the Past President committed Treason against the United States. Proof that their actions aided and comforted our enemies and caused the death of United States Citizens and Government Officials."

Julian looked at Jake saying, "WOW, What next?"

The news reporter continued, "The official word out of Washington is that the suspects are being held in seclusion and will remain there. Their case will be handled by the Supreme Court, as outlined under the Constitution, and will be closed to the public and all news media. We the media will not stand for this and will fight it to the highest court." He stopped and looked at the camera with a stupid look on his face and said almost to himself, "Dumbass, the Supreme Court is not going to make a ruling against themselves. "He stared at the camera and continued with the prepared speech. "This will be the first time that two former government officials, one being the highest office to be held and the other a step away from that same position, have ever been placed in custody. It is the scuttle butt that the trial will be closed and only the Justices of the Court will be involved."

Jake pushed the button again and the TV went blank and silent. He turned to Julian saying, "That will keep everyone's attention for a while."

"That is an understatement if I ever heard one. I bet the Sheriff is second guessing her decision to take charge. First the horrific tragedy with the President and his family involved, and now this, talk about reasons for citizen unrest, those two were held pretty high above just about everyone in Washington."

Jake just nodded replying, "Quite a mess, it should sure keep anyone from being interested in what we're doing here."

Julian picked up his folder and stood saying, "I'm heading home to digest all of this and start calling my team. We have a lot to do in a very little time."

Jake picked up his phone saying, "Okay, If Janet is home, I'm heading over there. If you need me just call."

Walking out of the Lab Julian said, "Thanks, I think."

Jake heard, "Sorry I missed you, please leave a message." He pushed the end button and decided he'd head home.

Jake packed up what he needed and closed and secured the rest, locked the Lab's door and headed for his truck

★★★

CHAPTER NINETEEN

JULIAN PULLED INTO THE PARKING spot next to the Sheriff's and got out taking the cup of coffee from the Waffle House he had stopped at. Locking the car, he turned and entered the building and walked to the Sheriff's office. He knocked once and entered.

The Sheriff was just hanging up the phone and turned to face him.

Julian looked at the Sheriff and said, "It sounds like you have most everyone in line. There will be a lot going on at the same time. I hope everyone keeps to the plan. If not someone will be hurt, hurt bad. These men do not hold anything back, life is cheap to them."

"Yes, I have tried to stress how important it is for everyone to follow the plan to the letter. There is so much that can go wrong, so quickly. One little mistake and we will lose it all, money, drugs and crooks. This is a chance to solve twelve cases, possibly more, and put a real hurt on the drug trade in this state. It will give me great pleasure to put Tyrone and Dr. Greenly behind bars for a long, long time."

Julian thought about his conversation with Jake yesterday, "If it goes the way Jake thinks, there will be no jail for those two." He did not express his thoughts to the Sheriff, instead he opened the folder he was holding and took out a sheet of paper. He handed the paper to the Sheriff saying, "We will need to get this authorization signed, by the Governor, for us to run as the lead dog in this action in three different counties."

"No problem, the Director of the GBI has been instructed to clear the way for any action we want. He is still living off the last bust we made, it made him look very good to a lot of people."

"Well, we all got a boost out of that one, but this one will make that one seem small." With that Julian stood and continued with, "I'm heading out to Jenkins County to look around. I'll be driving an old truck that my Uncle had behind the house, used it for the dirty jobs around the farm. It hasn't been on the road out of town for years. I will keep you informed on anything I see or find out. We will need to deploy around seven tomorrow night." With that he turned to head towards the door.

"Julian, that will not be necessary, go over to the Operations Center, we have a Drone in the air, compliments of the FBI. You can see everything from the air and be totally unnoticed. You will need to be in the Ops Center in the morning to run this operation, not in the field. I want you and Jake in the Ops Center running this whole thing, if it goes south I want my best at the helm."

Julian stopped and turned towards the Sheriff with a response at the tip of his tongue about his needing to be out there but before he could start she put up her hand saying, "No discussion. Use the Drone to do your surveillance and to be out there."

★★★

His phone beeped and Jake pulled it out of the holder on his belt and pushed the send button saying, "Jake here."

"Jake, Julian, change of plans. We have been ordered to run this operation from the Ops Center. The FBI has put a Drone in the air under our control. I'm going to place the five men out there as we discussed, they will be out there during the evening tomorrow. They will move in position at different times and from different directions. I'm heading over to the Ops Center now to have a look around."

"Okay, I'll stop by in about an hour or so."

"Great, see you then."

Putting the phone back in the holder he turned into the drive and pulled up to the garage. He was up in his apartment in just moments, and then he walked over and turned on the TV for some background noise. Then walked over to the refrigerator and opened the door, He stood there looking at the contents and was just to reach for a soft drink when the security panel beeped. He closed the door and turned towards the screen, it was Teddy at the front door. He called out, "Be right there." He stepped over to the button that released the door lock and pressed it. "It's open." He heard the door open and Teddy coming up the stairs.

"Hello Jake."

"Hey Teddy, How is everything?"

"Good," Teddy replied and stepped over to one of the counter stools and took a seat.

Jake asked, "Something to drink?"

"A beer would be nice. Is there anyone else here?"

Jake moved back to the refrigerator and opening the door took two beers from the door shelf while replying, "No, just the two of us." He moved around the counter and sitting on the stool next to Teddy placed one of the beers in front of him.

Teddy picked it up and opened it saying, "Thank you."

Jake opened his beer and nodded replying, "Something I can help you with?"

Teddy took a sip of his beer and turned a little to face Jake. He took another sip and said, "Two things, the first being, the information you passed along was fully correct, the objects we found have been removed and stored in a very safe place. There are a lot of people around the world that thank you very, very much. The finding of that which was ours and lost has brought new life to all involved."

Jake just nodded and took a sip of his beer.

"The second is a bit more confusing, the information you passed from Sir Eric of Garth was directly from him to you?"

"Yes it was."

"Jake, I know for a fact that Sir Eric of Garth died well over fifty years ago in a small town in the Midwestern area of this country. You are in your mid-twenties, how is that possible?"

Jake looked at Teddy and a moment passed before he replied, "Teddy some things should remain a mystery, now and for all time. I should think that the Brotherhood would understand something like that."

Teddy looked at Jake for a few moments then stood and walked over to the window and looked out on the river passing by slowly. He stood there for a few moments then he turned back to Jake saying, "So it shall be, I am the only one with the information about Sir Eric of Garth and it will die with me." He turned and walked back to Jake, he held his clenched fist to his heart and looking directly in Jake's eyes said, "On the beating of my heart and by the Brotherhood of the Cross you have my sworn word."

Jake stood and placing his clenched fist to his heart replied, "Under the Cross's reign and the Brotherhood's unity I respect your word."

Teddy nodded and walked down the stairs without another word between the two of them.

Jake was just sitting there thinking about the events that had just passed when a beeping came from the TV. He glance at it and one of the leading talking heads was almost shouting, "The Leader of Korea has died. My God, what is going on in the world? First the President and his family, then the Congress Majority Leader and her husband, then the former Secretary of State and the Past President are found to be traitors and now the Leader of Korea is dead. The entire world's leadership has changed in less than a year. What is next? My Go.........." The station cut off and the screen went blank.

Jake stared at the screen for a few more moments, shook his head and walked into the bedroom to change his shirt before heading down to meet Julian.

On the way to the Ops Center Jake stopped by Janet's house and was happy to see her studying and relaxing a bit. They agreed to meet later that evening for dinner at The French Market. Janet had mentioned that Snow Crab Legs were the special that night, something they both enjoyed.

★★★

Tyrone and Dr. Greenly were sitting on the deck at Tyrone's house sipping drinks and watching the river move slowly by. Dr. Greenly set his drink down and looking at Tyrone said, "How are you going to handle our security during this whole thing? I don't fully trust these guys."

Tyrone set his drink down and leaned forward a bit replying, "Well I've got two men that will be concealed in the building and we will have three with us on the floor. They will have four men with them at the building and two at the plane. We will also have two men in the small building that they use as an office. All of the men will have AR16's with thirty round clips and have been instructed to kill everything and anything that moves if something starts to go wrong. We will pick them and the drugs up at their plane and transport them in the 14 person passenger van to the building. The two rear seats have been removed, and a ten foot by twelve foot trailer is attached, for the drugs and then the money."

Their plane will touch down at 9:00AM, we should be there waiting. Will you have someone in the Fire Tower?"

"Yes, and a few in the woods along the drive route to the building, they will be there watching the coming and going. We will know at once if anyone is traveling on the road."

"Sounds like you have everything covered, I will pay the fuel supplier as soon as I get there and we need him gone quickly. Your men will have to see to that without spooking the driver. I'm sure it will not take him long to tell someone that a G550 landed in Jenkins County."

"I've taken care of that, the driver will be one of my guys out of Savannah. The only ones that will see the plane will be the passerby's on 25. Nothing we can do about them, if we stop traffic it will cause the local cops to investigate. We should be covered and be able to keep everything low key."

Dr. Greenly picked up his drink, took a sip and said, "Sounds like we have it covered, but we need to stay on our toes. These guys are pretty 'Bad Ass,' life doesn't mean much to them."

"Yeah, well we can be pretty 'Bad Ass' too."

"Just saying, you know, just saying."

"I know, I know, I've got it covered."

★★★

Jake and Julian were sitting at the table in Jake's Lab with papers and maps spread across it covering almost every inch of the top.

Julian sat back a little saying, "I'm sure eating the Snow Crab Legs and having a cold drink last night was a lot more fun than doing this."

Jake grinned replying, "That is an understatement if there ever was one." He picked up one of the photo's and pointed at a segment of the airfield shown on it saying, "This is the latest we can wait to stop the plane, if it gets on line and powers up the chance of hitting it goes way down. We have one shot and only one shot at stopping it. If it gets in the air it will be up to another aircraft to take it down. That would have to happen somewhere inside the three mile limit off shore. There is no way to take it down over land without a very high probability of many civilian injuries."

"I agree, if they are smart they will make a bee line straight to the ocean."

"Yes, we will see what unfolds in the morning. Lets go over it all again and then go over it with the Sheriff and her team. There can be no surprises by anyone."

"You got it, let's do it again."

The day went by slowly, meeting after meeting with group after group.

★★★

The two of the officers that Julian had picked for the onsite work for the operation had entered the woods south of the building's location and walked without speaking through the heavy undergrowth. They walked for about twenty minutes and came close to just walking out of the undergrowth into the field that surrounded the building. They separated and moved about twenty yards apart. It was close to full dark and they had to move very slowly to reach their positions. Once there they started to dig out shallow trenches to lay in, keeping the dirt removed close to one side of the trench and the leaves and brush removed from the spot on the other side. Once deep enough they laid stomach down and pulled the dirt in on top of themselves and then the leaves and brush. The only part of them above ground was their heads and one free hand. They each had a single night scope that allowed them to see anything that moved at the building. The scope had a switch that would allow them to use the scopes during the daylight. Now all they could do was wait for events to change. The lead officer pressed his ear bob and said, "South Team in place."

Three other officers were completing their two mile hike through the woods, their path circumventing the

airport. When they could see the airfield thru the trees
the split up with one moving east, one going west and
the third moved to the end of the runway where the
plane would taxi to just before starting the takeoff. The
third man took the tree climber off of his back and
picked a pine that had a view, through some light tree
branches, of the runway. He attached the climber and
slowly stepped into the foot pads and with a walking
movement he moved up the tree until he was about
sixteen feet above the ground. He turned and sat in the
seat, the light layer of tree branches almost completely
hid him from the airfield. His camouflage suit and face
grease made him blend in and become almost invisible.
He picked up the rocket launcher and scanned the area
of the airfield before him. He would have about forty
seconds to take the shot once the plane completed
the turn to face the runway. The other two men that
had moved in with him had dug trenches and covered
themselves just as the South Team had.

The officer in the tree pressed his ear bob saying,
"North Team in place."

It would be a long night for all involved.

★★★

Entering the Ops Center Julian turned and said to
Jake, "The South Team called last night at twelve forty,
two men walked up the drive and entered the building,
no lights and no noise."

"Sounds like Tyrone and Dr. Greenly planted some
insurance."

Julian nodded and walked over to the two seats in front of the flat screens and sat down. Jake took the other seat.

Jake and Julian watched the screens lighten up and everything come in focus. The cameras on the Drone were so good that he could see each leaf of the crops growing in the fields.

Jake positioned the Drone until he could see the man standing in the Fire tower, the man was slowly scanning the roads and countryside with a pair of binoculars. Jake watched him pick up his phone and talk into it for a short time. Jake moved the Drone and zoomed in on the area around the building and was satisfied that the two officers had camouflaged themselves correctly and could not be seen. Next he moved the Drone to the Airport and scanned the tree line very slowly looking for the other three officers. He could not find any trace of them, even with the magnification turned way up. Moving the control Jake moved the Drone in a large circle checking the position of the different agencies spread all across the county. As he checked each one of their locations he confirmed with them by radio that he was aware of their placement and movements. This was more to keep them following the plan then anything else, he wanted to make sure no one got hurt or killed.

Everything looked just as it should have, everyone seemed to be doing what they were supposed to, and being where they were supposed to. The largest screen, in the center of the five flat screens, showed the path of the jet that was moving northeast from South America. It was staying over the ocean, four miles from shore, at 31,000 feet, traveling at Mock 0.08. They expected it to make a low level entry into the states staying under the radar. All agencies had been told to ignore the plane should they pick it up on their screens.

"They will be here at 9:00 AM promptly," Julian said to whoever was listening.

Jake swung the drone around and moved it over the highway heading west, all the way to Augusta. He positioned it well out of anyone's range of sight and increased the magnification to where he could see the buttons on Tyrone's shirt as he walked out to the van and trailer. He watched them all get in and pull out onto the roar to State Highway 25, he also saw the two security cars move into place a quarter mile apart. One in front and one behind the van and trailer, the drivers were in constant contact with each other. Jake counted three in the van and two in each car, he was sure that the others Tyrone had out there were carefully concealed.

He moved the drone around to view Tyrone's house and then Dr. Greenly's house and saw the undercover cars moving into place to raid and search each of the houses once things began to happen in Jenkins County.

"Well, it's all in motion, the next few hours will be very long, and very event filled," Jake said, almost to himself.

★★★

The plane continued northeast until it was past the Navy base in St. Mary's, Georgia. Once past it the plane slowed and dropped down to 1200 feet and turned northwest. The pilot would take the plane across the state and back to Jenkins' County from the north out of South Carolina. He would put wheels down and chocked by 9:00AM as ordered. One did exactly what one was told to do, if he wanted to see tomorrow.

***

The first security car reached Brown Road at seven-thirty and waited for the van to turn onto the road. It pulled behind the van and the second car followed. The amount of dust was unbelievable, the two following vehicles were totally covered in seconds. It took them about ten minutes to reach the turnoff to the building. Once they arrived they pulled the van and trailer into the building.

Tyrone got out of the van and started barking orders to the men, they were scurrying around quickly, he wanted the money stacked on the opposite side of the building from the entrance. This would make it just a little harder to reload and take a few more seconds, seconds he might need to protect what was his. Once the money was unloaded he told one of the men to sit on it and stay there until he returned. The man did not know that there were two men concealed in the building and that they would see everything he did.

With the money unloaded Tyrone waved everyone back into the vehicle and they backed the Van and trailer out of the building and turned around and heading back to the airport.

After another dust filled trip the three vehicles were parked in the airport holding area, it was nothing more than a large parking lot.

Tyrone and Dr Greenly got out of the van and moved to the shade that the operations building provided.

Looking at his watch Tyrone said, "They should be landing in about ten minutes."

Greenly just nodded, then replied, "Once the plane is on the runway the fuel truck will pull out to it. We need to follow and be positioned to off load the shipment. When we pull out and start down Brown Road towards the building, one of our cars will stay here and the second will follow us. They are going to have three men with him and they will ride with us in the van."

"Sounds good, the rest will all be as good or bad as it turns out."

"I'm surprised you left only one man with the money, mighty trusting of you."

"Right, trusting," Tyrone turned and looked northward. "The man would die if he did not do what he had been told, The two men hidden and watching would report anything out of the ordinary.

The sound of the plane could be heard approaching from the Northwest.

★★★

Jake had the drone positioned in the southeast quadrant of the operations area, so that he could display the airfield and the building on one screen. They all watched the plane approach and then land at the airfield. It had barely stopped moving and there were two vehicles alone side it. The door of the plane opened and one man jumped out and moved to the fuel intake compartment. Once there he opened the compartment and unscrewed the cap. The driver of the fuel truck had pulled the hose to the compartment and handed it to the man from the plane. Looking at the name tag on the man's shirt said, "Jose, I'll be sending it, full flow, in about five minutes." The driver turned and walked away towards the truck.

Jose placed the end of the hose into the recessed space and turned the locking clamp. This locked the hose to the intake and pushed the seal open to allow the fuel to flow freely. It would take about fifty minutes to fill the two fuel tanks, there was a tank located in each of the wings.

EL Caapo Morta stepped out of the plane's door, he was wearing a bright red and white shirt with billowy sleeves, behind one of his men and walked directly over to where Tyrone and Dr. Greenly were standing. His second in command had a similar shirt and walked just behind him. They all shook hands and exchanged pleasantries EL Caapo Morta introduced the second man as El Greco. EL Caapo Morta turned back to the plane and gave a signal to his other two men. The turned and opened the cargo door and started moving the twenty-four by twenty-four by twenty-four inch bundles out of the cargo hole and putting them in the van. Tyrone's men joined them and started stacking them in the trailer. All EL Caapo Morta's men all had automatic pistols with thirty round magazines on their belts.

Once all was loaded EL Caapo Morta told his men to get in the van and he followed them. Tyrone and Dr. Greenly got in the front seats and Tyrone's man got behind the wheel and once he checked the doors he started the van. Tyrone said, "Go."

The man put the van in drive and moved off the airfield and onto Brown Road, one of the security cars pulled in behind it following closely. The plume of red dust billowed up and covered the security car to the point where they had to drop back just to be able to keep the windshield clean enough to see out of.

EL Caapo Morta looked out the rear window and laughed saying to EL Greco, "They are lucky to see themselves,"

His two men laughed, Tyrone's did not.

★★★

Jake, Julian and the other six men and the Sheriff stared at the largest screen and watched the van, trailer and the security car disappear in the huge cloud of dust.

Julian pushed the button that connected him to all of the people involved in the operation and said. "It is going down now, all, stay alert. South Team, five minutes to your site. North Team heads up, stay on full watch, GO on your determined time to act. It is in your hands, you will have the time to do it once and do it right."

There were eight "10-4's" almost at once.

★★★

The van and trailer pulled into the building after one of Tyrone's men opened the door to the interior. The van and trailer were pulled into the building and turned and stopped to cut the open space in half. It ended being positioned so that it could pull straight out of the building once loaded.

The man Tyrone had left with the money was sitting in the stacks of bills with his automatic weapon across his knees. He stood and watched the vehicles pull into place.

Tyrone got out of the Van and had his men, that had rode with him and the ones from the security car, start unloading the drugs. Once the trailer was emptied EL Caapo Morta's men started loading the money into it.

EL Caapo, EL Greco, Tyrone and Dr. Greenly stood to one side watching the transfers being done.

Once the drugs were unloaded and the money loaded EL Caapo Morta and EL Greco, his second in command, turned and moved closer to Tyrone and Dr. Greenly expressing their thanks and exchange words of encouragement about their future business deals.

EL Caapo Morta brought his hand and arm down sharply on Dr. Greenly's back yelling, "Morta!" When his arm made contact with Dr. Greenly's back the blade of his concealed knife cut through his shirt sleeve and entered the Dr's back. The blade glanced off of a rib and slid into Dr. Greenly's heart killing him instantly.

At that same moment EL Greco's arm hit Tyrone's back, and he also yelled, "Morta!" The knife blade shot out from under his shirt sleeve, intended for Tyrone's throat, but Tyrone had moved his head just at that moment. The point of the double edged knife hit his jaw bone and slid up the side of his face flaying it open until it reached Tyrone's ear. Blood exploded outwards in a fan like spray. The blade entered Tyrone's skull thru the ear opening and six inched of it sliced his brain in two, with a nerve generated jerk he turned towards EL Greco and fell to the floor dead.

At the sound of "Morta" EL Caapo Morta's men pulled their automatic pistols off of their belts and firing, cut Tyrone's men almost in half. The men Tyrone had hidden in the building stepped out of hiding and began shooting wildly. They were hit with the automatic fire and dropped to the floor dead. There were bodies everywhere leaking blood in pools across the floor.

★★★

"South team, undetermined amount of gunshots, the outside of the building it beginning to look like Swiss cheese."

"South team, hold your position until all is quiet or the vehicles leave the building. North team, it is about to get hot in your quadrant."

"10-4" came from both.

Julian barked into the mike, "Investigation teams Alpha and Beta, GO, GO, GO." With that command two teams of eight investigators busted through the doors of Tyrone and Dr. Greenly's homes and started a detailed search of everything, each team had a list of where, what and how to search the homes.

★★★

EL Caapo Morta, EL Greco pulled the remains of their sleeves, and the auto plunging knife devices, off of their left arms,. His remaining man stood next to them alongside the van, El Caapo Morta had a bullet graze on his arm, EL Greco, his second in command, had a bullet in his leg, the other man was uninjured. All of the rest were dead. El Caapo Morta pointed towards Tyrone and said, "Put him in the passenger seat and tie him upright," pointing at Dr. Greenly continued with "Strap him against the window behind the driver's seat. Put the two others in the third seat. When we get back to the plane, get out of the vehicle and kill everyone. When they do not see the second car, they will be ready to fight. We need to be in the air within five minutes of getting there."

The man started completing the commands, and EL Caapo and EL Greco started putting the bundles of drugs in the remaining room in the trailer and also in the van, once done, they got into the van and the driver pulled out and moved towards the road.

★★★

When the van and trailer were out of sight the South team moved slowly towards the building and entered through the open door. The sight in front of them was a little shocking. The bodies of all of the dead were piled in the center of the room and all of their throats were sliced open.

"South team, All in the building are dead and mutilated."

"10-4, Secure it and do not allow anyone to enter, that means no one."

"Yes Sir."

Julian looked at the dust cloud that was moving slowly down Brown Road, it was only moments from the air field. North team, you will be in contact in less than five. Team Leader, take the shot whenever you see fit."

"10-4, we are ready."

★★★

Julian pushed the mike's button saying, "Savannah, Macon, and Columbus Teams, Go, GO, GO. North

Team, members two and three, take out all on the airfield you can once the van is inside the perimeter fence, North Team Leader, if the plane starts to move take it out. Hot Team, when the first shots are fired come up ready, it's yours to take all occupants out in the Van. We do not want that Van with in three hundred feet of that plane. Five thousand pounds of fuel is going to make one hell of an explosion."

A group of "10-4's" replied.

"Jenkins County One, stop and detain that fuel truck and driver in five minutes." Then close down all traffic on Highway Twenty Five."

A "Got it" came back.

Julian looked at the large screen and saw the van crossing the highway and turned to enter the airfield lot. The driver gunned it as he swung around the perimeter fencing, that made it was obvious that he was trying to get to the plane as fast as he could.

They all watched the first two men at the plane go down, and one of the remaining quickly entered the plane. The other remaining men were on their knees returning firing towards the tree line. The driver of the van gunned it and the van surged ahead. The three men that had been buried in the shallow indentation of the old minnow pond came to a standing position with their weapons firing in three round bursts. The tires and the windows of the van exploded and those watching saw small puffs of blood escape out of the shattered windows on the far side of the van.

The remaining men on the runway took hits and fell dead in pools of blood on the tarmac. The pilot went to full throttle in his attempt to turn and take off, the engine noise was deafening, even to those in the tree line. The Hot Team members dropped to the ground and covered their heads just as the rocket hit the plane. The ground shook and a ball of flames shot skyward almost a hundred and fifty feet high, the energy way from the blast knocked the small operations hut's windows in and almost took the first row of trees down.

The North Team Leader had leaned way to his left so that the back blast of the rocket would miss the tree and not blow him out of it. He had just dropped the rocket launcher and grabbed onto the tree stand when the energy blast hit him. He was slammed into the tree so hard that it temporarily knocked him out.

It took the other two members of the North Team just moments to get to him and they had him down on the ground and fully awake in just a few moments after the blast.

Julian, Jake and the others all leaned back when the blast occurred. The images were so vivid on the screen that it was almost like they all were there on the tarmac. They saw the Hot Team all stand up and start to move towards the burning van. The van's gas tank had exploded from the excess heat of the burning jet fuel, the resulting fire insured without a doubt that the van's occupants were dead. The trailer, which the energy wave from the plane's explosion had turned over on its side, was blown another thirty feet away from the burning van.

Everyone in the room's attention shifted quickly to watching the other three screens and the joint teams entering the other three locations, Savannah, Macon and Columbus. These Teams were a mix of Local Police, FDA, ICE and FBI, insuring that all avenues of explanation were covered.

Jake stood up saying to Julian, "Its Janet!" He turned and ran out of the room without another word.

The Sheriff looked at Julian with a questioning look, he looked back and shrugged his shoulders and raised both of his hands. He did this as if to say, "I don't know." A quizzical look flashed across her face but the action on the screens quickly drew their attention back to them.

★★★

An alarm from Janet had gone off in his mind, "Jake I need you, Help, Please Help!"

He was speeding up Walton Way while trying to scan for Janet, everything he picked up was jumbled and not understandable. He ran the light at Fifteenth Street and was almost at seventy going around the vehicles in his way. As he came into the hard left and right turn on the hill he picked up, "Jake, I love y……." then nothing.

He made the turn onto Janet's lane and stopped the truck with it across the entrance from the driveway to the lane. He jumped out of the truck and ran as fast as he could towards Janet's home. When he cleared the trees and bushes and his view of the house was clear he saw two men pouring something on the outside of the house. They were so intent on their actions they did not hear him running on the gravel that covered the drive.

He reached the first man just as the second threw a lit rag, covered with the liquid, towards the house. The gun in his hand hit the man on the side of the head so hard that the pistol's barrel shattered and entered his skull. A wall of flames burst up the front of the house, six to eight feet high. Jake grabbed the second man and started beating at the flames with his body. The man was dead after the second time his body slammed into the ground, feeling the body go limp Jake tossed it over his shoulder like a wet rag. He darted to the front door and kicked it open, once inside he found Janet lying on the couch in a pool of blood with a knife in her heart.....................

★★★

Teddy and Marian got home a little after nine from visiting some friends, and as the SUV started to make the turn towards its garage Marian said, "Teddy there's an envelope hung on the rear door of the house."

Teddy stopped the SUV, and put it in Park, got out and walked to the door. He pulled the envelope off the door and the only marking he could see on it was a capital 'J' in the upper left hand corner.

Marian stepped next to Teddy just as he opened the envelope, in it he found one sheet of paper, folded in half, and the keys to the apartment in it. Teddy read it out loud, it read, "I cannot thank you both enough for the friendship and kindness you have shown me. I will never be far away, no matter where I am. I am and always will be with you in mind and spirit. Teddy I need you to complete the few things I have left up stairs to be done. I have left detailed instructions on how I would like them handled. I trust you to do them as if they were your own. You and Marian will always be in my mind."

Thank You, Your friend,

Jake

There was a small symbol sketched in the margin of the paper. Teddy touched it and nodded to himself.

Marian looked at Teddy with tears in her eyes saying, "I don't know why we lost him, but I wish him

God's Speed and Our Love." With that she unlocked the door and went into the house with a sob.

Teddy walked over to the door to the apartment and unlocked the door, turned the handle and pushed it open. He walked slowly up the stairs and turned on the rooms overhead light. There sitting on the counter were five large gray envelopes, three of the envelopes were taped to cardboard boxes of different sizes. He could see Jake's service revolver, credentials and phone also on the counter. He walked over to the counter and saw that there were notes attached to each box.

The first envelope, was tapped to a box about twenty-four inches by twelve inches by twenty-four inches deep, was marked Teddy and Marian. Teddy opened the envelope and read one of the two notes on half sheets of paper it held, "Teddy, this is just in case. 'J'.

Teddy opened the box and there were stacks of one hundred dollar bills and a piece of paper that read, 'Rent.' Counting the money Teddy found that there was Sixty Thousand Dollars. He looked at the second note and it read, "Please give the rest of these envelopes and boxes to Julian Brown, the contents will explain almost everything that needs explaining, and he will take care of what else I need done. 'J'.

Jake's phone began to buzz and vibrate.

Teddy picked it up, pushed the Send button saying, "This is Teddy on Officer Ken Smith's phone."

"Teddy? This is Julian, where is Jake?"

"Julian, you need to meet me at Jake's as soon as you can."

"Okay, I'm on my way, are you aware of the recent events?"

"No, Marian and I were at friends most of the night."

"Turn on the TV, I'm on my way."

Teddy walked over and turned on the TV and switched the channel to the local news. The talking head was going on about a large statewide drug bust that involved Augusta, Savannah, Macon, Columbia and Jenkins County. The screen switched to a photo of an airfield with the remains of a plane that was nothing but a large pile of melted metal. The screen switched again, it now was showing the remains of a small home that was burned almost to the ground. There were lines and lines of Police tape stretched between trees all the way around the house. Teddy sat down when they mentioned the occupant of the house's name, Janet Anders, they continued with the facts and that she was mutilated, murdered and the house burned down around her.

Teddy murmured, "Janet, Oh My God, Janet, no wonder." Shaking his head he muttered loudly to himself, "My poor boy, what must you go through." He sat there just staring at the screen.

The security screen beeped and Teddy turned to look at it, he saw two County Cars pull up and stop. "Jake must have installed a motion detector, smart."

The door buzzer sounded and Teddy saw Julian on the security screen, he called out, "Come in." He heard Julian coming up the stairs and it sounded like he had someone else with him. He stood turned off the TV and walked towards the counter and saw Julian stepping into the room. "Julian, Sheriff."

Both replied, "Teddy." Julian and the Sheriff walked to the counter and Julian put his hand out to Teddy.

Teddy took his hand and shook it saying, "He is gone." Pointing at the counter he said, "He left these for you."

Julian looked at the envelopes and boxes shaking his head said, "This is all that is left of him and him being here?"

"Sadly, yes."

The sheriff picked up the pistol and credentials case and put them in the purse that hung on her shoulder.

Julian pulled the envelope with his name on it off of the box and opened it. He read the letter that was inside the envelope and setting it on the top of the box reached over and took the last box off of the shelf and handed it to the Sheriff saying, "This one is for you."

She moved over to the table in front of the TV and pulled one of the chairs closer and opened the envelope and began to read the contents.

Julian opened his box and found three additional packages, a thumb drive and another note. He opened it and read to himself, "Julian, please give these envelopes to Martha, Dr. Andrews and you get the thumb drive and the envelope marked for you. Please open it and look at the thumb drive in private, your friend, Jake."

Julian put the note back in the box and put the cover back on it and lifted the box and placed it on the floor by the stairs.

Julian stood there staring at the last envelope and box, reading the name over and over. It read, "Janet."

Julian took the envelope off of the box and opened it slowly. There was only one page folded over once. Unfolding it Jake read the message, "There is one hundred thousand dollars in this box. Please have Paige manage it and give what is needed each year to give coats and shoes to Augusta's needy children in Janet's name. Please try and keep her memory alive."

Julian put the paper back and replaced the cover then took the box and placed it on top of the other, he turned around wiping his eye and saw Teddy watching him.

Teddy asked, "Do you think he will ever come back?"

Julian just shook his head to the negative."

The Sheriff put the top back on her box and looked at Julian and Teddy saying, "Everything, just everything on everything that occurred today to lock solid every action taken, in all five locations, There is also all of the data on the thumb drives to close fifteen to twenty murders and make over thirty more arrests of persons of interest, from everyday man to some very important people. Jake must have worked 24/7 since he got here."

She looked at the TV and once again they were showing the remains of Janet's home. The Sheriff stood there with tears rolling down her cheeks saying, "We, all of Augusta, have lost two very, very special people today my friends."

She picked up her box, turned and walked to the stairs, down them and out of the door, without another word.

Julian put his hand out to Teddy saying, "Thank you, please, please give Miss Marian my very best, if you or she needs anything. Please do not hesitate to call me, 24/7, I mean it Teddy, anytime." He turned and picked up both boxes and went down the stairs and out the door.

Teddy stood looking at the security screen and watched them both pull away. He turned and standing there for a few moments, looked around the room and felt a terrible, terrible emptiness. He turned and walked towards the stairs, flipped the light switch and walked down the stairs with the notes still in his hand....................................

***

A car pulled off the highway into the rest area and stopped just behind a parked S-10 pickup truck, a man in a gray suit got out and walked over and dropped two new eleven by twenty envelopes thru the open driver's window. Without so much as a glance around, he turned and walked back to his car, got in and drove away...........................

JULIAN'S EPILOGUE

J ULIAN STOOD BEHIND A PODIUM, on the top step in front
of the Richmond County Sheriff's Operation Center,
looking out at the crowd of thirty to forty people. Most of
them were reporters and cameramen from the local and
national stations. Standing on both side of Julian were
the Richmond County Sheriff, Lieutenant Governor of
Georgia, the Director of the GBI, Director of SLED
from Columbia, SC, Dr. Claude Andrews – Chatham
County's Director of Forensics, Southeastern Director
of the FBI, Southeastern Director of ICE, Ambassador
to Columbia, South America, County Sheriff's of
Jenkins, Chatham, Bibb, and Muscogee Counties.

He began, "This is a brief outline of the results of
Operation Stop Drugs Now - (SDN). The following
events occurred and the ensuing results will be detailed.

On Wednesday morning the officers of the agencies
represented here today put in place a joint operation to
apprehend, detain members of an International Drug
Cartel and their distribution network.

I will start with Columbus:

At 11:15AM At 11:15AM the task force comprised of
Muscogee County Sheriff's Office, ICE, FDA, GBI and
the FBI entered a residence confirmed as being used as
a Drug House for use and distribution. Twenty Kilos

of Cocaine were recovered and over two million dollars was found hidden in different wall cavities throughout the structure. Twelve illegal aliens were found involved and taken into custody. There will be additional arrests in Alabama in the coming weeks. The total estimated street value of the drugs is over another two million dollars.

Macon:

At 11:15AM At 11:15AM the task force comprised of Bibb County Sheriff's Office, ICE, FDA, GBI and the FBI entered a residence confirmed as being used as a Drug House for use and distribution. Twenty Six Kilos of Cocaine were recovered and over two million dollars was found hidden in different wall cavities throughout the structure. Eighteen illegal aliens were found involved and taken into custody. There will be additional arrests in the Atlanta Area in the coming weeks. The total estimated street value of the drugs is over another two and a half million dollars.

Savannah:

At 11:15AM At 11:15AM the task force comprised of Chatham County Sheriff's Office, ICE, FDA, GBI and the FBI entered a business confirmed as being used as a Drug Manufacturing plant and also for use and distribution of the drugs manufactured. Thirty pallets of the drug TAKE and thirty six kilos of Cocaine were recovered and over five million dollars was found hidden throughout the structure. Over a million dollars of equipment used for the manufacturing process was destroyed. Fifty Nine illegal aliens were found involved and taken into custody. There will be additional arrests in the Hilton Head Area in the coming weeks. The total estimated street value of the two drugs recovered is over forty million dollars.

Jenkins County:

At 10:45AM, There was a firefight between the two drug groups with Tyrone Mendez and Dr. Greenly of Augusta were killed along with other drug suppliers.

At 11:20, the task force comprised of Jenkins County Sheriff's Office, Richmond County Sheriff's Office, FDA, GBI and the FBI disrupted and stopped the delivery and sale of Sixty Million Dollars of Cocaine, both were recovered. Five illegal aliens were killed in the action. There will be additional arrests in South America and over twelve hundred and fifty acres of Cocaine producing fields will be destroyed. The total estimated street value of the recovery is over one hunded and twenty million dollars and the value of the destroyed the fields will exceed over seventeen hundred million dollars per year.

Augusta:

At 11:05 the homes of Tyrone Mendoza and Dr. Paul Greenly were entered under selected search warrants.

In Dr. Greenly's house drugs and drug paraphernalia, and over one hundred and eighty million dollars was found and confiscated.

In Tyrone Mendoza's house drugs and drug paraphernalia, and Thirty nine million Dollars was found and confiscated. There was also one hundred seventy five million dollars found in a pay Mail Office Area.

We also have additional information that has been compiled, documented, reviewed and confirmed that has closed twenty three open and cold murder cases in Savannah and Augusta. All related to this drug operation over the past eleven years.

The Richmond County Sheriff, Kay Winslow, has a list of names, positions held and addresses for forty seven individuals, with detailed information that has been compiled, documented, reviewed and confirmed. This list includes individuals in all levels of law enforcement, The Justice System, and the County, State, and Federal Government.

There have been four Richmond County Officers suspended without pay and awaiting trial for drug trafficking and the abuse of their law enforcement powers. These men are not part of the forty seven still on the list. The individuals on the list will be arrested over the next seven days, by the appropriate agency.

The last item I have to say is a bit more personal to me, during this investigation I, no, we lost two individuals, both dear friends.

One being a co-worker and officer of the Richmond County Sheriff's Department, and he was also the Deputy County Medical Examiner, his name - Kenneth 'Jake' Smith.

The other a very dear friend and the life partner of the first individual, her name - Janet Anders.

As of today the name of our Lab downtown will be known as the Kenneth 'Jake' Smith and Sheriff Kay Winslow Center.

There has been a Foundation set up in Janet Anders name for the sole purpose of clothing Augusta's needy children for all of our yearly different weather conditions. I ask all to donate as your personal situation allows, and keep this wonderful person alive in our hearts."

Looking out at all and then looking up said, "Thank You."

Julian led the twelve dignitaries into the building, immediately six State Troopers, three from Georgia and three from South Carolina, took their place outside the doors preventing any chance of entry by anyone.

★★★

Teddy entered the kitchen and hung his windbreaker on the back of his chair and took his seat placing the mail on the table next to Marian's tea cup saying, "It's getting a little cool out there. The weather sure changed quickly." He picked up the paper and glanced at the front page, noticing a small article on the lower left corner of the page he read the header out loud, "Janet Anders Foundation delivers two hundred pair of shoes and winter coats to over one hundred and sixty families." Looking at Marian said, "That is a wonderful thing."

She replied, "Good things from good people." She set her tea cup down and started looking through the mail and stopped suddenly and held a small envelope up in front of her. Turning it over a few times she could not find anything but her name and address on it.

She said, "That's strange" almost to herself. She opened the envelope and a card was all she found, she read it and started to cry, with a smile on her face.

Teddy looked over and started to say, "What …."

Marian handed him the card saying, "Thank God, God Bless."

Teddy read the card,

"All is well, God bless."

It was signed, Love J & J

TO BE CONTINUED ……………..